THEN A SOLDIER

THEN A SOLDIER

John Templeton Smith

**POCKET
BOOKS**

LONDON • SYDNEY • NEW YORK • TOKYO • SINGAPORE • TORONTO

First published in Great Britain by Pocket Books, 2002
An imprint of Simon & Schuster UK Ltd
A Viacom Company

1 3 5 7 9 10 8 6 4 2

Simon & Schuster UK Ltd
Africa House
64–78 Kingsway
London WC2B 6AH

www.simonsays.co.uk

Simon & Schuster Australia
Sydney

A CIP catalogue record for this book is available
from the British Library

ISBN 0-7434-1533-7

Typeset in Melior by SX Composing DTP, Rayleigh, Essex
Printed and bound in Great Britain by
Cox & Wyman Ltd, Reading, Berkshire

Acknowledgements

To Roger Read, aerial survey specialist, author, aviator, former journalist (amongst many other talents), who once started a novel with an IRA background. Regrettably the almost finished manuscript was shelved following the signing of the Good Friday Agreement (in those times of hope and optimism). A few years later when the 'troubles' had resurfaced with the emergence of the Real IRA and I was looking for assistance with additional research on this novel, Roger kindly sent me the manuscript of his earlier work. It proved invaluable in many ways, and I have utilized some of the scenes and a number of the plotting directions from his story. Although Roger's name does not appear on the cover of this book I consider it to be as much his as it is mine.

To Keith C. Boreland, whose experiences in Northern Ireland during the period depicted added greatly to the military background. Also for his in-depth technical details on guns and explosives.

To Dr Terry Phelps, Oklahoma City University, as always, for his scholarly advice on the many aspects of this story.

Apart from the above, I conducted four interviews prior to writing this novel, three of them with IRA members in Belfast, Dublin and Sligo, and one with a former SAS sergeant in Gloucestershire. Regretfully (and for obvious security reasons) I cannot name any of these men, but I am grateful to them for giving so freely of their time, and their keen insight into a political problem that I have been assured will never go away until the six counties of the North are finally absorbed into the Irish Republic.

I would point out this is a work of fiction. For those readers seeking a more factual account of the history of the IRA, and a deeper insight into the politics of the Anglo-Irish problem (which was already old when Columbus discovered America), I highly recommend the following: *The IRA* by Tim Pat Coogan, and *The Provisional IRA* by Patrick Bishop and Eamonn Mallie.

As a matter of record I did attempt to obtain an interview with the office of the then Secretary of State for Northern Ireland, Peter Mandelson, to obtain the official British viewpoint on the Anglo-Irish situation, specifically relating to allegations against the British government by Irish sources (and used towards the end of this novel but rewritten as a fictitious mortar-bombing scenario) concerning military tactics not in accordance with the Geneva Convention. My request has remained unanswered.

As a footnote I would add that the Northern Ireland town of Bantrain and the Derbyshire town of Hoddingham, as depicted in this story, are purely fictitious. In a similar vein and for purposes of verisimilitude, certain historical IRA and British Army actions follow a different time-line.

For Sam and Ita Spindlow

'Then a soldier, full of strange oaths, and bearded like the pard, jealous in honour, sudden and quick in quarrel . . .'

from *As you Like It* – William Shakespeare

'Perhaps there are times and places for all of us. In a more perfect world I would have wished ours could have been different.'

John Winter, ex-SAS

'History supplies little beyond a list of those who have enriched themselves with the property of others.'

Patrick 'Pat' Cavenaugh, Provisional IRA

Briefing

Long-term Objective: Democratic Socialist Republic.
Short-term Objective: Brits out.

February 1970

It is only a story. Your story. My story . . .

The mechanic was sitting with his back to a dry-stone wall. A temporary shelter from the bitter Arctic wind that was sweeping in from the north. He was looking down the hill, watching the two dark shapes making their way along the narrow, twisting road from the town of Crossmaglen, south Armagh. Unsure of their identity at first. Then as they got a little nearer he knew. One, a boy of twelve, the other, a girl a year younger. Brother and sister. Mikey and Majella Ryan. They glanced up suddenly – across the top of an overgrown hedgerow set between broken down dry stone walls – saw him sitting there. Waved. He half-lifted a hand in greeting. Then went back to his task: carefully tearing two sheets of white cartridge paper.

He was a little over 6 feet tall. Shoulder-length black hair. Blue eyes that matched the sky. A lovely soft voice the girls had said on more than one occasion. A Dublin voice. The young men of the area thought differently, but they knew of his reputation in the terror stakes. The latest being how he had got into a fight with half a dozen squaddies in a pub in Belfast. Big bastards, the story went. Four of the squaddies had been hospitalized; the other two had done a runner. The story grew with the telling, enough for the local hard men to give him a wide berth, even if their girlfriends were secretly in love with him.

He had been working in the farm's solitary barn all morning, changing the gearbox on a near derelict tractor. His labours complete, he had washed the oil from his hands, pulled on a ragged blue serge jacket over his denim shirt and jeans, and gone to the spot along the wall. Waiting for the 'comm'. He had been expecting the children's mother, Nancy. But not today it seemed. A pity, he thought to himself as he negotiated a difficult curve in the paper he was tearing. A great pity, for he was secretly in love with her. Even though she was at least ten years older than he, and a married woman. Not that he'd ever told her, or even intimated his thoughts. Even so, he sometimes caught her looking at him, and when their eyes met, they held each other for long seconds, as though sharing some carnal premonition. For his part it was a look of desperation and longing. Living on dwindling hope. For hers? He doubted he would ever know.

The children were climbing the green hill now, springing lightly through the wet turf – snatches of voices drifting in and out of the wind. They were dressed almost identically. Hand-me-downs. Or, more to the point, cut-me-downs. Clothes from a relative in the south, tailored by Nancy, something she was a fair hand at. Even so, the wide flapping dark flannel trousers and matching jackets gave the children an appearance of small adults. Comical to some, a matter of needs must for the poor.

'Your mother didn't come then?' he called, carefully tucking the white paper shapes into his pocket.

'Sure the car wouldn't start,' Mikey shouted back, out of breath from the steep climb. He was a tall boy for his age. Gangly. All elbows and arms. 'She said we'd to walk all the way here and all the way back.'

'No she didn't,' Majella said petulantly. 'She said that if it got fixed she'd be along to get us.'

'She said Dermot was too drunk to mend it,' the boy added with a knowing look in his eyes.

'But she's well?' the mechanic asked. 'Your mother.'

The boy just shrugged, put his hand in his pocket and pulled out an envelope. 'Said we had to give you this.'

'It's a pound note,' Majella added, her eyes wide. She made it sound like a king's ransom.

'Good money after bad,' the boy went on. 'She said that if you'd fixed the car right last month it'd still be running now.'

'Ah, so it would, but you see it's a very old car,' the mechanic replied, taking the pound note from the envelope. He turned it over in his fingers, noticing the numbers and letters written in pencil across the top of the note, before pushing it into his pocket. 'And you know what they say about old cars?'

'What?' the children asked in unison.

'You already said it: good money after bad. So, are you staying for a while?'

'No, Mam said we had to bring you the money and come straight home, and if we see any of the bloody English soldiers, we're to run and hide.'

'You are a liar, Mikey,' the girl cried, 'She said no such thing.'

'Did too,' Mikey shouted back.

The mechanic looked up at the low sky. It was darkening. 'Still, better if you start making your way. Snow's coming.'

'How do you know?' Mikey questioned.

'Smell. I can smell it.'

The boy wrinkled his nose. 'Cow shit!' he exclaimed. 'Sure, that's all I can smell.'

The mechanic laughed. 'That as well.' He climbed slowly to his feet, shivering slightly as the icy wind caught his face.

'When are you going home?' Majella asked.

'Later, I still have some work to do . . . You'll be sure to thank your mother for me, won't you.'

'I will,' the girl said, with a smile. Her mother's eyes all over again. Break a man's heart, those eyes. 'You like Mam, don't you?'

'Why'd you say that?'

'Because you always ask after her.'

'She's a fine woman,' he said, a little self-consciously, wondering how much more the 11-year-old girl going on twenty had seen in his stolen glances at her mother.

The boy sniffed before wiping his nose on the sleeve of his jacket. 'Anyway, she said you charge too much,' he declared, kicking at the turf with the toe of his boot. Not so much an admonition, more wanting the last word.

'Inflation, Mikey, it'll be the death of us all.' He put

his hand in his pocket and took out the paper shapes, separating them and handing one to each child.

'What is it?' the girl asked.

'Something I was going to give to your mother to bring you . . . open them out, you'll see.'

They did.

'Oh, that's lovely,' Majella said with a bright smile.

Mikey wasn't so sure, uncertainty in his eyes. 'How did you do it?'

'I'll show you one evening if you come round the garage.'

'You will?' A flicker of interest in the voice.

'Promise.'

A mumbled 'Thank you,' as he turned to go. As much as you'd get from Mikey. If you were lucky, and believed in miracles.

'Straight home now,' he called after them. 'Before the snow.'

They waved, and ran screaming down the hill.

The mechanic sat down by the wall and lit a cigarette, took the pound note from his pocket. An innocent enough transaction that served as a 'comm'. He examined the writing more closely. 1710DMAA – which translated to 5.10 p.m., Declan and Michael. The AA meant that the border crossing point was as previously briefed. Of course there would be diversionary tactics (something inferred but never disclosed to him); you didn't simply drive a truckload of Opus Dei-funded weaponry into the North. Maybe there were 'blind' eyes at Dublin airport, where the privately chartered flight from Antwerp – with a cargo manifested as 'steel plates' – had landed that very morning, but the British Army on the border of South

Armagh was something else. Even so, the Opus Dei connection had been the real body blow; a saintly mafia in which religion, politics and big business coalesced – with the help of a sympathetic cardinal or two inside the Vatican – and in turn became paymasters for a war against an old rival for hearts and minds, the Protestant church. That had quietly troubled the mechanic, raised in the Catholic faith. It still did, but for now there were more important things to consider – the first being that the big day was here. He was folding the pound note to put it into his shirt pocket when he noticed the X in the bottom right-hand corner. The same hand. What was that? A kiss! Had she sent him a kiss? He was smiling at the thought as the first flakes of snow caught his cheek. Needle pricks of ice. Melting instantly.

He looked down the hill. The children were moving slowly along the road. Back the way they had come. He flicked away the butt of his cigarette. Time to make a move, he decided. He had a radio concealed in his toolbox in the barn.

He was standing, turning away from his view of the children when the shapes drifted into his peripheral vision. He focused farther down the road. The visibility was deteriorating but he made out the two BA ferret scout cars. Patrol. Coming up from the border crossing point near Cullaville. Earlier today than usual. He checked his watch. One hour seventeen minutes earlier in fact. One of those little details he had been asked to observe over the previous weeks. His eyes moved back to the children. They had stopped.

As in that moment did the rural peace of a tiny corner of South Armagh.

The explosion coincided with the first scout car

lifting in the air . . . A flash-frozen frame . . . The dull
blast of a landmine shock-waving up the hill . . . A
bundle of startled rooks lifting like black rags out of
the trees around the farm . . . The vehicle seemed to
hang for a moment, defying gravity, then fell back to
the road . . . The secondary explosion the mechanic
guessed was the fuel tank going up . . . The stuttering
cracks of live ammunition followed . . . Soldiers from
the second vehicle, tumbling out . . . Running into the
flames to try and save their comrades . . . Shouting
voices . . . Confusion . . . Panic.

Diversionary tactics . . . merciful God.

The mechanic didn't wait any longer but started to
run diagonally down the hill. In the direction of the
children. Even as he was running, he saw the rusted
Ford Anglia on its way from the town. Nancy. The car
stopped – one more bend and she would have seen her
children. Instead she had witnessed the warning pall
of black smoke. His eyes went back to the road beneath
him. Mikey and Majella. They had disappeared.
Where? For Christ's sake, where? He quartered the
immediate area. Looking for the slightest movement.
Then he had them. They had found a way through the
hedge on the opposite side of the road. Were both
running across the open field towards a tumbled-
down barn some 200 yards away. A soldier from the
second scout car had also seen them, and had vaulted
a low stone-wall set between the hedgerow, his
crouching run surprisingly fast, carrying him in a wide
arc to cut off the two running figures.

It was the last movement the mechanic saw before
he reached the bottom of the hill. He scrambled
through the hedge and across the narrow road.

He never saw Nancy getting out of her car, throwing herself in blind panic over a gate as she caught sight of her children and the chasing soldier. In the same way he never saw her running across the field, mouth opening and closing in silent screams. By the time he had found a way through the hedge and in to the field opposite, he knew he was too late. Had heard the distinctive *zap-zap* sound of a high velocity weapon.

Then he saw her. Long red hair flying in the wind. Like the banshee of Irish folklore, whose wailing presence was said to signal imminent death! She was upon the kneeling soldier – SLR still at the aim – before he realized. Another crack. Softer this time. An almost harmless sound. Except when delivered from the hands of someone trained by the Provos. The soldier slumped forward in a half-roll.

'Nancy . . . Nancy . . . for God's sake . . .' he shouted, as he got nearer. But she hadn't heard. She had fallen beside the bodies of her children. Great keening screams coming from her mouth.

He dropped down next to her. Fighting for breath.

Startled back to the present, she turned on him, raising the gun in her hand. A Makarov. Pointing it at him. Then, seeing who it was, she dropped it into the grass. 'My babies,' she sobbed. 'Why? Why? . . . God in heaven, why?'

The mechanic rolled up the sleeves of the children in turn. Expertly checking their brachial pulse. The girl, a thready beat beneath his fingers. He pulled off his jacket and draped it gently around her. The boy was dead, of that he was sure. What was more it seemed he had been the reason for the shooting. He prised the Webley air-pistol from Mikey's fingers and tucked it into his waistband. *And if we see any bloody English soldiers we're to run and hide.* Except Mikey had never been one for taking orders. Especially if the orders came from an English soldier shouting for him to stop.

As for the soldier himself, he would have seen a silhouette in the lowering light spinning round on him. Gun raised. No way of knowing that the weapon was a harmless air pistol.

No need for Nancy to know. There would be time later. God willing.

And then the shouting from back across the field. He turned, and saw two squaddies racing towards them. He picked up the Makarov pistol, and grabbed Nancy by the shoulder. Spun her towards him. The eyes stared at him for a moment. No recognition. As though she was looking at a stranger. The green he noticed for the first time was flecked with hazel. He touched her cheek with his hand. 'Leave this to me, I'll take care of everything.' His voice was soft. Reassuring.

No comprehension in her eyes – only tears – as her hand closed over his. An unfamiliar touch. Sensual sandpaper roughness. Hands that had known too much hard work. But for all that they were elegant hands. Hands that you could hold and love for eternity.

He took a deep breath and stood up. Tossed the guns down and calmly raised his hands. The body of the dead soldier was some yards away, the familiar beret of the Green Howards lying near where he had fallen. A second lieutenant's markings on the epaulettes of his combat jacket. *Probably straight from public school where he'd served a few years in the CCF. Attracted to what? The uniform? The glamour of being a regular army officer! The eyes were still open –*

11

unblinking against the swirling snow, as though puzzling over what had brought him to this Irish field.

The mechanic could have told him, given the chance: *No British heroes in this Catholic roost, old son . . . they should have told you that much at least.*

The soldiers drew nearer. SMGs pointing straight at him. The old song came to his lips: *Shoot first; ask questions later.* He hoped he was wrong.

He half-turned his head back towards the children and the prostrate figure of their mother sobbing quietly. *Anything but this . . . anything . . . I'm so sorry, my darling girl.*

A gust of wind whipped across the field. A fluttering sound. And two pieces of paper fashioned into white doves of peace lifted and flew like mocking responses across the grass. For the briefest of moments they looked lifelike.

Almost simultaneously the frightening clatter of weapons fire. Familiar smell of cordite catching his nostrils. Not at him though. At the movement of the paper birds. Now shredded into a hundred pieces. He watched the smoke-blackened faces of the soldiers closing upon him. Sensed the hatred that projected from them in a dark aura.

First and last line of defence. *Seek a refuge against terror. Play the frightened man. No eye contact. Psychological games. Anybloodything. Start praying . . . out loud.* 'Hail Mary . . . full of grace . . . the Lord is with thee . . . blessed art thou amongst women . . . and blessed is the fruit of thy womb Jesus . . .'

He didn't see the stock of the SMG swinging in a vicious arc – felt it though. Steel on bone . . . toppling forwards . . . then, blackness.

PART ONE
An Irish story

Commitment to the Republican Movement is the firm belief that its struggle both military and political is morally justified, that war is morally justified and that the Army is the direct representative of the 1918 Dail Eireann Parliament, and that as such they are the legal and lawful government of the Irish Republic, which has the moral right to pass laws for, and to claim jurisdiction over the territory, air space, mineral resources, means of production, distribution and exchange and all of its people regardless of creed or loyalty.

– IRA Green Book

1

*No guide book to a tourist's Northern Ireland this; no
City Hall, no Grand Opera House, no St Anne's
Cathedral, no Linen Hall Library . . .*

There was winter night rain as Mouse scurried down
Cawnpore Street in the Clonard district of Belfast.
Through the place they called Little India, a Victorian
leftover lying in the one-time shadows of mills that
had supplied an Empire. Now a sordid, crumbling
assortment of mean red-bricked terraced houses, two
up two down, dry-closet out back. The smells of soot
and machinery trapped in stone. Sodden dreariness
under lamps of drizzling yellow.

Mouse was a small man, wasted by drink, who had
had his moment of glory in the early 1950s when he
had been part of an IRA arms raid on a British Army
barracks in Omagh. Something that had led to eight
years' imprisonment. He had been a hero then. Now,

little more than a messenger boy – and only that because he had kept his mouth shut. Had suffered brutal torture and interrogation. Had saved a few of his comrades from the same fate.

He checked his surroundings. A big old white dog, half starved, watching him from across the street. Mouse smiled and put his hand in his pocket, found the stale cheese sandwich wrapped in a piece of newspaper – his supper. He unwrapped it and held it out. The dog came slowly towards him. 'Not much for a cold night, owd dog,' he said soothingly. The dog took it. Gulped it down in one go. Let Mouse stroke his head for a moment, then turned and padded away. It was a kind of ritual between them. The dog sensing the old man was like him – a stray. They watched out for each other on the night streets.

Mouse took a last glance behind him at the bleak electric-lit emptiness before he slipped through a wooden door set in a brick wall at the end of the row of terraced houses.

A voice challenged out of the darkness. 'Who's that?'

'Mouse.'

The voice moved closer. Sean Fitzgerald. A pimply-faced youth with cruel eyes. Crew-cut fair hair that added to the brutal appearance. No more than twenty. A member of the newly formed Provisional Irish Republican Army (Provos). 'You're out late then.'

'I've got a message for Mr Cavenaugh,' Mouse said nervously. Then lifted his arms. He knew the drill.

Fitzgerald frisked him quickly and expertly. 'You never take a bath then, you old sod. Jeez, you stink to high heaven, so you do.'

Mouse stood still, or as still as he could manage. His legs were shaking uncontrollably. He knew Fitzgerald. Him and the others. They who would play games and smack him about. Just for fun, they'd say. He waited, expecting a playful punch, which would knock the wind out of him. But not tonight it seemed. Instead, the youth waved him past. He shuffled forward and instantly tripped over the outstretched foot. He fell, striking his head hard against the corroding brick- work. Lay for a moment, holding his face, grimacing at the pain. His blood warm and sticky on his hands.

Fitzgerald laughed. 'Next time take a fuckin' bath.'

Mouse fumbled through his trouser pockets, found a soiled handkerchief, brittle with dried phlegm. Dabbed at the wound, wincing as he did so. Finally, deciding he looked presentable, he struggled to his feet and felt his way along the side of the house, and opened the back door. It led directly into a kitchen. Two rings of a gas stove hissed blue flame – a vain attempt to keep the chill off the dingy little room, where condensation ran down the walls, dripping onto the rotting linoleum floor. Beyond the nicotine- stained lace curtain a gust of wind slashed rain against the window, rattling the panes.

There were two of them sitting at the Formica- topped table, the edges of which were scarred brown from cigarette burns. Pat Cavenaugh and Frank Ryan. A bottle of Bushmills 'Black Bush' whiskey and two glasses and a pack of playing cards set between them. They looked up when the old man entered and closed the door behind him. Cavenaugh, the Director of Intelligence/Belfast IRA, a man of medium height, friendly lived-in face, thick silver hair, kindly brown eyes, or at least one – the right one lost in the Omagh raid with Mouse all those years earlier. The black patch a benign reminder for the mild-mannered schoolteacher.

The redheaded Ryan, slightly taller, was a colder man altogether. Calculating grey-blue eyes. Something of the gunfighter about him, they said. He had served in the British Royal Air Force as an armourer years earlier, which had made him a weapons expert. Present occupation: OC of the Belfast Brigade.

Mouse took the letter from his pocket and moved forward and offered it to Pat Cavenaugh.

'Been fighting again?' Cavenaugh said lightly, noticing the blood on Mouse's temple. 'Now I would have said you were too old for that.'

Mouse still clutching the soiled handkerchief in his left hand dabbed at the cut. 'Oh it's nothing, sir . . . tripped in the darkness.'

Cavenaugh was thoughtful as he poured a glass of Bushmills and handed it to the old man. Noticed the shaking hand. The look of gratitude in the red-rimmed eyes. 'Wet night, Mouse.'

'That it is, sir.'

Cavenaugh opened the envelope and started reading. He looked up. 'You got this from Celia then?'

'I did. She said it was urgent.'

Cavenaugh nodded and forced a smile. 'That's women for you, Mouse. Making out that an invitation to a party is important. Still never mind.' He turned back to the table and put the stopper in the half-empty bottle of whiskey and handed it to the old man. 'Anyway, for your troubles, you won't go falling over again on the way home will you?'

'I won't, sir.'

'Oh, and tell young Sean to come in.'

'I will,' Mouse said, and disappeared quickly through the door into the darkness.

Sean Fitzgerald came through the door moments later (slipping the bolts into place, procedure when there was no outside guard). Water dripping from the spiky crew cut hair. Face red raw from the cold night. The jeans beneath the khaki anorak were soaked through. Even so there was a spring in his step. Youthful arrogance in his voice. 'You wanted to see me.'

'I did, I did.' Cavenaugh said with a smile. 'You're a bit of a hard man I hear, Sean. Is that so?'

Fitzgerald grinned. 'I can take care of myself.'

'Good. That's good. Always nice to know we have young men prepared to fight for the cause. To kill people. You are prepared to kill people if ordered, Sean?'

'Sure what else can you do? It's a war isn't it? People get killed in war.'

'What about if you get killed? Have you thought of the effect it will have on your family, your girlfriend?'

'Ah, sure they'll understand, they'll get over it. They know in their hearts nothin' else'll make a difference.'

'Good. That's good.'

'There's something you want me to do then?'

Cavenaugh glanced at the other man sitting at the table. A look of understanding passed between them. 'A small matter of a vendetta you might say. Stiffing a "B" Special.'

'Not a problem, you tell me when.'

Cavenaugh rubbed his chin thoughtfully, 'I will . . .

Oh, and one more thing. About Mouse. He happens to be a good friend of mine, you understand what I'm saying?'

Fitzgerald looked puzzled. 'Not exactly.'

'I mean, I don't like him tripping over and hurting himself. Not good for a man his age. So what I'm doing is putting you in charge of his welfare. That means anything happens to him I will hold you responsible. You do get my meaning, don't you?' A bleak smile.

'Yes . . . I do.' The tight-lipped acknowledgement was against his nature. What had the little bastard Mouse been saying? He'd kick his fucking head in, so he would.

'And I do mean *anything*, Sean. He catches a cold that turns into pneumonia, I'll make you responsible . . . Oh, and the op's tonight.'

Fitzgerald's anger faded in an instant. Now he looked anxious. Like an amateur poker player whose bluff had been called. 'Tonight?'

'Don't worry; Frank'll take care of you. That right, Frank?'

Ryan stared at the youth. His voice when he spoke was hard. Emotionless. 'Just do as I tell you and you'll be fine.'

Fitzgerald didn't seem too sure. He watched as Cavenaugh went over to the kitchen sink, opened a cupboard and took out a fresh bottle of whiskey and another glass, which he brought back to the table. He filled the three glasses.

'Ourselves alone,' Cavenaugh said solemnly.

They drank. And finally settled down to a game of cards. And in between hands, Cavenaugh briefed them on the night's work.

Then A Soldier

*

It was nearly midnight when Cavenaugh turned to Ryan. 'Time you were going then, Frank.' He slid a brown paper bag across the table.

'The bell?'

'The bell.'

'And the money you mentioned?'

'A metaphor for a united Ireland, if you like.'

Frank Ryan slipped the bag into the pocket of his donkey jacket. 'That fancy education of yours again is it, Pat?'

'Wins wars though.'

'You're wrong,' Ryan said, patting his pocket containing the brown paper bag. 'This wins wars.'

Cavenaugh smiled in that gentle way of his, and got up and went over to the solitary window. 'A bit of both then,' he said, pulling the lace curtain back and peering out into the darkness. Rain spattered on the windowpane. 'A dirty night but you won't mind that I'm thinking.'

Ryan let the remark pass and turned to the youth sitting at the kitchen table. 'Come along then, Sean. Work to be done.'

The two men left the house and walked to the end of Cawnpore Street. The rain had eased slightly, the smell of damp soot all the more pungent. Frank Ryan stopped under a streetlight.

Fitzgerald said, 'What are we waiting for?'

'A black taxi.'

'Oh.'

'Don't worry he'll be along.'

'What did Pat mean . . . about a bell?'

21

Ryan peered out into the darkness. Eyes unblinking. He was thinking about Pat and his way of force-feeding education into anyone who cared to listen. *What did Pat mean . . . about a bell*? Rousseau's conundrum, old son, that's what he meant. Better yet, if you haven't read Rousseau there's not much hope for you. He'd tried to convince Pat that the kids who were about to die for the cause didn't have time to read Rousseau – or anybody else come to that – to appreciate the finer points of literature and psychology, that all they needed was to learn how to become invisible to a sniper's bullet. Like Sean standing before him. How long did he have before he was cut down? A rewarding life right enough: there is no money in belonging to the IRA. It is a working-class organization and its members lead working-class lives. Home for most of the Belfast volunteers is a council estate or a terraced house in the remaining streets that have not been redeveloped. If you are in work you are expected to finance yourself. If unemployed there is a weekly handout of a few pounds (drawing dole is theoretically discouraged because of the state surveillance it entails), but only when the war chest is full. *A rewarding life*! Sometimes he questioned the sanity of it all. Sometimes he thought that knowing Pat had been a mistake, because it had given him perspective. And that was the last thing a soldier needed. Once you started analysing why you were doing it, you were on your way to Boot Hill as those lovely Hollywood shit-kickers would have it. Even so he made an effort to answer the young man's question. 'Something about when a philosopher gives you a bell and you ring it, you receive a large sum of money and an unknown

Chinaman dies.' His voice was quiet. Distant almost.

Fitzgerald shook his head and looked confused. 'I don't get it, Frank.'

'It's about not caring too much . . . not important.' The same quiet voice. He continued staring into the blackness a few moments longer, then with a resigned shrug turned towards Fitzgerald. 'The thing is, have you ever killed a man before?'

'No.'

'And you thought when you joined it would be like the old days, an apprenticeship in Na Fianna Eireann learning knot-tying and animal spoor recognition. Is that it?'

Hesitancy. 'No.'

'Something exciting then: like blowing up trucks and railways lines, that sort of thing.'

More hesitancy. 'I . . . I don't know.'

'What about shooting at the BA?'

'We were told we would be killing the uniform.'

'Same difference with our man tonight, we'll be killing the uniform. As Pat told you during the briefing, his name's Tommy Morris. "B" Special from Crossmaglen, up in town for his brother's wedding.'

'What did he do?'

'Killed the mechanic.'

'They said he hanged himself in his cell, so they did.' Uncertainty in the voice.

Ryan said bitterly, 'That's like suggesting St Patrick is alive and well and running the black fucking economy. Besides he was a better man than that . . . probably tried to escape, beat the shit out of six of them before they got a rope round his neck and strung him up.'

23

'Jesus . . . and you think it was this Tommy Morris who did it?'

'Does it matter? He was one of the bastards who had the mechanic in the cells.'

'I just meant . . . what of the others. What if it was one of them?'

'You think he should have a trial?'

'Well, no. I don't know . . . it's just that . . .'

A gust of wind rolled an empty beer bottle along the gutter, the thin clacking sound filled the street for a moment. Ryan watched it through screwed up eyes. The sound seeming to touch some exposed nerve. He reached out with his boot and stopped it. 'No, no, you're right, Sean. I can see that you believe in fair play, that's good. So let's have a trial.'

'When?'

'Here and now.'

Sean looked confused.

Ryan went on. 'I'll be the prosecution, and you'll be Tommy Morris conducting your own defence, does that sound fair?'

'I don't even know the man.'

'Don't worry; you've seen those American lawyer films on the telly. Just pretend we're in one of them. Okay? Remember though you're pleading for your life. Use the same tactics outlined in the *Green Book* . . . you have read the *Green Book*, Sean?'

Fitzgerald looked embarrassed. 'I did try, but then I'm not much of a reader.'

'Not much of a reader!' Ryan exploded, punching him hard in the shoulder. 'Is that what you tell yourself? Or is it that you subscribe to the tourist point of view that Ireland is a nation of saints and drunkards and blasphemers and priests and publicans . . . You need to do better than that, Sean. It's your life you're pleading for . . . Get it wrong and you're dead. Get it wrong and you could take me with you. Understand?'

Fitzgerald rubbed his left shoulder. He looked shell-shocked.

'Do you fucking understand?' Ryan yelled.

'Yes.'

'In that case we'll begin.' Ryan said. Quieter now. 'State your full name for the court.'

'Tommy . . . Morris,' Fitzgerald said hesitantly.

'And your job, Mr Morris. What is it you do?'

'I'm . . . I'm a "B" Special.'

'And where do you live?'

'Crossmaglen.'

'Ah, yes, a lovely place that. I've been there myself once or twice. So, can you tell the court what happened on the night of 7 February at the police station in Crossmaglen?'

Fitzgerald shook his head. 'I don't know what you mean.'

'No, well let me remind you, Mr Morris. That was the day a man was brought to the station, accused of shooting a BA . . . a British Army officer . . . a few miles south of the town. It seems he might also have been responsible for planting a land mine that blew up a BA vehicle, which killed another two British soldiers. He was known in the town as the mechanic. His name was Ben Casey. Now do you remember him?'

'I didn't see him,' Fitzgerald muttered.

'Oh, you're a smart one, Mr Morris.' Ryan's laugh was brief, sarcastic: a short expulsion of breath. 'You didn't see him!'

'I wasn't on duty that night.'

'But you know how he died?'

'He hung himself . . . in his cell. We returned his body to his relatives.'

'A good man, Casey was. A good man. And you're a "B" Special, and we know your feelings towards the Taigs.'

'I've got nothing against Catholics,' Fitzgerald started to plead, but even as he spoke he realized the stupidity of the remark. If he *were* a "B" Special he would regard Catholics as potential traitors and Sinn Feiners.

'You're a liar, Mr Morris.' Ryan hit him in the right shoulder this time. Two rapid jabs. Much harder. 'Next you'll be saying you haven't been spreading the word that if the Catholic church was giving out guns to the Provos, everybody would be joining the priesthood. Isn't that the truth?'

'Perhaps . . . perhaps I've heard it said.' Fitzgerald's eyes were beginning to glaze over.

'So, having established your mistrust of the Catholic church, let's go back to the mechanic. You accept the fact that we buried his body forty-eight hours ago.'

'I do.'

'And you expect us to believe he committed suicide! That he was put in a cell, where more than a week later he miraculously found a length of rope which he fashioned into a noose and then hung himself?' A playful tap to the cheek.

'It's the truth,' Fitzgerald sobbed, rubbing his face.

'You know what I think, Mr Morris? I think you haven't got the guts to admit that you killed a prisoner in cold blood.'

'I didn't do it . . . you've got to believe me . . .'

'And that's your final word?'

'What else? I'm innocent . . .'

'An innocent "B" special? That's an oxymoron, Mr Morris. You know what an oxymoron is?' A slap to the other cheek.

'No.' Raised hands now, to ward off further blows.

'A contradiction. Meaning you can't be both. You are a "B" Special, isn't that the truth?'

'Yes.'

Ryan fixed Fitzgerald with a bleak stare. The voice, little more than a whisper, was all the more chilling. 'It's very simple then. You must be guilty.'

Despite the cold rain Fitzgerald was sweating now, caught up in the game. 'I didn't fucking kill him. I never even saw the man.'

'Have you anything to say before the court passes sentence?' A vicious kick to the shin followed the question.

'I've got a wife and two children,' Fitzgerald whimpered, hopping on one leg, reaching down with a free hand to massage his ankle. 'For God's sake, you must believe me. He hung himself . . . I swear it on my children's lives.'

Ryan shook his head in mock disappointment. His eyes glittered. 'You, Tommy Morris, will be taken from this place, to a place of execution on the banks of the Blackstaff, and may God have mercy on your soul.' Ryan lifted his right hand, forefinger extended, thumb vertical, like a cocked gun. The 'gun' touched the back of Fitzgerald's head. 'Bang,' he yelled loudly. Loud enough to make Fitzgerald jump. Ryan blew away imaginary smoke from the tip of his forefinger, and laughed. 'I'm sorry, Sean, but you're dead.'

Fitzgerald tried to share in the laughter, but at that precise moment he felt sick. Trembling all over. His autonomic nervous system had seen to that. His glands working overtime. The chemicals stirring the blood. Muscles tightening. Belly going loose. Always worse when the danger had gone.

They were sitting in the back of the taxi smoking cigarettes when Ryan passed the paper bag to Fitzgerald.

'What is it?'

'Look inside.'

Fitzgerald reached into the bag and took out a pistol. 'We were told to use a silencer.'

'Were you now. And where would you get one of them?'

'I don't know, but we were told a modified coke bottle stuffed with tissue paper would do the same thing.' Fitzgerald replied knowingly.

Ryan snorted. 'I'll tell you something about silencers, Sean. It's good for one shot, after that the steel wool packing becomes compressed and the back pressure builds up so high that the user usually finds his hand is blown off . . . try it with a coke bottle son, and the shattered glass'll probably take your eyes out.'

Fitzgerald said nervously, 'What about the noise?'

'Not too much. What you're holding is a .32 calibre popgun. Not much stopping power. The muzzle blast is less than a .38 . . . quieter, especially when pressed up against the back of the victim's head. Then again you can doctor the bullets by taking out some of the powder to reduce the bang. An old trick when you want to shoot without drawing attention to yourself, and if done carefully and the gun is fired at not too great a range, the bullet's still lethal.'

'You can do that?' Fitzgerald asked.

'The only trade I've known.'

'Could you teach me?'

'We'll see.'

Fitzgerald went to hand the gun back. He looked paler.

'No, you keep it,' Ryan said.

'You want *me* to shoot the man?' Disbelief.

'Has to be a first time, Sean.'

'It's just that I've never . . .'

'Then again, there's Celia.'

Fitzgerald's eyes widened. Curious now. 'What about her?'

'She's with us; you know that, don't you? She's got this bastard Morris at a party. She's promised him a night of pleasure at the Europa Hotel. That's where this taxi's going now, to pick her and her fancy man up . . . well, him at least. Some night of fucking pleasure, eh, Sean.'

Fitzgerald was silent. Time was running out. He was sweating. Wondering if he had the courage to pull the trigger.

Ryan went on. 'Then again, she likes heroes, Celia does. After tonight she'll know that you're the new hard man on the block. Think of it, Sean. A night of pleasure with her at the Europa, wages for a job well done. I tell you, lying on top of those big beautiful breasts is like nothing you've ever known. Course you've got to be man enough to handle her.'

'You think she . . .'

'I've already told her about you,' Ryan interrupted

29

smoothly. 'I told her you're an iron man. She liked that, I could see it in her eyes.'

The taxi sped on through the night. The 'murder squads' that had been effectively silent since the fifties were about to be reborn.

Frank Ryan arrived back at the house in Cawnpore Street a little after three in the morning. He was soaked to the skin but even the rain had failed to wash away the sickly sweet smell of blood and gore that had spattered his hands and face and clothes. Even so he felt elated. Was on a high. All he needed now was a woman and a bottle . . . a way to round off the night. And perhaps still the slight tremor in his hands. Killing a man did that to you; no matter how many times the act was repeated the adrenalin rush never seemed to get any less. He'd thought young Sean would have gone through with it, but the boy had cracked up at the last moment, when the hooded figure of Morris kneeling on the ground before them, had pleaded his innocence in almost the same words that Sean had used in the mock trial. *I'm innocent . . . I swear on my children's lives.* Powerful stuff, especially given the emotion in the voice. Fucking lies of course, but powerful stuff.

He slipped quietly into the yard of the house, and felt his way along the side of the building to the door. Paused to remember the code of the day. He tapped three times and waited. Three taps were returned. He tapped once. One tap was returned. He tapped once more, and the door bolts clattered and the door opened on a pleasant warm fug of cigarette smoke and whiskey. Cavenaugh was not alone. Sitting at the table were Father Michael, and his wife, Nancy. He looked at the three faces for a moment. 'So, what's going on, Pat? Don't tell me you've arranged a party.'

Cavenaugh smiled and calmly ushered him to the chair nearest the gas stove. Then poured him a drink. 'Everything went all right then, did it, Frank?'

Ryan looked at his wife. She was combing her hair. It was longer than he seemed to remember, or perhaps he hadn't really been paying attention these past weeks. It was almost to her waist now. The coppery red colour glistening in the harsh light from the naked bulb above her head. 'What are you doing here?' The tone was harsher than he intended. Especially with what he had in mind once he got her away from here.

'Pat asked me.'

Ryan shook his head and turned towards Cavenaugh. 'What were you saying, Pat?'

'Everything went all right, did it?'

'And why wouldn't it?'

'Young Sean?'

Young Sean! Bloody magic he was, caught up in an immobilizing sense of terror, couldn't even hold the gun steady. Reason I sent him to the Europa to meet Celia. Perhaps when he realizes that there are benefits to the job he might try harder next time, either that or he'll die with a smile on his face. Thought it, but didn't say it. 'Oh, he's fine. I sent him home.'

'Just as well,' Cavenaugh said, poking a finger under the eye-patch. Gently massaging an imaginary itch. A habit which had developed when tiny slivers of metal had continued to eject themselves from the empty eye-socket for months after the Omagh bombing all those years earlier. Now nothing more than stress playing tricks. He withdrew his finger, adjusted the eye-patch. Added with a note of regret: 'It seems we might have got the wrong man tonight, Frank.'

Ryan was part-way through drinking his whiskey. He stopped, eyes wide, lowered the glass to the table. 'Wrong man? What's that supposed to mean?'

Cavenaugh turned to the young priest sitting opposite him. 'You want to tell him, Michael?'

Father Michael McVerry was a slightly built man in his early thirties, fair wispy hair, and pale eyes behind wire-rimmed spectacles. He had a permanent startled look, as though he had been frightened by something as a child and never really recovered. But for all that he was a diligent worker, having in the recent months set up what would become one of the best listening posts in Ireland, at the Clonard Monastery, strategically situated between the Protestant Sandy Row and the Catholic Falls Road. 'I received news from the airport tonight, Frank, one of the cleaners at the temporary RAF offices found a filing cabinet unlocked.' His voice was highly pitched and seemed – whilst seeking the correct level of humility for his calling in life – genuinely apologetic. 'They did the usual bit of checking, just to see if there was any news on future troop movements into Belfast. What they found was a movement from a few weeks ago. An Andover aircraft from Aldergrove to RAF Lyneham. What was interesting about it was the passenger. An SAS man named Winter.'

Ryan stared at the priest. 'I hope this is leading somewhere, Michael, I'm soaked to the skin, I'm tired, and I want to get home to my bed.'

Father Michael lit a cigarette, and pushed the packet

across the table to Ryan. 'It seems that Winter was working undercover, here in the North. Worse yet *he* was the man we knew as the mechanic . . . Ben Casey.'

There was a terrible silence as Ryan lit a cigarette with an unsteady hand and finished his whiskey. 'What are you talking about, Michael, you know as well as I do that we buried Ben Casey a couple of days ago.'

Cavenaugh, motioning Father Michael to silence took up the debriefing. 'The thing is, Frank, who knew Ben Casey before he arrived last autumn from Dublin?'

'Tim Daley recruited him from the south, you know that.'

'Sure I do. And wasn't Tim unfortunately killed in a car accident the very week he recruited Ben Casey?'

'I'm sorry Pat, I'm not altogether following you. It's been a long night,' Ryan said irritably.

'It seems likely it was set up by the SAS from the beginning. A lot of supposition, but just hear me out. What if the SAS had wind of the recruiting drive going on in the south last autumn at the time of the rebirth of the movement here in the North? What if they discovered that the mechanic – Ben Casey – was about to be taken into the Provos? Let's say they have a file on Casey and they find that they have a man on strength that is close in physical appearance to Casey. This man Winter. What if this man Winter has Irish associations and therefore can put on the Irish accent without any problems? So what is their next step? They take out Tim Daley, because he is one of ours, and is the only local man who can identify him. Next they take out the real Ben Casey, and slip their man in.' Cavenaugh paused long enough to take a sip of his whiskey. He leaned forward in his chair, his voice more intense now. 'Then comes the tricky bit. What to do with the dead body of Ben Casey? Sure, the easiest thing would be to bury him somewhere, or drop his body in the ocean. But no, somebody has a brilliant idea, why not put the body in a deep freeze . . . a sort of insurance policy if you like, just in case things go wrong in the North. And sure enough things did go wrong some weeks ago, when the landmine blew up a BA vehicle. The mechanic was there, as were your children . . . and Nancy here. The Specials pick up the mechanic and when they get him back to the police station he asks for a BA officer; he then explains the situation, which is verified through the SAS HQ in London. And this is where it gets really bloody clever, they take the real Ben Casey out of deep freeze and hand that body back saying that he had hanged himself in his cell, while the other man . . . Winter . . . has been quietly moved back to England. And if the cleaner hadn't been lucky enough to find that filing cabinet open, and read the right file, we would never have realized that our operation here had been compromised.'

Ryan closed his eyes and held out his empty glass for a refill. He sighed. 'Do you really believe they'd go to all that trouble?'

'Why not? The future eases open a fraction with each bold action someone once told me.'

'What about you, Nancy? You knew him, what do you think?' he asked, taking in the silver mini-skirt, the black stockings, the high-heeled shoes, the tight green sweater – he could almost smell the intoxicating perfume she wore – and at that moment he thought she was the most beautiful woman in the world.

'I think Pat could be right. Everything seems to fit sure enough.' No warmth in the voice.

'So that bastard Morris was telling the truth,' Ryan murmured to himself.

'What was that, Frank?' Cavenaugh asked.

'Nothing. You and your bloody bell again, Pat, I'm thinking there'll be a lot of dead Chinamen by the end of this. Still, I'd like to get my hands on that Sassman.'

'More or less what's been going through my mind; let them think they've got away with it and their tails will be up, but if we could nail the bastard, they'd know that we knew, perhaps that we had known all along and were feeding him false information.'

Ryan nodded and wiped his nose on his sleeve. The stench of blood filled his nostrils. 'So what do you want me to do?'

'Take a couple of the lads to England, see what you can find out.'

'Just like that.' A note of derision. 'You think our Intel is up to it do you, Pat? Up to last month we had a total of ten guns . . . how many men have we got?' Ryan took off his donkey jacket and held it out towards the blue flames of the gas stove. Steam rose in lazy tendrils.

'Just think what it could mean if we pulled it off though.'

'We need to get more funding in place . . . so you said.'

'The sparkle of America . . . I did. And it will come, but in the meanwhile we have to maintain some kind of momentum.'

'I wish I shared just one-tenth of your optimism.'

'You think it's impossible?'

'Of course it's impossible. I grant you we might have been lucky if we were trying to trace a regular soldier, but a Sassman! Those people are answerable to nobody. Even the regiments they served with before they transferred to the SAS couldn't locate them without all sorts of security checks through the SAS administration people at the Duke of York's Barracks in London. Quite simply they're invisible.'

'You'd have no objection if I sent Sean then?'

'What chance do you think he'd have?'

'I don't know. But he's young and wild enough.'

More like a risky piece of bravado, Ryan thought. Said: 'I'll give you that.'

'I could send Gerry and Conor with him.'

'Up to you, Pat, but you'll be wasting your time.'

Nancy Ryan said suddenly, 'I'll go.'

That was an attention getter. All heads turned towards her.

'You're staying here . . .' Ryan snapped, spinning round. Dropping the jacket to the floor. His voice failing when he almost found himself adding: 'To take care of the children.' *To take care of the children*! What children? They were gone. Dead and buried. In moments like these it was almost as if they had never existed.

'Give me one good reason, Frank Ryan.'

'You're my wife, that's reason enough.' He knew it was a lame excuse, but it was all he had.

The green eyes flashed, and the blood rushed to her face. And through the rising anger she remembered the time she was barely a teenager and had met Frank Ryan for the first time. A man of the world. Twenty-five, or was it twenty-six when she first saw him, on leave from the Air Force. He had come to call on her sister. She thought he was so handsome . . . a schoolgirl crush, which had turned into a competition with her older sister. And then the sister had fallen out with him, and she had met him one day coming out of school. He had given her a lift home in his car; impressed the hell out of the other girls. And she had told him she loved him, and that he had to wait for her. By that time she was sprouting little buds of breasts, something she supplemented with a bra stuffed with cotton wool. And when she was fourteen he had taken her. He was always careful. Always used a condom — against the teachings of the Church of course. But so was intercourse with a minor. By the time she was seventeen she was ready to marry him. Except by then she was not really in love with him. Even so the family expected it and she went ahead and married the man who was now past thirty. Not that she ever told him she didn't love him any more. And then, trying for the first baby. Six years of trying. Him telling her that she was barren. So that in the end she really believed it. And suddenly out of nowhere, in her twenty-fourth year she was pregnant. And a year after the birth of Mikey, she was expecting again. And then he had grown tired of her. Had some fancy woman called Celia, so she had been told. *You're my wife*. The thought made her flesh creep.

'In name only,' she snapped, letting the pent-up emotions of a lifetime flood out. 'My children were murdered before my eyes. Not your eyes, Frank Ryan, or the educated eyes of Pat Cavenaugh here, or the holier-than-thou eyes of Michael McVerry who talks

37

of God as though he drinks with him every Friday night trading free pints for promises . . . And the lovely thing is when your children are taken and the promises are cashed in they prove to be as worthless as all the promises you made me when we first married. How you were going to take me to America to start a new life. Chicago, you said. A house of my own. Your brother was going to find you a job with the big, fancy construction company he worked for. How he was even going to send us the air tickets. So no, Frank Ryan, I've listened to you and the church all my life and I don't give a flying damn what you and your friends here think or say, I'm going with your blessing or without it. I'll find the bastard if it takes me the rest of my life. Make sure you understand that . . . all of you.' She leapt up from the chair and stormed across the tiny room and grabbed her raincoat from a hook on the back of the door and slid the bolts back.

'And just how the hell do you think you'll find this Sassman in a country the size of England?' Ryan yelled.

The door was half open as she turned to face him. Defiance in every gesture. 'How do you think? I'm a woman.' She flung her arms wide, as if to emphasize the point: The raincoat hanging from her fingertips like a veil being discarded, her shapely figure, the thrust of her breasts, her beauty. 'Soldiers like women . . . you'd know what I'm talking about wouldn't you, Frank!'

Ryan, fists clenched, veins bulging in his neck, started up from his chair. Cavenaugh held him back as Nancy ran out of the door. The clattering of high heels on the pathway. The slamming of the door to the street. 'Let her go, Frank. Let her go.'

'She's my wife for Christ's sake.'

'And I'm sorry for the way things are, Frank,' Cavenaugh said soothingly, pulling him back into his chair. He poured another drink. 'You remember what you were telling young Sean last week – "The Army as an organization claims and expects your total allegiance without reservation. It enters into every aspect of your life. It invades the privacy of your home, it fragments your family and friends, in other words claims your *total* allegiance". You remember, Frank?'

Ryan glowered at Cavenaugh, who was standing over him holding the refilled glass of whiskey. *It fragments your family.* Like the woman he had planned to lie with. To work off the night and the drink and the shakes. 'Sure I remember,' he snapped.

'Little by little,' Cavenaugh said persuasively, 'That's the way I do it. A smile today, a song tomorrow . . . she'll be back, you see if I'm not right. Now drink this, and then get out of those wet clothes. You'd better sleep here tonight.' And while Ryan was drinking he escorted the priest to the door and helped him on with his raincoat.

'You have a way with the words, Pat.'

'I only hope that in the end they're the right ones.'

'It's just that I wouldn't want any harm coming to Nancy Ryan, she's a fine woman.'

'That she is, and you have my word I'll take care of her.'

Father Michael motioned Cavenaugh outside the door. 'There is something else,' he whispered, pulling the collar of his raincoat up against the rain.

'I'm listening.'

'The evening the daughter died from her injuries . . .

at the Mater Hospital here in Belfast. Nancy took confession the very next morning.' The priest took a deep breath as though summoning up the courage to break with his ecclesiastical vows. 'She told me it was she who shot the BA man, and that the mechanic gave himself up in her place . . . Until today I thought your man was a saint.'

A sharp intake of breath, quickly gone. 'And now?'

'Something for you to consider, Pat.' Sacramental circumspection in the voice.

Cavenaugh remained at the door long after the priest's footsteps had faded along the street. In his eye a flicker of interest. He could understand the real mechanic – the real Ben Casey – doing such a thing. But an undercover Sassman! *Until today I thought your man was a saint.* Something even rarer, Cavenaugh decided, as he went back into the house.

2

Under the glare of the moon the mountain had no colour. Like a day pushed inside out. Everything in negative. John Winter paused and looked down. He could even imagine the lights of Dorcas' farm below, welcome yellow beacons on the times he had been there on leave and had needed the solitude of a day's climbing to exorcise the blood guilt of the latest excursion. Places like Wayne's Keep in the hills outside Nicosia, Cyprus; Dhofar in the southern province of Oman; Crossmaglen, Northern Ireland; all had brought their mental wounds. Those that eventually scarred over. The nightmares, the blood guilt, took a while longer to dissipate. Sometimes they never did, the corruption remaining forever. The mountain before him was of course an illusion, something which for a fleeting moment and from a certain perspective had resembled Cader Idris in North Wales. In reality nothing more than towering cumulus along the line of a frontal system that August Gant had pointed out earlier in the weather office at St Johns, Newfoundland. A cold front they would meet up with about 500 miles before their Scottish landfall. And now they had.

August Gant, ex-USAF pilot turned soldier of fortune, looked across at the young man in the right seat. Mid to late twenties, military short white-blond hair and piercing blue eyes, somewhere around 6 feet tall, good physique, a combination that had brought the gals flocking at every watering hole from Florida to Newfoundland. But it was more than that. The young man had come heavily recommended, and Gant was on the lookout for new recruits. He adjusted the boom mike of his headset so that it was barely touching his lips. 'So, whad'ya think?' A thick South Carolina accent that came and went to suit his mood. He waved a hand at the vastness of the night sky. Decomposing starlight. A waxing moon flying through the wind-torn anvils of the frontal weather.

Winter considered the question. *Think?* Too many things, was his first observation. Six months after his discharge from a holding unit at Aldershot he was still struggling with his separation from the Army – his release from its womb-like safety, his release from its certainty: every day charted, daily routine orders posted on a notice board, a job to be done for which they clothed and fed you and gave you regular money. There had been no warning of what 'civvy street' would be like, for the simple reason that those who couldn't hack the withdrawal symptoms and had re-enlisted would never have the balls to admit failure, and those who survived those first few months were soon swallowed up in the seething mass of factory workers or miners, friendless in a way that only an ex-soldier would understand. Even so a trained eye would always pick them out, the straight back, the squared shoulders, the measured step full of confidence, a look of having lost a fiver and found a penny. The fiver: in once belonging to an elite corps where even the language defied translation. The penny: fading memories of their first RSM, and their glory days in Cyprus or Aden; there might even be a uniform hanging in a wardrobe – razor-sharp creases still – something that would eventually be thrown out when a growing family vied for space in a too-small terraced house in some soulless industrial town.

Some of his thoughts. The rest kaleidoscoped into making contact with Lieutenant Colonel August Gant, USAF (Rtd), who had put him in touch with a flight school in Florida, where he had learned to fly helicopters, and two weeks earlier gained his commercial ticket. Just the beginning, Gant had suggested, and had offered him a job, which started on the other side of the Atlantic. Hence he was here with the old-timer on a ferry flight to Wick in Scotland, in a single-engine Cessna 210 – the beginning of things. One engine at night over a big ocean. Something that had seemed commonplace over a beer in a Florida bar, but had translated to dry-mouthed uncertainty as he'd prepared to launch into a dark night over a dark ocean, even though he was only a passenger. In the cruise for the last nine hours at 11,000 feet he had become more accustomed to his surroundings. Strapped to a seat alongside Gant. Both wearing bulky survival suits. The dim red glow of instrument lights bathing the impossibly confined space. Sound but no apparent movement, as travelling in the register of outer space must be. Then there was the heat generated by the survival suit. Close to unbearable. He could feel the constant trickling of sweat down his chest and back – even though the air vents were wide open. With the help of the headset he had become inured to the noise of the 285 horsepower Continental engine a few feet ahead of the cockpit. Now, little more than a background hum.

So whad'ya think?

'You asked me the same question about an hour out of St Johns.'

'So, I gotta big backyard.'

'I think you like night flying.'

'Don't get any better than this . . . You know, some nights I could stay forever.'

'I still think you need to have a lot of faith in the maker of the engine up front.'

Gant chuckled. 'Safer than drivin' an' that's a fact.'

'What happens if it fails?'

'Hell, Wint, we ditch, simple as that. Reason we got that fancy little blow-up rubber boat stashed behind your seat. If we're real lucky we mebbe get picked up by a passin' ship at first light.'

'Lot of ships down there then?'

Gant scratched the day-old stubble on his chin. 'Could be some fishin' boats south of Iceland.'

'What about you, have you ever ditched?'

'Nope. Know a few who have though.'

'And got rescued you mean.'

'Negative. All bought the farm . . . havin' second thoughts I guess.'

'Not really, just like to know the options, the back-up plans. The "Ps" as we called it in the Army! Piss poor planning leads to piss poor performance.'

Gant laughed. 'I like that. That army trainin' of yours could save your neck, after all. Mind you, you're right in a way, this is hardly what I'd refer to as walkin' in tall cotton. Not enough money for a start. Still, once you've checked out that helo in Scotland we'll both be off to the Philippines.'

'You never did say what sort of job we'd be doing out there.'

Gant checked his watch. 'You'd better start windin' out the trailing aerial. Need to give Iceland a position report in five minutes.'

Winter picked up the spool with 300 feet of wire at his feet and began winding it out. 'What sort of work? You never said.'

Gant sniffed at the air. 'Smell any fumes?'

'Fumes?'

Gant pointed back to the internal ferry tank behind the two pilots' seats. It held 100 US gallons of aviation fuel, essential to extend their range. 'Gas.'

Winter sniffed. 'No. I thought it was vented overboard.'

'It is,' Gant replied as he lit a cigarette. 'Just wanted to make sure before I blew us both to hell.' He puffed at the cigarette for a while. 'Seems like President Marcos is havin' a spot of trouble in the south of the Philippines with a bunch of Marxist guerillas, wants a mercenary unit to fly a bunch of Skyraiders against them – ground-attack fighter-bomber if you didn't know. Great ship. Then again we need a helo and a helo pilot to mebbe pick up downed pilots.'

Winter finished winding out the aerial. 'Should be able to make your HF call now.'

'So whad'ya think 'bout it? Good pay.'

'Not my thing any more. I just completed a lot of years with the Army. I've had enough of killing to last me a dozen lifetimes.'

Gant scratched his balding head and twisted around in his seat, busying himself selecting a frequency on the HF radio that was strapped on the top of the internal fuel tank. When he'd passed the position report to Iceland Radio, he pulled out a thermos from beneath his feet and poured two half-cups of black coffee. Passed one to Winter.

'Airline stewardesses should be instructed to do the same.'

'What?'

'Only pour half a cup of coffee. Safeguard against turbulence . . . not forgetting a lapful of scalding liquid.'

'Good point.'

'So tell me, what sorta books do you read?'

'Books? Oh I don't know . . .'

'Poetry?'

'Not since my schooldays.'

'Robbie Burns?'

'Might have done.'

'Now that offends my Scottish ancestry.'

'I didn't know you were a Scot.'

'The name threw you, uh? It was Grant, got written down incorrectly by the immigration people about a hundred years back. Four generations to be exact. Fishermen from the very town we're going to.' He glanced across at Winter, noticed the look of uncertainty on the young man's face. 'Ye dinna believe me, laddie!' he rasped in a mock-Scottish accent. And reached down to the leg of his flight suit and opened one of the pockets. He handed Winter a knife.

'It's called a *sgian dubh*, the black knife of the Highlander. You know, the sorta thing you see in the stocking tops of Scotsmen when they're in the glory of national dress.'

'I've heard of it. First time I've seen one.'

'The Cairngorm stone set in the pommel balances it, makes it a good throwing weapon. Pretty neat, uh?'

'Very pretty,' Winter agreed, and handed it back.

'Goin' back to the books. Ever study military history?'

'Not really.'

'Clausewitz's *On War*, I thought every soldier had read that.'

'I was just a sergeant. Cannon fodder. The officers decide on strategies.'

'What about Alexander the Great, now there was a guy who knew how to win wars. Had a horse called Bucephalus, you'da heard of him?'

'Not offhand.'

'Jesus, Wint, I'd say your education is lackin'. What happened is that Alexander's father King Philip was presented this magnificent horse, they say it was tall in stature, courageous in spirit, and had the mark of an ox head branded on him. This horse was one of those fractious beasts whose breakin' by an unknown is the favourite staple of Western movies. You must have seen one of those?' A purely rhetorical question. He moved quickly on. 'Anyways, the horse defied the king, shying and stamping whenever he approached.

Alexander announced that he would mount him, seized his halter, turned him and leapt into the saddle . . . to the applause of the courtiers and his father. The son's trick was to have noticed that Bucephalus shied at his own shadow and to turn him towards the sun.' Gant reached forward and gently patted the coaming above the instrument panel. 'This little piece of aluminum confetti is my Bucephalus . . . once you've broken her there's nothing else you're ever goin' to do in your life that'll give you the same satisfaction.'

'As I said earlier, not my thing any more, August.'

The American smiled to himself. He had heard from a friend of his – a local car dealer back at Vero Beach, who had witnessed the incident and called the police – how three punks had decided to pick on a kid and his dog in the park. They had chains and, of all things, a crossbow. First, they shot the dog in the neck with a bolt then they set about the kid with a chain. It was at about that moment that a jogger came by. According to the car dealer, he floored the first guy with a chop to the neck, the second with a karate kick to the groin, and seeing the third coming at him with a knife, picked up the crossbow which happened to be loaded and shot him through the stomach. He then went over and checked the dog, then the kid, then jogged away. Minutes later the local police and paramedics arrived. The kid and the dog survived, as did the three gang members, except they ended up in the local hospital under police guard pending trial. Gant had subsequently found out that Winter's weak spot was cruelty to animals. He had wondered since that event – about a week earlier – if Winter would have intervened if an animal hadn't been hurt. Of course it had to have been the Englishman. He doubted there were legions of six-footers with blond hair and expert in the martial arts jogging in the park that morning.

Gant went on undeterred. 'Same sorta thing I used to say after Korea. Did I ever tell you about Korea?'

Winter shook his head.

'Nope, I guess I didn't. First jet war. Boy that was somethin'. But as you said yourself, at the end of it I was the same. I kinda figured I'd had enough, that I'd go home and find a job in a little bank on Main Street and marry my high school sweetheart. And you know what the problem was? After a month, or two, I realized I didn't belong there. Sure, it was my home town where I'd been raised and schooled. But it was a foreign land.'

Gant's voice faded. He took a last mouthful of his coffee. Stared out through the windshield at the threatening moonlit cloudscape that was very near now.

'So you left.'

'So I left.'

'And your high school sweetheart?'

'Smart as a whip, that gal. Know what she said to me after I'd been home three months? She said, "About time you were leaving, honey." Y'see she'd known all along that I didn't belong there any more. She'd seen a kid go off to a foreign war and witnessed a man – a stranger – who'd returned. Her way of sayin' she released me from my promise to marry her.'

'Did you ever regret it?'

'I guess it's about making choices. In Korea we were forbidden to fly north of the Yalu, to fight the enemy on his own ground. Same kinda thing's happening now in 'Nam, the pilots have their hands tied. Fighting for Marcos? My choice. Morality? My interpretation. Being a mercenary? According to the bible we're all mercenaries in the final analysis. My daddy told me before I joined the Air Force: "Be the best that you can be." This is my best, Wint. Not quite brain surgery, but my best.' He thought about that for a moment then added. 'You like music?'

'Some.'

'What sort?'

'Classics mainly. Mozart, Mahler, Stravinsky.'

Gant let out a sigh of relief. 'Thank the good Lord for that at least. Y'know, for a moment back there I thought I'd teamed up with a regular Philistine.' Then pointing ahead to the storm line added, 'You'd better finish that coffee and tighten your harness, things are goin' be bumpy for the next couple hundred miles or so.'

'How bumpy?'

'Hell, I don't know. Just let's say that storms like these have been known to tear the wings clean off an airplane . . . so if you see me startin' to pray, you'd better figure on joinin' me pretty damn quick.' Brief laughter followed. 'Then again usin' young Alexander's philosophy of attacking the line at the strongest point always seemed to work for me.'

Winter, uncertain how serious Gant was, just sat and watched the towering clouds growing near. Feeling the first signs of turbulence reaching out. Rocking the aircraft gently. Moonlight fading to pitch-black night. The rain followed. Light at first, like blowing sand on glass, then more intense, until the noise drowned out all else. The rocking intensified. The shock-mounted instrument panel vibrating so badly that the instruments were unreadable. A blinding white flash off the right wingtip. Lightning. He'd been caught up on the mountain once or twice when the weather had turned. This was a little different. No Dorcas' farm down below. No welcoming beacons of yellow light. At some point he saw Gant's lips moving – nearly panicked when he thought he was praying. It wasn't until there was a few seconds' lull in the storm that he realized the old colonel was singing.

It was more than two and a half hours until dawn and their landing at Wick. Even so, flying was something he had begun to love. There were no human killing fields here – no British Army who since time immemorial had taken the hardest 'animals' they could find and then let them loose on their enemies; their trick being to keep the percentage balance at 49–51 in their favour so that your 'animals' hated you marginally less than the enemy. No, here it was just man against the elements. Risks, certainly. But civilized risks. And even though August Gant had pointed out that a 'legitimate' flying job – rotary or fixed-wing – wasn't ever going to make a man rich, it would make enough. He could eventually save sufficient to buy a small cottage in the countryside somewhere. The future, despite the violent turbulence and the thunderous rain, looked brighter than he could ever remember.

3

The letter had saved him.

Even so the thought that Boston's Logan Field was one of the most depressing airports to have to fly from was foremost in Teach Cusack's mind as he made his way into the international departure lounge, threading his way between sprawling tourists packed into almost every square foot of the long, narrow, holding area. A single seat remained unoccupied facing the huge window, which looked out on to the ramp area. A Boeing 707 gazed back, rivulets of rain coursing down her bare aluminium skin. It was one in the morning. The London flight had been delayed for eight hours, first due to technical reasons, and then because the crew operating the flight had run out of duty hours. A few minutes after midnight the airline had assured the unhappy passengers (at least two of whom, on the realization that the date was now Friday the 13th, had cancelled their journeys) that a standby crew was on the way in. Even so the prospect of an extended sleepless night and the five time-slipped hours that went with it was not cheering to Cusack.

He was an average 5 feet 9. The thinning sandy-coloured hair belied his thirty-three years, giving him a fifty-ish look. Lifeless grey eyes. His pale, drawn and lined face giving him an appearance of permanent thoughtfulness. In Vietnam, they had called him 'Teach'; the name had stuck. He had been a bit apart even then, until it was patrol time, then like all the rest of the infantry grunts who all needed a brother in those hours, he had bitten the bullet and gone to find the enemy. Scared shitless at first, then as the number of patrols mounted he found he didn't really give a damn . . . until the last few days of his tour at least. Then he became scared shitless all over again. The stark realization that a VC bullet might find him just when he was about to go home!

He was wearing the free outfit given him by the Utah State Prison – packed in his shoulder bag a few spare shirts and pants and socks, his entire wardrobe – a maroon blazer over a green striped shirt, badly hemmed beige polyester trousers, black plastic shoes, and a black trench coat slung over his arm.

He rummaged around in his shoulder bag and pulled out a copy of a paperback novel. The *letter* was folded inside the book as a page marker. He opened it and read it again, for the fiftieth time, or so it seemed.

He had often wondered about incidents in his life, and the way things showed up when he least expected them. Like now. In jail for the past twelve months (robbery with violence at a convenience store in Utah, the three-year sentence reduced to one year by a sympathetic lady judge when the defence counsel had introduced Cusack's recent war record, heroism under fire, the award of two Purple Hearts) ever since his return from the war, when the succession of friends' apartments had dried up, and he had been forced to *take* what he needed. Getting out of prison and being met by an old ex-Nam buddy of his, who had given him a bed, with *sheets* – his first for twelve months – and as much beer as he could drink. Then one day suggesting there might be a job for him. A letter from another 'Nam vet who lived in Boston, which read: '*I don't know if you're interested, but we need a courier to travel back and forth to the UK/Europe. Up side is it pays well. Down side, you'll probably get sick to death of airline food. Let me know if you're available.*' Which he was.

And in the days that followed he had been introduced to a businessman by the name of William 'Big Bill' Fagan who was head of the Boston chapter of the recently formed Northern Irish Aid committee (NORAID), and who explained how American dollars were needed to help the newly formed Provisional Irish Republican Army to buy arms in the ongoing war with the Brits.

Not that Teach was particularly interested either way what the IRA, or even the PIRA as it was now called, wanted to do, even so he knew enough to play the patriot when questioned. And even though he didn't possess a degree in political science, he was his father's son. He had been weaned on Irish heroes and British injustices, was adept in potato politics before first grade, well before he had ever heard of Washington or Jefferson. Still, he didn't accept Fagan's words at face value, he asked questions. Besides, wasn't this an interview of sorts? And didn't he need the job?

'What about the Dublin government?' he had asked Fagan.

An almost imperceptible shrug of the shoulders. 'What about them?'

'I read something recently in one of the newspapers about Irish government ministers coming over to Washington and warning us against subscribing to the Provisionals; that it would only lead to more bloodshed.'

'A counter-productive move, Teach, something that has created a backlash shall we say. The working Irish-Americans don't altogether like the idea of foreigners coming over here to tell them how they should spend the dollars in their pockets. The movement's also got strong support from the unions, particularly the longshore workers' unions who've even offered work to exiled IRA members. In fact the Provisionals have already been given some pretty big subscriptions, which if it hadn't been for the veiled threats of outsiders they might never have gotten.'

Teach said, 'Freedom never comes cheap, and diplomacy keeps politicians in the style of life to which they've become accustomed, isn't that the truth.' An oft-quoted line borrowed from his father. It went down well.

Big Bill Fagan had patted the younger man on the shoulder. 'You'll do, Teach, you'll do.'

Now, armed with nothing more lethal than a shoulder bag that carried American dollars and a few bank cashiers' cheques, he was off to London to meet a man by the name of Frank Ryan. Ryan would buy him a drink at one of the Heathrow hotels, where he would hand over the money. The next day he would

catch a flight back home. The schedule was to make
four trips a month to London and/or Amsterdam. He
had naturally questioned the frequency of the trips
and what cover story he should have if questioned
by Customs. But his paymasters were one step
ahead. They had any number of false passports he
would travel on. European destinations could and
would be varied if deemed necessary. In every case
he was simply a tourist or an employee of a tour
company.

He put the paperback novel into his shoulder bag
and went off to find the toilet. Not that he needed to
relieve himself. Just that he preferred the solitariness
of a cubicle, where he could have a cigarette in peace,
and without screaming babies. A prison psychologist
had decided that Cusack liked small dark places
because they reminded him of a dugout – a shelter
against enemy 'incoming'. Cusack had said nothing,
afraid to admit that the Doc was probably right; afraid
to admit to the fact that he often awoke in the middle
of the night in tears and was afraid to go back to sleep
and be drawn into the same horrific nightmare where
his buddy, Rusty – a third-string Dallas Mafia type –
was being blown to pieces before his eyes. More afraid
that if he told the doctor anything he would end up in
some Psych Unit, being drugged day and night, ending
up a dribbling, incontinent, fucked-up war vet who
couldn't even feed himself any more. The reason he
had bitten his tongue and concentrated on the pain
and the promise of freedom.

And when they released him he had found a dark
place and cried for a long time. Not for Rusty and the
other guys from his platoon who had died in a

primitive land called Vietnam, but for himself. For winning his first war.

He was sitting on the toilet seat, looking through his shoulder bag for a pack of cigarettes. He pulled out the one sealed pack, which was obviously cash, and the large envelope with the bank cashiers' cheques in them. Naturally he hadn't been told the amount. And naturally he hadn't asked. He was a patriot after all. It was for the old Mother Country. Even so, the urge to open the envelope and the package was very strong. How much money was he carrying? Customs, he had been assured, wouldn't bother him, from which he assumed they had a 'sleeper' working for British Customs who would be on duty the following morning. They had obviously thought of everything. Including the fact that if he tried to steal the money he would be tracked down and killed. Same MO as the Mafia.

He lit a cigarette. What if this was just a dry run and he was carrying nothing more than blank paper? Better to play along for now, see how the land lay. Then perhaps, as had happened in 'Nam, with disillusioned infantrymen looking for a way out (the deserters the American press had never written about) he could get *killed*. Mugged on a Boston street. The muggers (apparently) getting away with much more money than they had ever dreamed of. As for his *dead* body. An old trick a number of disillusioned infantry grunts had used in 'Nam, something that had fooled everybody: Substituting body parts of a dead enemy soldier for your own. Leaving your dog-tag amidst the blood and guts of a dismembered trunk. Retrieving a hidden backpack filled with K-rations. Enough to get you to Vientiane, Laos. And a new life. He'd heard the stories about the place, about the fountain in the street in the middle of the town where the deserters congregated every day, pooling their resources to buy a few beers and cigarettes. Going out sometimes on night patrol he often found himself thinking that those who'd flown the coop were the really intelligent guys. At least they were guaranteed some sort of life. Night patrol carried no such guarantees . . . other than your buddies might get around to scooping you up into a body bag.

He finished his cigarette and flushed the butt down the toilet. When he returned to the lounge moments later the flight was starting to board.

4

Nancy Ryan had persevered. Nearly six months after leaving Belfast and finding a job as a barmaid at a public house in Aldershot, she had carefully screened the customers. Picking out the soldiers, and only then those of the rank of sergeant. She had been careful about whom she dated. Only those she thought might be able to give her the information she sought. She also kept a list of the men she had been with, including as much background information on them as she could obtain. Something for the future, Pat Cavenaugh had suggested, for the time those soldiers might be posted to Northern Ireland.

It was her eighth pick-up that proved to be the lucky one. His name was Peter Bradshaw. A Lancashire man. He had served on the same entry course with John Winter in 2 Para. Better yet he had been Winter's best friend. At least until he disappeared one day – Bradshaw after half a dozen double scotches and lying naked in Nancy's bed had confided that *disappeared* meant the SAS – 22 SAS Regiment to be precise. And he was good enough, was Wint, Bradshaw had rattled on, only the best get into that mob. Nancy had continued to play the tart – performing all the tricks her husband Frank had taught her, plus acquiring some new ones along the way – eventually picking the Lancashire man's brains clean of everything he had ever known about Sergeant John Winter.

Those months turned her into a harder woman, starting on the day before travelling to Aldershot to look for a job. She had stayed the night in London, and found a hairdresser who cropped her waist length red hair. More than a symbolic gesture, the severely short hair gave her face a hardened look, drew attention to the big green eyes. A clever woman can talk with her eyes, she had once been told.

Through all the weeks and months she wrote the obligatory comms to Pat Cavenaugh, keeping him informed of her progress. After all it was for the cause – nothing else. Besides which she knew that Pat would never confide her whereabouts to Frank.

As far as Frank is concerned, Pat had said, the information comes from a 'sleeper' in London, an old friend of mine . . . no names no pack drill, as the Brits would say. You have my word, darling girl, that he'll only find you if you tell me that is what you want. And never forget, to choose your victim, to prepare your plans minutely, to right a terrible wrong, is something we all have to learn to do.

Pat Cavenaugh: the handsome old silver fox as she thought of him, the black eye patch giving him a slightly roguish air. An unmarried man who had given his life to teaching, and loyal membership of the Irish Republican Army. Who had seen her off from Belfast airport those months ago, slipping a thousand pounds into her handbag (his own money), and telling her that she was the daughter he had never had, and if she ever needed for anything she only had to let him know. He was a dear and lovely man in a world devoid of dear and lovely men.

Her last communication to Pat had been twenty-four hours earlier. She had tried the Belfast number, using the code the Deputy OC of the Belfast Brigade had given her months earlier and been instructed to try him at a London hotel number. Room 415. Which she had. He had listened with great care and after a few moments' silence had told her exactly what to do.

Now on that Friday morning she was driving along a narrow dirt road, between narrow dirt road, between slate and stone dry-walls, looking for the house of Dorcas Volk, who lived 10 miles inland from Barmouth Bay in North Wales. It wasn't too difficult; it was the only house for miles. A big farmhouse, lying in the shadow of Cader Idris, set back 100 yards from the uneven track she had been driving on for the past fifteen minutes – an eighteenth century dark granite building with a sickle of white gravel driveway. It was nine o'clock when she parked her Mini hire car next to a Land Rover by a red-roofed barn and walked towards the house.

Somewhere, a motor mower was whining; the smell of freshly cut grass hung over the drive. The house and grounds were obviously well cared for. Impressive. The thought that money was no object in keeping the small estate in pristine condition came to Nancy's mind. What she would have given to own such a house.

She rang the bell and waited. Hoped that the long drive from Aldershot, started at four o'clock that morning, was not going to be in vain, and at the same time running over the cover story she had hastily prepared the previous day. After half a minute the door opened. The woman who answered it was nothing like Nancy had expected.

Dorcas Volk was at least fifty, and trying to look younger, or at least different. Shortish black hair, a red bandana tied around her head, black eye-shadow like bruises, black lipstick, a dead white face with sharp cheekbones. Slav-looking. She was wearing a paint-stained artist's smock, jeans, and ankle boots – the type one might use for climbing. No jewellery. The dark eyes were the give away. Sunken. Glaze hardened. Polarized by age.

'Mrs Volk?' Nancy asked.

'Dorcas Volk. Miss,' the artist said. The accent was a curious mixture of Eastern European and Welsh.

'I'm sorry to trouble you, but I'm trying to find John. John Winter. I'm Nancy by the way. My husband Peter Bradshaw came here for the weekend once or twice some years ago with John . . . on leave.'

The cover story given her by Pat Cavenaugh, one based on the recent friendship she had struck up with Sergeant Bradshaw at Aldershot. She tried to disguise the Irish accent, inflecting some of the flattened vowels that Bradshaw's Lancashire accent carried.

'You'd better come in.' She led Nancy into a darkly furnished sitting room and waved towards a chair. 'Peter Bradshaw,' she murmured thoughtfully. 'Possibly. He brought quite a few friends to stay. Anyway you're a friend?'

'Oh yes, for a long time now.'

'And what has that nephew of mine been up to now?'

Nancy made a mental note of that piece of information. *Nephew*. The exact relationship between Winter and the woman in front of her something Bradshaw had been unable to verify. She smiled. 'Oh nothing, it's just that a mutual friend of Peter and John is getting married next week, and we – Peter and I that is – have been trying to make sure that all the boys who were in 2 Para together would be there. Bit of a surprise.'

'That's nice. But you obviously know he's left the Army now?'

Another tidbit of information. Bradshaw hadn't seen Winter for some years. Had lost track. Had thought Winter was still serving with the SAS. 'Oh yes, that's why I took the chance on coming to see you . . . I was thinking of phoning but as I was staying with friends in Shrewsbury this week, it didn't seem too far to drive.' The background story she had rehearsed over the last twenty-four hours came out easily and convincingly.

'He's been in America,' Dorcas said chattily.

'Oh! He's gone there to live then?' Nancy tried to mask her disappointment. England was the enemy – fighting on their bog was quite all right. America? Something beyond the range of her capabilities. Even the language was different. She would stand out like a sore thumb. Too dangerous.

'No, no, just an extended visit. He went about six months ago, getting himself retrained to be a civilian was all he said to me before he left. Would you like a cup of tea, Nancy? It was Nancy, wasn't it?'

'Yes . . . A cup of tea would be fine.'

When Dorcas went to the kitchen Nancy got out of her chair and walked around the room, admiring the framed oil paintings that covered the walls, land and seascapes mainly, all signed 'Dorcas Volk'. She finally came to an antique-looking writing bureau in a corner of the room. The top of it crammed with silver-framed photographs. Family members it seemed. One stood out. A blond haired young soldier. A sergeant in the Parachute Regiment. He looked remarkably like 'the mechanic'. Remarkably!

'Only photo I've got of John,' Dorcas Volk said coming back into the room carrying a tray. 'Such a handsome man, don't you think?'

Nancy looked again at the blond-haired soldier. 'Yes, very handsome,' she mumbled. It was him after all – the shoulder-length black hair she remembered obviously part of his disguise. 'I was admiring your paintings,' she added. 'They really are very good.'

Dorcas brushed the compliment aside. 'Poor to average I'd say, but then I've got nothing else to do. Idris, who comes up to take care of the gardens twice a week, thinks I should get a husband. I think he fancies me.'

'Is he good looking?'

Dorcas took a cigarette from her smock pocket, laughing as she did so. 'Oh, very. Only problem is I don't think his wife would approve if I started chasing him. Besides, I've lived here for over twenty years and I'm still that foreign woman; being a female artist makes it worse, being an unmarried female artist! I think they call me the eccentric hippy.'

'But not your gardener, Idris?'

'He calls the local women a lot of belligerent old

sows, to their faces as well. We have a good laugh about that.'

One thing Nancy had learned in the preceding months was very evident in Dorcas Volk. Lonely people love to talk given the opportunity. 'So, how is John doing in civvy-street?' She liked the civvy-street reference, something that only a soldier's wife would say.

'I think all right. Not that he ever wanted to be a soldier,' Dorcas replied.

'Really,' Nancy said, returning to her chair, noticing the unlit cigarette held to Dorcas' lips. 'Would you like a light?' She reached for her handbag.

'No thank you, it's not real.' She took the cigarette from her mouth. 'Plastic . . . herbal. I've been trying to stop smoking for months now. This helps a little. Anyway, as I was saying, it was that father of his that was responsible for him going to the Army in the first place. A cruel man, Axel Winter. Made the boy's life hell. Then again there was my sister, Anna – she suffered terribly. Axel always said John was not his son. Said Anna had been unfaithful to him . . . and a lot more I can assure you. She had an even worse time of it. I think it was a blessing that she died so young . . . cancer, you know. Only thirty-eight.'

'Oh, I'm sorry.'

'Long time ago. So the boy was left, to be raised by the father. I think that man must have beaten the boy every day of his life, the reason why he ran away in the end and joined the Army. Never told his father about it, just packed a bag and disappeared one morning. Of course, Axel, his father came here looking for the boy, but I didn't say anything. It was our secret, John and I.

He always said he wanted to do something else, but without formal education . . . mind you he was a bright boy. Good at languages, history, that sort of thing. His father died seven years later. They never met again. I went to the funeral in Cornwall. John was there, at the cemetery at least. I think he was sad that his father had died before they had had the chance to try and become friends. Even knowing his father from the old time he was always ready to forgive.'

'A strange choice of professions though, to become a soldier.'

'Not by choice, Nancy, as I told you it was the only chance he had . . . either be beaten to death, and that would have surely happened. Or run away. He was only fifteen.'

'Fifteen . . . when he went to the Army?'

'Maybe a little younger. He found out that the Army took boy soldiers. That's where he went. Of course he used this address, and I signed his papers as his next of kin – he might have forged his date of birth to enable him to get in, to get away from that terrible life, that wicked man . . . You must never tell John I told you this of course.'

'Of course.'

'I went to see them a few times when my sister was alive . . . meal times were the worst. He made the boy kneel in the doorway and say prayers before eating. Not that he was religious, but because Anna was a Catholic and had raised her boy the same way, Axel used it as a weapon against the child . . . mimicked the prayers, turned them into dirty stories. Then again, if young John didn't finish every scrap of food on his plate he would be beaten. Not just a hand across the backside, oh no, Axel Winter was a big man. First he would start shouting, and I would see the boy, eyes fixed straight ahead in fear, shaking all over. Then the father would pick the boy up bodily and throw him across the room. The same thing he did to the boy's dog. A little mongrel – a stray that the child had found and looked after. Axel would use that dog like a football – of course it died in the end, broke the little boy's heart. I was there when it happened. I stopped going to visit my sister after that, I couldn't stand it.'

Nancy was visibly shaken. She knew terror. The BA. Her two precious children being shot before her eyes. But somehow the vision of prolonged physical and mental cruelty by someone in your own family seemed to be . . . she couldn't find the words. Heart-breaking seemed to be only the half of it. She said in a quiet voice, 'So why did your sister stay?'

'She was afraid. I think he beat her just as often. If she had left I think he would have found her and killed her.' Brief silence. As though painting other pictures in her mind. 'I hope your husband, Peter, is a kinder man.'

Nancy thought of her real husband, Frank. More kinky sex with him. 'Oh yes, he's a lovely man,' she lied.

'Anyway, that was John's life. The fact that he became a boy soldier meant he had to sign on for a long while . . . ten or twelve years I think it was. I think he realized long ago that he had made a mistake, that he would have rather done something else . . . He once told me he wanted to be a schoolteacher, I think he would have been good at that. A gentle soldier . . . a contradiction in terms. Anyway, once he had resigned himself to the fact that he was going to have to serve all those years he gave it his very best.'

Nancy remembered the field in Crossmaglen. The falling snow. The mechanic, as she had known him, kneeling beside her and her children, taking her hand, the soft kind voice. *A gentle soldier.* Perhaps not altogether a lie. 'Yes, we always thought he was gentle and kind.' She looked at her watch; Pat had stressed the importance of keeping the meeting to no more than half an hour. *Talk too much my dear girl, and you might say the wrong thing. Create suspicion.* 'Oh dear, is that the time. I really am very sorry, but I do have to be going. It's a long drive back home. Peter will worry if I'm late.'

Dorcas got up from the chair. 'I quite understand. Anytime you're back in the area please drop in, any friend of John's is always welcome.'

'I don't suppose you have his address in America then, Miss Volk?' Save the most important question for last, she had been told. By then most people's tongues are as loose as they're ever going to be.

'Call me Dorcas, everyone does. He's not in America as it happens; he left there this week. He was going to Scotland. Would an address there be any help?'

It was nearly two hours later that Dorcas Volk received a telephone call from a certain Sergeant Peter Bradshaw at Aldershot. He was calling to see if his wife was there and to remind her that it was a long drive home, and that if she felt too tired to make the journey that she should perhaps go back to Shrewsbury and stay the night there. Dorcas apologized and said his wife had left. The sergeant chatted on for a moment or two about the surprise wedding guests for the following week, and finally asked if she had known the whereabouts of his old friend, John. Except he used the word, mate. She gave him the same information she had given to his wife.

Such a thoughtful and polite man, Dorcas Volk thought, as she returned up the winding staircase to her attic studio. He didn't sound at all like a soldier!

5

There was a thunderstorm passing over London's Heathrow airport that afternoon when Teach Cusack was deposited outside the Skyways Hotel by the courtesy minibus. A brief hail shower – tiny pieces of ice hard as iron whipping across the wide concourse – spattering his face and hair.

He moved quickly inside and stood in line at the reception desk. Amazing, he thought in his punch-drunk state of no sleep, screaming babies, time-zone changes - which were now called jet lag – and too much alcohol, how the Brits like the Americans stood patiently in line, while the people serving them appeared to have little or no sense of urgency. Didn't they realize they had some seriously tired people on their hands? What the fuck did you have to do to get their attention?

A hand tugged at his sleeve. He spun round, half in anger (he didn't like being touched) and found himself looking into the calm eyes of a red-haired man. The man was wearing jeans and an old leather jacket, scuffed brown, zipped tight to the neck.

'Mr Cusack?'

'Yes,' he replied, noting the Irish accent.

'Frank Ryan,' the man said quietly. 'It might be better if we get you a cup of coffee. Wait for the morning rush to quieten down.'

Cusack allowed himself to be led away to a bright modern coffee shop, off the main foyer. There was another man sitting at the corner table they went to. An older man with a shock of silver hair and a black eye patch over his right eye. The American noted the dark blue suit, the spotless white shirt, blue and white polka-dot tie. The air of authority.

'Mr Cusack, this is Pat Cavenaugh.'

Cusack held out a hand, 'Pleased to meet you, Pat. Folks call me Teach, by the way.' He sat down. The exhaustion of the prolonged journey from Boston was sufficient to make him think he may never get up again.

Ryan went off to get the coffee.

'Long trip then, Teach. The plane got delayed isn't that right?' Cavenaugh questioned in that smiling way of his.

'Nine hours late in the end. I'm thinking of travelling by ship next time, at least I'd get a night's sleep.'

Cavenaugh chuckled. 'Oh, I don't know, I went to America by ship once, when I was young. Seasick all the way and that's a fact.'

Ryan came back and placed the tray on the centre of the too small table, then took out a packet of cigarettes, offered one to the American and lit it.

'Thanks . . . I tell you it's just great to get away from the constant noise.'

'So you brought our package okay,' Ryan said impatiently. His leather jacket creaking as he unzipped it. 'No problems over the way with the Customs people!'

'Bill Fagan said I should be given the code . . .'

'Oh jeez, there was me forgetting . . . "Think where men's glory most begins and ends." '

Teach completed the couplet, ' "And say my glory was I had such friends." '

'The bloody problem with the Irish in America,' Ryan said sardonically, 'it's all William Butler Yeats and Guinness and never-ending choruses of Danny Boy.'

'You won't get an argument from me there, Frank,' Teach said lightly, rummaging through his shoulder bag. He put the package and the envelope on the table.

Ryan slid the contents across to Cavenaugh. Turned back to the American. 'I hear you were in Vietnam. Is that right?'

'Yes.'

'What did you do? Soldier . . . infantry?'

'You got it . . . plus some time as a gunner in a helo gunship.'

'Rough time I bet.'

Teach shook his head at the memory. Stared blankly across the coffee shop. Finally: 'Had its moments I guess, the best you could say for it.'

'And you're planning to go back to Boston tomorrow, isn't that right?' Ryan asked.

'Flight leaves around ten . . . or maybe that's the check-in time. God knows if I'll survive if I have to put up with screaming kids again.'

'I suppose you'd like a few hours with your head down right now.'

'A shower and a couple of hours might make me feel more on speaking terms with the world.'

'And a drink or two this evening?'

'Sounds great to me.' Cusack's narrow face was relaxed. The stale clam colour of his eyes had a hint of life. He stood up to leave. 'Well, gentlemen, if you'll excuse me, I guess I'll go and check in.'

Cavenaugh half-raised a hand. 'Oh there's one other thing, did you ever get to fly those helicopters in Vietnam?'

'Officially, no. Unofficially everyone on board learned the basics, a matter of self-preservation in case the pilot got taken out. I flew with a good crew, got more on the job training than most.'

'What sort of helicopters were they?'

'Hueys.'

Cavenaugh thought about that for a moment. Poked a finger under the eye patch and absently scratched at the old wound. 'Would I be right in thinking that the Agusta Bell 205 is the civilian version of that?'

'Dead right. You a flyer then?'

Cavenaugh laughed and shook his head. 'Good heavens, no. School teacher. I've read a bit about helicopters though. So why didn't you get a job flying them after you got back from the war?'

'Good question, Pat. Money for starters, you know, to do all the courses and get a licence. Then again there happens to be hundreds of qualified helo pilots coming back from 'Nam with all the qualifications. Too many pilots, too few jobs. I guess if I'd known that I was going to end up on welfare, I'd volunteered for another tour.' He turned to Frank. 'See you later.'

*

After Cusack had gone Cavenaugh turned to Ryan. 'Interesting man, wouldn't you say, Frank?'

'What was all that about? You reading books on helicopters and all! Philosophy, I could understand. The history of Ireland since James the First; even Nazi experiments in eugenics . . . but, *helicopters*!'

'He might be a good man to have on the team,' Cavenaugh said evenly.

'What team?'

Cavenaugh thought of the phone call he had made earlier to a woman called Dorcas Volk in North Wales. The woman who Nancy had assured him was a relation of the Sassman, Winter. Using Nancy's background information, getting a telephone number from directory enquiries; passing himself off as Sergeant Peter Bradshaw. Never hurt to double up on intelligence. As for Frank, a case of play around with the truth but never tell it. He looked casually around the coffee shop – an elderly couple a few tables away, wife reading a newspaper, husband eating a late lunch – dropped his voice, a precautionary measure, lest a single word like gun, bomb, assassinate, should act like a bullet in some unsuspecting ear. 'The phone call I was making in my room whilst you were waiting for Mr Cusack. I got a tip-off from my sleeper in London. He gave me the address for the Sassman. He's in Scotland.'

Ryan's eyes glinted. 'Is that right. Where exactly?'

'At a place called Wick in Caithness. I got hold of a phone number and made a call.'

'What sort of call?'

'General enquiries shall we say. The address happens to be an aircraft company at the local airport.

I asked if they did pleasure flights; that I was coming up that way for a holiday. The man said they didn't normally. Just that they bought and sold light aircraft and helicopters. So I pushed him a bit further, and he said they might be able to give me a ride in one of their helicopters as a sales demonstration flight but that I'd have to pay cash. As luck would have it I asked what type of helicopters they had and he said it was an Agusta Bell 205 and that it was the civilian version of what the Americans called the Huey. Lots of them on film reports from Vietnam, on the television news.'

'I'm still not following you, Pat.'

'Oh, perhaps something of nothing. I was just thinking how your man there said he could fly them, and what a lovely idea it would be to *borrow* the Scottish helicopter and bring the Sassman to Belfast.'

Ryan shook his head. 'Kidnap him?' Incredulity in the forced whisper. 'Impossible. Too risky. Besides how do you think a pilot would get a stolen helicopter into Belfast? Or anywhere else in the North, given that the British Army have got their own helicopters and planes patrolling the entire area.'

'You haven't been reading the papers, Frank. That's the best bit of all. President Nixon is visiting Belfast early next week.'

'I'm aware of that.'

'Something you might not be aware of. As of yesterday there were thirteen US Army Bell Hueys – the helicopters Cusack flew in – on the Irish mainland, variously deployed in support of the visit.'

'Where did you get that information?'

'London *Times* this morning. One thing I'll say for

the Brits when it comes to security, more leaks than Father Michael's church roof.'

'And how do the thirteen American helicopters fit into the scheme of things?'

'Ah yes, that did seem a bit of a problem to me. Might still be. I assume the American ones would be painted in camouflage, is that right?'

'Easy enough to check. But I'd say so.'

'Whereas the one in Scotland probably isn't, being a civilian machine and all. So assuming we could get our hands on it, is there any way we could repaint it in camouflage?'

'A quick respray to match up with the US equipment you mean. Possible. I'd need to check.'

'We'd need to move quickly.'

'Too quickly.'

'Not necessarily.'

'We don't have the infrastructure . . .'

Cavenaugh patted the package and the large buff-coloured envelope on the table. 'Amazing what you can do with money, Frank. Just think of it. An American pilot – of sorts at least – flying an American army helicopter right into the lion's den. He'd know the right things to say, or at least confuse them long enough with his accent.' He leaned forward, soft-voiced, coaxing. 'We could even land at the main terminal and have a car waiting for us to escort our VIP passenger away into Belfast. A public hanging of a Sassman in the Falls Road! That'd be a hell of a story for the press wouldn't it?'

Ryan fought to control his enthusiasm. Even so, his voice when he spoke had the breathless quality of someone who had just won the sweepstakes and didn't know which way to turn for the sheer excitement of it all. 'You think Cusack will go along with it?'

'You heard what he said about being on welfare. Bill Fagan mentioned that he'd just come out of state prison. Jeez, I'm betting the poor sod would go along with anything he was offered, especially a bit of money and a few square meals.'

'So how long have we got to put this plan into operation?'

'Seventy-two hours. Four days at the most. Unless you think your way would be easier.'

'My way?'

'A sniper's rifle.'

'Up to you. Whichever it is, is fine with me.'

Cavenaugh looked down at his untouched cup of black coffee. A light scum floating on the top. 'Tell you what,' he said, getting up from the table. 'You can buy me a drink in the bar. I think better with something decent to line my stomach . . . and I'm not talking about that synthetic stuff they call chilled wine that you were drinking last night.'

'Just blending in, Pat. That eternal vigilance you're always warning me about.'

'You sound like one of those nuns who runs the ecumenical conferences and the diocesan seminars at the big house in Sligo.' A small shake of the head. A twinkle in the eye.

'Better to stay sober I was thinking.'

'Ah you would all right . . . and when was I ever any other way?'

'Fuck you.'

'Did I ever tell you that you take it all too seriously?'

'What else is there?'

'Enjoy the journey, Frank. Until I hear news to the contrary, I'm thinking it's the only one.'

They were still arguing as they left the coffee shop.

6

Winter and Gant went flying again that Saturday afternoon. With a difference – this time it was by helicopter and the Englishman was at the controls. The Agusta Bell 205 was due to be positioned to a maintenance company in eastern England for dismantling and crating for its sea voyage to the Philippines. Gant had suggested that Winter airtest it to ensure it was fully serviceable. A reasonable enough request, even though representatives of Philippine Airlines had been at Wick a week earlier and had completed acceptance checks, ground and air, and had paid Jamie Gunn (the owner of the helo, and the local sales company) for the aircraft in full.

'Amazin' that those Filipinos paid Jamie for this bird without even doing an airtest, wouldn't you say?' Gant squinted at the bright sunshine. A way to disguise the little-white-lie-smile on his face.

'Amazing,' Winter agreed.

'So, how you liking it?'

'Bit bigger than the stuff I was flying in Florida.'

'More stable though.'

'Seems that way. Where we heading by the way?'

'About fifty miles south-south-west. There's a fir plantation down there. Thought you'd like to practise flying in and out of the firebreaks.'

They reached the Douglas fir plantation about forty minutes later. Winter lowered the nose and started his descent. 'Looks a bit tight! What do you reckon?'

'I'd figure a good three to four feet rotor clearance each side. Just stick to the middle, I'll let you know.'

The aircraft plunged into the forest, getting up to full speed, clearing the flanking trees by what seemed to Winter only inches. Gant assured him it was more like the four feet he had originally estimated. Still it was quite a trick at almost 100 miles an hour.

At the end of the first long, straight cut line, Winter pulled up almost vertically to bleed off the speed, rolled the tail rotor hard over until the nose pointed straight back down at the ground, and then dived back in between the trees to rush headlong the way he had come. A thin film of sweat was forming on his brow.

He found a more winding forest road and made several high-speed passes from end to end, staying well below the tops of the trees each time. The next exercise was more demanding. He ran at high speed towards a cut line crossing and instead of staying on the straight road he hauled the helo hard left into the side road. Seconds later he was back, trying the same manouvre to the right. The occasional flecks of green foliage that passed his windscreen were evidence that Winter was trying. The concentration level was extremely high.

Next, he tried a couple of quick touch and away

shots on an old aerial survey marker that Gant had noticed on one of the side roads. One more end-to-end and they'd head back to Wick.

He turned sharply from the touch down marker and hit the corner at well over 60 miles an hour, nose down, aircraft pulling a good 45 degree bank. The whole ship was vibrating, and he could feel the tiredness creeping up his wrists and forearms. Halfway through the turn he flicked his head back and to the side, to look along the firebreak line he was turning into.

He couldn't believe it!

There was a rider cantering along on a horse, right in the centre of the firebreak. Not more than 40 yards away. Heading straight for him.

Cause and effect. Action and reaction! What was the problem? What was a possible solution? What would be the outcome? Words that his American instructor had drilled into him day by day.

He had the luxury of a few hundredths of a second to make a rational decision. If he maintained this line he would probably hit the horse and rider. If he tried a hard pull up with such a short distance between them from this very nose-down attitude, there would be an opposite dip first and the rotors would probably dig in.

To pull a turn up and over and away from the direction the horse was going – to the left – would likely put the fragile tail rotor into the trees and that would be that, the machine would be uncontrollable and the inertia would carry it up to more than a hundred feet only to crash back like some crazy fireball.

A less severe turn to the right, towards the horse and

rider, but in the direction of the shorter stand of trees, would just miss the horse, but would slice a brave path through the crowns of the Douglas Firs.

The horse in the meanwhile, panicked by the horrendous noise, had veered towards the trees and finding no way through had reared up and tried to turn back. Away from the oncoming terror. The rider hung on grimly.

Gant's voice said calmly over the intercom. 'Come right . . . through the top of the trees . . . GO.'

Winter obeyed. Listening to Gant's assuring voice. 'Only fir trees . . . looking good . . . looking good.'

Not so to Winter . . . The noise was horrendous . . . The vibrations even more frightening . . . He experienced instant dry-mouthed terror . . . Knew beyond a shadow of a doubt he was crashing . . . A numbing collision of machine and mind . . . Disappointment that it should end here and now . . . Like this . . . A silly accident . . . The faintly ridiculous thought that he would have liked a last cigarette . . . Clinging to the controls as the windscreen disappeared into a sea of green pine needles and branches . . . No time for constructive thought patterns to emerge . . . Just wide-eyed terror transforming during an eternity of milliseconds into mute acceptance . . . The sweat on his brow turning to holy water . . . A last benediction . . . He truly was about to die . . .

Then they were through! Miraculously they were back in clear air. It was almost silent as he rushed up through 80 . . . 100 . . . 150 feet. He let out a long breath. Felt the tremor in his hands. Adrenalin rush. *Too damned close.*

Gant smiled and said, 'Good job they weren't a

stand of oaks or elms, now they'd have got your attention big time. Like they have intertwining high branches . . .'

'Meaning we wouldn't have been so lucky.'

'Meaning we'd have been dead,' Gant said matter-of-factly. 'Douglas firs have regular, even top branches. Present minimum resistance to the blades.'

'I didn't know you flew helicopters as well.'

Gant chuckled. 'Don't. Always said helos fly in the face of nature. I mean did you ever see a bird with anything but wings? No, sir. And I figure, as birds have been doin' what they do for these past few million years they must have figured it all out.'

'So how did you know about flying through the tops of those firs?'

'Educated guess.'

'Jesus Christ.'

'Yep, it did cross my mind that we'd be shaking hands with him momentarily.' Gant said, looking down to see if he could spot the horse and rider. Ensure they were okay. There was no sign. Which was good enough. Both parties severely shaken. Both parties in need of a drink to calm the nerves. 'So much for the owner saying this place was free and clear at the weekends, uh?'

'You want to head back to base?'

'Unless you want to try that again.'

'Enough for me for one day.'

'I'm real glad you said that.'

A chapping wind with a metallic tone was blowing when they landed at Wick and walked across to the old wartime air traffic control tower that had been converted into the offices of North Flight Limited, the aeroplane sales company.

They went upstairs to Jamie Gunn's office. There was no one there.

'Probably gone down to the hangar to bring up the Cessna for me,' Gant said.

'What do you want me to do while you're away?'

'Hell, I'm only taking the plane down to Birmingham, to the new owner. Be back on the airlines tomorrow. Tell you what; let's see what Jamie's got on airline schedules from Birmingham to Inverness. You could fly down to Inverness tomorrow and pick me up.'

'You think I need the practice!'

Ways and means. Not that Winter had yet agreed to the job in Southeast Asia. But then, Gant knew something the Englishman was yet to learn. Any pilot would rather be flying than sitting on the ground. That Winter needed maybe a thousand more flying hours before one of the oil companies would take him on their books was a fact of life. Little by little. Get them hooked first. In the end they'll reel themselves in. 'Had crossed my mind.'

7

It was nearing sunset when Winter, with the aid of a
motorized tug and hydraulic dolly, finally manoeuvred
the helicopter away in the corner of the big empty
hangar. Jamie Gunn had gone home an hour earlier
and left Winter an old Volvo estate car to drive and
instructions on how to lock the hangar and the office
when he had finished.

With nothing else to do except go and sit in his hotel
room, he had spent the past few hours refuelling the
helo and cleaning dead bugs off the windshield. When
that was done he worked his way through the *Pilot's
Operating Handbook*, memorizing some of the more
important details. Walking around the helo, checklist
in hand, familiarizing himself with every nut, bolt and
rivet. Tomorrow he had a flight to Inverness. Unlike
the earlier episode at the plantation he intended the
flight to go off without a hitch.

He drove towards the town as dusk was gathering.
The roads empty. The desolate countryside faintly

swelling, faintly falling. Not a tree. Not a hedgerow. Fields divided by slate walls. The constant wind. A long road appearing to lead nowhere. Until he breasted a slight rise and dropped down towards the town. A melancholy hour this, he always thought, for a stranger in a strange place – nightfall, the brittle lights, the temperature falling, people hurrying home to their houses. A few youths hanging around a near derelict street corner – the only sign of life – as he drove through the town towards Union Street and MacKay's Hotel. He parked in the small car park, went into the hotel and collected his key from the reception desk.

In other times he might have guessed something was wrong when he entered the room and detected the faintest hint of a woman's perfume. Now his only thought, as he closed the door and fumbled to find the switch for the room light, was that one of the hotel chambermaids had been there to clean his room.

It was as he turned back into the room that he saw the woman sitting in the chair on the other side of the double bed. Caught his breath. A woman in a white raincoat. Brutally cropped red hair. High cheekbones accentuating a slight hollowing of the cheeks. She was holding a handgun. Which was pointing directly at him. More than that, she seemed vaguely familiar. Something about the eyes.

'It is John Winter, isn't it?'

Irish accent. He knew then who she was. It all came rushing back. *The field in Crossmaglen . . . A late February afternoon . . . the children*! As though it had been yesterday. He said nothing. His eyes never leaving hers. His mind desperately trying to find a way out.

'Cat got your tongue has it, Sergeant Winter. You'd remember me of course.'

'Nancy Ryan . . . yes, I remember.'

'You'd also remember that we have specific ways of dealing with people like you.'

'Did your daughter survive her injuries . . . Majella, wasn't it?' Training, nothing else. If looking down a gun barrel try and change the line of questioning – assuming you are fortunate enough in the first place to be offered one to change. Even so he could hear the edge of fear in his voice. Feel it in the pit of his stomach.

A brief hesitation. A flicker of pain in the woman's eyes. The gun dropped fractionally. 'She died.'

'I'm sorry,' Winter said. 'I truly am very sorry.' What else could he say? Do? He was trapped and he knew it. One of those moments of truth that all soldiers face sooner or later. 'So they sent you to kill me, is that right?'

She watched him closely. Trying to reconcile Dorcas Volk's words to the man who stood about 8 feet away from her. Now: tall, blond, a fading suntan marking out laughter lines around the blue eyes. Then: a boy who had been beaten every day of his life; who had run away to join the Army to escape his worst enemy. Her long drive to the north of Scotland. Spending the night at a cheap bed-and-breakfast in Glasgow, before continuing her journey that morning. Not phoning Pat Cavenaugh as instructed to tell him if she had located the Sassman. Too confused. Still wondering what to do. He was the enemy after all. The bastard British soldier who had infiltrated their organization. Doubtless passed back information that

would lead to others of her kind being captured . . .
and yet, he had spared her. In that Irish field, he had
taken the blame for her. Allowed her to walk free.
'Answer me one question, Sergeant Winter.'

'Mister. I'm no longer in the Army.'

'Why? Why did you do what you did? Allow me to
go free.'

'Not important.'

'It is to me.'

'Well just let's say I don't like harm coming to
women and children.'

'And I'm supposed to believe that?'

'There was something else . . .'

'Go on.'

'I liked you.'

Nancy Ryan laughed. A small bitter sound. She had
been with enough British soldiers in the past months
to categorize 'like' in the same breath they would term
getting inside your panties. And those were the nicer
words. 'Is that a fact?'

'It's the truth,' Winter said. Weariness in the voice.
Surrender. 'I've got nothing else to say in my defence.
If the rest of your cell is waiting in the next room I
suggest you give three knocks on the wall, or whatever
else your code is, and we'll get it over with.'
Diversionary tactics. Split her thinking. She would
need to get out of the chair. Move to the wall. Long
enough for him to reach down and grab the frame of
the bed and throw it up against her. Slim odds!

She didn't move. Her eyes never leaving his for one
second. 'They breed them tough in the SAS, is that
what you're telling me?'

'I used to like you when you smiled.'

'Don't patronize me.'

'I wasn't.'

'I'm here by myself.'

'Not the *Green Book* way of doing things.'

'Don't *you* talk to me about the *Green Book*.'

'Why not? I happen to agree with a great deal of it . . . for instance, how the British taxpayers have never been given the democratic right to vote for their soldiers being in Northern Ireland.'

'You're a bit late in the day for that.'

'Politicians, Nancy. They're your enemy. The soldiers don't get a say. They do as they are bid. Refuse and they go to the glasshouse.'

'I don't give a flying damn about that . . . and don't think I'm one of your bog-wogs or muck savages who doesn't realize what you're trying to do.'

Winter watched the gun hand. It was dropping further. Amazing how heavy even an automatic pistol can become if you hold it out long enough! 'Trying to do?'

'It's just that *I* wanted to kill you for what happened. *Me*, not a group of loud-mouthed men selected by committee over a bottle of Bushmills. Instead I've decided to give you the same chance you gave me.'

'And let me go?'

'There'll be others. You do know that, don't you? You need to get out of here.'

'And what about you? What happens if they find out that you've let a former SAS man go? You don't think they'll be overcome with gratitude do you?'

'No need for them to know what happened. That I've been here. I'll just tell them I've learned you're possibly in Scotland, at a place called Wick.'

'When?'

'After I leave here. I'll call when I get back down south. I wouldn't count on much more than twenty-four hours after that.' She lowered the gun into her lap. Looking at it for a moment, as though temporarily unsure how it had got there in the first place. Finally she slipped it into her raincoat pocket and stood up.

'Where are you going now?' Winter asked.

She looked at him in the same way she had in that field in Crossmaglen all those months earlier. A stranger's glance. The ridiculous thing is she had never even considered what she would do when it was all over. Back to Belfast, to Frank? Never. What then? Where? For perhaps the first time in her life she felt completely alone. She had no one. No children. No husband worth calling a husband. No family. No money. Nothing. Even the hire car had been due back in Aldershot today. She thought of her elder sister, who had lost her husband and children for different reasons, who now lived alone on the outskirts of Dublin. A lonely, bitter woman. Exiled from the world. God forbid that she should end up like that. She moved across the room towards the door. *Where are you going now?* 'Home,' she said.

'To Ireland?'

'Perhaps.'

As she moved past him he reached out and took her arm. She offered no resistance, staring at him in that same blank way. She looked tired. He noticed the faintest touch of pink lipstick, the hint of pale green eye- shadow. Breathed her perfume.

'I would never do anything to harm you, you do know that, don't you?'

'I know.' So quietly, he hardly heard it.

'Do you want to talk?'

'About what?' The green eyes flashed. A spark of the old anger.

'Your children.'

She raised a hand and slapped his face – hard, the heel of her hand connecting with the edge of his cheekbone. 'Don't you ever mention my children again, you bastard.' She tried to pull away but he held on to her.

'You need to talk about them, Nancy. You don't think you're going to go through life keeping it all locked away inside do you? You need to remember them and the happy years you had with them, but at the same time you have to learn to give up the anger.'

'Let me go.'

'No. I want you to talk to me. I want you to tell me about Mikey and Majella. They were the reason I didn't re-enlist. After what happened I knew I could never go on being a soldier. Even if they had given me a job as a clerk at some RAMC depot and I never saw a gun again, I would know that I was a part of something I didn't want any more.'

She didn't speak. Her head was lowered. She wavered slightly on her feet.

'Are you all right?'

'I'm fine.'

'Have you eaten?'

'No . . . it's not important.'

'Do you like Chinese? There's a restaurant a couple of hundred yards up the street. Or if you'd rather not be seen with me I can go and get you some take-away.'

A brief struggle to pull away from him. He held on. Finally she said, 'I'll come with you . . . then I must leave. The hire car I've got, it's overdue. Next thing I'll be picked up by the bloody police.'

'Where did you hire it from?'

'Aldershot.'

Aldershot! Very clever. The way she had tracked him, obviously. And all those 'Loose talk costs lives' posters that the Army put up on every free bit of wall space. Bloody joke. 'Have you got the phone number, I'll call them and extend it.'

'I can do that.'

'Just give me the number. I don't think you're in a fit state to do anything at the moment.'

She handed him her shoulder bag. 'There's a contract in there. Should have the phone number on it.'

Two hours later they were standing by the sea wall looking out over the desolate harbour. The street behind them was empty. The only sound, water slapping the hulls of a few ageing fishing boats that rode gently at anchor. A half-moon high in a near cloudless sky. The sea glistening silver. Away to the left an ancient castle perched on a high plateau pressed against the skyline – a derelict monument still casting a watchful eye for sea-borne invaders. The plateau itself eventually falling sharply to the North Sea in formidable cliffs. Their tall out-stacks rising like pillars ringed with surf in the moonlight.

'You enjoyed the meal?'

'Yes, it was lovely. And the wine . . . thank you.'

Winter looked out at the fishing boats. 'Did you know that a hundred years ago this was one of the busiest fishing ports in Scotland? In those days you would have seen boats in their hundreds. The herring catches were legendary. They even had an army of coopers who made the barrels – there would have been thousands of them stacked all the way along the harbour wall. Can't remember the exact figures, but August Gant – he's the chap I was telling you about over dinner, he told me about the export trade. How the town was built on the fortunes it brought.'

'He's the man who owns the aeroplane company, is that right?'

'No, that's Jamie Gunn. August is the American pilot I was telling you about over dinner, helped me to get my pilot's licence in Florida. His great-great-grandfather was a fisherman here around the 1850s. One of his sons emigrated to America, August's great-grandfather I think he would have been.'

America, she thought, the place Frank promised to take me. She would have loved it. Oh, how she would have loved it. Still, that was yesterday. No use dwelling on such things. A small sigh. 'So what happened to the fortunes?'

'I think the fish just went away. Or the sea was overfished until there were no more left. Sad in a way isn't it? All the families, all the lives, dependent on one little silver fish. And then having to up stakes and move away from their homes, and go off in search of a new life. Not too bad for the young people, but can you imagine the effect on those who were too old to move, to find employment?'

'We all survive the best way we can.'

'Perhaps. It's just that I always hoped life would be better than just surviving.'

'And it hasn't? For you, I mean.'

Winter forced a laugh. 'Oh I've been lucky enough.'

Nancy stole a glance at him. His eyes were fixed on some distant point in space. But the sadness she saw in his face was almost tangible. A hurting boy trapped in the body of a man. Hopelessly looking for a kind word. A loving embrace. *Anything.* She remembered Dorcas Volk's words. Tried to picture him as a child, being beaten half to death, day after day. How lucky was that! There was a moment of wanting to reach out to him. To put her arms around him. To soothe away some of the pain. Instead she chastised herself. Told herself over and over again that the man beside her was her sworn enemy. She shivered as a chill breeze coursed down the narrow street. The moment passed. 'It's late. I'd better be going back now.'

'Back?'

'To Aldershot . . . I have to return the car.'

'They said Monday would be okay when I phoned.'

'I know . . . it's just that . . .'

'Money . . . is that what it is?'

'Nothing to do with you.'

'I checked your purse when I was looking for the hire car contract. Ten pounds isn't going to get you far.'

'You're a nosey bastard, aren't you.' She regretted the words the moment they left her lips. Turned away from him and looked down the dark row of fishermen's cottages. Squat. Grey granite. Black lifeless windows. Too few streetlights. 'Which way to the hotel?'

They started walking. 'You can stay in my room tonight. A good night's sleep. You'll feel better in the morning.'

'It's the same line all you soldiers use isn't it? You can stay in my room, nothing will happen I promise.' A bitter laugh. A little voice telling her to remain the hard woman. Not to weaken. 'Didn't you ever think we women might prefer the truth?'

'I'm only offering you a bed to sleep in.'

'I'm a married woman, or had you forgotten?'

'I'll sleep in the bath.'

'And I'm supposed to believe that?'

'Believe what you like, but I'm not letting you get in a car to drive all that way at this time of night. A hundred miles at the most and you'll fall asleep at the wheel. What good would that do?'

'And if I don't obey you, you'll tie me up to prevent me leaving, is that it?'

'I'd never do anything to hurt you, Nancy Ryan, that aside you'll do as you're told for once.' A gentle voice.

Something that did not go unnoticed as she walked beside him, along the narrow streets and through the dark alleyways of the bleak fishing town, back to the hotel. Not speaking, but thinking that Dorcas Volk had perhaps been right. *A gentle soldier. A contradiction in terms.* She even decided she liked the way he said her name. The way he smiled with his eyes. Then told herself it was the wine talking.

He awoke early. Stygian blackness. Uncertainty of his surroundings. Lost for a moment in that fleeting moment between sleep and consciousness. Womb-like warmth. Comforting. Then the pulse in his ear fading. Remembering. He started to move. Stubbed a toe against something hard and sharp. *Shit.* That focused the mind wonderfully. *Bath in hotel room in Scotland.*

IRA woman with a gun, asleep in his bed. He thought he must be losing it. Some of his old (and successful) mates from the initial SAS selection days at the Duke of York's Barracks might have understood, but he doubted it. She had been right the previous evening. No soldier was going to allow a beautiful woman to sleep in their bed. Alone. The consensus would have been: *What a fucking waste* (with appropriate sign language for the hard of hearing). But that was the Army. Half a slow-march step either side of primeval. Raw, violent, loveless. Necessary on all counts.

He climbed out of the bath and fumbled for the light switch over the sink. The blanket dropped from his shoulders as he checked his watch – seven o'clock. He sat on the edge of the bath and rubbed the toe he had hit against the business end of the tap, and then spent a few minutes doing basic limbering-up exercises. An attempt to overcome the aches and pains of an uncomfortable night's sleep. And thought of the time, not so many years earlier, when he had gone through the selection process to join the SAS. A week's introduction to navigation and other skills, followed by three weeks of softening up with ever-increasing grades of difficulty. The fifth and final week had been the killer. Known simply as 'endurance', it entailed the individual travelling alone over 41 miles of difficult terrain – like the Brecon Beacons – carrying 55 pounds of equipment and with a time limit of seventeen hours. Few aches and pains then. He decided he had become too soft. Promised himself he would make a conscious effort to get into better shape.

After the brief workout he showered and shaved and cleaned his teeth; dressed in the fresh clothes he had neatly piled on the toilet seat the previous night and finally took the bulky envelope from his shirt pocket. The letter he had written before turning in.

Switching off the bathroom light he slipped noiselessly into the bedroom. There was a thin, grey light at the window picking out the horizontal weave of the curtain fabric. He moved to the side of the bed and put the envelope on the bedside table. Nancy was dead to the world. Still as beautiful as the first day he had met her in the town of Crossmaglen, a year earlier. Impulsively he reached down and kissed her lightly on the forehead. Pulled the rumpled sheet over her bare shoulder. Promised himself he would remember her perfume forever.

He took his nylon flight-jacket from the back of the chair and put it on. Then picking up his Jeppesen flight case, he left the room, closing the door quietly behind him.

8

It was a sunny autumn afternoon. The air still. Puffs of fair weather cumulus. Birdsong. The last of the flowers the only splash of colour. The occasional distant hum of traffic.

They were sitting in a walled-in, tree-lined garden at a house in Kilburn, north London. Pat Cavenaugh, Frank Ryan, Teach Cusack, Sean Fitzgerald – who had flown in that Sunday morning from Belfast – and the owner of the house, Feargal Walsh. An old man, Feargal, who in his youth had been present at the 1916 Rising, and had played at fringe politics throughout the twenties, thirties, and troubled forties. His wife called him an old romancer. Cavenaugh thought differently. Winning battles through energy, attention to detail, ability to do without sleep or food, disregard for personal comfort, contempt for danger, was one thing. Winning them with style by paying attention to history, something else.

They were all waiting for Feargal's son, who had the same Christian name as his father and was therefore known by friends and family as Young Feargal. He was driving down from Blackpool.

'So,' Cavenaugh said to the old man, referring to the 1916 Rising they had been talking about for the past twenty minutes. 'What do you think was the turning point?'

Feargal Walsh, still dressed in a black suit, white shirt and blue tie (he had been to Mass that morning), peered up at the sky, squinting back the sunlight. 'Oh that's easy enough. Numbers. When Padraig Pearse led the one thousand two hundred volunteers and members of Connolly's Citizen Army against the might of the British Empire, he knew the odds were twenty to one the wrong way. Knew that they'd be foot soldiers against artillery. Knew that they'd be cut off from all possible support from the country, or from reinforcement of any kind. The leaders also knew their rising was bound to fail, but in the numbers they knew their dreams wouldn't die. They believed the new generations would pick up the flag and fight on . . . and if the call came, know how to die.'

'And you think the thousands of people who bartered their lives that week really knew they were being sacrificed?'

The old man adjusted his steel-framed glasses. Cavenaugh watched him intently. Noted the pouched cheeks, like a suspicious hound's. You could pass this man a hundred times in the street and never notice him. Unless you looked at his eyes. They were still bright after all these years. A fanatic's eyes. 'Not those numbers, Pat. The twenty-to-one odds. That's what you've got to focus on. Pearse was before his time, that's all. Do you know why the Americans are losing the war in Vietnam?'

'Tell me.'

'Television.'

Young Feargal appeared at that moment, accompanied by his mother. Helping her to carry trays with tea and sandwiches, which were placed on a garden table. Maggie Walsh poured the tea into Sunday best china and disappeared into the house without a word. Young Feargal pulled up a chair next to his father, while Cavenaugh completed the introductions.

'You've got an aviation company up at Blackpool then, Young Feargal. Doing well, is it?'

The son was in his mid-thirties. Medium height. Healthy-looking pink face. A broad smile. His mother's boy in good looks. His father's in business acumen. (The older Feargal had run a big printing press company in London since the end of the war). 'Well enough, Mr Cavenaugh. Da says you need some help with a helicopter, that right?'

'Tell him what you're thinking, Frank.'

Ryan finished his cup of tea and lit a cigarette. 'We've got . . . or hope to have, an Agusta Bell 205. Need a quick respray in US army camouflage paint. First off, can you do it? If so, how quick?'

Young Feargal considered the question. 'Depends what quality you're looking for, Frank.'

'Completely secondary. It needs to last for a flight from England to Ireland, that's all.'

'A light sanding to take the gloss off and a once-over with water-based paint should do it.'

'How long?'

'Half a day . . .' Young Feargal started. Then correcting himself as he obviously considered his employees. 'Overnight. I'll have to do it myself, though if you could lend me one of your boys, it would help things along. Mind you, if you fly through any heavy rainstorms you're going to start to wash the paint off.'

'How badly?'

'Well I mean, it wouldn't all come off in one go, but you'd start to see the original colours peeping through around the door frames perhaps and on panel seams. The more flights in similar conditions, the more the water-based stuff would come off. Like a bad paint job on an old car when the surface hasn't been correctly prepped. Lasts for about five minutes.'

'How about registration numbers on the side?'

'Tell me what you want, and you've got it.'

'As easy as that?'

'You'll need to give me as much notice as possible so I can arrange to have my hangar empty on the afternoon you bring it in.'

Ryan stretched his hands before him. Seemed to be inspecting his fingernails. Lowered them to his lap. 'I wasn't exactly thinking of bringing it into Blackpool airport!'

'Ah!' A look of understanding flickered through Young Feargal's eyes. 'Out of sight, out of mind, you mean?'

'That too difficult?' Ryan asked.

'Not a problem, Frank. I'll give you the location of a disused RAF airfield before you leave, owned by a farmer friend of mine. Even got a big empty hangar, not much roof left, but it'll do.'

'And the farmer?'

'Comes from Derry originally . . . sympathetic you might say. Oh yes, and I'd need a picture or something of the camouflage design and colours you're talking about.'

Ryan motioned to Sean, who took a large buff coloured envelope out of a briefcase. Handed it over.

Young Feargal inspected the glossy photographs, which had been taken the previous day at Aldergrove airport. 'Who took the photos?'

'Is that important?' Ryan asked.

'I need to know what type of film they used. Agfa films tend to come out more blue. Kodak is closest.'

'What type of film, Sean?'

Sean, shook his head. 'Not a clue. Michael took them.'

'I'll phone you later, and let you know. That okay?'

Young Feargal smiled and nodded, and put the pictures back in the envelope. Then took his father's teacup and refilled it.

Thirty minutes later, as they were leaving, Pat went over to the old man. 'It was lovely to see you again, Feargal.'

'And you, Pat. You're still school teaching then?'

'Education. My literature lessons include the mention of people like you. Hopefully they wake up one or two of the young minds. Alert them to the fact that there's something more noble than pop music and television.'

'You remind me of Padraig Pearse; he was a school-teacher as well. Used to do and say the same thing. Not the television of course. But he believed our future lay in the hands of the young. The real boys, he used to call them.' His voice took on a wistful quality. As though he was back in the Dublin of his youth. Easter Monday, 24th April 1916. Manning the barricades.

Hearing the artillery fire. Watching his comrades being blown to pieces before his startled eyes. 'The *real* boys,' he sighed. 'Those for the better tomorrow.'

Cavenaugh wondered if Pearse had ever really said that, or if Feargal was colouring history. Still, it was a powerful epithet, whichever way it had been. 'You were saying . . . before your son arrived, how America was losing the war.'

'Television.'

'Yes.'

'No use hanging your Sassman in the Falls Road, Pat. You need an audience. Vietnam has an audience – the rest of the world. Now take next Thursday evening for instance. Craogh Parc in Dublin. A big football match. The game's being televised. What better place for stiffing a Sassman.'

'Tell me more,' Cavenaugh said.

So the old man did.

By the time they had returned to the Skyways Hotel, Cavenaugh was in high spirits. Had felt the old quickening under his heart the moment Feargal had told him his idea. A simple plan. But weren't they ever the best?

Paying attention to history.

He invited the rest of the boys to his room and opened one of the bottles of whiskey he had brought with him.

A lighthearted toast today. 'To the backdoor stuff. May the black economy always taste as good.'

They drank and refilled the glasses.

'What are we celebrating, Pat?' Ryan asked.

Cavenaugh stood by the window watching the lines

of traffic moving slowly along the Bath Road. The airport beyond. Poking a finger under the eye patch, gently massaging the hard, scarred skin. 'Could we perhaps take the Sassman to Dublin in that helicopter, do you think?'

Ryan turned to Cusack. 'Do you think that's possible, Teach?'

'Sure. Need to check distances, you know, to get an idea what the fuel requirement is. But according to the map you were showing me on the drive back just now, I think we'll be okay.'

Ryan asked, 'Why Dublin?'

'First things first, let's get the helicopter and the prisoner down to that disused airfield Young Feargal told you about.'

'As discussed in the car?'

'Right. Check the airlines for seats to Aberdeen. Once that's confirmed I'll put in the call to Bryan Russell.'

When the three men had left the room, Cavenaugh refilled his whiskey glass and went back to the window. Deaf to the soft thunder of a BEA Trident climbing out on a westerly heading towards Staines. The rattle of windowpanes. His mind conjuring with the permutations of increased media coverage, and heightened international support.

Nancy Ryan telephoned Pat Cavenaugh twenty minutes later. She had made good time. By then was south of Burnley. Had stopped for petrol and a cup of coffee. And in the cold light of day had formulated a story to explain her failure to make contact with him the same day she had spoken to Dorcas Volk.

'I was worried about you,' Cavenaugh said. 'What went wrong?'

He sounded like he'd been drinking, she thought. 'Wrong?'

'You didn't call as instructed.'

'Nothing too important. A woman thing . . . you know, time of the month. Do you want me to go into detail?'

Cavenaugh said, 'So where are you now?'

'Shrewsbury,' she lied. 'That's as far as I got on Friday.'

'You could have tried to make contact . . .'

'Fuck you, Pat Cavenaugh. Isn't that just typical of men, no compassion. All, me, me, me! Well let me tell you, I had a serious hemorrhage as in menstruation hemorrhage . . . you'll know all about that, won't you, Pat, the discharging of blood from the lining of the uterus? I had to find a doctor. Do you know how much blood I lost?'

'I'm sorry,' Cavenaugh said defensively. Taken off guard by the sudden outburst. 'I'm terribly sorry. I'll make it up to you. Why don't you come down to London? Skyways Hotel next to Heathrow airport.'

'I'm driving a hire car. I've got to get that back to Aldershot first.'

'You're up to driving then?'

'I think so. Anyway, I spoke to the woman in North Wales, Dorcas Volk on Friday. She gave me an address for the Sassman.'

'That's great news. You'd better give me the details.'

'It's an aviation company in Scotland, at an airfield called Wick. Have you got a pen?'

'Go ahead.'

She passed the details. 'So what do you intend to do?'

'Not on the phone. Call me from Aldershot, we'll plan to meet up.'

'Oh, and one other thing, it seems that Winter is no longer in the Army.'

'The Volk woman told you that?'

'Yes.'

A thoughtful silence. 'Makes things a bit easier, then.'

'Perhaps . . . Is Frank with you?'

A short pause. 'He's here, yes.'

'I don't know if I'm up to seeing him, Pat.'

'I thought you wanted to be part of the cell.'

'With Frank running things, you mean?'

'That's the way of things.'

'Not for me.'

'He's still your husband.'

She thought of the tart, Celia, who Frank had been messing about with for years now. 'We all make mistakes, Pat.'

'This is bigger than personal differences. You know what I'm saying?'

'I know.'

'And you forgive me for being so insensitive earlier?'

'You should give Frank lessons in how to handle women.'

Cavenaugh laughed. 'That sounds like my lovely girl. So you'll think about it?'

'I'll think about it.'

Another laugh. 'Anyway, it's great news, Nancy. You've done brilliantly. Last place we'd have thought of looking for the bastard. An aeroplane sales company in the north of Scotland. You'll phone me from Aldershot, then?'

'I will.'

'Any problem getting me here, you'd better try the Belfast number. Take care of yourself, darling girl.'

She left the phone box and walked back to the car. Opened the door and got in and picked up the AA road map on the passenger seat. And suddenly froze. *Aeroplane sales company in the north of Scotland.* She hadn't mentioned that. Just the address Dorcas Volk had given her. *North Flight Limited, Wick Airport, Caithness, Scotland.* The silver-haired old bastard. He hadn't even trusted her to question Dorcas Volk.

She opened her handbag and took out a packet of cigarettes. Lit one with a shaking hand. Opened the car window. There was rain carrying on the westerly wind. Blowing into the car. She ignored it. Tried to visualize the sequence of events with Pat in London. Frank was there. And no doubt Sean Fitzgerald. It was obvious what the plan was to be. Frank was a marksman. A sniper. High-powered rifle. Telescopic sights. Then again, what if Pat was lying to her? What if Frank had already left and was on his way to Scotland?

She took a last puff of the cigarette and stubbed it out in the ashtray. Went to close her handbag. And saw the letter and the money.

That had been an eye-opener. Not that she thought so when there was a knock on the door at eight o'clock that morning, and she had stumbled out of her bed naked, pulling her raincoat around her before answering it. Room service. An old man – the hotel porter – with a tray. For Mrs Winter, he'd said. Her husband had asked for it to be brought to her room at eight o'clock. She had nearly hit him. *Mrs Winter*. Instead she took the tray and put it on the small table by the window, then went to the bathroom to give Sergeant Winter a piece of her mind. Except he'd gone. The only sign he had been there, a neatly folded blanket on the toilet seat. Even so he couldn't have gone far. Some of his clothes were still hanging in the wardrobe. Pairs of highly polished shoes neatly lined up on the shoe rack below. Folded shirts and sweaters and socks and pants and handkerchiefs in the drawers. A few books and magazines. An orderly man. An ex-soldier of the Queen. To be expected.

It was after she had eaten breakfast, and was enjoying a second cup of coffee that she noticed the envelope on the night-stand. She opened it and found it was stuffed with money and a letter. Her first thought: Condescending bastard. She had screwed up the letter and thrown it across the room. The money followed. A blizzard of giant confetti.

It was half an hour later, when she was showered and dressed, and ready to leave, that she decided she needed every penny she could get. She picked up the money, note by note. Counting it as she went. Two hundred and fifty pounds. More bloody fool him. Then the crumpled letter, which she smoothed out and read. Then folded it neatly and put it into her handbag. She took it out now and read it again.

Then A Soldier

My Dear Nancy,

I'm not a letter writer, so please bear with me over what I'm about to say.

I will always share your grief over what happened to your children; I was very fond of them. Enough to question what I was doing in your country long before they died. I realize the futility of any words I might offer, but I would have gladly given my life to save them. Please believe that.

You asked me a question yesterday evening, before we went out: Why had I let you go on that day in Northern Ireland? Why hadn't I turned you in? One of the answers I gave you was because I liked you. Not altogether true, but then I was never going to tell you what I really felt. Not to your face at least. Lack of courage in that department, I'm afraid. The truth was (and I suppose if I'm being honest with myself, still is) because I loved you. I loved you from the first moment I saw you at Dermot's garage in Crossmaglen, when he introduced us. It was 19 September last year (five past nine on a rainy morning). Of course that presented complications. Even if I had been the loyal comrade you imagined me to be, I knew you were a married woman and a Catholic. As it was, I was the cold un-forgiving face of the enemy. No astrological star signs were ever going to unravel that celestial conjunction.

Perhaps there are times and places for all of us. In a more perfect world I would have wished ours could have been different.

My love,
John

PS. I know you'll throw a fit when you see the money. So let's call it a loan . . . until you find better times.

She smiled at the postscript. He had that way. Serious and quietly spoken, and once in a while a silly remark that could make you laugh. Then her eyes were drawn back to the earlier words. *I loved you from the first moment I saw you.* She read the words over and over again. Finally put the letter in her handbag. 'Damn you, John Winter! Damn the day I ever set eyes on you.'

She got out of the car and went back to the phone box and called the hotel in Wick.

'Has Mr Winter checked out?'

'No, he's booked in until the end of the week.'

'Is he in the hotel?'

A minute or so while they checked. 'I'm sorry. No.'

Next, she tried the number for the airport.

'Hello, North Flight, Jamie Gunn here.'

'Could I speak to John Winter, please?'

'Who's calling?'

'A friend of his, Nancy.'

'Well he's away flying at the moment, Nancy. Went down to Inverness a few hours ago to pick someone up.'

'Have you any idea what time he'll be back?'

'Not really. His passenger just phoned from Birmingham, said he was delayed and would be on a later flight.'

'How much later?'

'Early evening at a guess.'

'Thank you.'

'Will I tell him you called?'

'No, that's all right. I'll try and reach him at the hotel later.'

She hurried back to the Mini and sat staring blankly

through the rain-lashed windscreen. Looking at, but not seeing, the steady stream of cars and trucks heading south on the black cataract of the A682 towards Manchester. She remained like that for ten minutes. Then started the engine. Merged into the southbound traffic. She had warned him after all. What else could she do?

9

August Gant called it the Paradiso factor.

As in: the best was never quite good enough. Not for the sort of men he recruited. He was always looking for the rarity. The natural. The flyer with hand eye coordination that somehow embraced microscopic precision as though it was the most normal thing in the world. Technically perfect pilots were ten a penny. The naturals came along once in a very long while. The reason he had delayed their departure from Inverness until night had fallen and the storm was at its height. Anybody could do it when the sky was blue and the weather benign. At night, on instruments, flying close to the machine's limits, something altogether different.

They were airborne now. Level at 2,500 feet. Below, lost in cloud and rain and night, the Moray Firth. The turbulence had been forecast as moderate to severe. Gant, seeing the intense concentration on Winter's face, had offered to take over the radio duties.

The voice of the Inverness controller came up:

'Helicopter Golf Alpha Mike, Inverness Approach, call Kinloss Radar on one one nine decimal two.'

'Nineteen point two for Alpha Mike, 'night.'

'Safe flight Alpha Mike.'

'Top of our list, sir.' Gant replied cheerily, before selecting the new frequency. He paused to check for other transmissions, then keyed the transmit button: 'Kinloss Radar, Helicopter Alpha Mike's on the frequency.'

'Roger, Helicopter Alpha Mike, this is Kinloss Radar, confirm altitude and magnetic heading.'

'Okay, we're twenty five hundred on the Inverness altimeter nine-nine-two, heading's zero zero five.'

'Roger Alpha Mile, Kinloss copies altitude two thousand five hundred and heading zero zero five. Be advised this will be radar advisory service only.'

'We copy, sir.'

'And Alpha Mike, Kinloss Radar, confirm your flight conditions?'

'Alpha Mike's Popeye . . . correction . . . on instruments.'

The RAF Kinloss controller who had served on an exchange posting with the USAF at Nevada in recent years, picked up on the American military jargon. 'Air force or navy?' he asked.

'Not a night for the navy ladies, sir. This is strictly a professional operation . . . ex-air force, by the way, but we appreciate you askin'.'

Background laughter from a lady ATCO as the Kinloss controller keyed his mike switch again. 'How's the turbulence, Alpha Mike?'

'Confirm this is *Royal Air Force* Kinloss?'

'Affirmative.'

'Roger, my southern sense of fair play, didn't want to go upsetting the navy unnecessarily. Reference turbulence, enough to make the navy pukes seasick.'

More background laughter from the lady controller. 'Not so the air force, Alpha Mike?'

'Reason we call it the *air* force, sir. We carry out our commerce up here.'

A smile in the voice. 'Copied, Alpha Mike. Advise when you are VHF contact with Wick for release.'

'We'll let you know, sir, and we're glad we offered a moment of light comedic relief for your good lady there.'

'You heard that?'

'Air force pilots, sir. Known for our exceptional eyesight and hearing, our dashing good looks and our laconic sense of humour.'

More laughter.

Gant peered out into the blackness then transferred his eyes to the instrument panel. Winter was doing a pretty good job of maintaining altitude and heading. He noted the DME reading from Inverness. And as they slammed through brick-wall-like turbulence pulled his harness a notch tighter, until it bit into his shoulders. Then flipped the PTT switch to intercom. 'Thirty miles to go.'

'Copied,' Winter acknowledged.

'Shitty night.'

'Had crossed my mind. You'd better check Wick, see what their weather's doing.'

Gant selected the Wick frequency on box two and gave them a call.

Jamie Gunn's voice came back almost immediately. 'Didn'a think you'd be coming, Alpha Mike.'

'Oh it's not that bad, Jamie.' What the hell was he talking about! It was close to lethal. 'How's your weather?'

'Surface wind three five zero at three zero knots, with gusts up to five five . . . fifty-five knots. Cloud base estimated at 300 feet. QNH nine nine zero. Landing runway three one. Go ahead.'

Gant read back the information, then briefly selected box one and cleared with Kinloss.

'ADF coming in strong I see,' he said to Winter.

'Yeah . . . confirm the minima for ADF to runway three-one.'

Gant picked up the Jeppesen manual marked at the Wick plates, and flipped it open. 'Four hundred and seventy feet.'

'Cloud base for Wick?'

'Estimated three hundred.'

'Could be a little bumpy on approach.'

Gant suppressed a smile. Shit, he'd been feeling queasy for the past 40 minutes. How much more bumpy could it get than this? 'I guess you'll be stayin' as high as possible as long as possible, right?'

'Wind shear over the cliffs . . . Right.'

Winter eased the helo out to sea, planning a 3-mile approach to the beacon. Fighting the controls the same way he had been all the way from Inverness. His wrists aching. His calf muscles burning from the pounding his feet were taking on the rudder pedals. He commenced descent below minima. Calling out pre-landing checks as he went.

They were less than ½ mile from the coast at 300 feet when Gant called 'Lights . . . intermittent . . . eleven o'clock.' Adding: 'Could be the town.'

The spine-bruising turbulence intensified. It lasted for maybe sixty seconds. Long enough to increase the already high heart rate of pilot and co-pilot.

'Alpha Mike's short final.' Gant called on the radio.

Gunn's voice rasped back. 'I've got you in sight Alpha Mike, cleared land. Suggest you clear at first intersection and hover to hangar. I'll go down and open the doors for you the moment you've cleared.'

'Roger that.' Then to Winter, 'You get that?'

Winter gave a nod of the head. Acknowledging the fact that he'd picked up the instruction. He could have just as easily said as much over the intercom, but he hadn't. Without really knowing why he had opted for the unwritten law of the veteran about times and places for words. He reached up and flipped on the landing light. Easing back on the cyclic. Levelling off within feet of the runway, buffeted by the winds. Fighting all manner of forces as he departed the runway and followed the taxiway to the hangar.

As they were proceeding in a low hover towards the hangar, pounded by the wind and rain, Gant smiled to himself. He knew he had found a natural.

10

Ryan, Fitzgerald and Cusack moved north that night. The last BEA flight that Sunday from Heathrow to Aberdeen's Dyce airport. The turbo-prop Viscount was full, mostly with oil workers employed on the new offshore oil rig exploration work – the 'Montrose Field', the first British oilfield in Scottish waters, had come on stream the previous year, turning the city of Aberdeen into the new Klondike. The three Irishmen, casually dressed, did not look out of place, their accents unremarkable amidst the international flavour of the oil men. They were met outside the terminal by a small, nervous looking man named Bryan Russell, who escorted them to the car park and gave them the keys to a dark-coloured Ford Cortina that he had stolen from a hotel car park two hours earlier. It was raining heavily. A black night.

'Thanks again, Bryan. Can we give you a lift somewhere.'

A hurried glance back towards the terminal. 'No thanks, my wife's picking me up any minute now.'

'Everything we asked for?'

'In the boot.'

'Petrol?'

'Full, and there's a spare five gallon jerry can in the boot with the other stuff.'

'Map?'

'In the glove compartment.'

'What about the car . . . what do you want us to do with it?'

'Make sure you dump it before seven in the morning.'

'*Borrowed* is it?'

'Right . . . Oh, and I put a thermos of tea in the car, and some sandwiches. On the back seat. Thought you might welcome it.'

'Very thoughtful, Bryan. I'll make sure and tell Pat how thorough you were.'

Russell gave a thin smile. The last thing the self-employed Irish locksmith wanted was recognition. Moira, his Scottish wife, would never understand.

They were on the main A96, heading north-west towards Elgin. Fitzgerald was driving. Ryan was sitting in the passenger seat, opened-out map across his knees. There was no other traffic on the road at that time of night.

Cusack, who was sprawled across the back seat, said, 'I'm impressed, Frank. How did you put all this together at an hour's notice?'

'Served nine years in the RAF. Made it to corporal. I learned a bit about planning and execution. Time management.'

'And that guy, Russell?'

'Another of our sleepers. We haven't got many, but those we do have are strategically placed throughout the UK. It's been going on a long time now.'

'So, what's the game plan? Once we get to this Wick place?'

'We'll do a recce of the airport. See if we can find this helicopter.'

'What about local police?' Sean Fitzgerald asked suddenly.

'Just fucking drive, Sean . . . and listen.' He turned back to the American. 'Wick's a small fishing town. I'm guessing there won't be much in the way of a crime wave going on between midnight and six in the morning. So, first stop the airport. If we can find the helicopter we'll get you to check the fuel state and ensure the internal batteries are hooked up, so that we're ready to get out of there. If we should be stopped by a police car, which I'm thinking is highly unlikely, we tell them we're tourists looking for our way into town and MacKay's Hotel.'

'What about the topographical maps I asked for? The ones to get me to the disused airfield near Blackpool?'

'In the boot.'

'Boot?'

'The trunk, as you fellas call it.'

'Oh, right. I'd like to have a look at them. Need to check the height of terrain, especially with the weather the way it is.'

'Okay, we'll stop at the next lay-by we see. Got that, Sean?'

'Got it.'

'While you're checking the helo, Teach, I'll take Sean and pick up the Sassman in the car. We'll return to the airport, park the car somewhere and get out of there. You'd better plan a route that doesn't overfly the town. Anything else?'

'How did you know where to find this guy?'

'We got lucky there. Pat put in a call earlier and found the town has two hotels. He called them and said he had a package to deliver to a Mr Winter tomorrow morning, and could they confirm his room number and that Mr Winter was still staying in the hotel. The first place didn't have a clue what he was talking about. The second . . . we hit the jackpot.'

'Just as well it wasn't a city with a thousand hotels, I guess.'

'Didn't need to be a hotel. Could have been a private house, then we would have had to wait until the morning and try and locate him through that aircraft company he seems to be involved with.'

'Did you do any flying when you were in the air force?'

'Oh, a couple of rides. Officers wanting to impress junior NCOs. Why?'

'Thought you'd better sit up front with me, and map read. I'm going to have my hands full flying the bird. It's been a long while.'

'Might be safer to come west out of Wick and then head south over the water, there's a lot of mountains up there.'

'Yeah, right. That way we might be able to stay under radar . . . what time you reckon we'll get there?'

Ryan took a torch out of his pocket. Snicked it on and shone it down on the map.

Fitzgerald concentrating on the road ahead, said, 'It's about four hours.'

'How did you work that out?'

'There was a map in one of the in-flight magazines on the plane coming up.'

'Good man, Sean.' Turning back to Cusack. 'There's your answer, Teach. Should get there about one-thirty. Say two o'clock.'

'And airborne by what? Three?'

'Maybe.'

The American said nothing. He was wondering if he'd maybe overstated his qualifications. Sure, he'd flown Hueys in 'Nam. Done everything, right through from basics of climbing and turning and descending, straight and level, to practice autorotation. Only problem was the last time was more than a year earlier. Flying was something that required practice. *Especially* night/instrument operations. Then again the offer of a couple of thousand dollars for a few days' work had been too good to refuse. He put his head down on the seat and closed his eyes and tried to remember how flying a helo had been.

And instead found himself thinking of Rusty – the third-string Dallas Mafia type. The man reduced to red slippery meat that he'd scooped up and placed in a zippered black bag. Now found himself craving his M-16. There was beauty in the slow-motion film clip of a bullet homing on its target. There was beauty in a shell case falling to the ground. There was beauty in a gun – when you were behind it. A helo at night, in shit weather? Now that sounded kick-ass fucking dangerous. Or as the Belsen-thin Rusty with the big, frightened eyes had always said when they went out on night patrol against the Cong: *Bad karma, man. Can't you fuckin' feel it*?

11

Jamie Gunn was a thorough man. After moving the helicopter into the hangar he had gone back into the storm to get the fuel truck. Once the helo was refueled, he switched off the hangar lights and locked the main doors. Then he drove back to the old tower and put the kettle on. He had run the airport for a dozen years now, had been in aviation for nearly three times that long. A medium-height, medium-build, dour Scot with a craggy, lived-in face, he thought he had seen it all. Now, listening to the old air traffic control tower creaking and moaning in the wind, the rain smashing into the windows like ocean waves, he wondered how anybody could have got that helicopter in. He poured out three mugs of coffee, 'Tough flight, I'm thinking,' he said. Clipped Highland brogue. As impersonal as the weather. He handed out the drinks.

Gant nodded. 'Shitty. If it'd been up to me, I'd'a settled for a hotel in Inverness. Said as much to Captain Winter here, know what he said when I mentioned the horrendous wind that was blowing?'

Gunn shook his head. 'Hav'na got a clue.'

'Said, "August, we fly in a gale. What's the difference?" True as I'm sitting here.' A twinkle in the old eyes.

Gunn took a bottle of Old Poultenay Single Malt from his desk drawer, unscrewed the top, and poured a little into each mug. 'Distilled locally, you'll like it . . . He said that did he? Bit too brave for me, August.'

'Testosterone levels of the young,' Gant replied knowingly.

'Aye, I'm sure you're right . . . It's not catching by any chance?'

A snicker from Gant. 'You're thinking about your wife, I guess?'

Gunn fell into silent convulsions.

Winter, who was still trying to come to terms with the adrenalin and the relief of being on the ground in one piece, managed a weak smile and took a sip of his coffee. He'd been through similar ribaldry in his army days. Had learned the best way to handle being a 'rookie' was to say nothing.

Half an hour later on the drive into town Winter confided in the old American. 'Seems I've got a problem.'

'What sort of problem.'

'A few people looking for me, shall we say?'

Gant understood immediately. 'Civilian thing or Army?'

'Army.'

'D'you know who exactly?'

'IRA.'

'Shit! Who told you?'

'A lady friend.'

'What's her name?'

'Not important.'

'But it's good Intel?'

'I think so.'

'And she thinks they may have located you?'

Winter slowed and changed gear as he came into the old fishing town. Thought of Nancy's warning. Twenty-four hours after she left. Tomorrow at the latest. 'More than likely.'

'We could head out in the morning. First light. Take the helo down to the shippers in England.' Gant said, looking at the dark granite buildings that lined the road. 'Anywhere but here! Can see why my great-granddaddy left this place . . . damned depressing. Best I can say for it. Thought any more about the job in the Philippines?'

Winter eased the car into a parking space on Union Street, near the hotel's main door, and switched off the lights and the engine.

'You see,' Gant continued, 'You need something like another thousand hours before the oil guys will hire you on to fly their operations. Sure, I figure you're good enough. But they're looking for a bit more experience in the logbook. Put it this way, I'll get you a one-year contract with Jack Crane – he's the boss of the operation. In that time, you'll get the experience, plus a bit of fixed wing flying if you want it. You'll also get a sack full of duty free dollars which will mean you can drive up to your interview in a brand new car and in a real smart suit, instead of arriving in a pair of jeans on the last bus.'

They got out of the car. Winter locked it. 'I'll think about it.'

'Don't forget the sunshine . . . and those Filipino gals are the prettiest in Southeast Asia.'

'I'll say one thing for you, August . . . you don't give up.'

As they picked up their keys from reception and checked for messages the young man on the desk mentioned that there had been a call for Mr Winter that afternoon. No message. Although the young man seemed to remember it was a lady who had called.

'Your young lady?' Gant asked, as they made their way down the dimly lit corridor to their rooms.

Winter thought of Nancy. 'Had to be, she's the only woman who knows I'm here.'

'Any reason she'd call and not leave a message?'

Any reason? And he thought of the letter he had written to her in the dead of night. *I loved you from the first moment I saw you.* And hadn't they got on reasonably well together the previous evening. His pulse raced at the thought of hearing her voice again. 'I don't know.'

'What if we pack our bags and check out?'

'Now?'

'Sure.'

'And do what?'

'Spend the night holed up in Jamie's office . . . just to be on the safe side.'

'No need. Tomorrow morning will be early enough.'

'You sure?'

'Yeah, I'm sure.'

'You goin' to eat . . . in the restaurant?'

'Too tired, I might order room service. Get an early night.'

Gant smiled. 'I'm glad you said that, I'm dead on my feet. I enjoyed the flight by the way.'

They stopped outside Winter's room. 'You did?'

'Well, the landing part of it at least.'

Winter smiled back. He liked the American. A genuinely happy man with a dry sense of humour. He would have enjoyed serving under such an officer in the Army. Except the British didn't seem to understand that humour and leadership went together. An altogether American thing. 'See you in the morning?'

'Yeah, 'night.' Gant started walking away down the corridor. 'What time you wanna leave in the morning?' he called back.

'Seven o'clock okay?'

Gant stopped and turned. 'Sure, why not. What the hell else would I be doing at that time of the morning other than sleeping?' A grin from ear to ear. 'By the way, is your young lady a blonde or a brunette?'

'Redhead.'

'They tell me those gals got fiery tempers . . . that right?'

He thought of the slap he'd received the previous day, the sometimes-sharp tongue. The flashing green eyes. 'Could be.'

'Is she beautiful?'

'A world-beater.'

Gant grinned again, then turned and set off down the corridor. 'Naturally,' he called back, 'I'll be expecting an invitation to the wedding.'

The smile slipped from Winter's face as he unlocked his door and went into the empty room. *Wedding invitation*! There was a lovely thought. Highly improbable under the circumstances, but a lovely thought. The first time in his life that he had fallen in love. At his age! And he'd never even kissed her, held her close, made love to her. But he had known from the first moment he had seen her. How did such things happen?

He undressed and showered, then too tired to think about ordering room service, got into bed. The faintest hint of her perfume was still on the pillow. He closed his eyes and tried to remember every contour of her face. Every word she had spoken.

12

They arrived in Wick at two-thirty; the rain and poor visibility had slowed their progress. Following road signs they passed through the west of the deserted town and continued on the A99 road. The airport came into view on the right of the road about 2 miles later. Or at least a big hangar with a red light on the top of it. Further along the road was an open gate, which led onto the airfield. Fitzgerald switched off the car's lights and they followed what appeared to be a disused perimeter track towards the hangar. Out of the misty rain they now saw an air traffic control tower. Another red light on the roof of that structure. A high-winged single-engine aeroplane – minus its propeller, with ropes stretching down from the underside of the wings to large concrete blocks – was parked on a stretch of grass.

'No helicopters on the apron,' Ryan said urgently, as they drove at a walking pace past the tower. 'Let's try the hangar, Sean.'

The massive steel doors were secured by a rusted

padlock. Ryan went to the boot of the Cortina, and started searching for a jack-handle, or something heavy. When he returned the American was removing the lock from the iron hasps it had been linked through.

'How did you do that?'

Teach grinned. Water dripping off the end of his nose. 'Spent a year sharing a cell with a career thief. He taught me about picking locks. Pretty easy when you know how.'

'Glad we've got you along,' Ryan said meaningfully, pushing on one of the doors. It grated open about eighteen inches and the two men slipped inside.

It was a vast tomb. Pitch black. Icy cold. Ryan shone his torch straight ahead. Pitted concrete stained with black oil and spilled aviation fuel – the sharp toxic smell turning to taste as it picked at the back of his throat. No aeroplanes. Then he swung the beam to his immediate left. The Perspex windows of an Agusta Bell 205 helicopter threw back a dazzling reflection.

'Is that it?' Ryan asked.

'Looks like it.'

'We'd better check that it's serviceable before we go any further.'

'Seems in pretty good shape,' Cusack remarked, running a hand down the nose section. He opened the pilot's door and climbed up into the cockpit. Inhaled the faint leather smell of the seats. Looked around for a minute or so. Checking the instrument panel. Searching for the battery master switch. He found it along with banks of other switches on the overhead panel, flipped it on. The sudden whine of gyros coming to life. It took him another thirty seconds to locate the fuel gauge. And a final minute to run his hands over the instruments, levers and switches. Finally, he knocked off the battery switch and climbed down from the cockpit. 'The good news is we've got full fuel.'

'Good news!'

'Yeah, we still could have problems when we go to start it. Like the internal battery power being too low, or the starter generator on the fritz.'

'We'll take a chance on that.'

'Do you want me to try and get it out while you're away?'

'No. I'll close the door and put the lock back in place. Doesn't appear to be any security guards around, but better safe than sorry.'

'And you'll be about an hour then?'

'Less if possible. If anything goes wrong and we're not back in two hours, get out of here. There's a railway station in the town. I'd suggest you head there and take the first train south. In that case call Pat at the first opportunity. You've got his contact numbers?'

'Right.'

Ryan turned and started walking across the darkened hangar. 'The weather's not going to be a problem, is it?'

'If we can find the west coast like you suggested and follow it south, no.'

'And if not we'll be past caring, is that what you're saying?'

'Don't worry, Frank, we'll make it. I mean how difficult can it be?'

Ryan stopped and turned back towards the American. 'On second thoughts it might be better if you come with us.'

'Any particular reason?'

'I was thinking of your expertise in picking locks. It occurs to me we may need it at the hotel.'

Twenty minutes later Fitzgerald was parking the car in River Street, at the back of MacKay's Hotel. Like the rest of the town the place was deserted. The wind whipped the rain in horizontal sheets past the dim glow of a nearby street light. Ryan got out and hurried to the back of the car, opened the boot. He unzipped the canvas holdall. Three .32 calibre pistols. Close-range weapons. He checked they were loaded, dropped one in his pocket and got back in the car. He handed out the other two guns.

'You know what to do then, Sean?'

'You've told me ten times already.'

'Just want to be sure. What we've got here is an ex-SAS man. They're tough.'

'Not with one of these stuck in the back of their head.'

'Maybe. But remember, if things go wrong and he's armed, we take him out.' Ryan reached over and took a cushion from the back seat. 'If you have the time use that . . . it'll muffle the shot.'

They walked around towards the front of the hotel, checking the street. It was deserted. Then they returned to the back. A door marked FIRE EXIT. It was locked. Ryan went to the car and got Cusack. 'Seems I was right about the locked doors.'

The American had it open in less than a minute. He was left to stand guard. Ryan and Fitzgerald slipped quietly inside, securing the door behind them.

'Room twelve,' Ryan whispered.

Fitzgerald turned left into an offshoot of the main corridor. Raised a hand to Ryan. Then pointed.

'You got the tape?'

Fitzgerald patted his pocket.

Ryan took a piece of plastic from the pocket of his anorak. Slipped it between the doorjamb, in line with the Yale lock. The door gave with a slight click. He held it, returned the plastic to his pocket and took out the automatic pistol.

A nod to Fitzgerald and a deep breath and he was in the room. His hand searching urgently for the wall switch. He snapped it on, and immediately saw the bed and the man sleeping in it. 'Better be the right fuckin' room,' he said to himself as he leaped forward and grabbed the man's hair and pushed the muzzle of the gun into the side of his head. Thought he had made a mistake. He didn't recognize the man whom he had met a couple of times in Crossmaglen. Fuck it!

Winter, exhausted from the long day, and the mentally tiring instrument flight back from Inverness, woke with a start. Began to bring his hands up. Too late. His eyes slowly focused on the menacing face inches from his own. Felt the gun at his temple.

'No a sound, Sassman, or I'll blow your fuckin' brains out. Understand?'

Winter moved his head slowly to show he understood.

'What've you found, Sean?'

Fitzgerald was emptying the contents of Winter's flight-case on the floor. He found a pilot's licence inside a plastic holder. 'It's him.'

'Get that fuckin' tape here.'

Less than two minutes later, Winter – hands bound

behind his back, mouth and eyes taped over – was being bundled out of the fire exit into the rain. A blanket was draped around his bare shoulders. Fitzgerald opened the Cortina's boot and they pushed him into it.

'Start the engine. I'll pick up the rest of his stuff,' Ryan snapped, and disappeared back through the fire exit door.

Six minutes and some seconds later the Cortina drove slowly out of the rain-swept town in the direction of the airport.

13

It was nearly dawn when Nancy Ryan pulled into the car park in the red Mini. She switched off the engine and took a piece of paper from her handbag. *Skyways Hotel/Heathrow/Room 415*. Pat's contact details copied prior to her visit to Dorcas Volk in Wales. She checked her watch. Five minutes past five. Too early! Perhaps she should let him sleep a little while longer. She had arrived back at her bed-sit in Aldershot late the previous evening. Taken a hot bath and gone straight to bed. The alarm had gone off at 3 a.m. *Who the hell gets up at three in the morning*? So, fuck it. If she was going to do without a decent night's sleep, so could Pat Cavenaugh. Besides hadn't she decided that this would be the best hour to catch him? When his defences were down. Always assuming of course that her intuition was right! That the old silver fox was still playing games. She got out of the car and walked towards the brightly lit main entrance.

A bird sounded a tentative note from the hotel rooftop. As though seeking avian support for his suspicion that this grudging grey might be morning. No confirmation was forthcoming. There was no sky.

Ten minutes later she was going up to the fourth floor in a lift, carrying a tray with two cups of coffee and two packets of digestive biscuits.

There was a matter of a minute or more before a tousle-haired Pat Cavenaugh answered the door, pulling a wine-red silk dressing gown around him.

There was a moment of not recognizing the woman standing before him. The cropped Titian hair! Like a Joan of Arc marabous, he thought. Then he focused on the eyes. 'Nancy . . . God, is that you? I didn't recognize you . . . the hair!'

'I thought you'd like coffee,' she said, brushing past him, entering the room.

'What time is it?'

'A bit after five.'

'And aren't you the early bird.'

'I remember you once saying: "The enemy never sleeps, so why should we?" Or was that one of your Bushmill moments?'

An innocent smile: one way to handle a sharp tongue. 'I said that did I?'

She went over to the window. Placed the tray on the round table, pushing two empty whiskey bottles and four glasses out of the way to make space. Opened the curtains. Orange sodium lights in the car park below. The lines of car windows opaque with dew. A number of aircrew climbing onto a courtesy bus that had just pulled up outside the main entrance. She took off her white raincoat and tossed it on the bed, then pulled out a chair and sat down.

'I thought you'd be calling me from Aldershot,' Cavenaugh said, coming over to the table and sitting in the chair opposite. Noting the mini-skirt that left too little to the imagination. The black tights. The patent leather stilettos. The tight green sweater. The sensuous perfume.

'I got a flat tyre on the drive down from Shrewsbury. Then found the spare was flat as well. It took me four hours to find someone to fix it. By the time I got back it was too late, so I had a bath, got changed and came straight here.' She took a packet of cigarettes from her handbag. Lit one.

Cavenaugh stretched and suppressed a yawn. 'Frank'll be pleased.'

'When he gets back you mean?'

'Back?'

A blue shaving of cigarette smoke curled and broke against the white plaster ceiling.

'I checked with the young fella on the desk. He said my husband had checked out yesterday evening. When would that have been, Pat? Just after the time I phoned you the information?'

A moment of readjusting his eye-patch. A rueful kind of smile. Like he'd just been beaten at cards. 'We decided the element of surprise might be the best way to play it up in Scotland.'

Nancy shook her head. She was getting to know Pat Cavenaugh better than he knew himself. 'Did they get him . . . the Sassman?'

'I don't know. Frank said he'd call me this morning.'

'Why not last night?'

'A . . . a change of plans,' Cavenaugh said hesitantly. 'I, er, decided we should pick him up and take him back to Ireland.'

'And how do you propose to do that?'

'It's not important at the moment.'

'Not important at the moment! What the fuck's that supposed to mean? That I'm unreliable? You send my husband out there to kidnap a Sassman, and now you're telling me it's not important. What happens if Frank gets killed?'

Cavenaugh looked shocked. This was the last thing he had been expecting. 'I thought you'd had enough of him? The reason you left.'

'Jesus Christ, Pat Cavenaugh, why ever do they put men in charge of armies, especially men like you? You're no better than Father Michael. Never had a wife, never had kids, and yet you insist on pontificating over things you know nothing about. I lost my two children, or perhaps you'd forgotten. Perhaps after that I was having a breakdown, I don't know. But I blamed Frank for what happened. Wasn't it him after all who decided my children would be better acting as "dicks" to carry the comms? Then when you found out the mechanic was a Sassman I decided if it was left to you and Frank, we'd still be pissing about this time next year. So I located him for you. Now it's all the boys together, is that what you're telling me? So what am I expected to do now? It's you after all who's been so concerned about Frank. Now I'm ready to make things up, what do I get?' She stubbed out her cigarette in an angry gesture and leapt from the chair, grabbing up her raincoat, slinging the long strap of her handbag over her shoulder.

'Where are you going?'

'What the fuck does it matter? It's all lies isn't it, Pat? From cradle to grave! And you? Preaching your fine words about a united Ireland. You the eloquent scholar with the mighty education, and in the end you're just as bad as the bloody English. The best part is that we lesser mortals – the illiterate masses – believe you, do your bidding. Buy into your smarmy sincerity. And all the time it's just a con game. Is that why you never married, Pat? Sort of a power trip with you is it? Getting an orgasm every time you fuck one of us . . . metaphorically speaking of course.' She started to walk towards the door. A bitter laugh. 'You want to know what the saddest thing is? It's that I really thought you were better than that.'

'All right . . . all right.' He called after her. 'I'll tell you. Just come and sit down . . . please.' The old smooth voiced Pat. A repentant man who never liked to lose an argument. Or a friend.

She came back slowly, allowing him to take the raincoat and the handbag from her. To sit her down on the edge of the still warm, unmade, bed. Facing the window that framed the beginnings of a pallid eastern sky. He sat next to her. And told her about the plan to grab Winter, and steal the helicopter, and fly to a disused ex-RAF airfield near Blackpool.

'And then what?' she had asked.

'I haven't discussed it with Frank yet.'

She had put an arm around him. Squeezed his waist. 'But you'll tell me.'

Which he did. Not quite the truth. More the placenta that had nourished it and was now spent. Discarded. Its qualities suspect. 'Quite simply we move him to a rendezvous near Dublin early this week by helicopter . . . I would have preferred Belfast but with the increased British Army presence that looks too risky. Once we're in the Dublin area we'll move him to

Belfast by road.' He had raised a hand as she tried to interrupt him. 'I know what you're going to say. How do we smuggle him across the border? The answer is once again quite simple. There's an English Salvation Army bus with a children's choir touring various towns in Ireland this week. It's due to drive north across the border on Friday night for a concert in Belfast on Saturday. The Sassman will be concealed on that bus. With luck we shouldn't have much interference from the BA border patrols . . . I think they've got a soft spot for the Sally Ann.'

When he had finished she sat silent. Thinking. 'Not a very good plan is it, Pat?' She removed her arm.

'And why would you say that?'

'What about the stolen helicopter? Don't you think all the police forces and God knows who else will be looking for it?'

'Risk,' Cavenaugh said. 'We operate under cover of darkness, and at low level under the radar.'

'But there is a risk, you concede that much?'

'There's always that.'

'Perhaps not! Winter, the Sassman, has a partner. An American.'

'How do you know that?'

'Dorcas Volk. Winter's aunt. She told me.'

'Why didn't you mention it before?'

'Why didn't you tell me what you were doing, instead of sending Frank on some lame scheme? I didn't think it was necessary, that's why not.'

'So what's the significance of this American?'

'I don't know. I could phone him with some story about how Winter has borrowed the helicopter and try and get him, the Yank, to talk to whoever owns it, and explain it will be returned on Saturday. That way at least Frank won't have to run the risk of some plane spotter seeing the helicopter and reporting it to the police. And that, as stupid as it seems, is what will likely happen. Some innocent kid blowing the entire operation to high heaven.'

'I still don't see how you can convince him.'

'I found your Sassman for you didn't I, Pat?'

'You did.'

'Would you call that against the odds . . . yours or Frank's?'

'Yes.'

'So it's worth a try.'

'Perhaps.'

'So where was the Sassman staying in Scotland?'

'A hotel.'

'You've got the number?'

Cavenaugh reached over to the bedside table. Rooted through some papers. Found the scribbled note. Gave it to her. 'How will you find the American? Have you got a name?'

'No. But if they were together I'm sure somebody will know.'

'Okay. Once Frank calls me you can use the phone here. In the meanwhile I'd better shower and get dressed.'

Nancy pondered the proposal. 'Is that a good idea? Using the room phone? What if the hotel operator on the switchboard is listening in? I can hardly use the same code that we use to a complete stranger, can I? I'll find a public phone down in the reception area. I'll wait for you in the coffee shop; you can let me know if you've heard from Frank when you come down to join me. Then I'll call this hotel in Scotland.'

'Well enough.'

'Then you can perhaps trust me enough to tell me what you intend to do in Dublin with this Salvation Army thing, in a bit more detail.'

'Better than that! Once I've got Frank's call, I'm catching a flight there. You can come with me.'

She got up, tugging her skirt down, smiling for the first time since she'd entered the room. Then leaned down and kissed him on the forehead. 'If Frank calls, don't mention you've seen me.'

'You want to surprise him, is that it?'

'It's what wives do, Pat.'

A moments pause in the open doorway. 'Oh, one more thing. If I'm going to Dublin with you, can you remind me to phone the garage in Aldershot . . . they'll have to come and collect their car.'

After she had left Cavenaugh went back to the table and picked up the first whiskey bottle, checking the contents – it was completely drained. The other one had about a finger or two left. He felt quite happy. Hadn't he told Frank she would come round in the end. Maybe he'd never been married, but he'd known enough women. Smiling to himself he poured the remains of the bottle into the cleanest looking glass and threw it back. Jesus, she was some woman though. And that hair, cut back almost to her scalp, hardened her face in a way that was purely sexual.

He stared at the bottle he was holding. Remembered an American years ago asking why the Irish spelled whiskey with an, 'e'. Remembered his reply and the laughter it got: 'Oh, that's easy, we do it to be awkward.'

And as he went off to get his shower, he decided that was the thing about this operation. It was awkward. Out of the ordinary. Like the 3,000 word paper he had once written in his younger days, the opening lines as fresh in his mind today as the greater body of Yeats' work which he had drowned in as a boy.

The Price to Pay for the Irish Question
What is the price the engaged parties are prepared to pay in settlement of their differences? 'Differences' is of course, the crux: ethologists are not of one mind at all as to why primitives fight in the first place. Some insist on seeing primitive warfare as 'cultural', a channelling of masculine instincts to violence into collective form, as well as an expression of identity by the males who form a particular collectivity. Others regard fighting as a means of competition for scarce resources and point out that, though pitched battles appear to achieve little on the day, the stronger collectivities do, over time, appear to prevail over the weaker, by taking up the territory that they are unable to defend. Such territories are, nevertheless, separated from each other by recognized no man's lands, at or in which battle's normally take place. At some stage, however, the time comes when no man's lands disappear and frontiers assume tripwire function.

Impressive stuff for a poor undergraduate. Before its time. But now time was catching up. The people were getting the education. The no man's land of ignorance was shrinking. A prelude to taking their war to the enemy. He had heard the talk about future targets – one of which was the British government (including the prime minister of the day) on their own soil.

14

There is a place somewhere between sleep and consciousness where the mind dwells for a moment. A temporary purgatory where reality seesaws between two truths, either one seeming as valid as the other. The place Winter was now. Locked in battle with himself. On a 41-mile endurance march. SAS selection. Brecon Beacons. His mind telling him that trained airborne troops can travel at temperatures below −50 degrees Celsius for many miles carrying heavy packs, day after day. Thoroughly soaked with sweat, body-thin from weeks of inadequate rations and lack of sleep, they nevertheless avoid hypothermia so long as they keep moving fast enough to maintain their body core temperature above 33 degrees Celsius. His problem was, he was falling behind . . . He could see the Denison camsmock of the student that he had been tailing gradually pulling away through the grey morning . . . Heard his own voice telling him to fight the drowsiness . . . The leaden heaviness in his legs . . . Watched the student disappear into the mist somewhere on the ridgeline bottleneck of the Bwlch y Ddwyallt . . . He reached up and wiped his eyes . . . And knew he wasn't going to make it . . .

The banging sound might have been a gun. Except it wasn't, it was a door. He struggled to open his eyes and found he couldn't. The same thing when he tried to move his hands. His feet. Then he remembered. The Irishmen. Two of them. A gun at his head. Being tied up. Forced into a car boot. A short drive with his head resting on what felt like a car jack, every bump in the road pounding him near to unconsciousness. Then long minutes when the car had stopped and the engine had been switched off. Voices. Another engine sound somewhere far off, coming closer. Metallic sounds. Being dragged out of the boot into the wind and rain. Being hauled up into a cold metal tomb . . . the familiar smells were the give-away. The Agusta Bell 205.

After that, confused shouting. The engine spooling up. A rocky take-off. Shivering uncontrollably as the blanket came off his naked body. And still the shouting voices. He tried to make out what they were saying, but the noise was too great. The flight seemed to last for ever. He concentrated on staying awake, pretending he was again on the Brecon Beacons. Testing himself against the best of the candidates. He couldn't be sure if he had succeeded or if he had lapsed in to unconsciousness at some stage of the journey. He did remember the voices screaming again though. In the same way he felt the lurch of the helicopter as it descended rapidly. Something didn't seem right. Then they were rocketing up, leaving his stomach behind. The roller coaster ride seemed to continue for a long while. Until they hit the ground. Hard. Too hard to be a normal landing. A distant tearing of metal from somewhere. And then finally, the engine winding down.

Minutes later he had been lifted down from the machine. Had felt a cold wind on his face and body. Then a comforting warmth as a blanket was draped around his shoulders. The binding on his ankles was freed. The blood was pounding at the base of his shins, and squeezing down again into his feet. Hands held him upright.

An Irish voice started shouting again: 'Get the bastard in the hangar.'

'Where in the hangar?'

'Where do you think?'

'I'm not a fuckin' mind reader, Frank.'

'Just find a secure place, Sean.' Resignation in the slow measured voice, as though the speaker was mentally counting to ten, trying not to lose his temper.

Hands under his shoulders. Half carried, half dragged. His feet touching grass. Then sharp pitted stone. Or tarmac! Then the echo of his captor's shoes. The smooth stone under his bare feet. Concrete? Inside of the hangar? The creaking of an opening door, being sent sprawling onto a cold, damp floor. Trying to roll over and find the blanket. Hearing the door slamming shut. And then silence.

He didn't know how long it had been. But now there were hands lifting him into a sitting position, ripping the tape from his mouth. Untying his hands. Something soft being thrown at him.

'Get dressed, Sassman.'

Winter rubbed his wrists, trying to get the circulation

going. Fumbled around for the clothing. Found he was holding a shirt. He struggled into it, buttoned it slowly and awkwardly with unfeeling fingers. Then his trousers. His hand reached out for something else, but there wasn't anything else. 'What about the tape around my eyes?'

'That stays.' Hard Belfast accent.

'Afraid of being recognized, is that it?' Probing for weakness. Turning emotional rape on your captors, especially if you feel they are not trained professionals. Mileage to be gained.

Silence. That had obviously struck a nerve. He waited. Tensed himself for a blow to the body or the head. Punishment for insolence.

Instead a hand was reaching for the tape, tearing it from his face, hair and eyebrows being ripped out by the roots. He gasped in pain. Blinked in the thin grey light that came from a tiny skylight window in a sloping tin roof high above him. Focused slowly on the man before him. Recognized him then from his time working under cover in Crossmaglen. Nancy's husband. A big, brutish man. Lank, reddish hair, greying at the temples. He was holding an automatic pistol.

'Frank Ryan?'

No acknowledgment in the eyes or the voice. 'Sit down . . . on the chair, behind you.'

Winter sat.

'Not in the Army now, is that right Mr Winter?'

Winter, now becoming more alert, was thinking of the hours being taught AOPR: Awareness, Observation, Planning, Reaction. Should have reckoned that Nancy's warning was not guaranteed. Couldn't have been her fault, could it? And as he was thinking, allowed his eyes to dwell on the younger man standing behind and to one side of Ryan. Young, crew-cut hair, mean-looking eyes, flexing his fists like he was looking for a fight. Made a mental note that he could be the weak link. Hard men didn't need to show it until it mattered. 'That's right.'

'But you won't mind answering a few questions before we leave here?'

'Depends on the questions.'

Ryan paced quietly backwards and forwards in the small galvanized-clad room. 'We were interested to learn how you infiltrated our organization. Answer that question and we might go easy on you.'

'I've nothing to say.'

'They can't protect you now.'

Stating the bloody obvious. Tell me something I don't know. And the reward for non-answers? Pain! But then hadn't his intake been quoted as the toughest breed to date. Resist at all costs. Never crack. Hang on to the bitter bloody end. Queen and country they had been told. 'I've nothing to say.'

'That's a pity then,' Ryan replied. 'I mean, is it worth ending up a cripple? The Army won't give you a medal now.'

A bell rang somewhere. A regular two-note sound. A telephone extension. There was a knock on the door. An accentless voice shouting: 'Your phone call, Frank.'

Ryan moved to the door. 'Watch him, Sean. You know what to do.'

'Shouldn't we tie him up again?' Edgy. Nervous.

'You've got a fuckin' gun. If he moves kill him.'

Ryan turned and went out of the door.

Sean stood very still, the gun that he'd suddenly pulled from his belt waving unsteadily in his hand. His eyes were locked on Winter's. Expecting the Englishman to look away. Winter just stared back. Unflinchingly.

'So how long have you been in the 'RA, Sean?'

'Shut the fuck up.'

'Frightened are you, Sean . . . and you the man with the gun?'

'I'm not scared of fuckers like you.'

'You're not afraid that I could kill you?'

'I've got the fuckin' gun, remember.'

'Except I don't need a gun . . . plenty of weapons around here.'

'Like what?'

Winter shrugged. 'Oh, there's always a weapon handy. A brick, a belt, a pencil . . .'

'A pencil!' Fitzgerald roared with laughter. 'What the fuck would you do with a pencil? No, no, don't tell me; let's see if I can guess. You keep tapping them on the head 'til they pass out, is that about right?' More laughter followed.

Winter recalled his old instructor Nick Ashe telling him of the time he had driven a 4H 4 inches between the ribs of an assailant. 'Then again,' he suggested, 'there's a magazine.'

Fitzgerald looked disdainfully at a copy of an aviation magazine on a workbench that stretched along one of the walls. 'And what the fuck would you do with that, hope there's some jokes in it, and that your enemy would laugh himself to death?'

'Would you like me to show you?'

Fitzgerald stepped back, until he was pressed against the door. Gun wavering. 'One move . . . I fuckin' mean it.'

'I wasn't thinking of moving. I was thinking of showing you a trick that SAS soldiers are taught. You'd probably be the first 'RA man to know about it. Impress the hell out of them if you gave them a demonstration.'

Sean liked that. He grinned. Something he could tell Celia about. She liked hard men. 'Sure, why not.' Bravado in every syallable.

'I need to get up. I'll stay over here. If I don't you've only got to squeeze the trigger, like Frank said.'

Sean motioned with the barrel of the gun. Permission to move – granted.

Winter stood up slowly, enjoying the freedom of movement, felt that, given the chance, he could run for miles. Miles that would eventually work off the minor aches and pains in his body. His training had told him that the optimum escape moment was at, or very close to, the moment of capture. When you were still at your strongest. The optimum moment was also the time of maximum danger, when your assailants were most highly stressed, most irrational. He picked up the magazine from the workbench. Flexing his fingers. 'The secret,' he said quietly, 'is to roll it tight. Like this.' He demonstrated. 'You have to get it really tight. When it's compact it weighs more than a piece of wood of the same size. Then again the edges of paper are very sharp.' He looked at the Irishman, and as he maintained eye contact hooked his right foot around the leg of the chair, ready to kick it up to the gunman's left. The theory being that the eye and the gun hand would momentarily follow the flying object. He rocked gently back and forward on the balls of his left foot, timing the projected momentum.

'Then what?' Sean asked.

Seconds later the gun was skittering across the floor. Sean Fitzgerald was on his back, with Winter over him, the back of an inverted chair crushing hard against his larynx. Blood oozed from Fitzgerald's eye socket, where the end of the magazine had been jabbed home with a cutting twisting motion. The follow-up jab to the stomach had brought Fitzgerald's hands down and had left his nose undefended for the crunching upward smash of the magazine that broke it with a pain that eddied to his gut and the back of his throat. The flat-handed cymbals slap on his ears had punctured the eardrums with air implosion, so he could barely hear what Winter growled at him through clenched teeth.

'What are you going to do now, Sean?'

Except Fitzgerald couldn't answer. He was gagging under the pressure of the chair on his throat, and his temples throbbed with the pulse of blocked blood.

'What are you going to do now?' Winter's voice was guttural and subhuman. He was in the white fury necessary to key himself to put bigger men away so totally that they never thought of coming back after him.

Fitzgerald managed a strangled sound. He couldn't see well through the blood, but he caught a terrifying glimpse of Winter's wild blue eyes. He was still looking at those eyes as Winter pulled him up by his jacket, then snapped his head down sharply on the concrete floor, knocking him out.

Another two or three seconds and Winter would have made it. He was halfway to the gun when the door opened. He heard the click of a weapon being cocked. Froze where he was. He looked up and saw Frank Ryan standing very still, gun aimed at his head. Watched the trigger finger. Waiting for that smallest part of time when he would know he was dead.

Instead the Irishman smiled. 'Trouble with Sean, young and stupid. Doesn't know how to take orders . . . Back to the chair, Mr Winter. No sudden movements. Unlike the boy, I'd take pleasure in shooting you.'

Winter went slowly to the chair and sat down. 'But you've got orders to the contrary, is that what you mean?'

'Not important . . . you haven't killed my boy by chance?'

'No. Just roughed him up a little.'

Ryan looked down at Fitzgerald's bloody face. Shook his head. The expression read to Winter like: God help us. 'Half the reason I left you untied. Hoping you might try something with him. Only way he'll learn.'

'I'd say he's got a long way to go.'

'Something we agree on at least.' Ryan stepped back, opened the door and shouted out into the hangar. Seconds later two big men with skinned knuckles and hands the size of dinner plates ('minders' from London, supplied by Feargal Walsh) came in, pulled Winter roughly off the chair and tied him up. The tape went back over his eyes and mouth. No names, no conversation. Footsteps, feet being dragged, followed. The door closed. Leaving Winter to brood on the silence. Silence – a punishment every bit as effective as physical abuse.

*

At the far end of the hangar Young Feargal was inspecting the damaged left skid of the helicopter when Ryan approached him.

'Fixable is it?' Ryan asked.

'Oh sure. A bit of patching and welding. Not that the ARB would approve, but as we'll not be asking.'

'How long?'

'We'll do the paint first. While that's drying I'll get on to it. No delays. I'd reckon you can be on your way tomorrow night.'

'Apart from that I need another favour. Sean's got himself hurt. Need to get him back to Belfast.'

'How bad?'

'I don't know, but I'd rather he went to our doctor over there, you understand?'

'Not a problem, Frank. I'll get someone to fly over from Blackpool and pick him up.'

'Good man.'

'How did he hurt himself?'

'Not important. You stick to what you know best and leave me to worry about the rest.'

Young Feargal understood. Picked up on the coldness in the voice. 'I'll just be away to make the phone call then.'

15

Nancy was thinking about the early-morning phone call she had made when she boarded the Aer Lingus Viscount with Pat Cavenaugh at London's Heathrow airport. Nose pressed to the window — tiny raindrops streaming in shivery lines — watching the edges of the concrete taxiway, the grass, the side of the runway slowly accelerating. The sudden jolt. And then smoothness, and the ground falling away. A whine of machinery seconds later, followed by a dull clump as the wheels locked up in the undercarriage bays. Moments after that a two-note chime as the fasten-seatbelt and no-smoking signs went out.

Cavenaugh ordered a large whiskey (Irish, what else) at the first opportunity. She asked for coffee. By now they were above the clouds in bright afternoon sunshine. It felt warm on her face. She reached up and opened the air vent. Adjusted it until the cooling stream of air caught her forehead.

Cavenaugh took a sip of his drink. Sighed. 'A

mouthful of this, Nancy, and the poorest man is a Caesar in the purple.'

'Very poetic.'

'And you're not a one for poetry, is that what you're telling me?'

'I think you live in a world of your own, Pat. Using words to paint over the cracks of reality.'

He laughed. 'And listen to you: "Using words to paint over the cracks of reality", indeed. Allusion, a tool of the poet if ever there was one.'

'The problem with being around you too long! You've tainted us with your iambic pentameters, your allegorical references, your high-flown rhetoric, so that in the end we all sound like cheap imitations of the academics and the politicians. Talking meaningless twaddle for the pleasure of hearing our own voices. You and your kind have been at the party so long, Pat, that you've forgotten why you went in the first place.'

He thought of telling her what he had told Frank: to enjoy the journey. But he doubted she was in the mood for his homespun philosophy. Instead he leaned across and whispered: 'So tell me again, what was it exactly that you said to the American in Scotland?'

Nancy sipped her coffee. 'The truth! Easier if you have to go back over the story, isn't it?'

'No names though.'

'I may be a woman, but I'm not altogether stupid.' Her voice a low hiss. 'Of course no names. Just that Winter had been removed with the helicopter by our people for questioning. In all probability he and the helicopter would be returned by this weekend. Should Mr Gant notify anyone concerning a missing aircraft and person, he will never see his friend again . . . or the helicopter.'

'That's his name, then?'

'I told you that this morning after I'd made the call. August Gant.'

'Fancy name. Typically American, don't you think?' She didn't answer.

Cavenaugh went on. 'And he agreed? Just like that?'

'What else was he going to do?'

Cavenaugh lit a cigarette and caught the eye of the hostess. He ordered another drink.

Nancy looked out of the window at the white fluffy clouds below. Her mind wandering again. Recalling the opening lines of the phone call at 6.45 that morning to the Wick hotel.

Asking to be put through to the room of Mr Gant.

Trying to keep her voice calm. Business-like. 'Do you know a man named John Winter?'

'Sure, who's calling?' A deep, friendly voice. Like someone you've known for a lifetime.

'A friend.'

A short silence as though he was trying to remember something. He was. 'Say, do you have red hair by any chance?'

That had taken her aback. 'What?'

'Do you have red hair?'

'Yes . . . why?'

'Oh, that's okay then. Wint was telling me about you.' A smile in the voice now.

'He was what?'

'I asked him if you were beautiful, and he said you were a world-beater. Anyway, I just wanted you to know that old guys like me rarely get to speak to

155

beautiful ladies any more . . . so it's a real pleasure.'

She had felt short of breath. 'What else did he say?'

'Didn't have to. I could see it in his eyes. I told him I expected an invitation to the wedding by the way.'

She stopped breathing. 'The what?'

'Oops. Guess he hasn't asked you yet, uh?'

Why the hell was she having this conversation with a total stranger? 'Well . . . no. It's not exactly like that.'

'Ah, you're not too sure about the guy, is that it? Well let me tell you, I've met a few good men in my time, and he rates up there with the best of them. One thing I've learned in a long life is that people don't develop good hearts; they're born with them. Y'know what I mean by a good heart? Kindness. He's a real gentle man. You don't find guys like that any more. If you take my advice you'll hang on to him . . . I'm sorry, I didn't catch the name.'

'Not important.'

'Same thing he said. So what's the big secret?'

'No big secret . . . it's Nancy.'

'A genuine pleasure to meet you, Nancy . . . I'm August, but then I guess you already knew that. If you want to talk to him by the way, he's in his room.'

'No, he's not . . . that's why I'm calling.' Threat or favour? She needed to be careful how she phrased her words. 'I need your assistance, Mr Gant. It concerns his well being . . .'

The line went very quiet as she carefully outlined the practised words.

'Penny for them,' Cavenaugh said, leaning across.

She turned away from the window. Glanced at him. 'Just thinking.'

'Anything I can help with?'

'I'd like to start my life over again.'

'No easy requests with you is there, girl.'

A troubled smile. 'Did you always want to be a school teacher, Pat?'

'Sure I did.'

'And you never wanted to live anywhere else but Ireland?'

'No.'

'What about America?'

'America, the first and last great democracy if you believe their newspapers and politicians,' he said expansively. 'Went there once when I was young. New York.'

'What was it like?'

'I was there for the St Paddy's Day Parade down Fifth Avenue. Frightening. I've never seen so many drunk Irishmen in one place at one time.'

'Seriously.'

A shrug of the shoulders. 'It's different. It's impersonal. It's tough. It's a country where money rules, where people measure you by the car you drive, the house you live in, a place where people work twenty-four hours a day and sleep the rest . . . you're not still thinking about Chicago, are you?'

She stared at him, slack-mouthed. 'How did you know about that?'

'You don't remember the speech you gave us all that night in Belfast? When you stormed out on Frank?'

'No. But then I probably said a lot of things in the heat of the moment.'

'Not that that was the first time. I'd heard it all before. Frank told me years ago, how you were begging him to take you there. I think he was looking for advice.'

'And what advice did you give him?'

He turned and looked at her. Gentle. Kind. Avuncular. 'You really want to know?'

'Yes.'

'From my lips to God's ear, I told him that if you were my wife we'd be on the first westbound flight, first class all the way.'

'The truth?'

'The truth.'

She went back to staring out of the window. At the vast, empty, blue dome of sky. Wishing her memories were better. Wishing that there was something more gentle, and clean and nice to this life than war, and fighting, and killing.

As they were descending into a cloud-covered Dublin and the stewardesses were checking seat backs were in the upright and locked position and tray tables stowed, Cavenaugh asked, 'Do you want me to tell Frank that it was you who located the Sassman?'

'Is it important?'

'Not really.'

'You don't think Frank would resent the fact?'

'He's your husband. What do you think?'

What do I think? I think Frank pigeonholed women into the barefoot and pregnant category ever since the blood first rushed from his brain to his loins. His only comprehension of equality between men and women is in reaching an orgasm together. 'I think we should keep it our little secret.'

Cavenaugh patted her hand. No words. Just the beatific smile of an ageing scholar who had once belonged to a rather grand Cambridge college. A deep man, they had said, in those far-off heady days.

Then A Soldier

In these modern times (and given the opportunity) the same voices would have considered little, if anything, had changed.

16

Mouse's only mistake was being at the safe house in Cawnpore Street when Sean Fitzgerald arrived that afternoon in the care of Father Michael.

It started at about five o'clock. A bed had been made up on the sofa in the front room. A meagre coal fire burned in the grate. Sean Fitzgerald, head and left eye covered in bandages and dosed with pain killer tablets and a sleeping pill had been laid down. He was unconscious in minutes.

'So you don't know what happened?' Mouse asked, accepting the brimming glass of whiskey from the young priest.

'A car accident I think we'll call it,' Father Michael replied with a wink, and sat down opposite the old man at the kitchen table. He'd lit two of the gas rings on the stove to take the late afternoon chill off the room. The steady hiss of blue flame.

'Nobody else hurt then?'

'Not as far as I know.'

'The eye! What about the eye?'

'Don't worry, Mouse, just bruising so the doctor said.'

'Thank God for that. I remember Pat . . . Mr Cavenaugh that is, years ago . . . oh, that was terrible.'

'You did well I hear.'

'I got taken.'

'You know what I mean.'

Initially, Mouse tasted the whiskey like a connoisseur at a wine-tasting convention. A drunk's way of showing the world he was as normal as the next man. Then, when the world wasn't looking, the amber liquid disappearing faster than it had been poured. He said, 'I remember mixing "paxo" in somebody or other's kitchen . . .'

Father Michael interrupted, 'What was "paxo"?'

'A highly volatile mix of potassium chlorate and paraffin wax, ah, but sure, you'd know about that.'

The priest didn't. What was more he'd only ever heard Mouse mumble in words of one or two syllables. Potassium chlorate indeed. 'Then what happened?'

'Oh, that was a night, Father. There was Pat reciting Wolfe Tone . . . "Rise up, O dead of Ireland! And rouse her living men . . .", and young Dan Reilly – no more than fourteen he was, laughing and singing. Such a voice he had, like a bell. It went like clockwork that night . . . except for the time that is.' Mouse grinned at the thought. 'Owd Gerry and his time.'

'What happened?'

'Gerry Boyle, he was the one with this fine chronometer, bought it from a tinker at some fair in the west, so he said. Anyways, we all went according to that, anybody else lucky enough to have a watch left it at home, in case we got taken you understand . . . You wouldn't want the BA to get their hands on your personal possessions would you? Later on, when I was in prison, I found out that Gerry's great watch had been affected by the rain getting into it or something, so that it was gaining. Going haywire more like. It seems we were nearly an hour earlier than planned.'

'But it didn't really change anything!'

'Who knows . . . probably not. Anyway we drove in to the armoury in a stolen BA lorry, overcame the two guards, and began loading up with rifles and Stens and whatever else it was. Clockwork . . . except they said for a woman down the street who'd noticed something was wrong and stopped a BA officer. Pat and me were the last out . . . I locked the doors of the armoury and threw him the keys as this officer and some men came running, and shooting . . . Pat was hit in the head.' Grimy fingers toying with the glass now. Raising it to his lips. Draining the last dregs. Putting it down reluctantly on the table. Rubbing his mouth with the back of his hand. A sad smile in the watery eyes. 'Blood all over his face there was . . . terrible sight, and such a handsome man to be disfigured. They pulled him up into the lorry . . . I tried to follow but got hit in the leg. That was all. I watched the lorry driving away, bullets flying.'

'And you got taken.'

'And I'd do it all over again, Father. Just to see the look on the faces of those soldiers, when they finally broke the door down and found all the guns gone . . . but that wasn't the best bit. The best bit was how Pat auctioned the keys to the armoury in America. Raised a lot of money it did.'

'You're a hero, Mouse.'

A look as if to say: *Old soldiers and their stories,*

Then A Soldier

Father . . . always as bright as the sun that comes in the windows. I'm an old man, little more than a skeleton. Dressed in a ragged suit, and a filthy old shirt – with a frayed collar that's been turned twice – that's been on my back for weeks. You start talking like that, and they'll lock you away for sure. 'Away with you, Father. I was shaking with fear every minute. Pat Cavenaugh was the one. Planned it all. He's your hero.' A tremor in the dry, cracked lips as he glanced sheepishly at the empty glass. 'Is there any more of that whiskey going? Talking's thirsty work.'

Father Michael laughed and picked up the bottle.

Celia arrived half an hour later. Dressed up to the nines, reeking of cheap perfume. 'Grapes,' she announced, holding up a brown paper bag, 'for the wounded soldier.' It was at the same time Father Michael was leaving. She went through to the front room.

'You won't be saying anything to her,' the priest said to Mouse, as he opened the kitchen door. He didn't need to add that the woman had a mouth the size of Lough Neagh. It was common knowledge.

'What would I say, Father? Sure, I don't know a thing.'

Celia was a nymphomaniac with a mean streak. A big-busted peroxide blonde who performed for money, but also liked screwing married men and making sure their wives found out about it. Took a sadistic pleasure in breaking up homes. Other than that she doted on hero figures. Any man in the limelight was targeted by her. The hero figures, however, would soon find out that once their headline

163

status slipped, she would quickly cut them dead in the street, or the pub, or anywhere else; and should they have the misfortune to become less than ordinary, they would find her waspish tongue was the loudest in screaming condemnation.

She was sitting in a chair by the fire smoking a cigarette. She'd put a few more lumps of coal onto the embers. Was waiting for it to catch. She glanced across at Sean. Bandaged head. Sleeping soundly like a child. England, she'd heard. Sean had been shot or something. The story was going round the pubs already, and him only back a few hours on a *private* plane. She liked that. Important people flew on private planes. Sean must have done something very heroic.

He awoke an hour or so later. Dry-mouthed. Trying to make saliva. By then it was dark. His right eye picked out shadows on the walls thrown up by the now blazing fire. He turned his head slowly. It hurt. Saw somebody sitting in the chair by the hearth.

'Who's that?'

The figure stirred, slipped from the chair onto her knees, edged forward to the side of the sofa. 'Celia.'

He reached out a hand. Not quite believing. Touched her shoulder, the satiny feel of her blouse. The soft flesh of a woman beneath. His pulse quickened. 'How long have you been here?'

She said something he didn't quite catch.

'You'll need to speak louder . . . a bit of damage to the ears as well.'

She put her face next to his. 'What sort of damage? Guns and things?'

'Worse,' he lied. 'Lucky to get out with my life.'

'You've been giving OBEs to those English bastards then?' The current street slang: OBE — one behind the ear.

'Yeah . . . something like that.'

'Oh Sean.' She kissed him. Reached down to his crotch. A playful squeeze. Felt the instant hardness. 'No damage down here, then!'

His voice was a hoarse whisper. 'Is there any drink in the kitchen?'

'Whiskey you mean?'

'Why not! A celebration.'

'I looked a bit earlier. Mouse was sitting at the table when I arrived, looks like he's drunk the place dry.'

Fuck! That's all he needed. The old piss-artist wandering in just at the moment he was screwing her. Would impress her no fucking end, wouldn't it. 'Could you go and get a bottle . . . money's in my jacket.'

She found the jacket draped over the back of a chair by the window, took a five pound note from his wallet, then another two pound notes (more out of habit than wanting to steal from a hero) and put it in her handbag. She came back and kneeled in front of him. Arching her back slightly. Her breasts more prominent than ever, straining against the thin fabric of the blouse. 'Is there anything else you'll be wanting?'

He reached out and ran a hand across her body. She shivered. That excited him. He quickly unbuttoned her blouse, eased her huge breasts out of her bra, leaned into her, kissing and gently biting at her nipples, one by one. His left hand behind her back pulling her close, the other sliding under her skirt. Between her parted legs. No panties (she carried them in her handbag, she had once told him); the effect on

165

him, electric. As it was with her. He could tell she liked it. She was ramming her tongue into his mouth. Groaning without let-up. God she was a furious woman.

And just as suddenly she pulled away. Panting still. 'I can't, Sean . . . I want to . . . you know I want to . . . but not with him in the kitchen.'

'He hasn't touched you has he?'

'No, but after a skinful of whiskey he looks at me . . . you know . . . in a dirty way . . . It's just that I don't like him being near.'

'All right. You go and get the bottle . . . I'll take care of it.'

'I'll use the front door, will I?'

'Why?'

So that all the old dried-up cows down the street peeping from behind their lace curtains will see me stepping out of an IRA safe house. Then mouth slanderous insults at their henpecked husbands and anybody else within earshot. And all the while wishing they had the bodies to attract so many men. 'No reason,' she said meekly, 'It's just that I'd rather not go through the kitchen with him in there . . . You do understand, don't you, Sean?'

'There's a key for the front door on the hallstand. Don't worry, I'll kick the old bugger out.'

In the kitchen there was silence broken only by the dripping of a broken tap. Mouse was asleep at the table, head resting on his folded hands. Slackened mouth of old age. Spittle dribbling down the grey stubble of his chin. But more than that he was back at the Omagh barracks with Pat and Gerry, and young

Dan Reilly with a voice like a bell, and the gunfire was going off like firecrackers in the velvet night. And Gerry starting to climb off the back of the lorry to get him after he'd fallen. And himself lying there shouting, 'Get away, boys, I'll be fine . . . I'll be fine.' And as the lorry sped out through the gates and the dust and the smoke of the exhaust was settling, an English soldier reaching down. Grabbing at him. Fear showing in the eyes, as the wounded Irishman's chilling voice reached his ears. 'Put your hands on me you dirty bastard, and I'll tear your heart out.'

Mouse's mistake. Talking in his sleep. In his dream.

At precisely the moment Fitzgerald was grabbing him by his shoulder, pulling him from the chair. Being surprised at how light the man was. Like a sack full of feathers.

Mouse crashed on to the lino floor, letting out a cry as he did so. 'Who the fuck are you calling a dirty bastard?' Sean shouted. And when the old man didn't move, he kicked him hard in the stomach. And again. And again. 'Come on you fucker, I want you out of here, you stink the place up, so you do.'

Mouse, clutching at his stomach started to crawl towards the kitchen door. Fitzgerald's boot helping him along.

When he was outside on the pathway, Fitzgerald had a dizzy spell. Leaned against the side of the house. His head suddenly throbbing. 'Your fuckin' fault,' he screamed. 'Getting me all upset . . . and for what?' Another kick. 'For fuckin' what? You calling me a dirty bastard!' His boot kept raining kicks on the defenceless figure until his strength had gone. Then he staggered back into the kitchen and bolted the door.

He ran some cold water in the kitchen sink. Dabbed it at his sweat-covered face. His neck. Groaned at the pain in his head. Then made his way very slowly to the front room. Sat down on the sofa staring at the dancing flames in the grate. Thought of the Sassman in England. Another chance, that's all he needed. One more chance to show Frank that he could handle things.

After all wasn't it Frank who had told him he was impressed with his background? That he had the makings of a good soldier.

A good soldier. Sean Fitzgerald: the sixth child in a family of eighteen. His grandfather had been an IRA man in the thirties. He, Sean, who had left school at fifteen and worked as a labourer for a fruit merchant. In 1969 during the riots he turned up at the barricades and then joined the Fianna. During the gun battle around St Mathew's in the Short Strand he ran ammunition to Billy McKee and his men.

He denied himself those other thoughts: the "B" Special, Tommy Morris, from Crossmaglen earlier in the year. How he'd been unable to hold the gun steady at the back of the man's hooded head and squeeze the trigger.

And that very morning – being beaten unconscious by an unarmed man he was guarding with a gun. No forgiveness in Frank's eyes for that. Even though he had tried to explain that the Sassman had tricked him. Frank's parting words: 'Go home, Sean, for Jesus' sake go home . . . you're a fuckin' liability.'

Hip-swinging Celia – or 'Miss Breastfast' as she was called by the lecherous young men who congregated in pubs and invariably (at the three-pint and on stage) got round to discussing local girls, and which one had the biggest tits (the six-pint stage was when they grew really brave and the anatomical discussion moved south) – came back a minute or two later. Poured the whiskey. Undressed them both in front of the fire. Told him he was an iron man. A hero. That he was hung like a donkey (they said Celia had a way with the words). Things got better after that.

The slashing rain of the early hours had stopped, leaving a leaden sky to tramp slowly eastwards, clearing the area around dawn. By mid-morning a weak sun was trying to penetrate the thin fog lying over Belfast. The television forecaster had promised an exceptionally warm September afternoon, due to the extension of an Azores high-pressure system that was now prevailing over the area. Father Michael, whose faith gravitated in other directions, arrived at the red-bricked end-of-terrace house in a raincoat, and carrying a rolled umbrella. He was calling to check on the well-being of Sean Fitzgerald. Following instructions.

The paint-peeling, weather-warped wooden door set in the wall at the end of the terrace was off the latch. A few inches open. As he pushed it further he saw what at first appeared to be a bundle of rags and a big white dog lying on the dark brick pathway. The dog was whining gently in its throat. When it saw the priest the whining was replaced by a deep threatening growl and bared teeth. It scrambled to its feet. Rocking a little unsteadily, like an old arthritic person who had remained in one position for too long, or a drunk experimenting in equilibrium as he negotiated the first faltering steps from his local pub. Even so, the clouded eyes were fixed on the apparent intruder. Hackles up. Belligerent. Threatening.

It was when the dog got up that Father Michael saw the hollow-cheeked grey face. The bluish-tinged lips. Mouse.

Father Michael held out a hand to the dog. Palm upwards. The voice soft. Gentle. 'It's all right . . . It's all right . . . He's my friend too.' The umbrella was arced back, ready to take a swipe if the animal attacked.

It didn't. Instead, it edged away very slowly. Watchful. Teeth still bared. Ears pricked.

The priest kneeled down beside the old man, tried to wake him. Hopeful. Prayerful. *The faith that gravitated in other directions*. 'C'mon, Mouse. What did I tell you about getting so drunk that you go falling over and hurting yourself.' A desperate little smile of optimism as he felt for a pulse. Not with your thumb, Michael, with the tips of your fingers, he told himself, as he tried to remember a procedure that was some way outside his calling. Was that a beat? He tried increasing the pressure, holding his breath for a moment as he did so. Desperately searching for a sign of life. The little smile was now serious concentration. 'Sure, I don't know how you do it, Mouse. One small one is enough for me. Perhaps after this we'll have to think about taking better care of you. What you've got to realize is you're not the young man you once were, taking a bottle or more of that stuff can't be good for you . . . You know I'm right . . . '

He stopped talking as the lump came to his throat. It came in the same moment he realized there was no pulse. No life. He lowered the chill, almost childlike hand back across the body. Fought back the tears.

That was when the dog started whining all over again.

17

I was born in Prague. Raised in Odessa on the Black Sea.

Winter's torturers left him again that morning. He was not unconscious. That had been earlier, through the previous day and night. He felt detached from the pain in his feet. Was aware of what had been going on around him. He thought he was still in control of himself. He also thought that there was no longer any point in them beating him because the pain had begun to cancel itself out. He could not stand on his feet any more. He could see them in the morning light that came from the high window though, grotesque, bloody and swollen. He could not count how many times in those hours they had thrashed the soles of his feet with the heavy electrical flex. And how many times he had slipped into unconsciousness.

Now, with the tape removed from his eyes and mouth, and the bindings from his hands and feet, he had been left huddled on the concrete floor of the small cell-like room. Feeling the pain spreading from the soft rippled flesh of the soles of his feet, into his ankles. And shins. And calves. And up through his thighs, into his guts.

He understood the technique. This was the beginning of things. No questions. They were softening him. Beating him and hurting him. The questions would come when they thought the moment was right. When they hoped to get the answers they sought.

The pain throbbed in him. Welled in him. Enough to be unable to crawl a few feet to a plastic bowl of water he had been left. The second day and no food, but he'd got over that. Suffered the hunger pains that turned to writhing stomach cramps. Talked himself through it. As he did the stench from the bucket they had placed in the corner of the cell. Urine and faeces combining to foul the air that he breathed.

He tried to focus on Nick Ashe's course on Transcendental Meditation. Nick and his eastern mysticism. Close your eyes. Repeat your mantra. Over, and over, and over, and over, and over. Concentrate on the third eye. Try! It really is there. Like summoning a spirit – an occult pickpocket who has slit the soul's silk, drained the rejected dreams of a lifetime. Your mantra still humming. Like car tyres on creation's highway. No! Like nothing. Like nothing at all. Like . . .

It lasted a few minutes; then he found his thoughts wandering again as the pain coursed through his body. He saw Nancy standing by his side that night in Wick . . . at the harbour wall . . . moonlight on the water. Heard her voice. Felt her presence. Her footsteps ringing on the pavement as she walked beside him, along the deserted streets and through the dark alleyways. The look in her green eyes as he said goodnight; the panic, fear, mistrust, for a second gone – the real Nancy returning his gaze. What was it he had seen? Friendship? Love? The frames clattering on, like an old grainy black and white movie. Then seeing her lying, fast asleep, in his bed. Her beauty taking his breath away. Seeing himself bending down. Kissing her forehead. Breathing her perfume. A voice telling him that she would never have lied.

All trailing to another voice. A darker voice: *What did you expect of her? She is the enemy. Not only is she the enemy, she's a married woman. A Catholic. You're a fool, John Winter, to think that she would help you. You of all people!*

And all the time, in the last safe place in his mind – the farm near Cader Idris – working on the story over and over and over again; substituting part of Dorcas Volk's background, her fireside stories when he was a boy soldier on leave: *The days of the Northern Phantom (as she called his father, because he came from northern Germany) are now over. You understand, boy? Now I will tell you a much nicer story.*

Whose story?

My story, of course. Whose did you think?

Were you loved?

What a strange question, boy. Of course I was loved. Why do you ask?

I . . . I wondered what it was like.

The story first, then I will tell you about love. It was a long time ago. I was born in Prague. Raised in Odessa on the Black Sea . . .

He was sinking into unconsciousness again. The

pain ebbing away. A few minutes' sleep. He would feel better after that. Just a few minutes . . .

That was when the door crashed open and the two torturers returned. He lay still, looking through shuttered eyelids. Saw the pale faces. Saw the one with the heavy electrical flex, beads of sweat standing out on his forehead, as though it was already the end of another session.

'Is he conscious?' the first voice asked.

'He soon will be,' the second replied with conviction.

'What's the point? I'll bet money he's not goin' to talk.'

'He's a hard man, so he is . . . I'll grant him that.'

'So, what's the point?'

'Frank and his games, is all.'

'What sort of games?'

'You ask too many questions. We're taking him to Ireland tonight.'

'Then what?'

'What do you think? Then we kill the bastard.'

'How?'

The voice dropping to a conspiratorial whisper. 'I overheard Frank talking to Pat Cavenaugh on the phone. You'd never believe what the old silver fox has come up with!'

'Try me.'

Creaking hinges. The sound of a door opening slowly. 'What the fuck are you two doing? You're not paid to stand and talk. I need answers to questions . . . got it?' Frank Ryan's voice. The door slammed.

'You're not paid to stand and talk,' mimicked the first voice bitterly. 'Wherever did he get the notion we were gettin' fucking paid?'

'A working class movement right enough,' the second voice said thoughtfully. Or was it cynically?

The voices stopped. A bottle top being unscrewed! The bottle being passed. Back and forth. Back and forth. Until it was empty.

The shuffling of feet on concrete.

A rush of air.

Winter felt the huge, calloused hands grabbing at him. Smelled the whiskey fumes. The ice cold water in his face would be next. Then . . . the questions.

He took a deep breath. The truth. The whole truth. Nothing but the truth. Framed the words in his mind. *My name is John Winter. I was born in Prague. Raised in Odessa on the Black Sea.*

18

The weather forecast for that Tuesday evening was good. Clear skies. Full moon. The prognosis, towards the end of the period at least, showing a weak cold occlusion with light to moderate precipitation passing through Northern Ireland. Not a factor for their flight.

Indeed, it was a smooth, velvety night, as the Agusta Bell 205 doglegged the southern end of the Isle of Man, a few miles south of Spanish Head. Teach Cusack turned down the instrument lights to minimum intensity, allowing his night vision to improve. Off to the right he could see a brightly lit ferry boat and what might have been a few fishing boats. The altimeter hovered around 100 feet. The helo continued steadily on course, maintaining 100 knots. The noise and vibrations inside the machine, horrendous to the uninitiated. To any ground (or sea) observers within a 3-mile radius, a flat *whop-whop-whop* beat of the big rotor blades.

Ryan adjusted the boom mike of his headset closer to his lips. He had been watching the American ever since take-off. Low level north of Blackpool until they were out over the sea. Skimming the waves. Picking up the edge of the airway between Liverpool and Belfast, a place where possible primary radar returns might not be questioned. He was a little apprehensive but felt better as dusk set in and they climbed marginally higher. 'You okay?'

Cusack, who had swallowed an amphetamine an hour or so before take-off, was feeling ace. *Okay*? Shit, he was invincible. Jesus, he could make this bird do things that even the manufacturers hadn't considered. Fuck, he didn't even need a helo to fly, could do it all on his ownsome. Cool, the best part – no gooks shooting at him. 'I'm fine, Frank. Just fine.'

Ryan relaxed. He had to admit that after the horrendous night flight down from Scotland, he had had his doubts about flying with Cusack again. Especially when he buggered up the landing and damaged a skid. 'Getting used to it, I suppose.'

'You got it, Frank. I mean, the other night was the first time I'd been in one of these babies since 'Nam. You need time to get used to it . . . know what I mean? Then again . . . the weather, man, now that was just plain mean. Makes tonight's ride a piece of cake, huh?'

'As long as we don't get intercepted by British Army helicopters going in.'

'Why we're using their coastal low-level route for ingress . . . By the time they figure out it ain't one of theirs we'll be long gone. Landed. Covered up with camouflage. Drinking the pint of that Guinness you've been promising me.'

'What's the next checkpoint?'

'Portaferry fan marker according to the airways

chart. Once by that, we swing left and head down to Dundrum Bay. I'll stay off the coast on that leg, we wouldn't want to hit the Mourne Mountains would we?' Shit, he was feeling good. Spacey.

The flight continued to go like clockwork. Picking up the Newcastle NDB. Seeing the lights along the coast: Glasdrumman, Annalong, Ballymartin, Kilkeel. Across Dundrum Bay. Inland now, towards the western side of Drogheda.

Ryan knew the area reasonably well. With an Ordnance Survey map across his knees and a clear moonlight night it wasn't too difficult. 'Okay, I've got the River Boyne . . . come right a bit . . . bit more . . . steady.'

'What's next?'

'Little town called Trim, about twenty miles. After that we come left onto a southeasterly heading. Follow the R154 road for seven miles.'

'Those lights ahead! Is that Trim?'

'No. Navan. We come ninety degrees left there and follow the river. After about three miles it turns back onto this heading. Lead us straight into Trim.'

'Lose the river and we could be in trouble you mean?'

'Lot of lights down there . . . easy enough to turn at the wrong town.'

Two minutes later the oil pressure needle began flickering. Cusack said, 'Oh, shit!' with such feeling that Ryan thought they were about to hit something. Like the Hill of Slane – even though he could see the rising ground off to his right.

'What? What is it?' A moment's panic.

'Oil pressure.'

Ryan followed Cusack's pointed finger. Watched the flickering needle. Getting lower down the green scale.

'How far we got to run to the farm, Frank?'

'About twenty-five miles . . . what d'you think?'

'Once that needle drops into the caution range – that's the yellow arc – we'd better consider landing.'

'And if it gets into the red?'

'Then we don't get a choice . . . engine failure . . . autorotation . . . and whatever's beneath us is where we end up . . . Could be entertaining . . . Got a cigarette?'

'A cigarette!' As though this was hardly the moment to be thinking about having a smoke. When you were facing possible engine failure. And crashing.

'Sure . . . one of the few vices I got. I would'a asked for a woman, but as we don't have one on board I'll go with the second choice.'

Ryan lit a cigarette and handed it to him.

'Thing is, Frank. You keep me pointing in the right direction, and I'll keep an eye on the oil pressure and a lookout for a suitable landing site below.'

Cusack eased the helo up to a more comfortable 1,000 feet.

Ryan noticing they were climbing, said, 'What about radar?'

'Not going to make much difference now, we're out of the army low-level corridor from way back. We're just local traffic if anybody's looking on radar. Besides it's goin' to be easier to see the temporary flare path from up here . . . then again, if we lose the engine we'll have that bit longer to say our prayers and hope that the Lord is having a good day and is prepared to forgive us our transgressions.' Jeez, he really was enjoying this. Nobody could kill him the way he was feeling. He was fucking invincible.

The minutes passed. Following the dog-legging river. Glistening silver in the moonlight.

Ryan on the edge of his seat. Ever checking his watch. Watching intently for landmarks below. Mentally counting off the miles. Finally: 'Okay, that's Trim, in your one o'clock. Come left on to a south-easterly heading.'

The oil pressure was dropping further now. Cusack figured they had a few minutes at the most. He started looking around for flat terrain. Wind direction? That was something else. If push came to shove, he'd guess westerly. 'Okay, Frank, I've got what looks like a clear patch coming up in my one o'clock. Near a wooded area. I'm going down to take a look-see. If it's level enough I'll try and get us down there.'

Ryan, who had been keeping a visual on the narrow R154 road for the past minute or so, suddenly saw a white flashing light. Then green. Then white again. 'Contact the farm,' he said. 'A bit to the left . . . about a mile . . . maybe two.'

Cusack looked left and down. A few seconds quartering the area. Then he had it. 'Okay. One run, straight in, that's all we got. You sure it's not compromised?'

'It was okay when I spoke to Pat before take-off.'

'Your call, Frank! Once I put this baby down, it's staying down. We try and keep the weight off the skids and on the rotors for a quick getaway, that's the time we're going' to lose the engine.'

'You're sure?'

'EYEFULL. One of those left-field acronyms that stands for 'immutable law of fucked-up luck' . . . I'm sure.'

Ryan watched the white-green lights growing ever closer. 'We'll land,' he said.

'Roger, that,' Cusack replied and began his descent.

Car headlights came on as Cusack commenced his approach. The headlights were as previously planned. Pointing into wind. He passed what appeared to be a white farmhouse. Dark trees. No high wires that he could see. Then turned back onto a north-westerly heading. Final approach. The headlights away from him now, capturing a clear area of ground with a big white cross marked out. A last glance at the oil pressure. The needle was nudging into the red. 'Fuck. Fuck. Fuck. Keep turnin' and burnin', baby . . . do that and I'll love you forever.'

And on a night like no other, Teach Cusack's luck held.

Pulling back on the cyclic, working the rudder pedals. C'mon baby, just a little bit more, steady, steady, steady. Bump – bump. They were down. The American, grinning from ear to ear, went rapidly through the shut down checks. The thin, dying whine of the jet engine outside. The faint scent of hot engines and jet fuel. Aviator country.

The car headlights that had lit up the LZ went out, at the same moment Ryan moved back to the side door. Pistol ready. The helo landing light was still on as a man came quickly over a wall. Cusack saw he was armed. There was a Rusty-Dallas-Mafia-bad-karma-moment before he recognized Pat Cavenaugh. Then he started laughing. Hallelujah!

Ryan was out of the helicopter, ducking his head as he cleared the still turning rotor blades. Thankful to be on the ground.

Cavenaugh greeted him. 'Welcome home, Frank. Good flight?'

'Oil pressure problems,' Ryan complained.

'Like what?'

'Like practically nil.'

'Does our American friend think it's fixable?'

'He's going to phone Young Feargal and explain the problem. Thinks we might need spares.'

'Well, at least you're here.'

Ryan, relieved at losing the knot of anxiety in his gut from the very real fear of a forced landing during the preceding minutes, managed an uncharacteristic laugh.

Cavenaugh looked at the dark shape of the helicopter. 'On board is he?'

'Feargal's boys have got him in the back.'

Cavenaugh signaled to a dark figure that had followed him over the wall. 'Go and give the boys a hand, Billy. You know where to take him, and when that's done make sure you get the camouflage netting over the machine . . . This way, Frank.'

'What is this place exactly?'

'One of those battery-chicken farms. You know, the places they force-feed chickens to fatten them up quickly. Don't bother going inside one of the long huts to check, the stink of chicken shit is unbearable. Put me off eating them for life . . . Anyway, the owner and his wife have moved into a caravan for the few days we're here, so we've more or less got the house to ourselves. '

They climbed over the low dry-stone wall and followed a dirt path towards the farmhouse. The smells of silage and manure. Oceans of fresh air. 'Got a little surprise for you,' Cavenaugh remarked, a few yards further on.

'What sort of surprise?'

'Your wife's back.'

Ryan stopped. Grabbing Cavenaugh by the shoulder as he did so. 'Here?'

'She's gone into Dublin to see her sister. She'll be back later.'

Ryan took a packet of cigarettes from his pocket. Offered one to Cavenaugh. 'I don't think that was a good idea, Pat. You know her sister's record.'

'That was years ago, a bit of drug dealing, so what? Besides she got off with probation didn't she? How long was it? Two years?'

'Not the point, she's known by the Gardai. We wouldn't want anything leading them here, would we? Anyway, I wasn't altogether referring to that.'

Cavenaugh accepted the light from the match shielded in Ryan's cupped hands. 'The collaboration thing, then! Sleeping with the enemy, wasn't it? And as I recall she had her head shaved and was tied to a lamppost with a big sign advertising her sins. That drove her out of Belfast. What else do you want?'

'I don't want my wife associating with her.'

'I'll have a word with her then, not that I think she'll take a blind bit of notice . . . Anyway you never asked me how she was.'

They started walking again. Picking their way slowly along the darkened path.

Still the fucking comedian, Pat! She walked out on me, remember. Why should I be asking after her? Because she's decided to come back? 'Where's she been all this time?'

'Working as a barmaid.'

'Where?'

'England.'

'Where in England?'

'Aldershot.'

Army town. He knew that much. Felt a slow anger rising within him. His wife a barmaid to the enemy! And what else? He didn't like the pictures that that thought conjured up. 'I assume she made contact with you, and you told her we had the Sassman?'

'Very perceptive.'

And now she comes crawling home. Sure, Frank'll understand. Always a soft touch. 'Aren't I ever.'

Over supper, an hour later, Cavenaugh outlined the operation to Ryan. They were alone in the kitchen: low-beamed ceiling, peat fire burning in the range. The other men were eating in the living room.

'Craogh Parc on Thursday night. There's a football match. It's being televised. Apparently President Nixon's going to be a guest of the Prime Minister.' Cavenaugh pushed a copy of the *Irish Times* across the table. He had circled the headline – 'Presidential Visit to Craogh Parc' – in red ink.

Ryan looked up from the plate of stew he was eating. Stopped. Fork midway between plate and mouth. Why did he get the feeling he was not going to like this? 'And?'

'We take the Sassman overhead at five hundred feet at nineteen fifteen hours, fifteen minutes after the game's started, and drop him. At the same time, exactly, an IRA press release will be transmitted to the usual sources. Something like: "This is the body of an undercover SAS man, an enemy of the Irish people, who infiltrated the ranks of the Provisional Irish Republican Army in September, 1969, and murdered the innocent Ryan children in a field near Crossmaglen in February of this year. This is not an allegation. This is a statement of fact. This body of our sworn enemy is delivered with a specific message to the British government – *For every Irish man, woman, or child, shot by your army we will respond by taking the life of a British soldier.*" The point of the exercise is that the game's being televised. You've got to imagine the size of the audience that it will reach. Education for the masses, Frank. It's about time the rest of the world got a crash course on the continuing plight of the Irish people.'

There was silence save for the muted voices of the others in the next room. Ryan lowered the fork back to the plate. Felt a spasm of irritation. Too difficult. Too dangerous. *For those on the helicopter at least.* 'A bold plan, I'll give you that. But do you think the rest of the world really gives a shit one way or the other?'

'It's up to us to make them care.'

'And you think dropping an enemy soldier onto a soccer pitch in front of thousands of fans, and possibly hundreds of thousands of television viewers, is going to win us sympathy?'

'He'll be dead before we drop him. Bullet in the head. So we'll simply be returning the body for military burial . . . I can add that to the press release.'

'And you think the media will report the facts? You know those bastards, not an honest bone in their fucking bodies. They'll twist and contort it to suit their own ends.'

Then A Soldier

'It's about a united Ireland.' Cavenaugh the preacher again. Passion in the voice. The glittering eye. The body language. 'You know as well as anybody that there's no possibility of lasting peace coming to the North while the British link remains fixed and immovable. Stormont will fall . . . maybe not this year, but soon. Then what?' The lifted hand, the wagging finger emphasizing the rhetorical question. 'Then, Britain will preside over a political vacuum. There is no more stark indication that a society has failed than the presence of combat troops on the streets. It's about being brave, Frank. Seizing the moral high ground. How many Americans, for instance, realize how many centuries this country has been occupied by the British? One in every ten thousand? One in every hundred thousand? What about the other vassal states of the British Empire? Practically all handed back.'

'The old, "understanding that war is an extension of politics" argument,' Ryan murmured. He'd heard it all before.

'And strategy by this teaching becomes a crude form of economic theory. Of course. Hit them where it hurts. In the wallet. Systematic destruction of specific parts of their mainland infrastructure. Killing their soldiers along the way. Until the British man on the street rebels against the ever-increasing tax burden needed to foot the bill. Votes the traditional political parties out of office, decides it's time to join the twentieth century before it's all over.'

'A lovely thought.'

'The increasing British tourist industry,' Cavenaugh went on. 'The day tourists are afraid to come to England because of the threat of being caught up in

187

war and bombing and killing, is the day the politicians will start listening.'

Ryan raised a hand. 'You don't need to sell me, Pat.'

'No, no . . . my apologies. Me on my soapbox again, eh, Frank.'

'Going back to the Thursday night drop. We could have a problem with security.'

'For instance?'

'If President Nixon is going to be at the game there'll be US Army helicopters on patrol around the area.'

'The same sort of thing you'll be in.'

'Except we don't have the correct callsign and frequencies.'

'Which is why we'll be conducting a diversionary attack on the border fifteen minutes earlier, at exactly nineteen hundred hours.'

'And where might that be?'

'RUC post at Bantrain.'

'And what do we hit it with? Sticks and stones?'

'The arms shipment last February.'

'What about it? We got the stuff across the border didn't we?'

'Not all. We kept a consignment of mortar bombs here, plus a few rifles and ammunition.'

'Here? Dublin you mean?'

'No. *Here*. Out in the chicken sheds.'

Ryan pushed his plate aside. Let out a low whistle. Mortars! He liked the sound of that. Hitting power. 'So we find a suitable launch site on the southern side of the border, and knock out the RUC depot in the North.'

'The site's already been located. Except we need a mortar expert.'

'You've got one. Me.'

'No good. You'll be here running the final briefing for the helicopter mission.'

'So what do you propose?'

'Gerry Faul. He'll be arriving in the morning . . . Any objections?'

'No, no. Gerry'll do fine.'

'Good. So are we going to take the boys into Trim for the Guinness you promised them?'

'Who'll stay and guard the Sassman?'

'Billy.'

'Billy who?'

'Billy Costello . . . one of my Sligo boys.'

'He's good enough is he?'

'He's a member of the Legion of Mary.' A lay organization dedicated to good works. Ryan missed the irony of it.

'What sort of fucking soldier, I mean?' Impatience in every word.

The hand reaching for the eye patch. Habits of old age. 'Very good. Like Gary Cooper in *High Noon*. Reminds me of you, when you were young. Eyes of a gunfighter.'

Ryan snorted. 'Save your flattery for the women, Pat, the silly cows love that sort of thing.'

'You're a hard man, Frank.'

Ryan scratched his nose. 'You've still got that house in Sligo, then?'

'Left to me by my father. My sister takes care of it for me.'

'Do you ever go there?'

'A week or two in the summer.'

'Hardly worth keeping for that, is it?'

'Has its uses. You know who stays at Classiebawn

Castle, just up the road from me, every summer?'

'No.'

'Earl Mountbatten and his family . . . Spends a lot of time boating.'

'British establishment in spades, eh?'

'Always nice to have targets for the day we need to bring attention to the "cause".'

'So when are we going to stiff the old bastard?'

'Perhaps never. Just a name on a list, Frank. There's a lot more before him.'

'Assuming of course we can get past their security and get lucky.'

'We only have to be lucky once . . . They have to be lucky all the time.'

As they were walking out of the house some minutes later Cavenaugh said, 'Had some sad news from Belfast today.'

'About what?' Half-interest in the voice.

'Mouse died. Father Michael found him outside the house this morning, lying on the pathway.'

'The drink was it?'

'I don't know. They're doing an autopsy. But more than likely.' Softer then. 'He was a good man in his time though . . . one of the best.'

Ryan didn't answer, his good mood at getting this far with the operation, suddenly gone. He blamed his wife. He was thinking about her again. The news that she was here! The news about where she had been these past months. What she'd been doing. He was by nature a jealous man. The thoughts running riot in his mind at that moment only fuelling the impotence he felt.

Cavenaugh said, 'Talking of good men, what

happened to Sean, you never told me the full story.'

'Sean? Oh that's easy enough. He thought he could take on the Sassman in an unfair fight. Like, he was armed. The Sassman wasn't. No need to tell you who won.'

'Was it necessary?'

'Of course it was necessary. Only way we're going to turn him into a fighting man. He's got to learn by his mistakes. I'm not always going to be at his back to save him, am I? No pain, no gain. Isn't that what they say?'

The sound of the engine woke him. The slamming of a car door. He looked across at the thin-curtained window to see if there was daylight. It seemed not.

The pain wasn't as bad tonight. Even so, he had tried standing earlier, when they had brought him food. Left the tray on the bare wooden floor just inside the doorway. A tin plate of stew. No fork or spoon. He'd pulled himself off the bed, wincing as his feet touched the floor. He'd cried out as he lowered himself to the floor. Finally, his back against the edge of the bed, legs stretched out before him he picked up the plate. Burned his fingers trying to get the food to his mouth. When he was finished there was a tin mug of water. After that he had inspected the room. About fifteen feet by nine. About ten feet in height. Heavy wooden door. Curtained window at the opposite end of the room. Whitewashed walls. A bare light bulb – low watts – hanging by about 18 inches of braided flex from the ceiling. The narrow bed and mattress the only furniture.

The sound of voices suddenly from outside the house. He had struggled painfully to his feet, switched off the light. Hobbled on his heels across the room. As he did so the sound of car doors slamming. A car engine starting. He reached the tiny window and eased the curtain back. Red tail-lights disappearing down a driveway. He tried the window again, as though perhaps imagining the welding seams that had blackened the cream-coloured metal window frame in making a prison cell were not really there.

He had staggered back across the room. Tried the door. It was locked. Made it to the bed. Sat down. Relief flooded through his body. He lay back on the mattress.

Question: Could he unlock the door?

Question: How many guards downstairs? Outside his door even?

Question: Even if he got through the door and overpowered the guards, was there another vehicle outside?

Question: If not, how far could he get on foot?

Question: Get where? Where was he? Ireland?

That was when exhaustion had taken over and he had fallen asleep.

Now he had woken up. Annoyed with himself. Realizing it was too late. The car had returned. Or had it? He had counted four doors slamming on the car that left. This time only one.

The sound of footsteps in the corridor outside the room. Two sets of footsteps to be precise. A raised voice. Female. He lay still and closed his eyes. Heard the key in the lock. The door opening. Trying to assess what chance he had of overpowering two guards. Patience, he warned himself. The click of the light switch. He opened his eyes very slowly. Looked up.

Caught his breath. An automatic rifle was pointing directly into his face. Close enough to smell the gun oil. An olive-skinned young man with long black hair, said very quietly, 'One wrong move and I'll empty the magazine into you. Got it?' Quiet voice equals cool-headed killer. A professional, cool-headed killer. Object lesson: Proceed with caution.

Winter, acting the frightened man, simply nodded.

The young man half-turned his head without taking his eyes off Winter. 'Here he is if you want a look.'

Nancy Ryan appeared at the gunman's shoulder. Face pale. Scrubbed clean of make-up. No recognition in the eyes.

Winter found himself looking up at a total stranger. She was like a dream. But dreamed and gone.

She leaned forward suddenly and hissed. 'Bastard . . . you fucking bastard.'

The young man pulled her back. 'He's the Sassman that killed your kids, that right?'

'I've seen enough.'

'You want me to rough him up a bit for you?'

'You? What the fuck's it got to do with you? My husband'll take care of that.' She turned and stormed away down the corridor.

The gunman looked temporarily stunned at the venom in the woman's voice. But only temporarily. The cool look returned almost instantly. No more words. Then the door slamming closed. A key grating in the lock. Footsteps dopplering into the distance.

The dark voice ebbing back. *What did you expect of her? She is the enemy . . . You're a fool . . . Thinking that she would help you . . . You of all people!*

*

Later, some time after midnight, Cavenaugh, Ryan and the rest of them came back. A little the worse for drink. As they tumbled into the house Billy the gunman mentioned that Mrs Ryan was back. Ryan grinned and to the shouted encouragement of the others went up the stairs two at a time.

When he tried her door he found it locked. He beat on it a few times, calling her name, finally gave up and stumbled back down the stairs. He went to the kitchen and made himself a cheese sandwich.

He slept on the kitchen floor that night.

The other men didn't say a word.

19

Cold, oily darkness. A solitary window partially covered by sackcloth. An ancient paraffin lamp hanging on a hook from a ceiling beam. An inspection lamp rigged up over the workbench area – electricity supplied by an extension lead from the battery chicken sheds. An uneven earth floor, hard as stone. Rusting tractor parts stacked in piles at odd intervals. Suspended from another crossbeam, a block and tackle, a chain and hook.

Ryan had been busy in the workshop, about 50 yards from the farm, since six o'clock that morning. Thoughts of Nancy pushed to the back of his mind as he happily engaged in his trade. Happy enough that every once in a while he whistled a pop song to himself. Something that reminded him of his RAF days, working on aircraft in huge cavernous hangars. A place where fitters of all trades went about their work, singing or whistling. But more than that it was vindication. Vindication for nearly ten years of his life given to his enemy whilst he learned a trade that would benefit the 'RA. Freezing his arse off in Nissen hut barracks where coke stoves at either end warmed only the immediate area. Dragging himself off to lectures on dark winter nights to learn enough to pass his corporal tech's board, when he would rather have gone to the local village pub, or the NAAFI, or even the camp Astra – the 'flicks'. Vindication indeed. Now, at last, after all those years, he was on the threshold of making a significant mark for his army.

The ten mortar bombs were concealed under a couple of tons of chicken dung nearby. The rest of the items were strewn around the workshop floor. An 81 millimetre practice bomb was dangling from 4 feet of baling wire, firmly down a deep drain just below the workshop, being fished out occasionally for measurements and trials.

It had all the earmarks of a successful day.

Gerry Faul arrived at the workshop a short while later carrying two steaming mugs of tea. Early forties. Stocky build. Black hair and long sideburns, smelling heavily of Brilliantine. Gerry, a throwback to the 1950s 'teddy boy' era. Black-framed Buddy Holly spectacles. He was dressed in workman's overalls. Black boots, highly buffed toecaps – the only clue that he was an ex-soldier. Like Frank Ryan he had served in the British forces in his younger days, in his case Army. Like Ryan, he knew a thing or two about weapons and bomb making. 'Beautiful morning, Frank.'

Ryan pushed back the welding visor, shut off the gas tanks, and wiped his hands on a length of old toweling. 'Morning, Gerry. Yeah, not bad.'

'Looks like you've been busy.'

'Let's hope it fits. What sort of vehicle have we got?'

'Caravanette. High back. Burning a bit of oil, but it'll do for what we need it for.' He surveyed Ryan's work. Five steel tubes in rows of three and two were set against a double triangle of angle-iron frame. Various tags and brackets were spot welded on in carefully marked places, and pre-drilled bolt holes. 'Nice bit of welding.'

Ryan lifted the whole rig down using the towelling and pushed it upside down under the workbench, throwing in several lengths of angle iron to add to the confusion. A tractor gearbox casing lay in the corner of the workshop; he lifted it onto the workbench, and surrounded it with an offering of tools, giving it a being-worked on look. Lastly he threw the grating back over the drain and kicked a boot-full of chicken-soiled straw over it. 'It'll do. We'll drive up to the border this afternoon. Check out the launch site.'

'I stopped in Bantrain last night,' Faul said conversationally. 'Checked out the RUC station.'

Ryan took a mouthful of tea. 'God, I needed that. Anything out of the ordinary up there?'

'Depends. What time's the hit?'

'Nineteen hundred hours tomorrow.'

'Cutting it a bit fine.'

'Cutting what a bit fine?'

'There's a Salvation Army hall next door to the RUC post. Tomorrow afternoon there's a choir performing there.'

'You sure?'

'Sure I'm sure.'

'What time does it finish?'

'I didn't check. Starts at one o'clock though.'

Ryan picked up his donkey jacket off the workbench

and pulled it over his denim shirt, gave one final
glance around the shop, before pulling the door
closed. He looped the rough string knot over the peg.
High-tech security, he thought to himself with a rueful
smile, *a wooden peg and a string knot* – only in
fucking Ireland. 'What sort of choir?'

'Salvation Army.'

A deep frown. 'I guessed that, Gerry. I mean, is it
men or women. What?'

'Kids mainly, from Derbyshire according to the
poster.'

A desperate shake of the head. 'Shit.'

'Going to cause problems?'

'I don't know. I'll check with Pat.'

Faul motioned towards the white Bedford high-back
caravanette, painted with the legend: *County Meath
Medical Health Authority – Blood Transfusion
Service.* 'You want to check the vehicle?'

'We'll do it after breakfast.'

'I've found a good place to stash it for twenty-four
hours up by the border. Foolproof.'

But Ryan wasn't listening. His thoughts had
returned to Nancy. A slow anger building up in him
again. A barmaid at Aldershot! If he found out she'd
been screwing BA fuckers, he'd kill her.

He found Cavenaugh in the sitting room reading a
newspaper. The silver-haired Irishman was dressed in
a dark grey suit, white shirt, and dark blue knitted tie.
Save for the black eye-patch, which gave him a slightly
roguish air, he looked more like a banker about to
leave for his office in the city.

Ryan closed the door. 'We might have problems, Pat.'

Cavenaugh looked up unhurriedly from the newspaper. 'And such a lovely morning I was thinking.' The smile of a man without a care in the world slowly dissolving. 'What sort of problems might they be?'

Ryan joined him at the dining table. They were alone. The rest of the men had been fed and had left to carry out specific tasks.

'Gerry stopped off in Bantrain last night. Seems there's a Salvation Army kids' choir performing a concert there tomorrow afternoon. The problem is that the Salvation Army hall is next door to the RUC station.'

Cavenaugh closed the newspaper, folded it neatly, and placed it on the end of the table. Rubbed his chin thoughtfully. 'Yes . . . I'd heard about that. I thought it was today. Gerry's sure it's tomorrow afternoon?'

'I'm just telling you what he told me.'

'But you're thinking it might conflict with the mortar attack?'

'Last thing we fucking need. Hitting a soft target like that.'

'Quite right, Frank, quite right. I'll tell you what; I'm planning to go back to Belfast this evening . . . Mouse's funeral tomorrow, you understand?'

A sympathetic nod of the head. 'Of course.'

'I'll leave early and stop off in Bantrain and confirm the time the concert ends and if the area will be clear. I'll phone you. Code to proceed: *The funeral's going ahead on schedule*. Code to abort: *The funeral's delayed*.'

'Assuming delayed, what then?'

'Change your mortar sighting. Fire into open ground as close to the target as possible . . . make it look like the dumb 'RA getting it all wrong again. The English newspapers and television reporters will take great pleasure in reporting it.'

'You think quick, Pat, I'll give you that.'

A brief smile. 'That superior education of mine you're always knocking.'

'So assuming we receive the abort message on the RUC station we still go ahead as planned?'

'Helicopter will be fixed will it?'

'Young Feargal's flying in himself this morning to Dublin. Bringing a few spare bits and pieces. Doesn't think it'll be a problem.'

'If it is, Frank, you know what to do with your man up there.' A movement of the head towards the ceiling.

'Not a problem. One other point: how many people know that we're dropping the Sassman in Craogh Parc tomorrow night?'

'You and me and those that need to know in Belfast . . . We have their approval by the way.'

'So when do I tell Teach about the mission?'

'Up to you, but I'd suggest you leave it as late as possible.'

'It's just that we need to get rid of the helicopter afterwards.'

'Like I told you at Murphy's Bar last night . . . get it over to Sligo airport. There'll be a car waiting to take you to my house up there . . . my sister is aware you'll be coming.'

'Long way to Sligo.'

'You'll have cover of darkness. You can stay low enough to be off the radar. Besides, I'm thinking in the confusion and panic no one will notice a blacked-out military helicopter disappearing into the night.'

'Perhaps. What happens to the helicopter once we get it to Sligo?'

'You don't really need to know, but if it'll put your mind at rest it will be getting a high-pressure wash overnight to get rid of the military paint job, and will appear the following morning as a shiny civil machine visiting from England.' Then changing the subject. 'Have you seen Nancy yet?'

'No.'

'You up to a word of advice?'

'Try me.'

'Go easy on her. Remember she's come back to you. Whatever's happened is in the past. If you want her back then give her time . . . Oh, and one other thing, she's had her hair cut. You might want to say how nice it looks. That always goes down well.'

'How . . .' Ryan started and stopped as the door opened.

Nancy, dressed in jeans and a heavy knit sweater, came in carrying a tray. Bacon, sausages, black pudding, eggs, tomatoes, potato cakes and soda farls – an Ulster fry. Two mugs of steaming tea. 'Secret talks is it?' she said, sensing the sudden silence. Then looking at her husband, added, 'Aren't you going to welcome me back, Frank?'

Ryan stared at her, hardly able to believe it was the woman he had married all those years earlier. The hair, of course. He didn't think it did anything for her. In fact he considered it ugly. 'I came up to your room last night . . . the door was locked.'

A contrite smile. 'I'm sorry, Frank, it's just that I was afraid to be alone in the house with that Sassman and only the young boy as a guard. I locked the door as a precaution, that's all. I was so exhausted I didn't hear another thing 'til I awoke this morning.' She placed the tray on the table and put the plates and the mugs before the two of them. Paused before she turned to leave and leaned down and kissed Frank on the forehead. Ryan remained impassive. 'Of course,' she said lightly, 'You can always take me up to the bedroom now and welcome me home. Pat won't mind, will you, Pat?' A wink of the eye.

Cavenaugh laughed and began buttering a piece of toast. 'Don't you get me involved in your marital squabbles, I've got enough to worry about.'

'The hair's different,' Ryan managed, by way of polite conversation.

'Do you like it?'

'Very nice.'

She turned to Cavenaugh. 'So, when are we taking the prisoner to Belfast?'

'Still working on it. Probably towards the end of the week. That about right, Frank?'

Ryan had picked up on the subtle eye contact. 'That's right.'

Nancy smiled at them both and left the room.

'The hair's different, is it?' Cavenaugh mocked. 'Jesus, Frank, you certainly know how to sweet-talk the ladies.'

Ryan scowled and picking up his knife and fork attacked the food before him.

Four p.m. Frank Ryan was sitting in a lay-by about 3 miles south of the border, on the Dundalk road. He'd been there for the best part of two hours now and was getting nervous. He had been looked at by two Garda patrols already but they hadn't stopped. He looked in the wing mirror of the Ford Corsair. A procession of trucks and private cars. Nothing else.

The visibility was poor. A damp mist blanketing the rolling countryside. He could see barely 800 or 900 yards in either direction. Another white-and-blue-striped police car came from the direction of Dundalk, slowed as it approached the lay-by. It pulled in and stopped some 10 yards ahead on the gravel verge. A blue-uniformed Garda officer climbed out and closed the door behind him. The driver remained in the car. The man looked both ways, stretching his shoulders. Then walked slowly around the car, looking continually at Ryan, who was sitting very still at the wheel of the Ford Corsair. When he reached the kerb he paused momentarily and then dropped down through the hedge and out of sight.

Two minutes later the officer reappeared, buttoning his trousers and straightening his jacket. He glanced quickly in Ryan's direction and grinned, lowering himself back into the police car. With a ripple of gravel the car sped away, resuming its journey to the border.

The little event had distracted Ryan for a few seconds and when he looked into his rear-view mirror again, he saw it was filled with a white vehicle. He heard the slamming of a door, turning his head in time to see Gerry Faul approaching. Dark blue trousers. Matching anorak with a Mobil Oil logo. A grin on his face.

'Chatting up the Gardai then, Frank?' He grinned as Ryan opened his door and got out.

'Stopped for a piss,' Ryan said, gesturing towards the bushes. 'No problems getting here?' It was a dumb question. He was here, truck and all.

Faul walked alongside the caravanette smiling to himself. 'No problem. I'd taken a couple of precautions just in case I broke down and caught the attention of the Gardai.' He opened the side door of the van and showed Ryan inside. On the floor was the gearbox casing of a tractor from the farm workshop. Several tools strewn around. 'Taking an old gearbox up to Belfast to trade for a new one from a friend of mine.'

'How about the rig?'

'It's flat under the floor. Two bolts to get at it.'

'The roof?'

'Just have to kick out the Plexiglass skylight. The rack goes across the van instead of along.' They climbed in and discussed the assembly.

'What about the exploder?' Faul asked.

Ryan looked a little more serious. 'I've bolted on a plastic drain-pipe as number six tube, the bottom right corner one next to the firing position. It's a cascade sequence, so that'll be the last one to go. The frame looks complete with five, so any remains will look like a complete set. There won't be enough of anything else left. With a bit of luck it'll demolish most of the front of the van.'

'What's the delay on the sequence?' Faul asked.

'What you like, Gerry. Up to three minutes if you're really nervous.'

'Thirty seconds I was thinking.'

'Fair enough.'

'What about the mortar bombs?'

'You'll bring them up in the morning in the Corsair.'

'What about a driver?'

'You can have Billy Costello, Pat's convinced the

sun shines out of his arse, so I suppose we should give him a try. Make sure he's got the car pointed in the right direction before you light the fuse though. You want as much distance as possible between you and the van in that half-minute before the fun starts.'

'Right.'

'So where do we take the van now?'

'Found a nice little hideaway about ten miles from the launch site. Just follow me.'

Ryan pulled out of the lay-by slowly, following the white blood transfusion van, a cloud of oily blue smoke hanging over the now empty lay-by. A cheap enough vehicle, Gerry had mentioned earlier. He prayed that the engine would last long enough for what they had planned.

They drove on for almost an hour through Carrickmacross and Shercock and part of the way to Castleblayney before turning off into the forecourt of a small garage. Several vehicles were lined up, 'for sale' prices painted in white on the windscreens.

Ryan stopped and watched as Faul backed the van alongside the line of vehicles.

A youth came out of the building and after a few seconds talking with Faul went back into the workshop end of the garage, reappearing with a pot of whitewash and a brush. He then proceeded to write SOLD in massive letters across the windshield.

Ryan waited in the Corsair, grinning at the van. Simple. Nobody could be interested in that old van. Especially with 'SOLD' painted on the windscreen.

Faul waved to the youth, who was busy counting a handful of banknotes, and walked over to the car.

*

Following Cavenaugh's earlier directions Ryan drove on to Castleblaney, taking several minor roads to the north and west of the town. He eventually slowed on the crest of a small hill. A stand of perhaps twenty trees. The mist had lifted. Below them a narrow road leading to a group of derelict farm buildings. Beyond that a gentle rise, and beyond the rise they could see the thin line of rooftops of Bantrain. The one distinguishing landmark was a tall factory chimney gushing black smoke into a murky sky.

Ryan glanced at Faul. 'The chimney is exactly two hundred yards beyond the RUC station . . . directly in line with the last tree on the left edge of this wood. What do you think?'

'Range from here to the target?'

Ryan passed him a cigarette packet. 'Details written on the side of one of the cigarettes. Don't smoke the wrong one for Christ's sake . . . So what do you think? Good enough?'

Faul took the packet and put it in his pocket. 'Good enough? I'd say bloody perfect.'

Pat Cavenaugh went through the house looking for Nancy before he left for Belfast. He found her in one of the bedrooms changing the sheets. 'They're keeping you busy, girl.'

She stopped and looked up. 'A woman's work, as Frank puts it.'

'Ah, yes. I apologize for your husband, but he's a bit slow when it comes to the social graces. Give him time, he'll come around.'

'You really believe that?'

Not really. But I love you like a daughter and what

else can I say? 'Would I say it otherwise? It's just that some men don't appreciate what they've got until it's too late. It'd be a shame to see my two favourite people split up for good.'

She went over to him and kissed him on the forehead. 'Thank you, Pat.'

'For what?'

'For being kind.'

'My mother's teaching. She always said a helping hand and a kind word would thaw out the coldest heart.'

'A fine woman, your mother.'

'That she was.'

Nancy picked up a pillow and fluffed it up. 'You'll be putting a wreath for me at the funeral?'

'I will.'

'I've got a few pounds spare in my bedroom. How much will you need?'

'Not a penny piece.'

'I can't expect . . .'

'Why ever not? You're young and beautiful. You can expect everything and a bit more on Sunday.'

'And you're an old flatterer.'

'And you were twenty years too late for me, so there we have it. I'll let you cook me a meal when you get back home. How does that sound?'

'Whenever you say.'

He put his briefcase on the bottom of the bed and clicked the two catches. Opened it. 'You'd better have this, while I think of it.' He handed her a Makarov pistol. Part of a new NORAID-funded shipment via Europe that had arrived in Dublin a few days earlier. All very second hand, where doubtless some middleman had made a small killing, but it was better than throwing rocks. 'It came with the car this morning. Favour from a friend. Eight bullets in the magazine and about another thirty in this box.' He put the cardboard box on the bed. Closed the briefcase.

'You think I'll be needing it?'

'No, not at all, but I wouldn't want you left here all alone unarmed if anything did happen. Frank didn't leave you a gun before he went out this afternoon with Gerry, did he?'

'No.'

'No. Still you have one now. You'll take care of yourself.'

'And you, Pat.'

She went down the stairs with him. Watched him get in the dark green MG1100 that had been delivered from Trim that morning. She waved goodbye as he drove slowly down the track towards the open gate and the main road. Went back to changing the beds. Then remembering the gun took it to her bedroom and put it, along with the spare bullets, in one of the dressing table drawers. Threw some of her lacy underwear over them.

Such a thoughtful man, always kind and considerate, never angry; pity he had never married and had children, she thought. The world, her world at least, could have done with a few more Pat Cavenaughs.

20

It was early evening when the well-preserved but rather ancient Bedford OB motorbus threaded its way around the last corner into Bantrain.

Corps Sergeant-Major Estelle Manners of the Salvation Army sat in the front seat up alongside the driver. Watched their progress eagerly. It was the first time she had been to her home town in five years and here she was leading the Hoddingham Corps Songster Group on their very first Irish visit. They were to spend the night here followed by an early afternoon service and concert the following day, before proceeding to their wind-up concert in Belfast. The Bantrain concert was more of a last-minute fill-in for the benefit of Estelle and her parents, who had put so much work into arranging the tour.

. The songster group was a bright-eyed selection of twenty boys and girls, the dominance in this case very much in favour of the girls, between the ages of fourteen and thirty. The Hoddingham Corps had an enviable reputation in its juniors, with a good

selection of young instrumentalists and singers. Their
concert experience had brought praise and awards
both within Salvation Army circles and in non-Army
national competition.

With much hard work Estelle Manners had
managed to arrange for several Army families in and
around Bantrain to offer accommodation for that
Tuesday night visit. The Songsters, along with an
improvised junior band group, had borrowed the
corps bus, and had made the overnight journey on the
ferry to Northern Ireland a few days earlier. The only
change in personnel was the driver, Tiny Goodhall, a
Londoner who had taken over at the last moment
when the regular driver had gone down with 'flu.
Goodhall had come highly recommended, especially
as he was a fully trained mechanic – an essential with
the Bedford OB bus, which was prone to breakdown
on a fairly regular basis.

The bus crept slowly around the corner by the
police station, crossed to the opposite side of the road
and stopped. Estelle jumped out and was greeted by
her mother and father.

Inside the small hall two trestle tables had been laid
out with a late-afternoon tea of sandwiches and scones
and strawberries and cream. The excited voices of the
younger members echoed through the building.

Unnoticed by the band members, a smartly dressed
silver haired man with a black eye-patch paused as he
passed the main door and casually read the poster
attached to it with drawing pins.

THE SALVATION ARMY BANTRAIN CITADEL
present

Then A Soldier

THE HODDINGHAM SONGSTERS from
DERBYSHIRE
BAND & SONGSTER CONCERT
THURSDAY 1.00 P.M.

Cavenaugh turned away and walked a few yards down the quiet street. The bus driver had a large metal toolbox out on the pavement. He was tinkering with the starter motor, muttering under his breath.

'Nice old bus,' Cavenaugh remarked as he approached the man. 'Bedford OB, isn't it?'

Tiny Goodhall stopped what he was doing and turned to face him. 'Yer, that's right. A few too many miles on the clock for my liking though. Now I've got a sticking starter motor.'

'No spares then?'

'Nah. They're sending one down tomorrow morning from Belfast.'

'How long are you staying here in Bantrain?'

'Only overnight. Concert tomorrow afternoon, then we're pulling out at five o'clock for Belfast and the final concert before we go home.'

Cavenaugh poked his head closer to the grimy engine, muttering approvingly as though he was an expert on things mechanical. 'The weather is supposed to be nice for the next few days.'

'Indian summer, so they say.'

'Suit an outdoor concert. Bigger audience.'

Goodhall grinned. 'Talking to the wrong man, guv. I'm just the dogsbody.'

Cavenaugh pulled back and smiled. 'Hope you get it fixed okay,' he said as he strode away.

He crossed the narrow street and stopped at a small

newsagent's shop and bought a local map. And as he did so glanced over at the bleak building next to the Salvation Army citadel. It was surrounded by high, fine-mesh, heavy-gauge fencing. The local RUC post.

He paused outside the shop, half glancing at the map, half watching several vehicles exit the station, including two British Army Land Rovers laden down with amour plating. Saw a flak-jacketed constable watching him intently from inside the compound. He made a show of studying the map, the way a tourist might, then walked away to the end of the street and round a corner. He found the phone box 20 yards further on, and called Frank Ryan. The message was brief: *The funeral is going ahead on schedule.*

Nancy Ryan, dressed in jeans and sweater, was sitting on the window seat of her bedroom window, knees drawn up to her chest, watching the farmyard below. The fields beyond. Thinking about the visit to see her sister, Peg, at her ground-floor flat in Orwell Road, Rathgar. The marijuana, the amphetamines, the LSD. Muling it, not taking it – earning pin money, just for the hell of it. Ending up with a police record. The beginning of the end.

How Peg's husband had taken their two children away to America, telling her that she could follow when all the shame had died down. And after the eighteen months' probation had been served, finding that the US authorities would not grant visas to convicted drug felons. And when she had turned around, so to speak, finding the husband and the children had vanished into the melting pot of America. Nearly five years now. Five years and never a word.

Then A Soldier

Then in the last twelve months there was the British soldier, a Cornish boy called Richard, whom she had dated . . . and been found out. And received the mandatory IRA punishment for collaboration with the enemy.

And had said to Nancy as she was leaving to drive back to the farm: 'Take my advice, Nancy, stick with Frank.'

'You didn't.'

'He was just a schoolgirl crush. I soon got over him; besides you took my place.'

'What would you say if I told you there was somebody else?'

'Is he rich?'

'What's that got to do with it?'

'Everything.' Then seeing the look in Nancy's eyes said with dismay. 'Don't tell me you've fallen in love . . . and at your age, of all things!'

'I'm only thirty-five for Christ's sake . . . and I didn't exactly say I was in love.'

'So who is he, this mystery man who you haven't exactly fallen in love with?'

'An Englishman . . . an ex-soldier.'

Peg had stared wide eyed and open mouthed, and Nancy had wondered if her sister was about to laugh or cry or scream out in anger. Instead she drew her back to the kitchen and poured them both a large gin and tonic, apologizing for the fact that it was all she had left in the house . . . Well there was cooking sherry, she added, but you had to be seriously fucking depressed to drink that. Nancy had been quietly surprised to hear her sister use that sort of language. The sixties drug thing aside, she had always seemed

like a nice, quiet elder sister. The more recent crime of
consorting with the enemy – *collaboration horizontale*
as they called it – and having your head roughly
razored and being tied to a lamppost with a sign
hanging round your neck telling all your sins was seen
as something that could happen to any girl or woman,
especially a lonely widow or divorcee.

'Frank'll kill you if he finds out; you do know that,
don't you? Cold hearted inside . . . where it matters.'

'Like the unexpected bit when you take the loaf out
of the freezer you mean, and find the middle hasn't
properly thawed.'

'I'm being serious.'

'There's nothing to find out, Peg. I haven't made up
my mind one way or the other.'

'The truth?'

'I suppose . . . I don't know. Thirty-five isn't exactly
the first blush of youth, is it? You're probably right . . .
I'll stay with Frank to the bitter end, hating every
minute of it, and regretting the fact that I never had the
courage to do anything about it . . . what would you do,
in my place?'

Peg sipped at her gin. Pondered the question. 'It's
not as though you've got the kids any more is it? Then
again, Frank isn't exactly the big earner is he? Stay
with him and you'll be a widow soon enough. Then
what? No pension schemes with the IRA . . . Think
about your own life, Nancy. Nobody else is going to
take care of you after the guns have stopped firing.' A
pause to reflect on the great mistake of her own life,
something her conscience reminded her of every hour
of every day. And then in a smaller, less certain, voice:
'Even so, there's a lot to be said for what you have,

214

rather than what you might have. Anyway, love only lasts as long as the titles at the start of the film . . . isn't that what they say?'

That was Peg. Throwing up all the options and never picking one. Indecisive! Was she like that? Was she just a younger version of her sister?

That had been yesterday.

This was today.

She lit a cigarette, and smoked quietly for a moment. Looking out of the window. Thinking about tomorrow. And when she had finished the cigarette she put her shoes on. The men would want to eat soon enough.

She was at the bottom of the stairs. The ticking sound of the grandfather clock in the hallway. The smell of furniture polish. The kitchen door partially ajar. She was about to enter when she heard Frank's voice.

'Top secret, you understand that, Teach? Top secret.'

'Yeah.'

'Breathe a word and you're fucking dead, understand?'

'Sure.'

'Okay. I'll go over it one more time: Operation Freefall. Tomorrow night. Departure eighteen-forty-five hours local. Stage one: Position helicopter over Dublin. There's a football match kicking off at Craogh Parc at nineteen hundred. The guest of honour at that match is President Nixon. At nineteen-fifteen we descend over the pitch to a height of five hundred feet. At that precise moment we drop our prisoner. Following my command that the drop has been executed we exit the area as rapidly as possible. I would suggest that we depart in the opposite direction

– to the east – initially just in case we're being tracked on radar . . . but I'll leave that side of things to you. Stage two: Once we consider we are clear of Dublin, we need to drop down to treetop height, then proceed to Sligo . . . Got it?'

'Got it. Can I ask why we're going to Sligo? Bit off the beaten track.'

Need-to-know information. For the privileged few only. Teach Cusack was a long way outside that category. 'You can ask but I can't tell you.'

'Just drive the goddamned machine, uh?'

'You're sure it's fully serviceable?'

'Yeah, we changed an oil sender unit or something like that at lunchtime. Did three independent engine runs. Oil pressure's perfect . . . I guess I can talk to the rest of the team about this, though?'

'What team? You and I are it.'

'What about your wife?'

'Fuck my wife, she doesn't have the appropriate security clearance.'

'Oh.'

'So if she starts asking you questions, make sure I get to hear about it. That goes for the rest of them, understand?'

'Yeah.'

'Now, you're *absolutely* sure that helicopter isn't going to let us down. Last place I want to be is sitting up there with you after completing the most hazardous part of the mission, and finding that five minutes out of Sligo I'm going to die in some silly fucking accident.'

'Don't worry, it's working like a well-oiled Swiss watch.'

'Thank God for that . . . One last thing, I suggest that after dinner you get an early night and give some serious thought to how we can conduct the operation with minimal risk to ourselves, bearing in mind there'll probably be armed US Army helicopters patrolling the Dublin area tomorrow evening.'

A brief, nervous laugh from the American. The thought of going up against helos modified to carry a whole shitload of rockets. The only consolation: the initiative was with them. 'Minimal risk's my number one priority, Frank. Always.'

'Good man . . . now I'd better go and find that bloody woman and see if she can get some food on the go.'

Nancy withdrew from the cracked-open door and hurried back up the stairs. She stopped at the top, and as her husband came out of the kitchen into the hallway, called down to him. 'About ready to eat, Frank?'

He looked up. 'Yes. You need any help?'

'You offering?' she asked with a smile.

No amusement on his face. 'I'll send Billy in.'

Ryan went into the living room, closing the door behind him. The muted sound of raised voices and laughter. The clinking of bottles.

It was the way of things, Nancy thought, as she peeled the potatoes at the kitchen sink. Frank wouldn't change. He'd shown little interest in her from the time Majella had been born. That little interest had diminished over the years to a point that they were now two complete strangers sharing the same space. He hadn't been near her since she had been back. His idea of retribution for the locked bedroom door on the

217

first night – something for which she was secretly thankful. Even so, it was Frank all over. Behaving like a spoiled child.

And suddenly and more clearly than ever before she could see herself living out her years in a drab little flat on the edge of a drab city. Like her sister who was so indifferent about everything – especially her former husband: *No, I've absolutely no idea whether he's working or whether he's lying in a gutter being moved on by big American cops with sticks. I never cared. Honestly, I never gave him a thought. It sounds like someone protesting, I know it does, but it's funny: I have great trouble remembering what he looked like then and I never, until you just brought the matter up, wondered how's he aged. Probably got fatter. There's a family picture somewhere. His parents were fat.* Such indifference was chilling. You could understand hate or bitterness even. You could forgive a slow fire of rage and resentment. But she talked about him just as you would some minor celebrity who had been in the news one time. Is he dead or alive? Who knows, who remembers? On to another topic.

And the last thing Peg had said – and there was more to it than Nancy wanted to admit – *No one is going to look after you after the guns have stopped firing.* The truth of the matter was they had stopped firing a long time ago.

In the Lower Falls, Belfast, later that evening, a minor squabble between Prods and Catholics had developed into a full-scale skirmish, resulting in the Army, supported by amoured vehicles, conducting amongst other things a house-to-house search. A fog of CS gas wafting through the streets. The soldiers behaving with a new harshness; axing down doors, ripping up floorboards, disembowelling furniture, smashing the garish plaster statues of the Madonna, the Infant of Prague and Saint Bernadette that adorned the tiny front parlours.

The reason why Pat Cavenaugh was staying the night at the Europa Hotel – an imposing building in the heart of the Golden Mile. He had been joined by Father Michael who, an hour earlier, covered in his silk vestments, had been a mythical figure, shrouded in the smoke of incense, raising the golden monstrance with the body of Christ in the Host above the heads of innocent choir boys and pious sisters and a greatly diminished congregation (the majority being too afraid to take to the streets). Now in his shabby black coat and slightly sweat-stained white collar, he was just another agent of God. One of the poorer, more wretched ones.

They were sitting around a low glass and chromium table in a corner of the plush, carpeted hotel bar. Crystal tumblers of whiskey and a bowl of peanuts set before them. Bright. Glitzy. Sterile. A far cry from the squalor of their usual meeting place in Cawnpore Street.

'You picked a bad night to come back,' the priest suggested. He bowed his head. Prayerful posture.

'What started it . . . do you know?'

'An informer tipped off the BA to where they might find hidden weapons.'

'The problem with our kind of war, Michael, you never know who you can trust.'

'True enough. And it isn't as though we're going to

put up our hands and let them take the weaponry, is it?'

'No, but we're not strong enough yet to manage the sort of confrontation that's out there tonight. The news on the car radio mentioned as many as three thousand troops being drafted in.' Cavenaugh cast an eye around the bar. At the smart suited businessmen and the well-dressed ladies. The cocktail set. The subdued buzz of polite conversation. No straight glasses with the dark brew here. It could be New York. Paris. London. Anywhere. Amazing what the thickness of double-glazing and concrete could hide you away from. 'Then again there's a bright side.'

'There is?'

'Most certainly. After tonight the recruiting figures will increase five-fold.'

'I hadn't considered that.'

'Most people will not struggle, never mind vote, for abstract things. They will not fight for ideas. They will fight to bring material benefits, to improve the quality of their lives, to guarantee the future of their children. The "big ideas" which we have concerning liberation, nationalism, independence and socialism must develop out of the "small ideas" concerned with local grievances, local protests and local aspirations. A few good men will doubtless die tonight . . . martyrs to the cause. All because of a local grievance. Just as well the British are not as intelligent as they believe themselves to be or they'd understand they are only helping to strengthen that cause. Adding to our numbers.'

'Put like that we can't lose.'

'Just a matter of time, Michael. Ten years. Fifty

years. A hundred years. We'll get there in the end.' Cavenaugh gathered up a few peanuts from the bowl and put them in his mouth. Took a sip of his whiskey. He was tired. It had been a long day. 'Anyway, what of the funeral tomorrow?'

'No problem there. Everything's going ahead as planned.' The priest adjusted his glasses. A small, nervous gesture. 'The autopsy though, that was something else.' A pause, as if to marshal his thoughts, his words. The moment he had been dreading. 'It . . . it seems that Mouse didn't die of natural causes. He was badly beaten . . . internal injuries, that sort of thing. The doctor said he could have been lying in that condition for quite some hours before he died . . . I'm sorry, I know how close a friend he was.' He waited for Cavenaugh to say something, but the other man just sat, staring into empty space. Mouth slightly open. The face suddenly older, more tired, than he had ever known it.

At last, a dry whisper. 'Now why would anyone do such a thing?'

The priest cleared his throat. Fiddled with his glasses again. Looking, as his calling had long taught him, for a few placating words. 'Perhaps we should take comfort in the thought that death is a gift of God. A release from sickness, pain, loneliness, and misery . . . an entrance into eternal life where there's nothing to fear.'

Cavenaugh, who was not a religious man, was not in the mood for a sermon. 'Perhaps it would have been a damned sight easier if He'd admitted us all to eternal life from the beginning.'

'You can read about that in the Bible. Man, paradise, the fall . . .'

'The fall, the eviction from paradise, original sin, and with it the curse of one hundred thousand generations. The God of the longest wrath on record.' An uncommon despair in the voice.

'The God of forgiveness,' the priest replied meekly.

'Try telling that to the people being beaten and abused by the soldiers tonight, Father.'

The priest looked for a while into the drink before him. 'The Church has rules. She has rules for prevention and for education. God has none. God is love. Which of us can fathom His judgment?'

Cavenaugh shook his head and smiled. He was suddenly thinking of Nancy on the flight to Dublin. What was it she had said? *You've tainted us with your iambic pentameters, your allegorical references, your high-flown rhetoric, so that in the end we all sound like cheap imitations of the academics and the politicians.* And perhaps the holy men? Too many words, that was the problem. Perhaps it always had been. He thought he would like to get drunk when all of this was over. Not just for one night. But for the rest of his life.

As Father Michael was leaving Cavenaugh said, 'Sean's staying at the house, is he?'

'That's right. He didn't notice anything out of the ordinary if that's what you're thinking.'

'You asked him, did you?'

'I did. Besides, his hearing seems to have been damaged following the *accident* in England. I doubt he would have heard artillery fire if it had started up in the next street.'

I don't like Mouse tripping over and hurting himself.

Then A Soldier

Not good for a man his age. So what I'm doing is putting you in charge of his welfare. That means anything happens to him I will hold you responsible. You do get my meaning, don't you? His words to Sean those many months ago. Cavenaugh smiled. 'Oh, I'm not looking to apportion blame. Frank thinks he has the potential to be a good man, that's all.'

'Perhaps you should drop in and see him in the morning, give him a pat on the back for his work over the water.'

The lightest of penances for the sin of doubt perhaps! Cavenaugh's hand reached up. A finger slipping under the eye patch, gently massaging the old wound. 'Why not? Why not, indeed. A good idea.'

'We all need encouragement, Pat. A kind word.'

'True enough.'

'Will I let him know you're coming?'

'Is he by himself?'

'Celia's staying with him. Playing Florence Nightingale.'

The smile was still there. *Florence Nightingale!* That was a new one. She was better known on the street for her first-class Carrara marble breasts. Mary, Joseph and Mother Theresa, what an army this was. Hookers, empty-headed boys, whiskey-swilling priests, and a few over-the-hill good men. 'That's kind of her. Perhaps you could phone her and get her out of the house by nine in the morning. Give me time for a private word with him.'

Cavenaugh had walked out to the front of the hotel to make sure the priest got a taxi. It was a clear, starlit night above the neon lit street. A chill in the air. Words

223

marked by a coda of near-transparent smoke. 'Did we get a name on the informer by any chance?'

The priest offered Cavenaugh a cigarette from a half-empty pack. He lit it. 'Keep the packet, Pat, I'm trying to give up . . . bad for your health so they tell me.'

A taxi pulled in to the kerb. 'Good night, Michael. I'll see you at the funeral tomorrow.'

Cavenaugh watched the taxi pull away into the stream of traffic along Great Victoria Street. Then opened the packet of cigarettes. He emptied it into his hand. Along with the cigarettes were two cigarette papers stuck together. *The 'comm'*. Written in small capital letters, a name and an address. He memorized the information then took a cigarette lighter from his pocket and lit the paper. It flared briefly before he let it go. He dusted the ashes from his fingers and went back into the hotel.

21

'DON'T FRATERNIZE'. A Republican News *headline
that autumn. To press the point the Belfast
Provisionals had started taking measures against
those who befriended soldiers. Housewives who
persisted in giving out cups of tea found their homes
daubed with vile slogans. Women foolish enough to
socialize with off-duty squaddies? Something else all
together . . .*

The 'little witnesses' returned to the farm early. It
was the nickname Pat Cavenaugh had given the two
minders they had borrowed from Feargal Walsh in
London – the pale-faced giants who hardly ever spoke,
who never smiled, who could frighten you to death
with a look. As Cavenaugh pointed out to Ryan, the
term referred to testicles, and if you had the usual
number how they were inseparable. Ryan had said it
was a load of bollocks. The words had left his lips
before he realized the humour in the remark. They had
both laughed until they cried.

No laughter on this particular evening however. The

little witnesses had been to Trim on some minor errand in the farm's Land Rover. As they were leaving the town they had seen Nancy making a call from a public phone box. Non-approved telephone calls – a *Green Book* breach of security during wartime operations. They had reported the incident to Ryan immediately upon their return.

That Nancy had gone into town an hour earlier to pick up some provisions from a late-night shop, saying that there wasn't sufficient food for the following day, was something Ryan had not questioned. Now he went to the kitchen and systematically checked the cupboards. The food supply was low, but not uncommonly so. That was when his mind started playing tricks. Feeding his jealous imagination. Throwing up scenes of his wife with British soldiers in Aldershot . . . working as a barmaid . . . and something else when the evening's work was over he shouldn't wonder. She had obviously had an affair. Been fucking one of them? What else? Was she now phoning the English bastard? He went to her bedroom and started searching through her belongings.

Nancy might have guessed something was wrong when she pulled up outside the house some time later and picked up the wicker shopping basket from the passenger seat. Frank was standing outside the farmhouse. No jacket or sweater, despite the chilly evening. Shirt sleeves rolled up. Behind him, caught in the yellow light that spilled from the open doorway, the two pale-faced minders. The wind had changed, was now out of the east. The heavy scent of lilacs drifting up from the gardens replacing the stink of manure from the chicken sheds.

Ryan was quietly seething. Even the rest of the men, sensing trouble was brewing, had slipped away quietly to their beds. No one enjoyed being around Frank Ryan when a black mood descended upon him. The two minders were different. They were trained pit-bulls. They did precisely what they were told. And Ryan had told them what was to happen the moment his wife returned.

'Took your time,' Ryan snapped as she moved away from the car.

'Oh, I was talking to the shopkeeper.'

'Were you now . . . and the phone call?'

She stopped. 'What phone call?'

'You were seen in the town . . . in a phone box. You know the procedure about phone calls during an operation!'

A moment's hesitation. Raw-eyed, frightened apprehension on her face. Even so she came back on the offensive. Her way of doing things. 'Oh, Christ, Frank, grow up . . . I was only calling my sister.'

'You saw her yesterday.'

'She's not doing too well.'

'The silly bitch is back on the drugs, is she?' Ryan asked. More than a little sarcasm in the voice.

'She was never on the drugs as you put it, Frank. You know that as well as I do.'

'Got herself involved with another British soldier, then?'

'It's her health if you must know.'

'So if I phone her now, she'll confirm that you called her a short while ago?'

'What is this exactly? Are you saying you don't fucking believe me?'

'Give me one good reason!' He thrust a hand into his jacket pocket and pulled out a letter, waved it angrily in front of her.

'What's that?'

'What's that? What's that?' he mimicked. 'What's that, is a fucking letter from your Sassman upstairs . . . Let me see now, what did it say? "I loved you from the first moment I saw you." Is that right? Is that fucking right, you bitch?'

She lunged forward to snatch the letter from his hand. 'You bastard . . . you've been going through . . .'

It was as far as she got before Ryan's hand caught her a stinging blow across the face sending her sprawling to the ground. The shopping basket and its contents went flying. She cried out as he grabbed her arm and pulled her roughly to her feet. She could smell the stench of whiskey on his breath. Another slap to the face followed . . . 'And the money . . . the bastard gave you money.' . . . Another slap . . . 'You charged him for it, did you? . . . so what the fuck are you now . . . a fucking whore?' . . . Another slap . . . And another.

The two minders came forward silently., each taking an arm, thrusting her down on her knees.

Ryan was prowling around her now, muttering to himself. Beside himself with anger. His eyes glittering. 'Do you know what this is?' He held something up. It glinted in the yellow light that angled across the driveway from the open door.

She tried to focus on the object, but found it impossible. Her head was ringing with the blows she had received. Her eyes full of tears, blurring her vision. 'Go to fucking hell.'

Ryan grinned at the minders. 'Listen to the whore . . .

telling *me* to go to fucking hell. There's only one of us who's going to fucking hell.' He motioned to the two men to pull her to her feet. They did as they were told. And on some unspoken order began to undress her. She struggled as they began tugging at her clothes. It was a one-sided battle. First the sweater was pulled over her head and tossed aside. Then the shoes. Then the jeans were unzipped, tugged down over her hips, pulled away from her feet. Like the sweater, thrown aside. The bra and panties followed. She stood naked before him, shivering. The minders' iron fingers locked painfully on her arms. She was slammed back to the gravel, skinning her knees in the process.

Ryan's face came near. The whiskey fumes again. 'Go to fucking hell! . . . That's you, you whore. That's where collaborators go . . . where you're going with your fucking Sassman tomorrow.' He brought the object up in front of her eyes again. Much closer this time. Now she saw it. The glint of metal. Cried out in fright. A cut-throat razor. Felt the cold steel pressed hard against her cheek. 'Let's see if he wants you when I've fucking finished with you.'

'Please . . . please, Frank,' she sobbed, 'Please . . . I can explain . . . please, God, don't hurt me any more . . .'

Ryan spat at her, and grabbing at her hair began to savagely shave her head, cutting her scalp as he lunged back and forwards. She screamed over and over again at the stinging pain. But the more she screamed the more violent he became. 'You think what happened to that sister of yours was bad? . . . You think she was hard done by for fucking an English bastard? . . . Wait 'til I've finished with you . . . No man will ever want to lay a hand on you again . . . fucking whore . . .'

By the time he had finished her screams had died to nothing more than low animal whimpers. The tears were still streaming down her cheeks. Her body shaking all over.

Ryan ordered the two men to stand her up. The gravel cut viciously into her bare feet. Her head was completely shaved now, blood running down her face and neck from the numerous wounds that had been inflicted.

'See what your fucking Sassman thinks of you now,' he screamed as he placed the blade an inch under her left eye.

'Oh, God, please, Frank . . . not my face . . .' She struggled against the powerful hands that held her. Her eyelids fluttered. Like a trapped bird. She felt the blade turn through ninety degrees. Felt it press lightly into the skin. And harder. She let out a gasp as the sudden white-hot pain shot through her. A quick downwards movement. A trail of warm blood down the left side of her face, running to her lips. The pain suddenly too much too bear.

She screamed once. And fainted.

She was being dragged up the stairs. Her feet banging against each one. She could taste her blood on her lips. In her mouth. There was the sound of a door being unlocked. A door opening. The next moment she felt herself being thrown bodily into the darkened room. Her head colliding with a wall. The door slamming behind her.

She didn't know how long she lay there. Seconds. Minutes. Numb with shock. Huddled into the fetal position. Sobbing like a frightened child. Then a light went on and she felt hands touching her bare shoulders.

'Please . . . please, no more . . .'

'It's all right. I'm not going to hurt you.'

She recognized the quiet voice. John Winter. Allowed herself to be lifted to her feet. He guided her to the bed and sat her down carefully.

'Let me see.' His fingers under her chin. Gently lifting her face. 'Jesus . . . who did this to you?'

'Not important.' Her voice barely audible.

Winter took off his shirt and ripped one sleeve away at the seam. He slid her arms into the shirt and buttoned it. She continued to shiver. 'Not much I can do,' he said, ripping the sleeve into strips. He picked up the mug of water they had brought with his supper. The water he had left until he got really thirsty. Dipping one of the strips of fabric into the water he began to bathe the long cut down her left cheek.

She winced and cried out.

'I'm sorry. It's going to hurt.'

'How . . . how bad is it?'

He looked closely. 'Not too deep. It could do with stitches though. I'll bathe it the best I can and hold it together. It should knit okay.'

'It'll scar though?' A stupid thing to say. She realized that the moment the words had left her lips. But it was all she had left. Her looks. Without those, what? What was left?

'Don't worry. A plastic surgeon can get rid of that in no time, you'll see.'

'Poor Catholic girls from the ghettos and plastic surgeons . . . sounds about right.' Bitterness through the pain.

She was right and he knew it. He bit his lip. Wished he had better words to offer. He dabbed at a few cuts on her head. Then picked up two strips of cloth and soaked them in the water and held them to her face. 'Lie back very slowly . . . good.' He lifted her feet on to the bed.

'It hurts . . . oh, God it hurts.'

'Don't talk too much. You'll open the wound. I'll ask you questions. Tap my arm with your fingers. One tap, yes. Two, no. Got it?'

One tap.

'Who did this to you? Was it Frank?'

One tap.

'Do you know why? Did he tell you why?'

One tap. Then her finger began to trace out letters on his arm. L.E.T.T.E.R.

'Letter?'

One tap.

'What letter? I'm sorry . . . do you . . .'

She was tracing letters on his arm again. F.R.O.M.Y.O.U.

He removed the first piece of blood soaked cloth and took more strips from the mug and held the compress two handedly to her cheek. Holding the wound lightly together. Gentle pressure. 'The letter from me . . . the one I left you in Scotland, you mean?'

One tap.

'I'm sorry . . . I should have never done that.'

Her fingers briefly touched his arm. No message.

'So Frank knows you were in Scotland with me . . .' He looked at her shaved head.

She closed her eyes and tried to look away.

'Don't move. Please. Just lie still. I know why he cut

off your hair . . . it's the punishment for women who collaborate with the enemy. Is that right?'

One tap.

'Do you know what's going to happen? To you? To me?'

One tap.

'Tonight? Is it going to happen tonight?'

Two taps.

'When? Tomorrow?

One tap.

'Good. We'll talk about it in the morning, then. Close your eyes.'

She closed them. The pain throbbed through her head.

'One more thing. They take me to the toilet every morning and evening. There's a bucket in the corner otherwise. Let me know if you need it. I'll rig the mattress up to give you privacy . . . understand?'

One tap.

'I wish I had some pain killers to give you.'

The fingers touched his arm. Stayed there for a moment.

He sat through the night tending the wound the best he could. Talking to her from time to time – trying to take her mind off her pain – telling her stories he had heard from Dorcas Volk about his grandfather, a man who had served on India's North-west Frontier earlier in the century, not about war though, but about the family life in an Army garrison at Quetta. About children growing up in what had always seemed a fairy tale environment of hot days and dusty bazaars of snake charmers and beggars and holy men. Of monkeys coming down from the hills at meal times to chatter and claw at the wire mesh that covered the verandah. Of an adventurous life that seemed to mirror every word of, Kipling's *Kim*. And when he had finished weaving the tales, with hopefully a little of the same magic that Dorcas had, and Nancy had fallen into a troubled sleep, he sat on the floor and thought other darker thoughts.

Like, if he ever got his hands on Frank Ryan he would break every bone in his body.

PART TWO
Then a soldier

Deep peace of the running wave to you
Deep peace of the flowing air to you
Deep peace of the quiet earth to you
Deep peace of the shining stars to you
Deep peace of the Son of Peace to you
                              – Celtic blessing

22

Piss poor planning leads to piss poor performance . . .

Pat Cavenaugh stood on the corner at the end of Cawnpore Street, reading the *Irish Times,* briefcase at his feet. Following a leisurely breakfast at the Europa he had taken a taxi to City Hall. He was dressed in a black raincoat and a black suit – ready for the funeral that afternoon. He had walked from there. It was a dry autumn morning, a freshness in the air. A good-to-be-alive day, as he thought of it. He had arrived at the end of Cawnpore Street a few minutes before nine. Was now patiently waiting, reading the paper, the head-lines and lead story given over to the rioting of the previous evening, not least the revelation that at least 1,000 canisters of CS gas had been fired by the BA in the space of ten hours.

Celia came out of the front door of the house a few seconds later. Her high heels clacking noisily along the pavement. When she had turned the corner at the far end of the street, Cavenaugh rolled up the newspaper and walked up to the door in the wall. It was off the latch. He pushed it open. A big white dog, filthy and underfed, was lying on the pathway. It stood up, rocking on its feet. Tail between its legs. Looking up at him with big brown, sorrowful eyes. He reached down and stroked the dog's head. 'I'm sorry, old son, but your master's not coming back. You'll have to find somebody else to feed you now.' The dog just flopped back down on the path. Eyes fixed on the paint-peeling door at the end of the path. A low whining sound coming from its throat.

The back door of the house was open. He placed the briefcase carefully in a corner of the kitchen. Called out Sean's name through the open door that led to the tiny hallway and the stairs. Stood for a moment, as the familiar smells of the ghetto – cold, damp, cooking fat, stale cigarette smoke – rose to overwhelm him. The grime, the filth, the detritus (including a saucepan on the side, half full of something now covered in green mould) was equally as depressing. More so after the five-star luxury of the Europa.

He sighed and shrugged and filled a kettle and put it on the grease-caked gas stove. Then cleared some plates off the table. Took off his raincoat and hung it on the back of the door, along with his suit jacket. Rolled up his shirtsleeves and ran some hot water in the sink. Squirted a generous measure of washing up liquid into it. Began work on the dirty crockery and saucepans. Florence Nightingale was obviously not house-trained. Then again perhaps 'professional' ladies did not consider it an essential part of their curriculum vitae.

When the dishes were washed and the table wiped, and the last dregs of a bottle of disinfectant used to scrub the sink clean, he called out to Sean again.

He had made a pot of tea and poured a cup and was sitting at the table reading the newspaper when Sean Fitzgerald staggered into the room. He was wearing jeans and a vest. Nothing on his feet. His head was still bandaged. He looked terrible. Cavenaugh couldn't decide if that was due to his injuries or a night with Celia. Perhaps a combination of both.

'There you are, Sean. A cup of tea would go down well, I'm thinking.'

The young man dropped down in a chair at the table. 'Thanks,' he muttered, and reached over to one of the drawers and retrieved a packet of cigarettes. He lit one.

Cavenaugh put the mug of hot steaming tea before him. 'Frank tells me you did a good job over there . . . picking up the Sassman and all.'

Fitzgerald looked doubtful. Decided to come clean. 'Did he also tell you I screwed up and got jumped by the bastard?'

Cavenaugh laughed. 'Oh, Christ, don't worry about that. We've all done the same in our time. Me, Frank, Gerry Faul – every last one of us. We learn by our mistakes, that's all.'

'I suppose so,' Fitzgerald mumbled, brightening up a little.

'We had some shooting last night then.'

'Yeah, I saw it on the news on the telly. Three Prod bastards stiffed, they said.'

Cavenaugh indicated the newspaper front page. 'And one of our lads from the Third Battalion.'

'The telly said they sent in three thousand soldiers.'

'They did. Pretty bad, so I hear. Doing a house-to-house search, smashing down doors, breaking the furniture.'

'Bastards,' muttered Fitzgerald, picking up the mug of steaming tea, blowing on it to cool it. 'As if we're not poor enough.'

'They were tipped off.'

'The BA you mean?' Attentive now.

'Yes.'

'Do we know who?'

The altar-boy innocence of Father Michael McVerry and his confessional. A dangerous place for Belfast sinners. 'We do, Sean. Name and address supplied.'

Fitzgerald's face lit up. His chance to do something that would show Frank he was up for it. 'Anything I can do?'

A benevolent smile. 'In your condition? No, I think you need a bit of a rest. Don't worry, there'll be plenty of time for that. I'll get one of the boys round shortly. He can deliver the package.'

'Package? What sort of package?'

'One of those little things they invented up in Derry. The Durex bomb.'

'Oh, sure, I know all about them.'

'You do?' Genuine surprise in the voice. Frank had told him that Sean wasn't one for paying too much attention to anything that didn't wear a skirt.

'Sure. Frank got me to make up a few back in the summer; practice sort of. Sulphuric acid sealed in a candlewax phial, put inside a Durex, which is then put in a large thick envelope with some sodium chlorate . . . explosive chemical used as a weedkiller, that stuff is. You walk the bomb to the target, place the package and squeeze the phial . . . that releases the acid. The acid eats through the rubber Durex and . . . BANG.'

'I'm impressed. That's very good.'

'So why don't you let me take the bomb?'

'I would have thought you'd had enough excitement for one week.'

'Where does it have to go?'

'House in the Short Strand.'

'And the informer?'

'Oh, we know him well enough, a good Catholic boy from way back.' For once the heavy irony was not lost on Fitzgerald. 'In fact it might not be a bad idea. You calling in all dressed up in your bandages. You can make it a social call on my behalf if you like. Say we're looking for help tonight, that we need a spare taxi to do a bit of transporting for us . . . as in delivering a letter to me at the Europa Hotel at seven p.m.'

'Drives a black taxi does he?'

'He does. You could perhaps have a cup of tea in his kitchen; give him some instructions to read . . . a route of places to call after he's delivered the envelope to the Europa. Tell him he needs to memorize the places and the times then destroy the list – that should keep him busy long enough. Then squeeze the phial and leave the envelope on the table. The phial is contained in three Durex sheaths. So you've got a good sixty seconds to get out of there. I've checked it out very carefully.'

'You've got it with you? The bomb!'

Cavenaugh brought his briefcase to the table. The one delivered to the hotel by one of his young men that very morning. He opened it and took out the large sealed envelope. Placed it on the table. 'Oh, yes. And a small present for you. We got a shipment of these down south.' He gave Fitzgerald a Makarov automatic. 'A bit old, but they work well enough. Eight bullets in the clip . . . and a spare box of shells.' He put the box on the table. 'You better keep that with you, just in case he suspects something.'

Fitzgerald weighed the gun in his hand. Felt the awesome power flooding through his body. 'Suspects something?'

'Then you use that.'

'Ah.' A nod of the head. Now he got the picture.

Cavenaugh took out his wallet and removed a ten-pound note. Written along the top of the note in pencil a name and a street address. He handed it to the young man. 'He's the target.'

Fitzgerald looked stunned. 'Jesus, I've been in his fuckin' taxi, so I have.'

Cavenaugh nodded sympathetically. 'You and me both. The reason we need to be very careful who we speak to.'

As Cavenaugh was putting on his raincoat, Fitzgerald said, 'You'll be going to the funeral this afternoon, then?'

'Yes. Terrible thing that, Father Michael told me Mouse had been badly beaten. And him such an old man . . . not a threat to anyone.'

Fitzgerald felt himself breaking out into a cold sweat. Panicking. Thinking that there was no Frank Ryan to save him this time. 'I didn't hear a thing,' he lied. 'My ears . . . the doctor said it could take weeks before I hear properly again.'

'Oh don't worry, Sean. I'm sure he was scrounging drinks down the street and upset a few lads who were the worse for it themselves. Might have even run into a few off-duty squaddies somewhere who decided to use him as a punching bag. It was always going to happen . . . and if not that then the drink would have killed him soon enough.'

'It's just that you told me once that I was responsible for his safety. I was worried, so I was.'

Cavenaugh patted the young man on the back. 'I can't expect you to be your brother's keeper and go off across the water and pick up one of the enemy all at the same time, can I? And you with your injuries.' A quick glance at his watch. 'More importantly, I'd like you to leave here at exactly three o'clock this afternoon to take the envelope. Our man doesn't go to work until six. Go on foot. We don't want anybody else knowing about your errand. Got that?'

'Sure enough.'

Cavenaugh opened the door. The big half-starved white dog looked up at him with the same pleading eyes. It started whining. 'There is one other small thing you can do for me. Call it a personal favour if you like.'

Personal favours for Pat Cavenaugh! Things were looking up. 'Name it.'

'When you leave at three, shoot this dog will you?'

'The dog?'

'It was Mouse's in a way. It'll just sit and pine until it dies anyway. Cruel to be kind. You understand? I'll send someone round at three fifteen with a sack to pick up the body and dispose of it.'

Fitzgerald looked out of the door at the flea-bitten mongrel. A grin spread over his face. 'Not a problem.' He'd take pleasure in shooting the mangy fucking thing. It had kept Celia awake half the night. 'What about your ten-pound note?' He started to hand it back.

'It's yours, Sean. Take your girlfriend out tonight. Have a meal and a drink; maybe take her to the pictures. You'll deserve a bit of fun after this afternoon's fireworks.'

23

With John Winter it was never a case of *What you see is what you get*. He was deeper than that. Perhaps his wretched childhood had fostered the need to secrete things, even knowledge, in some dark recess of his mind. Not least when August Gant had once asked him if he had read Clausewitz, and he had responded by saying it was only the officers who studied the strategies of war. Not quite true. But that conversation had had little significance. It had been a 'feeling out' exercise. And Winter only ever gave minimum information. The wretched childhood reinforcing the soldier's iron discipline. The result: an implacable adversary. A reason why he now turned to Clausewitz. Or at least a small illustration of a thesis on strategy: *Attack when your opponent thinks he has won, and then at the point where he least expects it.*

It was mid-morning and he was standing at the window sharpening the edge of a sliver of metal. Through a slit in the curtains he watched the farmyard below. Frank Ryan was there with a group of his men.

He seemed to be doing all the talking. The men — five of them — were listening intently. Obviously some kind of briefing. This was D-Day after all.

He turned back to the bed. Nancy was sleeping now. After a long night, the young man whom he now knew as Billy Costello had come to the door and had escorted him at gunpoint to the bathroom, where he had been allowed to empty the bucket, and go to the toilet, and this morning — for the first time since his capture — wash and shave and clean his teeth. Folded up on the floor of the bathroom a change of clothes — a complete number two dress of a sergeant of 2 Para. He had dressed slowly, finding the experience of putting on an army uniform again quite alien. He had found a first aid kit on top of the bathroom cabinet and had persuaded the gunman to allow him to take it to tend Nancy's wound. He had washed the facial cut with hydrogen peroxide from a small plastic bottle, and taped a wound dressing to her cheek. The cut had knit together. Even so there was too much swelling yet to know how bad the scar would be. Bad enough for any beautiful woman, of that he was sure. Lastly he had given her four codeine tablets. Billy had escorted her to the bathroom after that.

Later he had returned with two mugs of hot sweet tea and a few slices of buttered toast. He also brought a pair of jeans and a sweater and ankle boots for Nancy. She had dressed quickly. No conversation or eye contact this morning. Winter didn't make an issue of it. Sensed the effect the uniform was having on her. One of Frank's little mind games perhaps! A part of her IRA training profile: learning to kill the uniform. The one that had murdered her children. Now she was locked up in the same room with it – it was not John Winter any more, not even a close facsimile, but a generic and abhorrent and faceless soldier. That close. And she, branded as a collaborator. Possibly destined to share the same fate. She would have seen her razored scalp in the bathroom mirror. The black, congealed blood from a dozen small cuts. The red, puffy eyes. The large wound dressing concealing what to her mind would now be a hideous scar – something she would bear witness to every day of her life (if there was to be a life). Plenty of little voices from training lectures and teachings of the Mother Church to remind her of her crime. Hammer blows to the soul – something Catholics feared more than anything else on earth.

Purgatory would be no better: it would lay the deaths of her children firmly at her own feet. Given time such a prisoner would start to question his or her own involvement. Given more time they would begin to believe they really were the guilty party. Given a way out – like a conveniently discarded razor blade on a bathroom floor – they may well slash their wrists. A cardinal sin from which there could be no forgiveness. The only drawback with guerilla forces linked to the Church of Rome: general lack of selection and training hindered by Latin incantations from birth designed to promote fear and superstition. No IRA manual yet conceived could produce the calibre of soldier they were up against. Time and money and the ever-present Vatican bogeyman would always prevent such comparisons. Even so, the IRA possessed something that even the British Army's finest did not – *a country under siege, a country to fight for*. Winter's thoughts as he stood at the window staring out at the fields beyond the farm.

And the rest of it?

Once during the night she had told him what she had overheard about the plan to drop him on Craogh Parc. The obvious reason for the uniform. Which didn't leave much time for him to get out of this place. Problem was, how? And even though the boots he was now wearing gave some support to his badly bruised feet, how far would he get, assuming he could break out in the first place? Notwithstanding that, he now had Nancy to consider.

Fortunately, Billy had made two basic mistakes. The first was that he had allowed Winter to take the first-aid box to the bedroom to clean and dress Nancy's wound. What the gunman failed to notice was that Winter had slid the bottle of hydrogen peroxide under Nancy's body along with a packet of plasters. The second mistake was in giving Winter the army uniform so early in the day – especially as Nancy had told him they were not planning to airlift him out until later that evening. The boots provided him with a possible means of escape, in that they both had curved steel tips nailed to the toes and heels. Winter had successfully removed one of the heel tips. The one he was now sharpening on the steel window frame.

Teach Cusack had completed refuelling the helicopter after breakfast that morning, with jet fuel delivered in 5-gallon drums from one of Ryan's contacts at Dublin airport. As he hauled himself up into the cockpit to recheck various airway charts and topographical maps (and even a current road map torn from a motorist's road atlas), Ryan appeared. Cusack had picked up the movement in his peripheral vision. He now watched the Irishman approach through the eerie green light that filtered through the camouflage netting pegged out like a marquee at a summer fete. 'Everything okay?' Ryan asked easing himself up a few more inches on the skid.

'Just checking the real estate between here and Sligo.'

'How long a flight?'

'Still air conditions: One hour. Problem tonight – according to the weather office over at Dublin airport – is that there's a low-pressure system coming in off the Atlantic. Forecast to hit the west coast at about twenty hundred. Given headwinds and shit visibility, I figure our eta Sligo about twenty thirty. Possibly later. Any chance of bringing the op forward by an hour?'

'No chance at all. We go as briefed earlier. To the second.'

'Had a feeling you'd say that.'

'When did you get the weather update?'

'Few minutes ago.'

'Any chance it'll change?'

'Same question I asked. Weather guy seemed pretty negative. I'll check later though.'

'Anything else you need?'

'Any luck with the frequencies the Army will be using tonight?'

'We've got one of our lads trying to get that right now from a tame air traffic controller over at Dublin.'

'But even without it, it's still a "go" situation. Right?'

'Right.'

'One last thing. What sort of guns have we got?'

'AK-47, that's all . . . What about the Army helicopters?'

'Miniguns at least. Rockets. No chance of either until they've got us away from any built-up areas . . . usual procedure a few shots across the bows, then escort you to nearest airport for landing.'

'And if you fail to comply?'

'Difficult one to call. As I said, no one would want to shoot down an aircraft over a heavily populated area, especially if the threat was seen as unknown or minimal – like a civilian airplane straying into classified military airspace by accident.'

'And as it'll be dark they won't see the camouflage, right?'

'Likely not. Except there'll be an American president down there . . . They might consider this an attempt on his life.'

'Which means what?'

'Beats the hell out of me. Shoot first ask questions later, I guess.'

'What about the odds of being spotted?'

'As I mentioned earlier, with sunset at nineteen hundred we'll be operating initially in that fifteen-minute twilight period – I monitored it last night. Might be darker tonight though, given the gradually lowering cloud cover spreading in from the west. If we can stay down in the dirt and pull up for the drop as late as possible I'd say the odds were pretty good. The problem arises after that. We'll be picked up in the light from the stadium high intensity floods . . . that's when any helos out there on patrol are going to see us.'

'Then it's all down to trying to outrun them.'

'I'm going to strip out all the surplus weight today – every damn thing I reckon is non-essential – make us as light as possible, see if we can squeeze a little more than the hundred and ten knots the manufacturer intended. The military version of this bird is seriously heavy. Armour plating, guns, rockets, extra crewmen. So we should have an edge. Only problem is . . . we can't outrun their rockets if they get a good bead on us and decide it's showtime.'

Ryan remained emotionless. 'Anything else you want to tell me?'

'Remember the flight in? Oil pressure problems? It's that fucked-up-luck thing again. Always expect the unexpected, that was what they used to tell us on night patrols in 'Nam. So we did. The gooks had a real uncanny knack of coming up with new ways to kill you . . . In the meantime I'll try and remember some of the tricks our helo guys used in 'Nam. Might save our necks.'

'Big payday if you do,' Ryan said. 'See you later.'

Cusack watched him move away and duck under the netting. A cold-hearted bastard if ever he'd met one. The way he'd conducted the briefing outside the farmhouse that morning, explaining to all gathered how his wife had been found guilty of being a collaborator, the reason she had had her head shaved the previous night. (Billy, who had helped him with the refuelling, had told him she'd also had her face opened up from eye to jaw. Said she looked like shit. Then laughed and added quietly to the American that you'd probably need to put a paper bag over her head before you fucked her now.) But it was after the briefing that Ryan had taken him aside and dropped the bombshell. *Four on board tonight, Teach. You, me, and the two prisoners. The two prisoners will be tied up prior to loading on to the helo. Once you have confirmed that we have a clear run into the DZ I will go aft and execute both prisoners and untie their hands and feet. We will be in contact throughout via headsets. You will keep me informed of progress to centre of DZ and altitude. When you state DZ NOW, I will throw out both bodies. Once they are clear I will state COMPLETE – COMPLETE. You will then vacate the area rapidly. I will remain at door with the AK-47 in event we are approached by unfriendlies.*

As simple as that. Two prisoners. No names, but it was obvious who they were. The British Army guy he could understand. But his own wife for Christ's sake!

All of which made him wonder whether he was going to get paid at the end of the mission, or receive the time-honoured reward of Stateside pilots who had performed a successful drug run for one of the Latino mobs – a bullet in the back!

His options however were extremely limited. Bankruptcy was one, assuming of course he could find someone dumb enough to lend him a lot of money to spend that he had no hope of ever repaying . . . some fucking joke. Going back to jail, another – halfway decent food, free uniform, maybe even a recreation room where you could shoot a little pool in the evenings. Then again the sex wasn't all it was cracked up to be. Which left what? Re-enlisting! Going back on a troop transport to the flipside of the over-the-rainbow Oz? Where the yellow brick road of darkness had been his best friend. Risking being butchered on some patrol by a bunch of miniature brown NVA bastards. He had the distinct feeling that his future wasn't quite as peachy as he had first thought.

24

It had been raining spasmodically for the past hour – light warm front drizzle – as the Saracen armoured personnel carrier with four heavily armed and bulkily clad British soldiers rocked and swerved its way past City Hall heading towards the Markets and the Short Strand. They had been out since early morning and were cold, wet, and smelly. They were also sweaty under the heavy flak jackets and thick army woollens.

'Another waste of fookin' time then,' the Geordie corporal spat, as he peered out through one of the letterbox slits.

'What we lookin' for again?' The driver. A Brummie with a distinctive nasal twang.

'Some bright spark phoned HQ. Said there was shootin' in Cawnpore Street . . . that the gunman was headin' this way . . . that he was wearin' a white bandage round his head.'

'How the fuck would they know he was headin' this way exactly?'

'Because they fuckin' follered 'im,' a third soldier chipped in. 'Not like it's important is it?'

'Just keep a fookin' lookout, man,' the corporal ordered. A nervous edge to his voice. He had spotted the trouble up ahead.

Overspill from the previous night. A single-decker bus on its side. Well ablaze. A small group of youths started grabbing stones and empty bottles to throw at the Saracen. Another youth was lighting a length of cloth that hung from a milk bottle. Molotov cocktail. The youth threw it. A dull explosion as it hit the vehicle. Flames. Black smoke. The group grew braver at that, their ranks seeming to swell in number from no immediately apparent source. Fists punching the air. Mouths screaming obscenities. Rocks raining in like meteorite showers. Another Molotov cocktail arcing against the leaden sky but falling short, igniting a patch of tarmac roadway. And another . . . and another . . .

The corporal had had enough. Could now see the hatred in the eyes of the stone-throwing boys . . . they were that close. Found himself picturing the fate of two of his mates – both corporals – who'd taken a wrong turning a few months back and found themselves in the middle of a crowd attending a Republican funeral. They had been stripped naked and beaten to death outside a nearby pub – which was now jokingly referred to by the Sinn Feiners as the Corporals' Rest. The same thing was not going to happen to him. Especially with only 181 days to go to demob. 'Let's get the fook awaah from here, Mills.'

The driver began to slowly turn the vehicle.

Too slowly it seemed for the corporal. 'Any fookin' time this week, man . . . Move it, for Christ's sake!'

John Templeton Smith

*

A little over 2 miles away the Republican funeral was drawing to a close. The rain had eased for a moment. The wind smelled of it even so – all 2,000 miles of an Atlantic crossing distilled into every breath.

The earlier procession for Cathal Kennedy, the little-used (or known) real name of Mouse, had become an occasion for a huge display of nationalist solidarity. It had turned into a spectacular and moving affair due mainly to the rioting of the previous evening and the rumour that had spread like wildfire that one of the legendary 'forties men' had died in the battle (no one asked how, but laid the blame squarely on the British Army). The procession, numbering as many as 5,000 mourners (*And not a dry eye amongst them*, a newspaper article was later to report) had been led by a pipe and drum band, while the coffin had been flanked by a black-clad guard of honour. The clatter of British Army surveillance helicopters overhead had only served to intensify the emotional cohesion of the crowd.

Now, moments before interment six smartly uniformed men materialized at the graveside and fired a volley over the coffin. A great cheer went up from the mourners. The IRA men melted away into the crowd where women held up umbrellas to shield them from the helicopters as they stripped off their uniforms which, along with the guns, magically disappeared.

The silver-haired Pat Cavenaugh, face grey as the day itself, watched as the coffin was lowered. Listened to the words plucked from Father Michael's mouth by the blustery afternoon wind. Felt the numbness of the occasion. Glanced down at his watch. Then offered his own silent prayer: *Deep peace of the quiet earth to you, Cathal Kennedy, if ever a man had a loyal friend it was you . . . So a safe journey to you now . . . Oh, and I sent your old dog along, he was missing you.*

And back across the city. The Geordie corporal spotted their man a few hundred yards further down the street. Quite by accident as it happened. He'd been eyeing up a girl in a mini-skirt and tall high-heels tottering along the pavement – fantasizing what he could do to her given half a chance. She had stopped to speak to someone half-concealed in a shop doorway. *A man with a white bandage around his head.* Had to be the gunman! Couldn't be anyone else. He yelled for the driver to stop. Told his oppo to give him cover. Clambered out of the Saracen, SMG raised.

Sean Fitzgerald saw the armoured car stop and the soldier tumbling out of it a number of seconds after one of his old girlfriends had cornered him coming out of the shop where he'd stopped to buy a packet of cigarettes – someone else who had heard the stories of him with his injuries being flown into Aldergrove on a private plane, and she, another Catholic ghetto girl like Celia, loved heroes. She was reaching out to take his hand, asking if he'd like to take her out tonight, when he pushed her aside and started to run down the street. Heard the pounding boots closing on him. He snatched the Makarov pistol from his pocket, half-turned and let off a shot. A clatter of SMG fire was returned. He dived behind a parked car. He was sweating now, despite the cold. His skin prickling. From under the vehicle, just below the rusted silencer, he saw two pairs of soldier's boots slowly advancing.

Shit. *Shit.* He took aim with a shaking hand and started firing.

The corporal, joined by his oppo, ran for cover behind a van on the opposite side of the street.

'Down there,' the corporal motioned to his number two, who sprinted for the cover of another vehicle on the same side as the van. Two rapid pistol shots followed him. Thin cracks across the now deserted street.

The Geordie corporal edged closer to the end of the van. 'The things we do for glory!' he muttered softly, trying to gee himself up for the big moment. He looked down the pavement. Gave a hand signal. His number two started firing. That was when he braced his body and peered around the end of the van. Across the street. And saw the strangest thing. The gunman was in the clear, standing up, struggling it seemed to open the zip on the windcheater he was wearing. Clawing at it with both hands. The gun nowhere to be seen. A comic figure, a jerking marionette, feet dancing a jig. No comedy in the face though . . . It was filled with panic.

Sean Fitzgerald had dived for cover flat on his stomach, terrified that the bullets would hit him. Completely forgetting that the large bulky envelope was concealed beneath his windcheater. It was only when he had fired the third time, across the street at the running shape of a soldier, that he had remembered the home-made bomb. The candle wax phial. Now squashed from his impact with the pavement. The sulphuric acid, slowly eating its way through the condom . . . *Three condoms . . . Sixty seconds at least . . . I've checked it out very carefully.*

How many fucking seconds had it been now? How many more seconds before the fucking acid made contact with the sodium chlorate . . . the weedkiller? Except the fucking zip was stuck. He looked down in terror; saw a corner of the envelope meshed into the zip. Panicked even more. Reached for the tight elasticated waistband of the windcheater. Forced a hand up inside. Grabbed the bulky envelope with sweaty, shaking fingers . . . Started tugging it clear . . . 'Jayzus-Jayzus-Jayzus.'

The last words Sean Fitzgerald ever uttered.

From across the street the Geordie corporal and his number two had moved out of cover. SMGs raised to the aim. The number two was making the first tentative step off the pavement, when the gunman opposite him simply exploded. No shout. No scream. It was that quick. Disintegrating flesh and bone and blood, flying in all directions . . . Taking the glass out of the parked car he was next to, as well as windows in a building behind the spot where he had been standing.

Both soldiers were thrown back. Concussion from the blast.

'What the fuck was that?' the number two yelled in horror as he staggered back to his feet.

'Looks like he was fookin' carryin'.'

'You think it was meant for us?'

The corporal looked up the street. The stone- and bottle-throwing youths had reappeared. Soundlessly. Like a flock of starlings. Winging there way towards them. 'Move . . . move . . . move,' he screamed, pointing his SMG purposefully towards the flock. *Rules of engagement: No firing unless fired upon first.*

The starlings hesitated at the sight of the aimed weapon of the running soldier. Just long enough.

That fookin' close, the corporal thought, as they drove away at high speed. Jesus Christ, he was getting too old for this game. He picked up the radio mike. Hit the transmit button. A momentary mental block as he tried to remember orders of the day. The latest colour code. Then he had it. 'Red One Seven to Blue Six Two.'

A surf-shingle sound carrier wave pause as someone keyed their transmit button. A calm voice said: 'Red One Seven pass your message.'

The corporal took a deep breath and started.

His number two was staring wide-eyed out of his letterbox, shaking all over. The nineteen-year old private from Leytonstone in north London had never seen anything like it in his life. The thought that the bomb had been meant for them was all the more terrifying. When he accidentally brushed a hand against his combat jacket and found the small flap of wet flesh – hair still attached to it – stuck to his fingers, he started to gag. When he looked down and saw he was covered in blood and body parts, he started screaming.

25

Winter was lying on the bare wooden floor. He had taken off his jacket earlier and rolled it into a pillow. Laid his head back and closed his eyes and gone over the plan time and time again in his mind. Looking for the one solitary mistake. The one little overlooked detail that would cost him his life. And when that line of self-questioning was exhausted, trying to find a possible flaw in the enemy's thinking that would give him the one and only chance he needed to break out. Remembered tracts of the IRA Green Book. The way his enemy played the game:

The Army as an organization claims and expects your total allegiance without reservation. It enters into every aspect of your life. It invades the privacy of your home life, it fragments your family and friends, in other words claims your total allegiance.

All potential volunteers must realize that the threat of capture and long jail sentences are a very real danger and a shadow which hangs over every volunteer. Many in the past joined the Army out of romantic notions, or sheer adventure, but when captured and jailed they had afterthoughts about their allegiance to the Army. They realized at too late a stage that they had no real interest in being volunteers. This causes splits and dissension inside prisons and divided families and neighbours outside. Another important aspect all potential volunteers should think about is their ability to obey orders from a superior officer. All volunteers must obey orders issued to them by a superior officer regardless of whether they like the particular officer or not.

Was Billy Costello, the young gunman, someone who would question Frank Ryan's orders? Winter didn't think so. The other IRA man, Sean, had been altogether different. Untrained. Fearful even. A look in the eyes that told you he was incapable of handling himself well in an emergency. Billy was different. He was trained to kill. Would squeeze the trigger without a moment's hesitation. And yet, everybody carried weaknesses. The problem was in discovering and exploiting them.

He got up from the floor and went over to the window. Looked out through the slit in the curtains. Overcast sky. No sun.

Nancy stirred. Opened her eyes. 'Is it time?' she asked. A small frightened voice.

He looked across at her. A battered and bruised rag doll. Her head was turned slightly away from him, a hand held up to the dressing on the left side of her face. And he felt a great sadness: sadness for her, because she had at least tried to offer compassion to her enemy, and in so doing had lost the only thing she had left. Her beauty. 'Time?'

'Did I tell you they were planning to take you this evening?'

'Yes.'

'I think they said seven o'clock.'

'A few hours to go yet.'

'I might still have a gun . . .'

'What sort of gun?'

'An automatic.'

'Where?'

'In the bedroom at the other end of the landing.'

The bullets would need to be scooped and a deep cross cut into the head of each. No range. No accuracy to speak of. The bullet would begin to tumble 5 yards from the barrel. But when it hit, it would splat as wide and thin as a piece of tinfoil, and a nick in the forearm would slam the victim down as though he had been struck by a train. *If you had the gun and the bullets in the first place.* 'Where in the bedroom?'

'The top left hand drawer of the dressing table. Frank obviously searched the room while I was in the town last night . . . He might not have found it.'

'Ah.'

'That was when he found the letter,' she added.

'Did you try and explain . . .'

'Explain what? That it was all innocent and nothing ever happened?'

'That you returned favour for favour.'

'He doesn't know about what happened at Crossmaglen, that I shot the soldier . . . that you took my place and let me go.'

'Perhaps if he did he would understand.'

'Understand!' A bitter laugh. 'He's past under-standing, that man. He's so caught up in hatred, in the mob violence thing, that he only sees what he wants to see, only hears what he wants to hear . . . Besides, I wouldn't give the bastard the pleasure of seeing me beg for my life.'

'How many of them?'

'Five plus Frank.'

'All armed?'

'What else . . . not much chance is there?'

'Not much, no. Do you know how many are going to be on the helicopter?'

'I'm not sure. I think Frank and the pilot at least.'

'Who's the pilot?'

'American. Irish-American.'

'Name?'

'Cusack. Teach Cusack. I heard him and Frank talking. Seems he was in Vietnam.'

Ex-military. That was something worth knowing. 'Nothing else?'

She could have told him how she had come back to Ireland out of a feeling of guilt. That she felt she had somehow betrayed him by allowing Frank to pick him up in Scotland earlier than she had promised. She could have told him that when she arrived at the house on the first night and heard he was there, that she had tried to persuade Billy to let her see him by herself – a half-thought-out idea that perhaps she could give him the chance she had promised in the hotel room in Wick, and let him escape. But Billy had refused point blank. Which had left her to play the hard bitch. Proving to the gunman that she really was who he believed her to be. An IRA woman with a score

to settle. She could have told him a lot more things . . .
But what was the use? It was all a little late in the day
for miracles. 'No, nothing else . . . except I think
they're taking me as well.'

He moved slowly across the room and sat on the
edge of the bed. He'd been afraid of that. 'I'm sorry,
Nancy. I'm sorry I got you involved.'

'You didn't . . . Whatever happened is my own
fault. Besides what is there to live for? I've lost my
children . . .'

'And your husband.'

'Oh, I lost him a long time ago. The problem with the
'RA, they take everything. Give nothing in return.'

Winter picked up a boot from the floor and examined
the sliver of metal he had sharpened and reversed and
nailed back into the heel, using the heel of the other
boot as a hammer. *Means of escape.* The problem was,
how many minutes would he have? 'What do you
know about Billy?'

'Nothing.'

'Is he a friend of Frank's?'

'No . . . I think he was brought in by Pat Cavenaugh.'

'Who's he?'

'Sort of Intelligence Chief of the Belfast 'RA.'

'Ex-soldier?'

'Who, Pat? No. A schoolteacher.'

His old training still at work. Here he was a civilian,
about to come face to face with his maker, and he was
still acting as though he belonged to a regiment. What
the hell did it matter what this Pat Cavenaugh was,
had been or was about to be? There was no 'green
slime' (SAS argot for Intelligence) of his own to whom
he could pass on the latest field report. He wondered

how long it took for an ex-soldier to become a fully paid-up member of civvy-street. To finally forget the language, the discipline, the umbilical-chord-like loyalty!

'Does Billy get on with Frank okay?'

'I suppose, why?'

'Nothing. Just wondering if I could play one off against the other.'

'I think our only chance is getting that gun . . . if it's still there.'

'Billy only usually comes twice a day . . . I doubt he'll be paying his usual visit this evening.'

'You could bang on the door to get his attention.'

'Then what? He's hardly going to allow you to take a walk to your bedroom.'

'Maybe not, but there is one thing most men have an aversion to.'

'Like what?'

'Leave that to me. If you had a gun what could you do against five of them?'

'Not five. Two.'

'Two?'

'On the helicopter. That's the only realistic opportunity I'll have to use it.'

'And if our hands are tied?'

Winter lifted his boot and showed her the heel and the razor edge sliver of steel standing proud. 'Cut through the rope or tape with this.'

'So what were you intending to do assuming you didn't have a gun?'

The slit in the inside seam of his left trouser leg. The plastic bottle of hydrogen peroxide he had retrieved from her side earlier whilst she slept. Now taped to his calf. Something to blind his captors with, perhaps. 'Try and jump whoever's holding the gun.'

'No expense spared with the SAS in teaching its men how to overcome adversity, is there?' Some of the old fire back in the voice.

'What you have to remember is: it will be practically dark. We will be in an alien environment of noise and movement, and we will have the element of surprise on our side.'

'You'd better see if you can get Billy's attention then,' she said. She swung her legs off the end of the bed. Stared at the blank wall opposite. If she was afraid she didn't show it. Another of the IRA's lessons.

The luck of the Irish was running for them both that afternoon. Winter had no sooner reached the door and was about to start banging on it when he heard footsteps in the corridor. He moved back to the other side of the room and sat on the floor. The key turned in the lock. Billy Costello had put a tray down on the floor. He eased it forward into the room with the toe of his boot. All the time his eyes watching the occupants of the room. Gun hand as always, very steady.

Nancy looked down at the tray and the two tin mugs. 'What's that?'

'Coffee . . . The American guy said Frank had told him to organize it.' He started to pull the door closed.

'I need to go to the bathroom.'

'You've got a bucket. That's what it's for.'

'It's not that. It's my period,' she said sharply. 'I thought it was over. It isn't. I need you to get me some sanitary towels and clean knickers from my bedroom . . . then I need to go to the bathroom to clean myself up, before there's blood everywhere. Naturally you can watch to make sure I'm not doing something I'm not supposed to.'

There was a look of embarrassment bordering on horror in Billy's eyes. 'Jesus, woman, I wouldn't even do that for my own girlfriend. You come and get the fucking things.' He waved the gun. Motioned for her to move.

She got up from the bed and stepped over the tray and out into the hall.

Winter looked on in disbelief. Watched the door close. Listened as the key grated in the lock. That simple. That bloody simple.

Before any potential volunteer decides to join the Irish Republican Army he should understand fully and clearly the issues involved. He should not join the Army because of emotionalism, sensationalism or adventurism. He should examine fully his own motives, knowing the dangers involved and knowing that he will find no romance within the Movement. Again he should examine his political motives bearing in mind that the Army is intent on creating a socialist republic.

He shook his head and started to laugh softly to himself. . . . *he will find no romance within the Movement.* That was a good one. No man in any Movement would find romance in sanitary towels.

26

It took the Italian-looking Billy Costello a leisurely two hours to reach the garage on the road to Castleblayney, by way of Navan, Kingscourt and Shercock – by way of thatched cottages with tidy whitewashed walls, sleeping ruins of Benedictine priories, crumbling round towers, decaying high crosses. All under a lowering sky.

Even so he'd felt like flooring the accelerator to see how fast the Corsair would go. He'd been told about the hotted-up engine, the 11.4:1 compression ratio. Had felt the firm ride of the lowered suspension. Loved the wire wheels and the gaping black hole where the radiator grill had been removed for improved cooling. Even the wood-trimmed racing steering wheel gave him the feeling of being at the controls of something slightly lethal. The reason he was wearing the chamois leather driving gloves was not so much a rally-driver image thing, more a *Green Book* directive: *All Vols [Volunteers] on operations must wear gloves and also hoods in so far as circumstances will allow.*

The engine note faded as he pulled into the garage

forecourt, being replaced by a low throaty burble from the tuned straight-through exhaust.

'Nice pleasant drive,' Gerry Faul (or 'Brilliantine Man' as Billy had nicknamed him because of the excessive use of the stuff on his fifties-era teddy boy hairstyle) remarked.

'Let's hope it remains that way . . . Where's the van stashed by the way?'

Faul pointed to the line of vehicles.

'Clever, very clever,' Costello conceded. 'Better clean the "sold" sign off the windshield, wouldn't want the Gardai stopping you to check on the registration documents would we?'

Five minutes later the van was driving away from the garage, leaving an oily blue smokescreen in its wake. The Corsair followed at a discreet distance.

They reached the launch site twenty minutes later. Everywhere was quiet. A perfect rustic stillness. Costello backed the Corsair up to the big white van which Faul had positioned on the grassy knoll by the copse they'd recce'd the previous day. The two men set about unloading the mortar bombs from the boot of the car. The light was fading fast by the time Costello drove the car back down to the road. Pointing it the way they had come. He got out and lifted the bonnet. Propped it open. *Reasons for being here.* He now stood by the driver's door, keeping a watchful eye on the deserted country road.

A few minutes later Faul jogged down to him. 'You . . . could have parked a bit bloody nearer . . . so you could,' he complained, bended nearly double, fighting for breath. Winded at the enforced hundred-yard exercise.

'Need to be on the road, Brilliantine Man. Good vis in both directions . . . anyway, what's the problem?'

'Thought we'd better do a time check,' Faul suggested. 'You know what Frank's like for punctuality in operations.'

Costello didn't, simply because he didn't know Frank Ryan that well. Even so he played the good soldier and looked at his watch. Paused for a moment. 'Eighteen-forty-five in ten seconds . . . five, four, three, two, one . . . mark.' A line he had picked up from some old American war movie. Anything to appease the boys from Belfast.

Faul glanced at the .22 Hornet rifle with the telescopic sight that Costello was nursing, and grinned. 'I see you've got the elephant gun.' It was the same reference he had made earlier at the farm when he had told the young man he might as well be carrying a fucking peashooter, that he'd be lucky to stop a tortoise at 20 fucking yards with a thing like that. Small-calibre bullets, he'd gone on. Need to be a first-class marksman with a thing like that, or else you're dead. Costello had told him it was his lucky gun, omitting the fact that he was using specially made-up Hornady 45 grain (2.9 gram) .22 Hornet hollow-point bullets. Nothing more had been said about it until this moment.

Now, the slim young man with the olive-coloured skin brushed the long dark hair from his eyes, and said quietly, 'You do your job, I'll do mine.'

'Time to get started then,' Faul replied, not unaware of the total coolness of the other man, and trying (more out of personal pride than anything else) to keep the nervousness he felt out of his own voice. He jogged away, back up the grassy incline to the stand of trees and the parked van. He had positioned the vehicle precisely on the line with a blue and white marker post he had driven into the soft earth – and in accordance with the written instructions passed to him the previous day – and the distant chimney at Bantrain. He now chocked the wheels with the house bricks he'd stowed in the back of the vehicle. Then he climbed in the van and sprung open the loose panels to bring up the mortar rack. Hammering in the tapered bolts in the base plate he sighted the rack against the distant skyline. There was a dim orange glow from the village lighting, throwing up the chimney in sharp silhouette. He aligned the blue and white marker with the chimney . . . dead in line with the RUC post.

There was no wind, and he spent the next two minutes taking up the threads on two bolts to get the angles correct, adjusting his black-framed Buddy Holly-style glasses to squint along the line of the rack.

With a final push upwards he popped out the Plexiglass roof, giving a clear run for the bombs on their initial trajectory.

He looked at his watch. Noticed his hands were shaking. He tried to hold them still by spreading his fingers wide. It didn't work. If anything, the shakes got worse. Concentrate, he told himself. *For fuck's sake concentrate.* Seven minutes to go to the 1900 deadline. He quickly loaded the six bombs into the terry-clips suspended above the mortar tubes. Pulling out the homemade safety pins, he threaded a line of dimex fuse through each of the eyeholes in the springs of the safety pins. As the fuse burned at one foot per second it would trigger each safety pin, move the terry-clip back fractionally, and drop the mortar bomb down into the tube. The detonation at the bottom of the tube would send it on its way. The first five would take four seconds to leave, the sixth wouldn't go anywhere, but would explode inside its plastic tube leaving the van unrecognizable. The four spare bombs were placed on the floor at the back of the van. Possible secondary explosion, which would add to the destruction of the vehicle.

Faul began running out the fuse wire. Thirty feet. Thirty seconds' burn time. *Then again he had to cover a hundred yards to the car.* Fifty feet might be better. He checked his watch again. Watched the sweep second hand counting off the final minutes.

At the Salvation Army Citadel in Bantrain, Corps Sergeant-Major Estelle Manners was becoming rather anxious. The Bedford OB bus parked outside was still not ready. Not that she could blame the driver, he had done everything possible to get the replacement starter motor. The fact that they had sent the wrong one that morning had been followed by a string of apologies from the Belfast garage responsible, and a promise that they would deliver the correct one that afternoon. By the time the concert had ended a few minutes before five o'clock there was still no sign of it.

The local army members had been wonderful even so, and had put on another late-afternoon tea. Trestle tables groaning under the weight of sandwiches and cake, ice cream and lemonade. The younger members of the Hoddingham Corps choir seemed quite happy with the unexpected turn of events.

The driver, Tiny Goodhall, came hurrying in to the

hall at that moment. Wiping his hands with an oily rag. 'We've got the bit,' he announced. 'The lad from the garage down the street just dropped it off.'

'Thank the Lord,' Estelle said feelingly. 'How long before I can start loading everybody up.'

'Right away,' Goodhall replied.

'What about fitting it . . . the bit you mentioned?'

A wide grin. 'Already done, innit. As I told you before, five minute job once I got the right part.'

Estelle smiled. 'I'll start right away then.'

Goodhall looked at his watch. 'Give me a couple of ticks . . . gotta pop up the street to pay the guv'nor at the garage and get a receipt. All right?' He hurried out of the hall.

Estelle turned to the choir and band members, the smile still on her face. 'Good news everybody. The bus is ready to go.'

A loud cheer rang up through the rafters.

Back on the south side of the border, Costello had been keeping a watchful eye on the narrow country road. The last few minutes had been the most nerve wracking. The thought that a Gardai car would suddenly appear out of nowhere seeming more and more likely with every heartbeat. But it hadn't. Just the gentle sounds of the Irish countryside at dusk: The occasional flapping of wings as the last of the birds winged their way homewards, the rustle of a wild animal in the hedgerow opposite, the hunting call of a solitary eagle owl.

He laid the rifle on the roof of the car and checked his watch. *Sixty-five seconds.* He tugged the chamois leather gloves tighter on to each hand in turn. Flexed his fingers. Took a deep breath to steady himself and picked up the rifle and focused the telescopic sight on the van.

Watching.

Waiting.

Saw Brilliantine Man kneel down.

Saw him checking his watch – imagined his voice counting off the seconds.

Saw the cigarette lighter coming out of the pocket. The brief flickering yellow flame being touched to the dimex fuse.

Saw him stand up and turn towards the waiting car.

And that was when Costello zeroed in with the .22 Hornet rifle. With such a small-calibre bullet he needed a head shot. The rifle had followed the figure with smooth precision as it stood up and turned to face him.

Costello squeezed the trigger. The rifle was zeroed for 100 metres, so the 45 grain hollow point bullet, muzzle velocity 2,400 feet per second, required 2½ inches aim-off. There was no further sound. No movement. Billy Costello was good enough to know that the bullet had penetrated Brilliantine Man's skull (probably through the left eye, where he'd been aiming) and gone into the brain, fragmenting as it went. Little chance of survival from that kind of wound. *He knew from experience*. He swung the rifle over his head and hurled it into the nearby bushes. Dropped the bonnet. Then leapt into the Corsair and gunned it down the road.

Calmly counting the seconds as he racing-changed through the gears.

Then the mortar bombs were cascading – *ploy, ploy,*

ploy, ploy, ploy . . . the blue-note sound of wind in a drainpipe. The final bomb in the plastic tube exploded inside the van, taking out the front of the vehicle in a spectacular explosion. The four spare mortar bombs went off a fraction of a second later, a secondary explosion that ricocheted flaming fragments of what had once been the pride of the County Meath Medical Health Authority through the small copse.

The sound, as Costello knew, would cover a radius of perhaps ½ mile. Half a mile in a backwater area. And if anyone heard it at any one of the few scattered farms within that radius, how long before a phone call to the authorities would be acted upon? Assuming, of course, the farm in question had a telephone. Assuming of course they thought it important enough to get involved in the first place. He eased his foot off the accelerator and reduced his speed slightly. Foolish to get stopped for speeding at this stage of the game. He mentally went over his route home to Sligeach (he never referred to it by its Anglicized name of Sligo), before reaching forward with his left hand and switching on the radio. He tuned it until he found a music station. They said it affected gunmen who took part in rural operations in different ways: a few spoke of being so excited after a job that they shot the wee birds in the wires as they drove away from the killing ground, others that you felt like eating a big dinner because you felt so exhilarated afterwards; some how they could not stop whooping with joy. With Billy Costello it was music. Nat King Cole was crooning the old standard: 'I Love You For Sentimental Reasons'. Billy sang along at the top of his voice.

As for shooting Gerry Faul, aka Brilliantine Man,

without hesitation and without regret, he didn't give it
a second thought. In wartime killing was a way of life.
IRA lectures taught its members not to become
emotionally involved.

Besides which he had simply been following orders.
Still was.

27

They had come for them as darkness fell. Winter had been watching from the window for some time by then. Had observed a distant, shadowy figure – the pilot he had decided – remove a camouflage net from the chopper prior to climbing up into the cockpit. Had heard the 1400 shaft horsepower jet engine whining into life. The massive two-blade rotor beginning its slow beating sweep. That empty feeling in the gut before a patrol, heightened by the fact that this time the survival chances were limited to a very tight timeframe. He had briefly thought of the letter he had sent to Nancy, the one responsible for her being here. Had wanted to go to her and hold her and tell her that whatever happened he still loved her; that he always would. But he didn't. He sensed she was being brave enough as it was. Perhaps holding the memory of her children as close as she could. Better that way if things were going to go wrong.

It wasn't the young gunman, Billy, who came for them, but the two pale-faced minders he knew from that unknown airfield somewhere in England. The ones who had beaten him and questioned him incessantly. *My name is John Winter. I was born in Prague. And raised in Odessa on the Black Sea.* Something else that had caused him concern! Why had they stopped the beatings? When the pain had become too much and he was losing consciousness, had he given them the answers to the questions they had asked? Was that why? Or was it because they had decided it was unimportant? A new-found strategy? Like taking him over a football stadium in Dublin and throwing his body out, as Nancy had told him! The reason for such an elaborate plan went beyond revenge. Not that it mattered either way. If he were dead he would be past caring. If he survived, he had no intention of hanging around long enough to ask questions of his captors or their associates. Nancy's children had finally made his mind up: that it wasn't his war. And in a way it was because of them that he had read something of the history of Ireland during his months in America. Had come face to face with too many centuries of brutal oppression.

Their hands had been tied and he, in his soldier's uniform, had been patted down. One of those training disciplines that he'd mentioned to Nancy – the reason she was carrying the gun she had retrieved from the bedroom concealed amongst underwear and sanitary towels (perhaps the reason they had not bothered to do the same to her; or perhaps Billy had joked with them about it: *Jesus, you wouldn't want to get that sort of blood on your fuckin' hands!*). After that they had been escorted at a 20-yard interval to the helicopter. He had been expecting a blindfold. Nearly right. It was a black hood. Standard IRA execution kit. Before they made you kneel and shot you in the back of the head. He hoped he hadn't miscalculated.

He watched as the hooded figure of Nancy was hoisted up into to helo, rolled across the floor. He was next. The hood was tugged over his head, the smell of clean linen briefly filling his nostrils, before the familiar scent of jet fuel overpowered it and every-thing else. Then being half-lifted. Thrust with big powerful hands over the bare metal floor. He felt her body next to his. The door slid closed, locking out the rotor wash and some of the noise. He listened. A momentary increase of noise as another door opened. Shouting voices. An increase in engine power. The noise, without headsets, overwhelming. He reached his tied hands down towards the heel of his boot — something he had been practising all afternoon. Feeling for the sharpened edge of metal with his fingertips. A sharp stabbing pain as the metal stabbed into his hand. He worked the rope against it and began a slow seesawing motion.

Up front, Cusack — who had taken his customary amphetamine tablet an hour earlier (washed down with a small glass of whiskey) — waited impatiently as the two minders retreated back across the grass area. Caught in the landing light. Hair and clothes blowing wildly.

He looked across at Ryan who was holding his AK-47 upright between his legs. He flipped the intercom switch on. Laughter in the voice. 'Showtime, Frank! Ready for this?'

'Let's go,' Ryan snapped.

Cusack increased the power and eased the helo up and back in a slow hover, controlling the small pendulosity, before turning the aircraft away from the makeshift helicopter landing pad, switching off the landing light as he did so. He tracked across a field in the last of the twilight, floating upwards to some 50 feet or so, glancing at the extent and height of the cloud beyond the small valley that was his initial routing before turning southeast for the DZ.

'Time check?'

'Nineteen-o-four,' Ryan replied. 'How long in to the target area?'

'We'll be there on schedule . . . nineteen-fifteen.'

'Right. I'll be going back two minutes before the drop to do what's got to be done. Then I'll open the door.'

'Make sure you lock it in the open position like I showed you earlier.'

'I know . . . Once I've gone back I'll wait for you confirming we are over the DZ and you are in the hover at five hundred feet. Got that?'

'Got it.'

Ryan peered out, watching their steady progress towards Dublin. Felt the occasional thump of turbulence through the floor of the cockpit. 'What about the Army choppers patrolling the area?'

'I've got our one and only radio selected to the Dublin radar frequency your guy passed back to you.' He reached forward and checked the volume was turned up, then increased the squelch – a loud scratchy noise filled their headsets, before he decreased the knob fractionally until the noise was cancelled. Max tuning. 'Nothing yet . . . they could be operating on UHF though. Using this VHF frequency as a back up . . . other than that we'll be lower than them and they'll have their position lights on, so hopefully we'll see them first.'

'How much weight did you manage to strip out?'

'All the seats in the back. All the radio gear except for the ADF and the one radio. Not as much as I'd hoped but I still figure we'll be able to outrun the Army guys if it comes to that.'

'What about the weather?'

'Getting worse. By the time we get across to the west coast later we should have pretty heavy rain.'

'Something like that night flight out of Scotland then?'

'I seriously hope not.'

'Did you give any more thought to evasive measures?'

'The US helos patrolling the area you mean? Yeah, sort of. I figured the only plan would have been to drop your prisoners at the end of the game instead of the beginning.'

'Why so?'

'By that time the security patrol guys would be running out of "playtime" – you know, getting low on fuel. So even if they gave chase they'd only be able to do so for maybe thirty minutes. But then you did say there was no possibility of changing the insertion time. That right?'

'That's right.'

A wide grin. 'Not a problem, Frank. Look at it this way. No one's expecting us. Our only problem will be reducing speed to the hover over the stadium . . . That leaves us wide open for about thirty seconds. After that we hightail it outa Dodge.' He wasn't even thinking about a posse. He was feeling way too good for that.

Ryan checked his watch. Looked down at the road below. A few car headlights. People driving home from work. Others taking wives or girlfriends out for the night. *Lucky for some.* Ahead the city of Dublin was a welcoming myriad of white and orange light.

Ghostrider One was one of three US Army Hueys slated for the night patrol of the Dublin City area due to the presidential visit to Craogh Parc stadium that evening. That at least had been the SOP (standard operational procedure). The three helicopters had launched from a secure ramp location at Dublin airport at 1830 and had been on station for thirty-seven minutes now. Ghostrider One was patrolling the stadium area, whilst the other two machines (Ghostrider Two and Ghostrider Three) were covering the north–south perimeter lines of the city. Each helicopter carried a crew of five: two pilots and three gunners. Three back-up helicopters were on the ground at Dublin airport, fully crewed and on standby for immediate launch.

The SOP was compromised at 1909 hours.

'All Ghostrider aircraft this is Rambler.' An American voice. Calm, matter of fact. 'Condition RED. We have unconfirmed report of inbound "bogey" to *Chicago*. Planned ETA nineteen-fifteen. Intentions unclear. *Quarterback* has left the area.'

'Rambler from Ghostrider One, any height info?'

'Negative on the altitude, Ghostrider One, er, be advised "bogey" could be a helo.'

The other voices of the two remaining helicopters

came up in turn, verifying information copied and looking out.

The army captain who was commander on Ghostrider One, knew that the coded transmission, *Quarterback has left the area*, meant that the President of the United States had been whisked away under a tight security cordon by his private army of Secret Service guys. Whilst *Chicago* was the code name for Craogh Parc. He said to his number two. 'Whad'ya figure on the "bogey"?'

'Operating in blackout conditions that's for sure. Low-level if it's a helo.'

'How low?'

'If it was me, my ass would be draggin' the sidewalk.'

That concurred with the captain's thinking. He checked his altimeter: 1,250 feet. Glanced right and down into the bowl of light that was the football stadium. Quartered the area, expanding his scan. Too much background light. Any helo coming in at low level would be at the stadium before it was seen. He rolled the machine to the right and descended towards the stadium, at the same time switching on the high-power searchlight that was fitted to the left of the nose. He then called his flight and stated his intentions. By the time he was over the north edge of the stadium at 100 feet, the other two helos were approaching at high speed to join him around the stadium perimeter. In the meanwhile the second flight of three – Ghostriders Four to Six had been scrambled from nearby Dublin Airport.

Cusack had been following Ryan's map-reading instructions, even though they were unnecessary – it was a pretty straightforward run into the stadium. In fact from 700 feet he could already see the glow of the stadium lights on the base of the low cloud that blanketed the city and suburbs. What he couldn't make out though was the aircraft landing lights. He had picked up one, then two. Had thought they were airliners being radar-vectored into Dublin airport. Except they didn't seem to be moving. As he approached approximately six miles from the DZ he suddenly realized what they were.

'Fuck,' he shouted.

Ryan looked at him anxiously. Touched the boom mike to his lips. 'What?'

'See those lights . . . over the stadium area? Two . . . now three . . . look like helos. Shit, there's another two . . . above.'

'You're sure?'

'Watch. They're turning . . . see . . . top two have just turned away.'

'How many?'

'Four at least . . . Five. Like I said, the bastards gotta be operating on a UHF frequency . . . woulda heard somethin' by now otherwise.'

'Can we get under them?'

Cusack took a cigarette from his shirt pocket and lit it. Wished it was a joint. *Under them*? What the fuck did that mean? You went under them and into the stadium area and they fucking had you. Like a swarm of killer bees they'd lock on to you and escort you quietly away. And blow you out of the sky. And why not? They wouldn't know this was just a private little vendetta between the IRA and the Brits. They'd figure this was some serious shit, like a bunch of foreign mercenaries trying to take out the President of the United States. 'Under them? Then what?'

'Like you said this afternoon. They're hardly going to shoot us down over a heavily populated area, especially if we're down in the rooftops.'

'Except we can't stay over the city for fucking ever.'

Ryan partially unzipped the dark anorak and pulled out a pistol from his waistband. 'Just do it. I'm going back . . . I'll open the door first.'

Cusack eased the helo down. He was following a main road. Could clearly see the cars and trucks. The shadows of trees and lampposts from the street lighting. Difficult to acquire good night vision. He couldn't see any obstacles ahead, like high wires, or bridges or tall, unlit chimneys. 'You reading me?'

Ryan's voice came back angrily. 'The fucking extension lead isn't long enough, thought you said you checked it out.'

Cusack was breathing hard. His concentration high. 'Could be caught up around your seat . . . here at the front.'

Ryan came forward and grabbed for the AK47. 'I'll do without the headset . . . just get me to the middle of the park.'

'What height?'

'Couple hundred feet should do it . . . give me a count of ten in the hover.' Ryan was reaching up to pull off his headset when the entire cockpit was trapped in blinding white light.

'Shit,' Cusack cried, lifting a hand to shield his eyes.

'Just get us there,' Ryan screamed. He pulled off the headset and moved back with the AK-47. Slid open the side door and locked it. Then leaned out into the airflow and let off a burst of fire at the helicopter searchlight that was bearing down on them.

The pilot of Ghostrider One saw the twinkle of weapons fire almost immediately. His last tour of duty in 'Nam had involved a night extraction of marines trapped on a beach at Koh Tang. A very sobering night op. One on which he had witnessed enough perimeter muzzle flashes (looking like a string of flashing Christmas tree lights was how he always remembered it) to last him a dozen lifetimes. He didn't hang around, but immediately took evasive action. At the same time he thumbed his transmit switch. 'Ghostrider One is under fire . . .'

'One this is Two, roger that . . . we're coming in low from the "bogey's" left side . . . pull up, pull up.'

Ghostrider One complied as the second ship of the flight closed in. A marine marksman poised in the door, feet dangling over the edge into space. Searchlight coming on at the last second. Framing a gunman with an automatic weapon in the open doorway. The marksman tried to get a steady bead. By now the helicopters were less than 30 yards apart and half a mile from the stadium.

Winter had finally freed his hands and pulled the hood from his head. He was a matter of 3 feet behind Ryan. Could see the figure braced in the open door way. The second burst of fire blanketed the engine sound for a moment. The stink of cordite washed back into the ship. Winter screwed his eyes against the acrid smoke as he reached over to Nancy. Slipped a hand under her loose-fitting sweater and retrieved the pistol from the waistband of her jeans, pulled the hood from her head almost simultaneously. Then as the firing continued he moved into a crouched position. That was when Ryan was swung off balance by a violent maneuver of the helicopter. And in that moment his eyes saw Winter; caught in the beam of the other helicopter's searchlight.

The Irishman's mouth screamed something as he raised the AK47. His forefinger closed on the trigger.

He was a fraction of a second too late. The sniper's bullet hit him in the leg, spinning him round. Ryan's finger jerked back on the trigger – nothing more than a reflex action – sending a burst of fire forward into the cockpit. Despite his injuries he was trying to bring the gun back to bear when the helicopter rolled over on its side and he was pitched towards the open door. Dropping the weapon. Hands scrabbling to find a secure hold. But there was nothing to hold – just empty air. He disappeared soundlessly into the roaring slipstream. Winter and Nancy could do nothing but watch with horrific fascination, both certain they were about to crash as the top storeys of buildings with lit windows flashed past the open door.

The helo righted itself as it careened over the row of rooftops. Winter reached behind Nancy and quickly untied her hands and feet. Motioned her forward. He stayed close behind.

He reached over and pushed the gun into Cusack's neck.

The mottled face, sheened in sweat, turned towards him.

'Keep flying,' Winter yelled.

He pushed Nancy into the co-pilot's seat.

'Which way to Dublin airport?' he shouted at the pilot.

Cusack waved a hand back over his shoulder.

'Have you got a frequency for them?'

They were out over the suburbs to the south-west of Dublin now. Pitch black night. They passed through an isolated rain shower. An intense peckling sound on the aluminum fuselage. That was when Winter noticed the altimeter. Under 100 feet. That was when the searchlight of one of the pursuing army machines reacquired them. Winter snatched up the headset from the floor and slipped it over his head. 'You reading me?'

'Forget trying to get to Dublin,' Cusack yelled breathlessly, 'I gotta distinct feeling these guys intend to shoot us down at the first opportunity . . . besides the radios are out.' He jerked his head at the centre pedestal. Torn up by gunfire.

Nancy was tugging at his sleeve. He pulled the headset clear from his left ear and leaned close to her. 'Sligo,' she shouted.

'What's there?'

'Doesn't matter . . . trust me.'

Holding the gun as steady as he could against Cusack's neck, he said. 'We're going to Sligo . . . can you do that?'

'If we can lose that hotshot on our tail.'

Winter passed the gun to Nancy. Motioning her to keep it on the pilot. Before he removed the headset he told Cusack: 'I'll go back and give you a few seconds firing from that automatic. As soon as the searchlight pulls away, climb immediately. Try and get into the cloud. Then turn left through ninety degrees.'

'What about radar . . . we'll get picked up by Dublin.'

'You got any other suggestions?'

'No.'

Winter moved quickly back, picked up the AK-47 from the floor, and leaned out into the 100-knot slipstream. He let off a three-and-a-half-second burst before the magazine was expended. The chase ship veered sharply away. Then they were climbing and turning. Winter secured the door and went forward.

By then they were in the cloud. In the dim red glow of instrument light, he saw the dark wet patch on Cusack's sleeve. He put on the headset. 'You've been hit . . . how bad is it?'

The pilot reached over and touched his sleeve with his right hand. Grinned. No Purple fuckin' Heart for this one. 'Didn't feel a thing . . . nice thing about shock.'

At 900 feet they were in cloud. There was a steady rain falling. Steady to those on the streets below that is. Here, at 110 knots, it sounded like being caught up in a waterfall. 'What's your track for Sligo?'

'From Dublin . . . about three zero zero.'

'Okay, let's come right onto a south-westerly heading for the time being . . . what about high ground?'

'There's a map down between the seats . . . I've marked off MEA's on a direct track to Sligo . . . don't know what's to the south-west.'

'Better climb to 3500 for the time being . . . I'd hate to hit anything.'

Cusack took a cigarette from his pocket with a shaking hand and lit it, and started a steady climb. He wasn't so much thinking of escape and survival as the fact that he hadn't been paid. And as spacey as he felt, that really pissed him off.

Then A Soldier

The helicopter carried on through the black night. The weather conditions grew progressively worse as it continued in the general direction of the west coast.

28

The Provisionals issued a statement to the BBC (amongst others) at seven o'clock that Thursday evening. In its précised form it claimed responsibility for the mortar bombing of the RUC post at Bantrain, Northern Ireland, that evening, *and* the execution of an SAS sergeant whose body was dropped (at the same time as the mortar bombing) from a helicopter onto Craogh Parc, Dublin. The statement was signed with the traditional pseudonym P. O'Neill and issued by the Irish Republican Publicity Bureau in Dublin.

There was one hour and twenty-nine minutes to go before BBC television's nine o'clock evening news bulletin went out. It had taken shape slowly, and the frenetic atmosphere was no different from most weeknights.

The attractive lady presenter, Angela Ambler, still in slacks and cardigan, was mouthing words slowly, establishing cadence and emphasis, and trying to commit the gist of each item to memory. The autocue was still being set up so that a final run-through, time permitting, would not be ready for a while. She put down the handful of papers she had been reading and picked up the cup of coffee. A moment of relaxation.

Looking up at the producer's lair she could see a tight group of people gathered around a monitor. With the studio lights dimmed as they were, she could see through the double glass. When they were on air she sat in a pool of bright light, seeing nothing much beyond the edge of the table itself. She now witnessed tense glances in her direction from members of the group gathered around the monitor.

It was a quiet news day, the only item of lukewarm interest: the Far Eastern royal tour, which unfortunately had precious few quotable quotes or memorable news film.

A voice came over the public address system. 'Sorry, Angela, we've got a hold-the-lead story developing up here . . . we'll keep you posted.'

That was all she needed. An evil day trying to cobble together this crap, and now a last minute insert to throw the whole thing into even more confusion. She mouthed a word in the direction of the producer's booth. One which would have caused comment among the admiring WI members throughout the country who had just voted her their TV Woman of the Year.

She finished her coffee, then got to her feet and made her way up into the noisy nerve centre of the newsroom.

The first thing she saw was a colour monitor showing a blonde-haired girl in big close-up, eyes closed, the face a mosaic of white dust and blood. The camera panned up to a uniformed man, tear-stained face gazing in dead-eyed confusion at the scene around him. The news presenter's eye caught – for a fraction of a second – the metal 'S' badge on the man's uniform collar. Next came the smoking shell of a windowless bus hanging at a crazy angle across a road. People milling around: Carrying, pulling, holding, pleading. Dust and smoke drifting.

The big white-faced clock jerked relentlessly on. Eighty-three minutes to airtime.

A production assistant was pulling a sheet of paper from a teleprinter.

Everyone seemed to have a sense of purpose, crossing and recrossing, between, in front of and behind each other. Several shouted conversations all taking place at the same time.

The production assistant thrust a long, folded pair of teleprinter pages into the newsreader's hand, pleased it seemed, to pass the parcel. She looked down at the cryptic heading: 'AP BELFAST 1930', followed by codes, names and distribution data.

She started reading: 'Children's Choir Bombing. In a horrific bomb attack this evening in the Northern Ireland town of Bantrain, more than sixteen Salvation Army boys and girls – members of an English choir – are feared to have died. Official Army sources say that the mortar bomb attack was probably aimed at the Bantrain RUC police depot, the building next door to the 33-year-old Salvation Army hall.

'Five mortar bombs fell as the twenty-strong choir, from the English town of Hoddingham in Derbyshire, were boarding a bus to take them to Belfast in preparation for a final concert tomorrow, prior to returning to England. Several adults accompanying the choir were also in the building but no accurate casualty figures are yet available. End.'

Then A Soldier

She read on.

'Background: *Bantrain*. Eight thousand inhabitants. Farming community. Market town. RUC depot never serious target. Stable, mixed Protestant/Catholic community. No known terrorist activity. Nearest IRA incident: Crossmaglen (15 miles east) Feb '70, terrorist reprisal on new British Army post being built near Cullaville.

'*Salvation Army*. Protestant. Founded 1878 Rev William Booth. Membership worldwide. Choirs called 'Songster Brigades'. Bantrain Corps sixty-eight members. Opened September 1937. Hoddingham Corps, Derbyshire, ninety members, band, senior choir, junior choir. Officer for contact: Major Apping. Number following.'

There were several other peripheral details, of use to other members of the production team, and more would be coming in. The presenter sat wearily on the edge of one of the desks and watched the monitor. The local Northern Ireland correspondent had made it to the scene and was being shown live. Another camera was also channelling in the general scene, which was no doubt being recorded for further editing. The editor was quizzing the on-screen correspondent for details and for a framework for a 'from-the-scene' clip. So much for the opening they had been working on for the last two hours.

The editor's gofer thrust a neatly typed sheet into her hand. 'Try that for size, Ange. Openers.' The longhaired young man rushed off.

Ange, God how she hated that.

The presenter mumbled her thanks to no one in particular and crept off to a quiet corner to get the rest of her act together. Literally.

Pictures kept coming in. The editor and producer flicked from screen to screen as the carnage was presented from BBC, ITN, and Radio Telefis Eireann cameras – all looking for markets. The Midland's Pebble Mill news team had made it to Hoddingham in record time and were offering tearful faces of the families of the bombed children, gazing up at a monitor linked in, courtesy of a Midlands newsroom, to almost the same material as they were watching.

A suave presenter was offering quiet, syrupy words of sympathy and pseudo-help, hoping for that magical quote that would get into the next two or three bulletins, or even longer. The power of television.

The editor watched this footage quietly, impressed with the effort that had been made in the time available. He paused to glance at a message that had been pushed into his hand concerning the execution of an SAS sergeant at Craogh Parc, Dublin. The message read: 'Negative. P. O'Neil statement concerning this could have been hoax. John Fielding, Radio Telefis Eireann.' The editor let the paper drop to the floor, and went back to watching the Bantrain footage.

Angela briefed an assistant to get on the line to the Midlands presenter to set up a live forty-second piece from Hoddingham. She would also remember to congratulate the Midland newsroom. A personal touch that had kept her in this seat (despite pretenders) for several years.

Some library material was now being run past at triple speed, of the recent bombing near Crossmaglen. She delegated an assistant to pull thirty seconds with a suitable voice-over. Another sheet of A4, a second or third copy of the presenter's text, dropped on to the editor's console. She speed-read it and pushed it off to one side.

A red-nailed hand jabbed out at a monitor showing two heavily armed RUC officers staring from the roof of the fortressed police station, down into the detritus of what had been the Salvation Army hall. 'Get that!' she ordered. 'Pre-title with voice-over!' The opening shot of any news broadcast was the 'catcher' that kept the audience on channel, not wandering off for a cup of tea or flicking over to another channel for sport or light entertainment.

Angela was back at the news set console now. Changed into the dark-blue 'conservative' dress. She still had the comfortable trousers on but they were well hidden under the table.

The originally bland news bulletin was now coming alive.

Good news didn't sell. ITN wasn't going out until ten p.m. She had it all to herself. This one might even run over. That was always a talking point the following day. If the Beeb considered it was worth extending the news programme for – even that was news!

Her half-sunken monitor was now showing live scenes from the demolished hall. Blanket-covered bodies were lined up in one corner. Ambulances were carrying away stretchers. A new paragraph was coming up on the autocue.

She cleared her throat. Put on a suitably impassive, here-is-the-news expression, and went into her private rehearsal.

She was cheering up.

It had the makings of a decent show after all.

29

'Sounds like a cow pissing on a flat rock,' Cusack said.

Nancy had gone into the back. Winter had taken off his jacket and laid it down on the floor for her. Then he had torn a sleeve from his shirt and bound up Cusack's left arm the best he could. Now he was in the co-pilot's seat. They were at 3,000 feet. Battling violent headwinds and turbulence and heavy frontal rain towards Sligo.

'Ever had one of these flame out?' Winter asked.

'Not as long as the relight switches are on.'

'You flew these in Vietnam, that right?'

'Not exactly . . . I was a gunner. A few of the pilots reckoned it was good insurance to break the rules and put us in the right seat as often as possible, figurin' if they got badly injured there'd be somebody on board to get them and the ship back home. No point in everybody dyin' because of some impractical rules and regulations.'

'So how did you get mixed up with the IRA?'

'Shit, man, it's nothing to do with the IRA. More

about money. As in I ain't got none. As in I came back from 'Nam and got greeted at the airport by a bunch of longhaired flower-power hippies, spitting on me. Then I couldn't get a job . . . Not a lot of vacancies for trained killers who can fieldstrip an M-16 in seconds flat in the real world. Got to the point I was literally fuckin' dyin'. As in malnutrition. I was going three or four days before I could find something to eat. In the end I held up a convenience store, took some food. Even left the guy an IOU; said I'd pay him back when I got a job. At about the third attempt at feeding myself I got caught. Went to prison. So that's it. Now I'm an ex-con. And you know what the kicker with that is? I'll never get a job again . . . ever. So when these guys offered me a bit of part time work I took it. Only problem was the guy who went out of the door back in Dublin, Frank Ryan, he never got around to payin' me.'

The rain eased slightly and they flew for about thirty seconds in relatively smoother air. 'So what are you going to do now?'

'Do? Shit, man, I'm dead in the water. I ain't even got my airline ticket home . . . come to think of it I ain't even got a home.'

Winter was probing for answers. The last thing he needed was to fly into a trap. 'What about Frank Ryan's contacts at Sligo? He must have made some arrangements.'

'Like I told you earlier, only thing he said to me was that a woman, a sister of one of the Belfast guys, would be picking us up to take us to her house for the night, and that a couple of guys were goin' to high-pressure wash the water-based paint off the ship.'

'Then what?'

'That's all I know . . . I swear it.'

They ran back into the weather. The turbulence suddenly lethal. High frequency jolts drilling the helicopter from nose to tail. Winter was trying to check a topographical map, folded and lying across his knees. He reasoned that the increased turbulence was possibly due to the fact they were on the lee side of the Slieve Gamph. Which would mean they were at least 10 miles south of course. 'Come right . . . ninety . . . degrees.'

'Nine-o?

'Yeah, I think we're south of course.' Winter leaned over the centre pedestal and reselected the ADF frequency. The needle on the instrument panel indicator continued its lazy sweep of the dial.

'I think that got hit, same time as the radio,' Cusack said.

Winter raised a hand for silence. 'Listen . . . hear that.'

Cusack strained to hear the morse on his headset. A weak two-character ident repeated endlessly.

DIT-DIT-DIT . . . DIT-DIT . . . DIT-DIT-DIT . . . DIT-DIT . . . 'SI . . . got that? Sierra India.' He turned the volume down until it was just a faint echo at the edge of his hearing.

'Yeah . . . the Sligo beacon right? What sort of range has it got?'

'About twenty miles at night . . . maximum.'

'Let's hope we find it soon.'

'Fuel?' Winter asked with concern. His eyes looking for the fuel gauge.

'I need a piss . . . the sound of all that water outside.' He laughed wildly at the thought. The helicopter slammed through some more brick-wall turbulence.

Five minutes later the ADF needle steadied.

'About twenty miles now,' Winter said. 'Seven minutes at the sort of ground speed we're making.'

'And the runway's north–south?'

'Right.'

'Except we've got no way of knowing if there's anybody on the ground to switch on the runway lights.'

Winter knew exactly what he meant. To conduct a night approach in severe weather with no radio communication and no runway lights, when and if you broke cloud before you hit something, was suicidal. He looked at the letdown plate again. The decision height – the height at which if you had no ground contact you poured on the power and conducted a missed approach procedure – was 1,250 feet. The problem was that the cloud base would be a lot lower.

Decision time. 'I'll call out the approach,' he said firmly. 'When we see the field I want you to hover well away from the terminal. I'll jump clear with Nancy. You then take the helo up to the building and land and shut down. Who knows, you might even find the woman meeting you has your money!'

That brightened Cusack's day a little. Until he considered the approach at least.

They had reduced speed. Were now in the descent. The ADF needle indicating 50 degrees of right drift. The wind gusting. The turbulence bone-jarring. Winter alternately glancing from the altimeter to the windshield. Looking down. Waiting for the first sign of ground contact. Anything. Like lights from houses near to the field. The thought that they could suddenly collide with something, frighteningly real. He had taken Cusack's watch. Was holding it forward in the instrument panel light monitoring the sweep second hand. Sixty seconds . . . Perhaps . . . They were through their decision height now . . . Cusack was muttering to himself, his face a mask of concentration, dripping with sweat . . . Five hundred feet . . . Winter called off the passing height . . . Kept up the sweep . . . Instruments to windshield . . . Four hundred feet . . . A quick glance up at the landing light and windshield wiper switches, something he would activate the moment he saw the ground . . . *If he saw the ground* . . . What seemed like a wall of water smashing against the windshield . . . Hollow sounding . . . Three hundred feet . . . A ground effect cattle grid rumble through the seat of his pants . . . Instinctive feeling that they had just skimmed the top of a small hill . . . Felt the involuntary movement of his sphincter muscle . . . Two hundred feet . . . Eyes wide now . . . Unblinking . . . Unmoving . . . Willing something to appear . . . The machine shuddered through a down draft . . . The VSI momentarily dipping dramatically . . . The altimeter jerked . . . Lost a hundred feet almost instantly . . . Eighty feet . . . Ten seconds . . . It came from his peripheral vision . . . A flicker of white lights . . . He looked left . . . Buildings . . . His hand reached up snapping on the landing light . . . Then the windshield wipers . . . He looked forward and right correcting for the drift angle . . . The landing light arced across an open area as the helicopter drifted right, picking up shiny blackness . . .

'RUNWAY BELOW YOU . . . come left ninety

degrees.'

Cusack settled into the hover at the far end of the field. Rocking in the wind. The windshield wipers metronoming back and forth. The landing light cutting across a swathe of white light to a distant boundary wall and hedge, a sparse line of black, dripping trees. 'All yours,' Winter said with relief. 'If anybody asks, you haven't seen us. Anything different . . . I'll come and find you.' The Makarov automatic in his hand seemed to emphasize the point. He pulled the headset from his head, tossed it down on the seat, and moved aft.

Nancy was huddled in a corner clinging to a bulkhead. Her face and skull, even in the thin light that spilled back from the instrument panel, were deadly white. He opened the door, grabbed his jacket, and bundled her out of the door. He followed closely behind. Both of them caught in the rotor downwash. Stinging rain whipped against their bare faces. Winter led her quickly away to the edge of the airfield.

They were lying in the dripping hedgerow 30 yards from the single-storey terminal building. There were lights on in the building. No sign of life. The helicopter was on the tarmac ramp. Engine shut down. Rotor blades rocking up and down in the westerly blow. A few yards beyond it a line of light aircraft, chocked and tied down, facing towards Sligo Bay.

'What now?' Winter asked.

'I'm not sure . . .'

'What do you mean, you told me . . .'

A car's headlights suddenly appeared from the road. The throaty sound of a 'blown' exhaust. The car sped quickly up to the front of the building. Skidded to a stop. The driver got out. Looked across at the helicopter and then ran through the rain to the building.

'Billy Costello,' Nancy said with surprise.

'What's he doing here?'

'I don't know. Perhaps he was sent to pick up Cusack and Frank.'

They watched and waited. A few seconds later he re-emerged. Cusack was with him. The pilot was pointing down the airfield. Waving his arm frantically.

'Bastard,' Winter muttered under his breath. And watched as the young gunman opened the boot of the car and pulled out what looked like an AK-47. Saw him bang a magazine into place with the flat of his hand. Then the two got in the car and drove off at high speed down the runway.

Nancy pulled herself up. 'Stay here . . . I'll be back.' She ran across to the building. Winter held the pistol in his hand, wondering what the hell was going on. He looked back down the field. Through the driving rain he could make out the car headlights working their way slowly along the perimeter. He looked back over his shoulder seeking a place to run and hide. There was nothing to be seen. Just pitch black night.

Perhaps a minute had elapsed when Nancy reappeared from the building. With her a man in a parka. Hood up. They paused for a moment. Then he started to run towards a high-wing single-engine Cessna parked at the end of the line of light aircraft.

She reached Winter, out of breath. Flung herself down. Her face shining with rain. She glanced down the airfield. The car headlights were working their way gradually nearer. 'There's your lift back to England,' she said urgently. 'You'd better be quick.'

Even as she spoke the starter engaged on the aircraft. A clunking mechanical sound carrying faintly through the wind and rain. The propeller turned through two blades and fired. A brief puff of smoke dissipating quickly. The low rumble of the engine as it settled at idle.

'How did you do that?'

'Not important.'

'What about you?'

'I'm repaying the favour, John Winter, that's all. Don't give me another thought. I'm Irish remember, I'll get by. Now, for Jesus' sake go.'

'You'd better have this then.' He pushed the gun into her hand, paused as if to say something. But he'd heard the resolution in her voice. Whatever he thought there might have been was gone. She was more a stranger now than ever. He dragged himself out of the hedgerow and limped over to the aircraft.

The passenger door was partially open. Buffeting in the slipstream. He pulled it back and climbed up into the instrument lit cockpit. Looked at the familiar face in amazement. It was August Gant. 'How the hell did you get here?' he shouted above the engine noise.

'Not important at the moment, seems like you've got some problems though . . . What the hell happened to that woman's hair and face?'

'IRA revenge for helping me.'

'That wasn't her, was it? . . . Nancy?'

'Yes.'

Gant looked shell-shocked. 'I didn't realize . . . she just said she'd brought my passenger. Where is she?'

'Back there.'

'You'd better get her then.'

'Get her? She won't come . . . We're not exactly on the best of terms.'

'You don't ask her. You tell her. She was the one who's kept me in the loop on this damn thing ever since it started . . . Reason I'm here. Jesus, Wint, how many more signals do you want. The damned woman loves you.' He glanced out of the side window through the sheeting rain. The car headlights were halfway up the airfield now. 'Those guys looking for you?'

'Yeah.'

'IRA?'

'Yes.'

'You'd better be quick then.'

Shit. Winter leapt down from the aircraft and hobbled back out of the propwash towards the hedgerow. Calling her name in the darkness.

'What the fuck are you doing?' she yelled angrily as he reached her.

He took her arm and pulled her up. 'You're coming with me.'

She shook her arm free of him. 'With you . . . like hell.'

'You remember the letter I left you in Scotland . . .'

'What's that got to do with anything?'

'I meant it. I love you. I'm not leaving without you.'

The defiance in her voice was replaced by pleading. 'Please . . . go . . .'

He leaned forward. His lips briefly brushing hers. 'Not without you. I'll die by your side if you ask me to . . . but I'm not leaving you.'

'I don't want your damned pity.'

'Who said anything about pity . . .'

'Look at me,' she sobbed. 'Take a good look. What is it? You feel responsible because I've been scarred for life.'

'I mean it . . . I'm not going without you.'

'Please . . . leave me.'

He put an arm around her waist and started walking towards the aircraft. Half dragging, half carrying her.

She continued to fight against him. 'Please . . . if you really love me . . . you'll go.'

He stopped. Pulled her nearer so that their faces were nearly touching. 'Have you ever considered it's just that I prefer older women?'

'You bastard.' She nearly smiled at that. Nearly, but not quite.

His grip tightened on her waist. 'You're a stubborn woman, Nancy Ryan.'

Her hand came up between them. Holding the automatic pistol. She held it unconvincingly towards his head. '*You* calling *me* stubborn, that's rich. What don't you understand about me telling you to go?'

'Look me in the eyes and tell me you don't love me.'

Her head dropped. 'I don't love you . . . now will you go.'

'In the eyes.'

She tilted her head. Eyes unblinking. Fixed on his. 'I don't . . .' she started. Then stopped as she saw the sadness of a little boy in his eyes. Too much loneliness. Too much suffering. Her left hand touched the side of his face. Moved slowly to his neck. Then she was reaching up, kissing him with a passion that was almost violent.

The car headlights had turned now. It was back on the

runway, moving rapidly towards the terminal. They had noticed the Cessna had started its engine. Winter pushed her in to the rear seats, and started buckling himself in the co-pilot seat. He looked at Gant and jabbed a finger in the direction of the lights. 'Look like we've got company.' Turned back to Nancy and took the gun.

Gant reached down to the switch panel above his left knee and flipped on the landing light. At the same time his right hand selected the flap lever to 20 degrees. As the flaps were travelling he opened the throttle. He held the plane on the brakes until the car had cleared the runway and was heading up the short taxi track towards them. He then slid his feet down the rudder pedals – off the toe brakes. The Cessna moved forward across the grass to the runway. The car spun round in a handbrake turn and gave chase.

Winter cracked open the door, aimed back at the headlights. Emptying the clip. Saw the return fire. Heard the dull pecks of bullets hitting the fuselage long before they were airborne.

30

The BBC's Angela Ambler was on her way home after a traumatic day. The Bantrain Bombing – as the incident had been headlined – was still very much on her mind. How could the IRA be so callous? They were nothing more than animals. She had always thought of herself as the ideal reporter. Observant, impartial, and believing in both sides being given fair and generous opportunity to state their case. Heaven knows she had witnessed enough intolerance and bigotry even in her young and middle class life, but this form of terrorism was absolutely unacceptable. It was almost as if they were deliberately inviting condemnation. How did you justify the killing of innocent children? She knew the images would stay with her for a long while.

The police turnout in Bantrain was impressive. The explosions had come as a surprise in the normally quiet Northern Ireland town. The high steel fencing that had been erected around the police station a few months after the troubles had started had been quite a joke to the inhabitants. Not so any more. The twenty officers and men, although sticking strictly to the book and wearing all the necessary heavyweight equipment, had become extremely bored by the past year and more of nothing ever happening. The duty sergeant and the evening's small patrol group had been getting their refreshment when the explosions came. The blast was surprisingly small, a mere rocking of pictures on the walls. Muffled noise. By the time they got outside to the street it was filled with dust. The bus had been thrown across the road, the front wall and windows of the hall lying across the rear wheels and rear half of the vehicle. Inside they could see a number of figures deep in the mass of seats, blood masking their faces and clothing. The hall itself was barely visible. The roof had fallen from one side and beams were forming a huge triangle, under which figures could be seen moving. Smoke and dust swirled as bricks and pieces of wood were moved and the search for survivors began.

The alert had been sounded and assistance was soon on hand. Very soon in fact. Mallin Fire Service had been the first, closely followed by two British Army troop carriers and an RUC squad who had been on patrol within radio range of Bantrain. The RUC squad was well equipped, having been prepared for a planned exercise situation. The Army was able to call in four ambulances. In less than half-an-hour some sixty men were hard at work inside the demolished building. The ambulances, the civilian pair from Bantrain Cottage Hospital and the Mallin and Army vehicles were soon coping bravely with casualties. A young British Army major had assumed direction of the operation very quickly. The RUC sergeant had called out his superiors but no one had arrived before the Army squad, so the major's assumption of command seemed natural. It was, after all, a question of experience. He had taken immediate control of the TV people who were soon on the scene. It was, amazing how many different groups seemed to have been on the move in this area of Northern Ireland on this particular evening. By nine o'clock that evening two full news crews had arrived, as had a complete outside broadcast van, intercepted on its way to overnight positioning for live coverage of a motor-cycle race meeting the following day. A lieutenant had been assigned to monitor the press and media and, along with a sergeant, had kept the cameras mainly on the street side of the operation. The death toll, according to the army major had risen from the early figure of sixteen, to twenty. A group of covered bodies could be seen in the far corner of the hall, well clear of the hanging beams. The TV crews pleaded for access to get better shots of the bodies but the lieutenant and sergeant held their ground, knowing that time would eventually beat their inquisitors. The ambulances were busiest. The civilian vehicles were surrounded by survivors and helpers, being used as medical centres – triage units – rather than as transport. The Army vehicles were coming and going with casualties and bodies.

An Army captain was brought forward for interview with the media and a full, brightly lit press conference was called. It came just in time for live coverage on the *BBC's Nine O'clock News*. The captain was a square-chinned bomb expert and in the introduction the Beeb's Northern Ireland correspondent introduced him as an expert in defusing bombs and landmines.

The lieutenant had added the extra touch. He'd positioned the captain in front of the bomb disposal Land Rover with its dayglo red stripes for effect.

Yes, it was definitely a mortar attack, probably intended for the police station next door. Judging from the damage involved, the attackers were almost certainly on the Irish side of the border. Yes, it was a standard IRA form of attack, and once again, as seemed to be the norm these days, had gone horribly wrong. These things were notoriously tricky, especially the home-made variety of mortar the IRA favoured, and the bomber had been very optimistic in trying for the small police depot. And no, there had been no prior warning.

The captain did his work well and mentioned the IRA at least four times, as was expected of him by his superiors. He supplied a considerable amount of extra detail later for the press, much of which would form the basis of 'background' articles for the following day's papers and the Sundays. The dailies had all photographed and gone long since. The first editions of most of the dailies were already heading for the streets, but several were able to reblock the front pages of the later editions to show the extent of the massacre.

ITN had countered with a series of newsflashes preceding and interrupting the chat show and the late movie. Similar coverage was being poured out to the Continent.

The busiest survivor had been the very photogenic Salvation Army driver, Tiny Goodhall. He became the real spokesman of the scene, the only person alive, or at least available, who knew what really happened.

They were delayed, he said, due to a starter motor problem. Even so they were starting to load up. He had gone down the street to pay the garage for some spare parts he had just fitted. He was returning up the street when there were a lot of bangs. He was thrown to the ground. Yes, he saw the front wall of the building fall outwards onto the bus. Like a Buster Keaton film, he'd told the young Radio Telefis Eireann reporter. The youngster had looked puzzled at the analogy.

Tiny's arm was bandaged and in a sling, and a wide graze mark wept on his left forehead. He was indefatigable. He was everywhere. Two Sunday paper correspondents had written him up for bravery awards, a third had suggested something along the lines of a paid exclusive for his real story. A medium close-up of Tiny, head in hands (presumably weeping) sitting on the step of the remains of the bus, framed in the shattered doorway, sliding door ripped from its mount and leaning precariously away from him, closed the Beeb's extended news bulletin. At the end of the bulletin the presenter's beautiful brown eyes had twinkled sadly as she wished the viewers goodnight.

Thank you, Tiny Goodhall, whoever you are, Angela Ambler thought as she finally pulled into the gravel driveway of her Sunningdale home; I'll mention you as one of my most poignant moments in my next women's magazine interview.

31

In the house on Cawnpore Street in Belfast they had been holding a wake of sorts.

Father Michael holding up his glass, declared. 'To another martyr to the cause . . . Sean Fitzgerald.'

Given time and gossip, he'd probably become a legend, Cavenaugh thought, as he raised his glass. 'Such a waste, Michael, and him so young.'

'They said the Army just gunned him down in cold blood, and then planted explosives on him to make it look like he was a bomber.'

Cavenaugh got up from the sofa and went over to the fire. Picking up a poker from the hearth he prodded at the coals. 'Just the beginning. The Army are deliberately provoking trouble in certain selected areas where Catholics live, to justify saturation of those areas by troops.'

'Even so, *that* was an unfortunate error.' The priest nodded in the direction of the now blank screen of the television set. He was referring to the BBC news they had just watched, and the massacre of the majority of a Salvation Army choir in Bantrain.

'We couldn't have known . . .' Cavenaugh started.

'If we'd had somebody in Bantrain, we could.'

'And what of the Dublin operation? Bantrain was nothing more than a diversionary tactic to focus attention, something to give us a clear run at Craogh Parc.'

'So why haven't we heard anything about it? Nothing on the television or the radio.'

Cavenaugh shook his head. He looked worried. 'I don't know . . . Perhaps they had problems with the helicopter. Don't worry, we'll hear something.'

There was a rumble of thunder over the colonial city. The rain, which had been light until now, suddenly increased in a dramatic heavy shower. Driving down the street. A berserk timpani beating against the windowpanes.

Father Michael, weary from the long day, got to his feet. He removed his glasses and squeezed the bridge of his nose. Then took a handkerchief from his pocket and polished the lenses before putting them back on. 'I hope so, Pat. Well, I'll be away to my bed. Early mass tomorrow.'

'God is love, eh, Michael.' The old cynicism.

'Doubt is the other side of faith,' the priest replied, playing his 'tower-of-faith-that-nothing-can-shake' role.

Cavenaugh smiled and followed him through to the kitchen. Helped him on with his raincoat. Then unbolted the door.

The priest slipped outside, raising his umbrella against the rain, shivering at the cold, miserable night. 'What has always puzzled me,' he said in parting, and on a lighter note, 'Is why anyone in their right minds would have political aspirations to maintain even six counties of the wettest country in Europe.' A brief high-pitched laugh as he raised a hand and set off down the pathway.

Cavenaugh had bolted the door and returned to the fireside. A last nightcap before he turned in had been his intention. He had settled down on the sofa, watching the pattern of flames from the burning coals, reviewing the day's events and considering what had to be done tomorrow in this death trap of the poor. It was not a gratuitous description for this part of the city – his city, as he liked to think of it (even though he had been born in Sligo). It was a fact. His part of the city stood unchanging on the edge of time. A place where the flowers still rusted along with the memories of the industrial revolution. He smiled to himself, he liked that, thought he would make a note of it before he went to his bed. Notes for the great book of poetry he was going to publish one day . . .

His wanderings were interrupted by a loud banging on the front door. He started. His mind immediately going on the defensive. *British Army acting on a tip-off? A few brave RUC members on a reprisal raid for the execution of Tommy Morris earlier in the year*? He put his glass down and reached for his gun, which was taped under a fireside easy chair, checked the safety was off. Cocked it. Picked up the green and white checked tea towel that was draped across the back of the chair. He now put it over his right wrist, covering the gun. For all the world looking like he'd just come from the kitchen and the washing up.

He went out into the tiny hallway. The banging continued.

He slid back the oiled bolts. Opened the door in a fast flowing movement. The tea towel hand raised. Finger poised on the trigger.

And let out a sigh of relief. It was Celia. Hair plastered to her skull. Looking like a drowned rat. Mascara running down her cheeks.

'Come in, girl, come in.' He reached out with his free hand and pulled her into the hallway, quickly closing and bolting the door behind her. Not noticing the towel slip from his arm.

He turned to face her. She was standing transfixed in the half-light that reflected from the parlour. Staring at the gun in his right hand.

An apologetic smile. 'Oh, I was thinking it was somebody else come for me . . . that they'd heard it was open season on us poor sinners.' He pushed it into the waistband of his trousers.

She stood there dripping water onto the threadbare carpet. 'Is it true?' she asked in a shaking voice.

'Give me your raincoat . . . Jesus, you're soaked to the skin. Is what true?'

'Sean! I heard he was killed this afternoon . . . up by the Markets.'

Cavenaugh took the raincoat and shook off the surplus water and hung it on a peg. He led her through into the parlour and sat her down in front of the fire. Knelt down before her and took off her shoes, the soles of which had the saturated consistency of blotting paper. He poured her a large whiskey in Father Michael's glass. 'Here . . . Drink this.'

'Is it true?' The eyes crushed by grief, as if she already knew the answer.

He pushed the glass into her hand and sat beside her.

She put it to her lips.

'All of it . . . straight back.'

She drank it and shuddered.

He put an arm around her shoulders. There was no easy way. He had learned that long ago. 'The Army shot him I'm afraid . . .'

'But I was told it was a bomb, and that . . .'

'Shot. By a sniper. That's as much as you want to know, Celia. One of those things in war. Wrong place, wrong time. I'm sorry . . . I'm truly very sorry.' He picked up the bottle from the floor and refilled her glass. 'He was a good man, Sean, that's the important thing . . . the thing we need to remember. And as all good men, he knew what he was doing, and he knew the risk.'

Celia sat sobbing quietly.

'Would you like me to make you a cup of tea?'

'Yes . . . Please.'

He got up and put some more coal on the fire. Lit a cigarette and gave it to her. Then went off to the dingy kitchen that smelled of cooking fat and dampness, and made a pot of tea. Took out the Sunday best china from the top of a cupboard. He brought it back to the parlour on a cheap tin tray, set it down on the hearth and poured her a cup. Dropped one of Sean's sleeping tablets into the hot liquid. Sleep. A short-term way to deal with shock.

She took it. An attempt at a brave smile. 'I'm sorry, I'm keeping you from your bed.'

He smiled back. 'Don't worry, you just get yourself dried out.'

It was at that moment that the phone rang. Cavenaugh left her and went out into the hall, closing

the parlour door behind him. It was Billy Costello
calling from Sligo (or Sligeach as he insisted on
saying). He spoke for nearly twenty minutes. No
names. No specific bullet words that could be picked
up by possible eavesdroppers. More the memorized
litany of being raised to Master Mason. Substituting
the badge of office of a white lambskin apron and the
working tools of a stonemason, for a black hood and a
well-oiled AK-47. Cavenaugh made mental notes.

'Nothing else then, Billy?'

'That's it.'

'I'll talk to you tomorrow then.'

He put the phone down and went back to the
parlour. Celia was curled up on the sofa, eyes closed.
Fast asleep.

He sat for a moment in the fireside chair. Imagined
the old dull ache beneath the eye patch. Reached up to
massage it. Frank Ryan dead! The Sassman escaped.
And Nancy? Whatever had happened to his beautiful
girl? Head shaved! Taken with the Sassman on the
helicopter. Both hooded! That wasn't the way things
had been planned. Not the way at all.

Quietly, he backed up the fire and put the guard in
front of it. Then went off to the spare room to find a
blanket. He draped it over her, taking a last look at the
clown's face of thin-pencilled eyebrows and smudged
mascara and bright red lipstick. The matted blonde
hair showing dark at the roots. A tart with the best
years behind her. There was something a little tragic
about that.

32

Nightmare scenario: There are places you never want to be. One of them, a single engine aeroplane at night over a stormy sea . . . when the engine stops!

They had crossed the Irish coast in the vicinity of the Devil's Glen and Mount Usher, a few miles north-west of Wicklow, bathed in the warm red glow of instrument panel lights. A few feet ahead of the panel the Continental 285 horsepower engine rumbled contentedly. After Mount Usher they had descended over the Irish Sea to 100 feet. Their track would take them into UK airspace over North Wales, then up through central England and Scotland to Wick. The frontal weather was further east than forecast, so that they were still running through heavy showers.

'What about Dublin radar,' Winter asked. 'Do you think they would have painted us?'

'I don't think so. I figured Wicklow was on the end of their primary radar range. Put another way, I came in more or less the same roundabout route this afternoon, and nobody at Sligo questioned me when I told them I was out of Dublin. No local Customs officer, tipped off by Dublin that they'd monitored an unidentified aircraft heading their way, came calling.'

'What about radar heading up towards Scotland?'

'Weather should be clear enough to fly low level through the mountains . . . some moonlight. Radar don't see too well through granite.'

Winter smiled at that. 'You never told me where you got the plane from.'

'Jamie Gunn. This is the one that was sitting outside the tower with the propeller removed. He'd sent it away for overhaul. Came back the same day you disappeared. I've sorta rented it for the day.'

'But you didn't mention what you were going to be doing with it.'

'Hell no, if I'd'a done that he'd have expected me to buy the damn thing.'

'You're quite enjoying this aren't you?'

'Sure, I am. All you gotta do is consider the alternative. Nine to five in an office or factory for the rest of forever. This way at least I get paid for having fun on my own time schedule. Anyway, how's your lady doing in the back?'

Winter glanced over his shoulder. She was lying down across the two seats. Eyes closed. 'Sleeping. I think she's exhausted.'

'I'm sorry about what happened to her.'

'She'll be all right now, I'll make sure of that.'

'Which I guess is your polite English way of telling me you'll be taking a raincheck on the Philippines job, uh?'

'Thanks for the offer, August, but I'd rather dig ditches.'

'You're walking away from a lot of money,' Gant replied. 'We're talking seriously big bucks, you know.' He said it, but there was little conviction in the voice. He knew nothing he could say or do would change things. And as he flew on steadily through the night he thought of his High School sweetheart. Tried to remember her pretty face. Thought it might be fun to go back home just once and see if she was still there. Laughed at himself. Hell, she'd probably be a grandmother by now. And even if she wasn't and had miraculously remained unmarried all these years he doubted she would even look twice at a balding old guy with a beer belly and liver spots, whose sole topic of conversation was airplanes.

He checked his watch. Shook his head in mock disappointment. He'd forgotten to switch fuel tanks. Chuckled to himself. *Anno Domini, August, gets us all in the end.* He reached down and selected the right tank. The engine ran for a few seconds, then began to surge, then die. Shit. His heart missed a beat as his fingers groped for the selector lever, quickly reselecting the left tank. The engine picked up. Silky smooth again.

Winter started in his seat. 'What's wrong?'

'At a guess I'd say they holed the right wing tank on take-off when they were shooting at us. Seems it's been draining away ever since.'

'How about the left wing?'

Gant pointed at the gauge. It was below a quarter. 'Not a lot.'

'Enough to make the Welsh coast?'

'If we climb, maybe. Burning too much down here.' He eased the control column back and started a cruise climb up into the weather. 'You'll find some maps stowed between the seats, check on the nearest field. Somewhere that's closed, preferably. Last thing we need is to start explaining what we're doing to a Customs guy.'

Winter pulled a sheaf of maps onto his knees. Started leafing through them. 'Llanbedr's used by the military, that's just north of Barmouth Bay.'

'Twenty-four hour operation?'

'I don't think so. I think they carry out trials on military stuff . . . could be a Ministry of Aviation place.'

'How'd you know that?'

'I've got an auntie who lives in that area. Used to do a lot of hill walking around there.' He pulled out a Southern England map. Refolded it. Ran his finger up the Welsh coast. 'What time did you estimate landfall at the Welsh coast?'

Gant checked his watch. 'Another ten minutes . . . puts us about thirty miles out.'

Winter gauged the distance on the chart. Held it up so the pilot could see it. 'Puts us about here.' The finger traced a direct track to an airfield circle. 'That's Llanbedr.'

'Keep your fingers crossed. If we make it, I'll drop you off at the end of the runway. You and Nancy can get out and disappear. I'll try and find somebody, gotta have security guards. Explain I ran out of fuel.'

'What about the bullet holes in the wings?'

'Just act dumb and surprised I guess. Don't worry I'll think of something.'

The Cessna continued bumping up through the weather. Both men on the edge of their seats. Both suffering that leaden feeling deep in the gut when engine failure is imminent. At night over an unfriendly sea – terrifying.

Winter was trying to estimate their landfall. 'We're going to have to descend,' he said eventually. 'With this tailwind it's hard to say where we are exactly, but we need to be visual before we hit the coast. Lot of high ground.'

Gant said, 'What about beaches?'

'Barmouth Bay. Big beach. Gently shelving for a long way out.'

'How far's that from this Llanbedr field?'

'Six or seven miles south.'

'Good enough.' Gant reduced power slightly and lowered the nose. The rain came and went in squally showers. The turbulence light to moderate. They started to break out of the cloud at 2,000 feet.

At 1,500 Winter picked up distant coastal lights. 'Looks like Barmouth,' he said, pointing. 'Llanbedr's about seven miles north of there. Come left about five degrees.'

Gant leveled off and altered course. Checked the mixture was leaned out as far as possible. The fuel gauge needle was near the red line empty marker. 'You'd better wake Nancy. Just in case.'

'Any life jackets on board?'

A sheepish grin. 'Nah. Took them off the other ship in Scotland when we first arrived, along with the raft. Never gave it a thought.'

Winter reached over the seat. Nancy was awake. She looked at him with concern. Had realized something was not quite right. He explained what was happening. Ran over the ditching drill twice. Made her repeat it back to him.

Then he turned back to the front. The lights of the coast nearer now. 'How far do you reckon?'

'Couple of miles . . . thought I'd try and get closer in, just in case.'

And in that passing moment the engine surged and died and surged ....

Gant was waiting. He quickly brought the blue-topped propeller lever back through the gate. The result was a feathered propeller, blades edge on to the airflow – minimum drag. There was no need to bring the mixture control back to idle cut off. The engine had finally quit by itself.

The silence was overwhelming. Gant trimmed for the glide. Heading directly for the lights. 'That the place with the big beach?'

'That's it.'

'Okay . . . I'm coming down to say three hundred feet, then if it looks like we ain't gonna make the beach I'm goin' to have to turn back to the west . . . into wind for the ditching . . . they do tell me that these light planes tend to go over on their back if you don't get it exactly right. You'd better tell Nancy quickly to adopt the brace position . . . then jam your door open with something . . .' His eyes were monitoring altitude and airspeed. Hands feeding in gentle corrections on the control wheel.

Winter turned back to Nancy. Reached over and took her hand in his. 'Looks like we're putting down just off the beach . . . make sure your lap strap's tight . . . put your head on your lap . . . hands on top of your head with your fingers interlaced . . . got it?'

She nodded. Eyes wide.

'Once we stop moving I'll reach over and pull you

out of my door . . . Don't worry, I won't let anything happen to you.' A last reassuring squeeze of the hand.

He turned back to the front. Quickly reached down and untied his boots. Opened the door. Worked the boots into the gap. The aircraft was out of 300 feet now. Perhaps half a mile or less from the beach. Gant turned gently back into wind. Lowered the flap. Switched on the landing light. Winter watched as the sea came into focus . . . Whitecaps breaking . . . Two hundred feet . . . It was very quiet . . . Light rain pattering on the windshield and fuselage . . . One hundred feet . . . The gentle shushing sound of slipstream.

They hit once in a fairly flat attitude . . . Bounced . . . Remained airborne for what seemed an impossibly long time . . . The second impact wasn't good . . . Gant had eased back too far on the control column so that the tail struck the water first . . . The nose pitched sharply down . . . An instant nerve tingling sound of tearing metal . . . The aircraft shuddered . . . Began a slow somersault.

It happened too quickly to fully come to terms with fear . . . The fuselage was rapidly filling with water . . . Winter unbuckled his seat belt and twisted round, feeling in the darkness for Nancy . . . The water over his head now . . . He didn't feel the cold . . . Just the panic that he couldn't breathe . . . His hands grabbed her shoulders, started pulling . . . She didn't move . . . He reached down and fumbled with her seat belt . . . Unfastened it . . . Pulled her over the back of the seat through the open door . . . A moment's terror as he tried to work out which way it was to the surface . . . He started to swim, pulling her with him . . . The landing light saved him . . . It was still on . . . An eerie green yellow glow angled across his path . . . His lungs were bursting . . . He expelled air from his mouth . . . And in the ghostly glow of the landing light noticed the bubbles were going down . . . Not up . . . He was swimming the wrong way . . . He stopped, expelled more air . . . followed the bubbles . . . Broke the surface gasping for air . . . His chest burning . . . He trod water, pulling Nancy towards him . . . She was unconscious . . . He struck out for the beach as hard as he could . . . Two hundred yards further his feet struck the bottom . . . They had been that close.

He stood up, gasping in great lungfuls of air, and carried her through waist-deep water to the beach. Laid her down. Put her head to one side. Inserted his fingers into her mouth to check she hadn't swallowed her tongue. Started to pump her chest. Lift and depress her upper arms. He kept going. She coughed suddenly. Water gushed out of her mouth. He kept pumping. More water. She stirred. Opened her eyes. Started coughing. He sat her upright and slapped her back hard. Then he held her.

'You okay?'

'Yes . . . I think so.'

'Will you be all right for a few minutes? I need to go and look for August.'

She had her arms folded tightly across her chest. She nodded.

He hobbled back down the beach and into the sea.

The moon broke through the clouds briefly. Shining silver on the waves.

He waded out a long way. Swam even further. After half an hour and totally exhausted he crawled back up the beach and collapsed alongside Nancy.

She put her arm around him and held him close. Both shivering. No words. They stayed like that for what seemed like a long time. She holding him. He, looking out to sea, not believing what had happened. Expecting to see the American walking out of the surf at any minute, cracking some corny joke about being held up by a bunch of mermaids on a girls' night out. But in the end there was no loud American accent, just the sound of the surf crashing onto miles of empty beach.

'We need to leave,' he said. Then realizing that neither of them had shoes he removed his army tunic, and ripped the sleeves away. He then tore both sleeves down their seams until he had four long pieces of cloth. Kneeling down he started to bind her feet first. And when that was done, his own. Then he put the remains of his wet jacket back on and pulled Nancy to her feet.

They set off along the beach. Away from the lights of the town.

Nancy was shivering more than ever now. 'Where are we?'

'North Wales.'

'Where are we going?'

'I've got an aunt who lives about ten miles over that mountain.'

'Dorcas Volk?'

He looked at her with surprise. 'How did you know that?'

'I've met her,' Nancy said.

'You've what? When? How?'

'The way I found you in Scotland.' She told him the story as they moved along the edge of the bay.

Then A Soldier

For two hours they went on well despite the darkness and the driving rain. A steep climb of 2,000 feet over broken ground. Keeping up speed to generate body heat.

They were at the summit of the high ground. Had paused for a brief rest. Winter knelt down and rebound her cut and bruised feet. Pulled her back up.

'Couldn't we stay a bit longer?'

She was already shivering. He knew the signs. The subtle symptoms of hypothermia. He had taught a good few young soldiers how to recognize the dangers of exposure. He also knew how to avoid its onset despite the very worse conditions. Rule one was to realize that, no matter how clever a man may be at spotting others becoming hypothermic, no one can be sure of recognizing his own deterioration, simply because, as the body core temperature drops, the body draws heat from the head. The brain begins to slow down, taking away the normal state of awareness and the will needed for self-preservation. 'No . . . we've got to keep moving. Keep up our body core temperature. If that gets below 33 degrees Celsius we're in serious trouble.' He started to lead her down the mountainside. Muscles burning. His feet cut and bleeding.

'John . . . please . . . I can't go on.' The words came in great sobs.

He stopped and held her for a moment. The dressing had come off her face in the sea. The dark line of a scar ran down the length of her left cheek. He leaned down and kissed her. 'Now aren't you glad you came?'

'What?'

'What other man would take you walking through the mountains at night in a storm in your bare feet.'

She tried to laugh.

He picked her up and started to carry her down the mountain. *Not exactly a 55 pound Bergen backpack.*

'I'll try and walk now,' she offered.

'Keep your hands clasped tightly around my neck,' he ordered. Once again on endurance with the SAS over the Brecon Beacons.

'How much further?'

Too far. He concentrated on putting one foot in front of the other. 'Not far.'

They dropped down into a valley in the pre-dawn light. By then Nancy had passed out. Winter's arm muscles were burning with such intensity that he knew if he stopped and put her down he would never get started again. That they would then sit together. Bodies rapidly beginning to lose body heat through convection, conduction, radiation and evaporation. How long before they died was anybody's guess. But it would happen.

Finally, when his blood-sugar level was at its lowest, he found himself on the unmade track between the dry stone walls that he knew so well. *A little further, he told himself . . . a little further.* The pain diminished when he saw the grey, mist-shrouded outline of the Cader Idris in the distance. Cader Idris – the chair of the giant and bard, Idris. A 7 mile ridge, which fell steeply into the Mawddach valley to the north-west, dropping more gently on the other three sides to the outlying hills. Cader Idris: his ridge. He'd climbed every foot and every side of it over the years. He managed a grim smile. Felt the leaden weight of inertia beginning to lighten.

The farmhouse came into view next. That spurred

him on with renewed energy. *A little further. A little further.* He turned in at the familiar five-bar gate. Hobbled down the gravel drive. Crying out as the sharp stones cut into the soles of his feet. Eyes focused on the front door . . . nothing else. He reached it and collapsed on the doorstep.

Holding Nancy to him with one hand, he took a deep breath and began to bang weakly at the door with the other.

By the time the door opened he had passed out.

33

Winter wakes up to an early morning light. Nancy is
sitting on the edge of the bed watching him. He tries to
move his hands, his arms. Finds he cannot. Muscular
spasm, a kind of ataxia, he thinks, trying to recall
some long-forgotten SAS lecture on physiology. He
looks at her. She is wearing a sleeveless forget-me-not
blue summer dress (near-transparent fabric, plunging
neckline, tight bodice that pushes her breasts together,
pronouncing her cleavage, flared skirt a few inches
above the knee) and a green silk headscarf fashioned
into a fortune-teller's head covering (all borrowed
from Dorcas Volk) tied at the back. Her face is pale.
The only make-up, the merest touch of eye shadow
and pink lipstick. The scar down her left cheek is livid
red. (When she speaks or looks at him she self-
consciously lifts her left hand to touch the scar, as
though trying to hide it). She tells him that Dorcas has
taken the Land Rover and gone to town to do some
shopping. That she will be away all morning.

He tries again to move his hand to reach for her.

Finds he cannot. 'I want to touch you,' he says. His eyes never leaving hers for a second.

She leans over and kisses him gently. A faint unfamiliar perfume. Intoxicating.

'I want you next to me.'

'I am next to you.'

'You know what I mean.'

She stands up and reaches behind her neck. Fingers scrabbling to find the hook and eye. She unzips the dress in one long electric movement. It slips to the floor with a faint rustle. She is wearing a white bra and black lacy panties (something else borrowed from Dorcas). Nothing else. She takes them off and pulls back the bedclothes. He is naked. She moves up close to him. Above him. Her soft breasts hovering for a second over his chest. He watches as she brushes her pink nipples lightly against his skin. Then she is pressing her body tightly to his. So tight it takes his breath away. 'Is that close enough?'

'Nearly.'

She laughs. 'How much closer do you want me?'

'I don't need to tell you, do I?'

She looks into his eyes with a longing bordering on desperation. 'No.'

She kisses him. Explores his mouth with her tongue.

Eases her body to one side. Slides the sensual sandpaper roughness of her hand down his chest, over his stomach, until she takes hold of him. Squeezing him gently until he can hardly bear it. Then she slides her right leg across his body, eases herself on top of him. Guides him slowly into her. A tiny gasp escapes her lips.

'Is that close enough,' she whispers. Hot breath in his ear.

'I love you.'
'I know.'
She begins to move on top of him.

There was warm sunlight spilling though the window. Patterning the window frame across the bed. 'We didn't have any protection,' she murmured, lying close to him, nuzzling his neck.

'I'm glad . . . you'll have to marry me now.' He turned his head and looked at her for a long moment.

She turned her face away. 'Don't.'

'Why not?'

'I'm ugly.'

'You're beautiful . . . will you marry me?'

Brief pain in the eyes. 'You don't have to. I'll stay with you as long as you want me . . . Until you tire of me . . . But you don't have to marry me.'

He struggled onto his side, managed to push his left arm across her body. Trying to hold her. Dismayed that the sensation of touch was absent from his fingers. As though he was touching her with somebody else's hand. 'I'll never tire of you.'

'You remember what you said to me in Sligo, about me being an older woman?'

'I was joking.'

'But it's true . . . Ten years from now I'll . . .' She stopped. She couldn't go on. She had seen her naked body in the bedroom mirror that morning when she had been dressing. Had been dismayed at the sagging breasts. The thickening waist. True, her legs were long and shapely, but for how much longer? Even worse, she had found her first grey pubic hair. That had been a shock.

'Do you love me?'

'You know I do.'

'And you'd do anything for me?'

'You know I will.'

'Without question.'

A sharp intake of breath. 'Yes.'

'Will you marry me?'

She touched her lips to his. As if afraid of what she would say.

He repeated the question.

'Yes . . . if you're sure.' A whisper.

'Do you want children again?'

'Yours . . . yes.'

Suddenly, as if remembering, he said, 'What about Dorcas? What happened? What did you tell her?'

'Everything.'

'When?'

'Yesterday.'

He looked confused. 'Yesterday?'

'It's Saturday morning. You've been asleep for more than twenty-four hours, after we washed you and bandaged your feet.'

'I don't remember a thing . . . What did you mean, everything?'

'Everything . . . all except for the plane crash. I didn't know if I should mention August to her.'

'I'll tell her later. So what does she think? Of us?'

'She's a very modern woman your aunt. She made a point of picking that dress for me . . . I'm certain it was because it was the sexiest thing she possessed. Other than that I don't believe she had any reason to go away shopping for an entire morning.'

'You think so.'

'I know so. She was as good as telling me that I should come up to her nephew's bedroom and seduce him.'

'Sounds like Dorcas. Get to know her a bit better and she'll come out with it in plain English . . . not refined either. The pure Anglo-Saxon diluted with Czech stuff.'

'She wouldn't!'

'Wait until I tell her that her shopping trip this morning is in all probability the reason for you being pregnant.'

Nancy coloured slightly. 'Oh, you wouldn't say that.'

'Why not . . . it's the truth.'

'You'd embarrass me.'

'Where have you been sleeping?'

'In the next bedroom.'

'You'll sleep with me now though?'

'What about Dorcas?'

'I'll tell her we're getting married, the minute she gets back.'

'And that makes it all right does it?'

'You can go back to your own bed before she gets up, if you like.'

'You've thought it all out then.'

He closed his eyes. Felt the warmth of the sun on his face. 'From the first moment I saw you.'

34

Billy Costello was feeling pleased with himself. And not without reason. He had first heard the news on the radio. Then the television. Then read about it in the papers. The reason why Pat Cavenaugh had driven to Sligo from Belfast.

It was Monday lunchtime, and the two men were at Hargadon's bar. An old, atmospheric institution, complete with a dark, wooden interior, snugs and a grocery counter. A quiet table (beer mats laid out with mathematical precision) near a window, that looked out directly on to the street. A few late season tourists, Americans mainly, were sampling their first pint of Guinness, much to the amusement of one or two of the locals. Others were conferring on the poet William Butler Yeats, whose grave was a stone's throw away in Drumcliff churchyard.

'You were lucky to have made it back in time,' Cavenaugh said.

'Right enough.'

'And lucky you realized what was happening even then.'

'Not at first. Like I told you, I saw the helicopter parked outside the terminal and I went inside to look for Cusack and Frank. There was another guy there, smoking a cigarette. I thought he worked there. I was just walking over to him when Cusack came out of the lavatory. Took me outside and told me they'd forced him at gunpoint to drop them off at the far end of the airfield.'

'Winter and Nancy?'

'Yes. And that Frank was dead.'

'So you and Cusack went looking for them in the car?'

'All I could do . . . then as we were working our way back towards the terminal I saw somebody moving around by one of the light planes. I headed back as fast as I could but by then the plane was moving. They started shooting.'

Cavenaugh smiled and lit a cigarette. Blue smoke mingled with dust motes in a shaft of sunlight. 'Just like in those television movies then . . . You chased him down the runway, firing back.'

'And like the papers and the radio and television said, the plane's crashed.'

'Missing,' Cavenaugh corrected.

'Same difference isn't it? I know I hit him. I saw sparks jumping off the wing. What was it the Scottish owner said to the news people? He'd rented the plane to an American for a few days. The American said he was flying from Wick down to England and across to Dublin and then to Sligo to pick up a friend of his, and would then be returning to Scotland. When the owner

hadn't heard anything by last Saturday morning he
started making phone calls. The local man at Sligo
airport confirmed the plane came in on the Thursday
afternoon, but was told it would be staying the night.
Next morning it had gone.'

'Which is why the search and rescue people are
scouring the land and sea from here to the north of
Scotland.'

'Does it make any difference?'

Cavenaugh finished his whiskey. 'Not a bit. You did
a grand job.'

They were getting up to leave. 'The Cusack fella was
asking to see you, by the way. Something about
money.'

'He's staying up at my house, isn't that what you
said?'

'Yeah.'

'In that case, Billy, we'd better go and pay him.
Perhaps you'd be kind enough to sort out a flight for
him from Shannon back to the States.'

'I'll get on it right away. What about you?'

'Oh, I think I'll stay for a few days with my sister.
Might even do a bit of fishing.'

'Anything else I can do?'

'Did you walk here?'

'No, I've got the Corsair.'

'Good enough, I'll see you at the house in a while.
I've got a couple of errands to run.'

When Costello had left Cavenaugh got into his car and
drove out to the airport. He wasn't thinking about
Winter. Or even the news about the light aeroplane
that had left Sligo airport late the previous Thursday

night. It was more the helicopter. The one Frank had hijacked from Scotland. And Nancy had telephoned Winter's American partner in Scotland and made a deal with him, on the very morning she arrived at the Skyways Hotel at Heathrow. Telling the American that the helicopter and Winter would be returned by that weekend, and if he said a word to the police he would never see Winter again.

Question: Was the light plane from Wick owned by the same people who owned the helicopter?

Question: Was the American pilot who picked up Winter and Nancy the same man she had phoned from Heathrow – August Gant?

Question: Why hadn't the owner of the helicopter reported it stolen to the authorities (the weekend had passed after all. It was now Monday)?

The first two questions would be easy enough to check – a phone call would do that.

The third, a bit more difficult.

The three questions threw up other questions however. The most important perhaps: how did the American pilot know about Sligo? How could he have even guessed Winter would be there, when the operation had called for something else altogether? Then again there was Nancy.

He recalled a meeting at the house in Belfast many months earlier when Father Michael had confided in him about her confession, that she had killed the British soldier in a field near Crossmaglen, and how the 'mechanic' had taken responsibility for the act himself. And later finding out the 'mechanic' was in fact an undercover Sassman, Winter. *Until that moment I thought your man was a saint.* Father

Michael's words. At that time he had considered the reason was something far more simple. That they had been having an affair. Then had dismissed the idea as fanciful. Not his Nancy. Not his beautiful girl.

The point was, did it make the least bit of difference that he had perhaps been wrong all along? It was all over now, one way or the other. And didn't he have to arrange the funeral of Frank Ryan later in the week (His broken body having been found in a street near Craogh Parc).

He pulled into the small airport. No apparent activity. Not a soul in sight. Drove up to the wooden shack that passed as a terminal building. Saw the camoflauged helicopter parked on the apron, a few yards away from a line of small planes. His local boys had obviously thought twice about washing off the paint. Had sensed the operation had been compromised.

He looked at it for a few moments longer. Tapping the steering wheel with his fingertips. Thinking. Perhaps the wisest thing was to leave it. Asking questions about a helicopter that had apparently appeared out of nowhere all by itself might raise suspicion.

He turned the car around and drove back towards the town.

35

October 1970

You and I are immortal – we've been saved so often it's our duty to survive . . .

Winter and Nancy made love that Saturday afternoon high on the grassy slopes of Cader Idris in the last hours of what had been an Indian summer. And afterwards they had lain in each other's arms and talked of their future. How they would go to Reno, Nevada, in late December to be married. Then drive across America to the Florida Keys for their honeymoon. A wedding present to be paid for by Dorcas Volk to the young man she thought of as a son, and his bride.

Eventually they dressed and set off back down the mountain. Hand in hand. She, wearing his too-large sweater over the forget-me-not blue dress, green silk headscarf and white tennis shoes. He, shirtsleeves rolled up, and baggy corduroys and climbing boots left in a wardrobe from his army days.

Then A Soldier

As they came in sight of the farmhouse far below and to the north-west he pulled her to a stop. His head tilted to one side, nostrils dilated, sniffing the air, listening. Eyes carefully surveying the dirt track road that went north-east from the house towards the distant town of Dolgellau. Looking for signs of traffic. Or people.

'There's nothing to worry about,' she said, reading his mind.

'Perhaps,' he said softly. Not quite believing it. Thinking of the cover story he had put out three weeks earlier. The phone call to an old friend in the regiment. How he had got him to call Jamie Gunn at Wick airport in Scotland.

One version of the conversation might well have gone something like:

'Hello, can I speak with John Winter or August Gant, please.'

'I'm sorry but they're not here.'

'Not there! But they left here late on Thursday night. They assured me they'd be back at Wick the following day. Or today – Saturday – at the very latest.'

'Where's here exactly?'

'Sligo . . . on the west coast of Ireland.'

'And who am I speaking to?'

'Oh, I'm sorry, Peter Miller here. I'm a friend of John Winter's. Look, if he gets back in with August today could you ask him to call me. He's got my number . . . On second thoughts, perhaps you might want to check with the authorities, just in case they've gone down.'

'GONE DOWN?'

'It was a pretty bad night when they left . . . Storms.'

'Have you any idea where they were landing first?'

'Dublin.'

'I'll get on to it right away, thanks for contacting us.'

'Hope it turns out to be nothing significant . . . I'll check back with you later.'

He had monitored the news reports through his army mate, whose real name was Christopher Fleet. Not exactly headline news in Ireland – that had been taken over by an IRA bombing at Bantrain in Northern Ireland, where a number of young people from an English Salvation Army choir had been killed – but enough to hopefully satisfy any interested party (IRA) that he (and Nancy) had in all probability been killed in a plane, which had initially been reported as missing (one enterprising Dublin editor going as far to suggest it had become the *Marie Celeste* of the skies – a ghostly aeroplane flying on until the end of time, with no hope of landfall), and was now considered to have crashed. A large-scale search operation had been going on for some time now. The young gunman, Billy Costello and the American, Cusack, had after all witnessed them leaving Sligo on that stormy night. Even so, and despite his precautions, he was apprehensive. Especially as Dorcas had gone away to stay with friends in London for the weekend.

'Perhaps nothing, your imagination getting the better of you. What was it you told me last night about being immortal?'

He turned his eyes to her. 'You and I are immortal . . . we've been saved so often it's our duty to survive.'

'I like that.'

Then A Soldier

He slipped his hands under the sweater. Caressed her body through the thin material of the dress.

'What's that for?'

'I like touching you, that's all.'

'The feeling's mutual.'

'Is that so.'

In a playful mood she unbuttoned the front of his shirt quickly and expertly. Ran her hands over his body. Around to his back. Raked her nails gently from shoulder blades to waist.

He closed his eyes. Wanting more. Knowing he could never get enough of her. 'I'll give you fifty years to stop that.'

She laughed and kissed him on the chest. Lay her head there. Sighing contentedly.

'So how did you like making love on the top of a mountain?'

'Is that why you asked me to wear this dress?'

'I've become an expert on the zipper.'

Mock reproach. 'Ah, that explains it . . . I've become nothing more than a sex object to you now.'

'You didn't say that when I took it off up there.'

'What did I say?'

'Not repeatable.'

Bright laughter. 'Were you shocked?'

'I'll need a replay before I can be certain.'

'You'll have to wait 'til after supper.'

'Is that a promise?'

'The second I've cleared away the dishes.'

'You didn't answer the original question. Did you like making love on the top of a mountain?'

She kissed his chest, then reached up. Mouth to ear. Whispered: 'Yes, yes, yes, yes, yes.'

'Would you like to come back again tomorrow?'

'The television weather man said it's going to rain tomorrow.'

'Better still, we'll stay in bed all day.'

'And here was me thinking you were so quiet and so shy.'

'I am.'

She dug him in the ribs playfully. 'Liar. You're nothing of the sort.'

'Are you complaining?'

She held his hand to her lips. Showered it with kisses. 'Never.'

They continued their descent.

'Tell me about America again,' she said.

'I was only there for about six months.'

'The Florida Keys . . . please.' The innocent excitement of a schoolgirl.

'Leaving Miami and heading south you eventually find yourself on a road that has been bleached white by the sun. On the left of the road is the Atlantic. On the right, the Gulf of Mexico. There's sunshine and palm trees, white pelicans skimming the green water, places like Key Largo where you can . . .'

They arrived back at the farmhouse as the sun was dipping low over Cardigan Bay. A faint breeze had sprung up carrying the scent of mown grass. Above, a few gulls wheeled in lazy circles. As they were passing the east end of the granite barn, a short cut through a swathe of Flander's poppies that had taken over what Dorcas called her wild garden, Nancy suddenly grabbed his arm. Gasped in shock.

Winter looked round. Saw a man in a hiker's kit

Then A Soldier

The hood of his anorak down on his shoulders. Thick, wavy silver hair and a black eye patch. He was holding a pistol and it was aimed at them. Nancy's fingernails bit into Winter's arm.

'There you are, Nancy. You're looking well, better than I'd thought you'd be . . . after the terrible stories I'd heard.' The eyes turned from her. 'And this must be Mr Winter . . . is that right?'

Winter had picked up on the Irish accent, faint though it was. 'And you are?'

'Pat Cavenaugh. An old friend of Nancy's. Isn't that the truth, Nancy?'

She stood petrified, clinging to Winter's arm. Words paralysed in her throat.

Winter tried to assess the situation. His mind spinning. Cursing himself for his own stupidity. He had sensed it back up there on the mountain. Known something was not right. His old friend, Nick Ashe, had tried to teach him about what he termed the heart's code. That primitive basic instinct that man had possessed in abundance when he was a cave dweller. *If you feel something is wrong, it is. You therefore have a momentary advantage.* But he had ignored it. Decided that it was erroneous information. Now? He looked at the gunman. He'd heard the name Cavenaugh from Nancy. Back In Ireland. Something to do with IRA Intelligence. 'Whatever it is, Nancy has got nothing to do with this. You do understand, don't you?'

A deceptive smile. 'Is that right?'

'How did you find us?' Winter asked. Trying to buy time. Eyes desperately seeking out the nearest cover. Wondering how good a shot the man off to his left

347

side was. His wrong side! Nancy was in direct line of fire.

'Bit of luck really. We'd given up. Decided that you'd both been killed along with the pilot who picked you up from Sligo a few weeks back. Then, two days ago, we found out from a local pilot who'd just flown back from Liverpool that a crashed plane had been found some miles up the coast from here. A bit more checking with the right people and we learned it was your plane. When I was told that only one body had been recovered from the wreckage, I remembered Nancy mentioning you had an aunt who lived in this area. We decided to come here. Stake the place out, as they say.'

We decided. Winter wondered how many 'We' was. At least one more. A sniper perhaps! He tried to work out the best place for such a shooter. Trying to run for cover from a pistol was one thing. An unsighted sniper with a high-powered rifle and telescopic sight!

'I'll do a deal with you,' Winter offered.

'I'd hardly think you're in a position . . .'

'Take me, but let Nancy go.'

'No,' she cried. Held him even tighter. Tears filling her eyes.

'A terrible thing a collaborator, Nancy.'

She looked at Cavenaugh. 'We're going away . . . A long way away, I promise . . . Couldn't you say you never found us?'

'If it was up to me, girl, you know I would. But like your man here when he was serving in the Army, we all have to take orders.'

Winter was starting to pull her away from the line of fire. Planning a run to the back of the barn. Twenty yards. No more. Staying between her and the gunman. Last gasp desperation.

Cavenaugh's finger squeezed the trigger in that very second. A sharp, thin crack. The bullet struck Nancy Ryan in the chest as Winter was turning her away. The angular trajectory of the bullet modified by striking the edge of her third rib, carrying it straight to her heart. She died almost instantly. A look of surprise in her eyes.

Winter dropped down with her. Cradling her body in his arms. Lifting the sweater, putting his hand over the wound. Dark blood staining the pale blue dress. He reached for her neck. Checked the pulse. There was none. His hand moved to her face. Closed her eyes.

The skin was drawn tight on his face as his head came slowly up. The look in his eyes chilling. Controlled hate. He started to move.

'Don't even think of it,' Cavenaugh ordered. He raised a hand. 'There's a rifle aimed at you.'

Winter followed the hand. Saw the dark-featured gunman from Ireland. Billy Costello. He was on the barn roof, by a chimney that had been added at some time to accommodate the old forge that was at the end of the building. He turned back to Cavenaugh. 'You might as well finish it then, you bastard.'

The older man smiled. 'Oh, it's finished well enough, Mr Winter. You're free to go.'

'Free to go . . .'

'Let's just say that we are on the same side. I was sent to take care of matters, to give you another chance if you like. Nancy's death will be added to your tally, along with Frank and their children. The IRA has you at the very top of their hit list. Even so, you have the

opportunity to leave the country and start a new life
. . . but don't forget they'll always be looking out for
you.'

'The same side?' Winter asked. 'You work for the
British you mean?'

'Something like that.'

'Who? MI5?'

'Not important.'

'Not important? What the fuck does that mean? That
you lead the IRA into clever little traps of your own
making . . . Like planting bombs and blowing up
innocent civilians, and making sure the IRA take the
rap?'

'The ends justify the means.'

'The day I left Ireland there was a bombing in
Bantrain . . . on the border. Was that something to do
with you? Surely to God you weren't responsible for
sacrificing all those English children . . . for what? To
enable the British government to win a few more votes
at the next election. To trick the world into believing
that the IRA have plumbed new depths of depravity!'

'We intend to win this war.'

'At any cost?'

'The British Army has lost 12,000 men in the last
two years. Deserters. Most of them have gone to
Sweden . . . a safe haven for such people. The government is understandably concerned. It thinks we have
created the first thinking soldiers . . . soldiers who do
not want to go to Northern Ireland and kill who they
consider their own people. All we are doing is tipping
the scales back in our favour. Creating a new
awareness, a new hatred for an old enemy.' He
signalled up to Costello on the barn.

Then A Soldier

The young gunman slid down the pantile roof and jumped, holding his weapon two handedly above his head. Like a parachute. He landed lightly on his feet, bringing the rifle quickly to bear on Winter. Cavenaugh moved back to join him. They began walking towards the dirt track road at the end of the driveway. Costello covering the withdrawal.

'You're making a mistake leaving me alive,' Winter called after them. 'You'd better kill me now . . . Fail to do that and I will come for you . . . Are you listening, Cavenaugh?'

The two men melted into the gathering dusk. Contract complete. They offered no reply.

Winter sits down in the wild garden. Amongst the late Flander's poppies. He holds Nancy's hand – finds it has already grown cold – the time of year he tells her. He rocks her gently in his arms. Then lowers his face to hers and kisses her on the lips. Warms her with his tears.

Debriefing

John Winter buried the body of Nancy Ryan in an unmarked grave high on Cader Idris that night. He kept a lonely vigil over her grave for twenty-four hours. Two days after that he left the UK for Manila, Philippines. His contact there – a mercenary by the name of Jack Crane – a close friend of the late August Gant. *Against all his hopes and wishes he went back to the only profession he knew – soldiering.*

On the first anniversary of Nancy Ryan's death, Pat Cavenaugh returned from a minor errand to his house in Cawnpore Street, Belfast, and found a vase of flowers on the kitchen table. It was something that tapped into the old Celtic superstitions. Red and white flowers in an Irish house. A sign for sure of an impending death. He had a team of three young 'RA men guard the outside of the house that night. Despite the security, he was found the following morning hanging by a rope from above the stairs. *The three IRA men swore on their mothers' lives that nobody went into the house that night, and nobody left it.*

Billy Costello died at his mother's house in Sligeach on the same day. *His execution turned out to be a carbon copy of Cavenaugh's.*

Then A Soldier

Father Michael McVerry, disturbed by the macabre killings, turned more and more to the bottle. He died in 1977 at the age of thirty-nine. *The cause of death: cirrhasis of the liver.*

Although Teach Cusack was paid for his work, he never again sought employment with the IRA or NORAID. *He is currently serving time in a Florida jail for drug dealing.*

As for the IRA, there is little kudos to be gained in becoming a member. Unlike the soldiers and policemen they have few of the compensations of a regimented life. The IRA gives no medals. Nor does it offer much extra status or reward to those who rise through the hierarchy. There is not much praise or recognition. A singular truth is: 'You are not as good as your last job, you are as good as your next one.' The price of treachery is high: interrogation in a slum back room, a haphazard 'trial', then a hood, a piece of wasteland and a bullet through the back of the head. Mere suspicion can be enough to doom you. This is wartime justice and these are wartime privations, yet there is not even the compensation of an end in sight. *Why then would anybody want to join the IRA? The answer is very simple: It is in the blood.*

Author's Note

John Winter first appeared in the novel *White Lie* when, as a respected professor of history at a small American university and living under the alias Deavas Carrol, his wife was brutally raped and slain by a city drugs gang. To avenge his wife's death, Winter reverted to his former persona of ex-SAS soldier turned soldier of fortune (code name Sibelius) and sought out those responsible for the crime. He systematically executed each one. Not stopping there he recruited a former ally/soldier of fortune, Charlie Riker. Together they went to Colombia where Winter masterminded a plot to rid the world of the head of the notorious Cali Cartel. During this low-key/low-budget operation (an object lesson for first-world Western governments perhaps) Winter crossed the path of two figures who were to play an important part in his future: the first was Tanner Williams, CIA; and the second, a semi-retired SIS (British Secret Intelligence Service) operative, Edeyrn Owens. At the end of this story Winter engineered an aircraft crash in the Gulf of Mexico in which he was believed to have perished. Matters should have ended there, with Winter retiring to a quiet life (under a new identity) in some equally quiet backwater of the world, perhaps picking up the threads of his history teaching profession, or possibly writing a definitive history of the Cistercians – the Roman Catholic monastic order founded in 1098 at Citeaux, France – his pet subject. It didn't quite happen that way.

The second book of the series, *Saigon Express*, shows why. Some months after the Cali operation, Winter's accountant, a Frenchman from Martinique by the name of Patrick van Fleteren, attempted to launder 7 million US dollars through a Nassau merchant banker – a Lithuanian by the name of Mehdizadeh. Unfortunately for the Frenchman the banker had close ties with the CIA, and upon discovering that the multi-million cache was in the name of a company bearing the name Sibelius (a name that appeared on a CIA black list), informed his CIA contact, Sam Yeo, in Freeport, Bahamas. What followed was seizure of the Sibelius account by the CIA's clandestine services division. Winter, very much alive, was naturally perturbed at the loss of his fortune (used primarily to support the widows of orphans of men who had fought under him over many years of mercenary activities) and justifiably so as Tanner Williams had given assurances during the Colombian operation that the CIA would turn a blind eye to proceedings and even provide Winter with a full pardon (a deal reneged upon by the CIA Langley mandarins).

Thus it is that Winter conceives an idea to ensure the return of his stolen money. The operation hinges upon lifting a consignment of weapons grade uranium from a nuclear plant in Tblisi, Georgia (being closed down due to leakage/contamination problems – a commonplace occurrence throughout the former Soviet bloc in the post-Cold-War era). Once this phase is completed the uranium is transported by air to the military base of Bien Hoa, Vietnam. With the assistance of a Vietnamese colonel in the Ministry of Defence, Winter notifies the CIA that should they fail to return the funds they have unlawfully seized within a certain timeframe he will deliver the weapons grade uranium to Iraq. CIA man Tanner Williams is brought out of retirement and once again teams up with his old British ally, Edeyrn Owens. The two men track Winter to Vietnam where they attempt to retrieve the missing uranium and orchestrate the death of Winter. Near the end of *Saigon Express*, Winter has a conversation with Edeyrn Owens, in which Owens questions his morals, asking him how he can justify betraying his own country (Britain) by selling weapons of mass destruction to a tyrant like Saddam Hussein. A reasonable question from the establishment man, one would assume. Winter holds his counsel, but suggests that if he (Owens) is really interested in the truth (*Which truth do you want?* is a phrase often used by Winter) then upon his return to the UK he should look back into Winter's history – the key to it all being Northern Ireland at the start of the most recent (1969) troubles. At this point, the protagonists of *Saigon Express* execute a smart half-turn to the right and march away into the gathering dusk to meet their respective fates.

In this story, *Then A Soldier*, we return to Winter's army roots. We find out what Edeyrn Owens (now in comfortable retirement at his home in Surrey, where the rose garden is still flourishing) might have uncovered had he carefully and systematically researched the early life of a young British soldier by the name of John Paul Winter (formerly of 2 Para, followed by a short stint with the SAS). For the reader, as for the establishment man Edeyrn Owens, the unpalatable truth is systematically laid bare.

Perhaps the final word should go to John Paul Winter (aka Deavas Carrol, aka William Durack, aka Sibelius) – a fictional character – based upon a real former SAS trooper, who once answered a question I put to him about his undercover work in Northern Ireland many years earlier, and his present occupation: *How can you morally justify turning soldier of fortune, when you were once a soldier of the Queen?* His answer turned out to be the genesis of three novels: *Which truth do you want?*